The Murder Diaries
Seven Times Over

An Inspector Walter Darriteau Murder Mystery

David Carter

TrackerDog Media

The Murder Diaries – Seven Times Over

An Inspector Walter Darriteau Murder Mystery

© David Carter & TrackerDog Media 2019

Follow David on Twitter @TheBookBloke

www.davidcarterbooks.co.uk

ISBN: 979-8524-332196
Third revised and updated edition
The right of David Carter to be identified as the author of this work has been asserted by him in accordance with the Copyright, Designs and Patents Act of 1988

Edited and Updated: May 2021

This book
is dedicated to the memory
of the late
Cecil Norman Carter
1918-1998

Highly medalled sailor, signaller, swimmer,
D-Day Veteran,
rower, grower, and father

Much missed
Never Forgotten

By the same author:

The Inspector Walter Darriteau Books:

The Murder Diaries - Seven Times Over
The Sound of Sirens
The Twelfth Apostle
Kissing a Killer
The Legal & the Illicit
The Death Broker
Five Dead Rooks
Old Cold Bones
The Walter Darriteau Box Set – One
The Missing Man
Falling

Other Books:

State Sponsored Terror
The Life and Loves of Gringo Greene
The Inconvenient Unborn
Grist Vergette's Curious Clock
Drift and Badger and the Search for Uncle Mo
Down into the Darkness
The Fish Catcher
The Bunny and the Bear

Chapter One

The orange streetlight bounced from the wet tarmac. 2.30 in the morning. No one about. No traffic, no pedestrians, no wildlife, nothing. The dark car approached the green lights. The driver saw a man coming from the right. He crossed the far lanes to the centre island. The lights turned amber. The driver slowed, coming down from fifth to third. The man glanced at the car and half nodded and set out to cross the road.

In the vehicle, the right designer clad training shoe switched from B to A. Brake to acceleration. The car surged forward. The man heard the engine roar and stopped dead like a fox caught in headlights, frozen in formaldehyde, as if in some sick art exhibition. The man couldn't believe what he saw. The lights were red; he was sure of it. He tried to move, to jump away. Too late. The bumper smashed into his knees, shattering both. The bonnet crashed into his falling body, breaking ribs, sweeping the guy high into the night. He bounced on the roof, cracking his left arm, somersaulted through the air, and crashed to the pavement.

The driver glanced in the mirrors. An impression of moving black shadows, a black bundle hunched on the pavement, growing ever smaller as the car sped away. The bundle didn't move.

It would never move again.

Darriteau yawned like a hippopotamus. Karen glimpsed his tonsils and glanced away.

'Excuse me,' mumbled her boss.

'Don't mind me,' she said under her breath.

'Well, Greenwood?' he said. 'Anything new?'

'Not much. We arrested Gary Jones at Ffrith Caravan Park, but you know that.'

'Ah yes, Gary Jones,' the crazy man who had been in and out of borstal and prison for twenty years. Hooligan, drug dealer, burglar,

1

wife beater, scourge of society. At least this time he would be put away for good, but too late for some, and as if Karen was following his train of thought she said: 'It's Millie I feel sorry for.'

'Course,' said Darriteau, pulling a face, and pondering on how the courts could have handed down one lenient sentence after another.

'Anyway,' said Karen, 'this time it's open and shut. He's confessed. His fingerprints are all over the knife.'

'Mmm,' said Darriteau, thinking of Millie and her mischievous face, that curly, mousy hair that framed her milk white phizog, those big blue eyes that entranced men so, they certainly entranced Gary Jones. Probably cost her her life. Entrancing partners wasn't all it was cracked up to be. Millie should still be here, and Darriteau felt responsible for that.

'Anything else?' he mumbled, trying hard to sweep the image of her smiling face from his tired brain.

'Not much. A hit and run on the by-pass.'

'Oh?'

'Just waiting for the post mortem.'

Right on cue, Mrs Carney swept into the office. Lobbed a file on the desks.

'Hit and run?' she mumbled.

'Yep,' said Karen.

Mrs Carney looked down and saw Walter Darriteau nod.

'Two smashed knees, three broken ribs, broken left arm, and right ankle, but none of that killed him.'

'So what did?' asked Karen.

'Cracked his head on the pavement. No one could survive that. This is the prelim; you'll have the full report before I go home.'

'Thank you, Sara,' mumbled Walter.

Sara Carney pursed her lips, and glanced at the pair of them, bobbed her head and left them to it.

'So who is he?' asked Walter.

'Who was he?' corrected Karen.

Walter gave his sergeant a look and she began again.

'Colin Rivers, aged forty-six, lives, or lived in a newish detached house in Saltney. Married, two daughters.'

'What did he do for a living?'

'Insurance salesman, office based, so I believe.'

2

'Family been told?'

'Yep.'

'What's his wife's name?'

'Marian.'

'Is she in the house now?'

'Probably.'

'Find out, will you? If she is, we'll pop down and see her.'

Karen drove the unmarked BMW. She adored driving, while Walter was happy to be driven, in the city anyway, where she couldn't speed.

A modern redbrick detached house, dull but comfortable, like a million others. The curtains were closed. A small flowerbed in front of the main window, crocuses out, daffodils considering their options. There were two five-year-old cars on the driveway. Walter took a quick peek at the bumpers and bonnets. No scratches or dents, no blood, and no sign of any recent hurried cleaning.

Karen rang the bell.

Marian Rivers came to the door, cigarette in hand. She glanced at the ID and invited them through to the sun-streaked conservatory at the back of the house.

'Do you want a coffee?'

Walter shook his head.

Karen said, 'No thanks.'

'Sit down, please.'

They sat in the cane chairs and wondered who should start.

'Your daughters are out?' asked Walter.

'Sent them to school, thought it best.'

'So sorry to hear your news,' said Walter.

Marian pursed her lips. Didn't say anything.

'Tell me about your late husband.'

A short silence and then she said, 'Not much to tell.'

'Did he have any enemies?'

Marian's mouth opened. She flicked ash into an empty coffee mug.

'I thought you people said it was an accident?'

'Yes, it probably was, but we are keeping an open mind.'

3

'So did he?' asked Karen.

'He was a man. What do you think?'

'Serious enemies?' asked Walter.

'No-ooo, just piddling things.'

'How did he get on at work?'

'OK, I suppose. An occasional promotion, occasional pay rise, that kind of thing; he was not a high achiever. Steady as he goes kind of bloke, and anyway, he was more interested in God.'

'God?' said Karen.

'Yeah. Didn't you know? He was a Lay Preacher. Didn't your people tell you anything? That's where he'd been, to a late night God squad meet up; they were planning a big service, something like that, that's why I said he had enemies. They appointed him over the heads of four others, two blokes and two women. You wouldn't believe how jealous and zealous some of them get in the church.'

She was smiling as she said that, and Walter guessed it had been a bone of contention in the Rivers' household.

'Did they make a habit of meeting late?'

'Recently they had, crazy isn't it?'

'What church?' asked Walter.

'United Reformed, Curzon Park.'

'And did you attend?' asked Karen.

'Nope. I can do without that kind of thing.'

'So, to your knowledge, did he have any enemies who'd want to kill him?'

'I can't think of anyone.'

'How are you fixed, financially?' asked Walter.

'Not bad, it looks like the mortgage will be paid off, and he was well insured too, with him being in insurance. There should be a big paycheque coming,' and then as if reading the detectives' minds she added, 'And before you say anything, I didn't do it, if that's what you think.'

'Course not,' said Walter, 'but just to be clear, where were you between two and four o'clock in the morning?'

'In bed, on my own, asleep.'

'And your daughters, they were in the house?'

'Yes, course, they were asleep too. They have big exams coming up, they are working really hard.'

4

'I want to ask you a personal question,' said Karen.

'It's your job.'

'Was he ever unfaithful?'

Marian threw back her head and said, 'Hah!' and glanced at the bird poop on the conservatory roof. 'I wish I knew the answer to that. No, I don't think so, but he was a man, wasn't he. Who knows? I'll probably never know now.'

'Did he get paid for his church activities?'

'Good God no, sorry God if you are listening, not a penny, no offence meant.'

'Thank you, Mrs Rivers,' said Walter, standing and fastening his raincoat. 'We'll be in touch if there's any news.'

During the ride back to the police station that overlooked the Roodee, Karen said, 'Forgive my ignorance, but what exactly is a Lay Preacher?'

Walter thought back to his childhood in Jamaica, and his Uncle Collis who was a Lay Preacher. He was always coming round to bless this house, or so he said, when in reality he was on the lookout for a free chicken meal.

'They stand in when the pastor is away or sick, a kind of first reserve if you like. Sometimes it can be an initial step towards higher things, but more often than not, they are just happy to help the main man.'

'Or woman,' corrected Karen.

'Yeah, that too.'

'You don't think one of his spurned rivals could have run him down, do you?'

'You heard the lady, they are jealous and zealous in the church, a catchy phrase, don't you think?'

Karen pulled a face.

'Anyway, check them out, these two men and two women who got the hump because Colin landed the job, a position that pays nothing and carries no qualifications.'

'They can't have killed him for that,' said Karen, guiding the car into the underground car park.

5

'It's been done for less,' said Walter, getting out and limping toward the lift, and as he did so, he shouted back over his shoulder, 'And another thing, we only have Marian's word that she was in bed asleep.'

Chapter Two

The driver hadn't slept. Jumped out of bed and booted up the Internet. Typed in: How to kill people. Twenty-seven million articles and features on How to kill people. Who writes all this crazy stuff, and more to the point, why doesn't someone do something about it? Scrolled down, began reading, started making notes, flipped on the local radio.

Appeals every hour on the hour for witnesses to come forward who may have seen the tragic accident on the ring road where a man was killed in the early hours.

There'll be no witnesses, pal. There was no one about.

The driver was surprised at how pleasurable it had been. To kill someone, and so easy too. One designer trainer lifted from B, set down on A. Acceleration! That was all there was to it. Man hit. Man dead. Job done. Such a tiny movement, such a tiny line between life and death.

An article that looked interesting caught the eye.

100 Ways to Kill People.

Click, and we're in.

Stabbing, no.

Strangulation, no.

Plastic bag over the head, no.

Shotgun, pistol, rifle, I don't think so.

Hit over head with a hammer. That would be messy.

Douse with petrol and set alight. Too risky. Too dangerous.

Poison, perhaps, maybe a possibility.

Sabotage brakes on victim's car. Too technical.

Grind up glass and hide in food. Goes to work on the stomach, causing an excruciating death. The trouble is you wouldn't be there to see it, to witness it, and that was half the fun.

Take out a light bulb, fill with petrol, refit and wait for victim to turn on the light. Would that work? Not for me.

Cut off head. The less said about that, the better.

Wait for victim to have a bath and lob live electrical appliance into the water. Ouch!

Drowning. Sounds too much like hard work.

Cut off hands. Very messy, and too hands on, or not, as the case might be, and presumably any old limbs would do. Perhaps not.

Run up behind someone with a heart condition and yell Boo! That was getting freaky.

Inject with pig's blood. Repeat dose if necessary. Yeah right, I just happen to have a pint of porky's blood in the fridge.

Or inject with thirty different substances, getting weirder the further down the list. Come on!

No, there was nothing there, nothing that leapt out, nothing that shrieked: Use me! Use me! Just have to think of something better, and then out of the blue, inspiration struck. The driver knew precisely how to do number two.

Threw on a coat, went outside and ambled to the paper shop. Bought the local paper, and there it was in the smudged LATE EXTRA. The nationals must have missed the deadline.

A man, Colin Rivers, aged 46, was knocked down and killed in Chester in the early hours of the morning. Police are appealing for witnesses. He was happily married with two daughters and was believed to be a Lay Preacher.

Well, of course he was.

Happily married? How the hell would they know that?

Took the paper home, cut out the article and pinned it to the cork tiles glued to the spare bedroom wall. Stood back and admired, yet it seemed awfully bare, that wall, one small article, 'One small step for mankind,' spoken aloud, a grin, a clicking of the fingers, left the room, closed the door, locked up, for it was time to get ready for work.

Karen's enquiries bore little fruit. The four spurned Lay Preachers admitted to having been mighty miffed at Colin's promotion, especially as they were all senior to him, but they were surprised and shocked he had died, killed on the highway, and more than that, each possessed a cast-iron alibi, for they had been sleeping with their partners at home, two men and two women, though not in the combinations Karen had expected.

'Take a more detailed look at Marian,' ordered Walter. 'Dig up everything you can. Something isn't right. Something stinks.'

Chapter Three

Harry Wilkinson had worked for the Chester Parks and Gardens department for forty-five years, almost exactly the same time he had been married to Bethan Jones. Through the years Harry gained steady promotions until he landed the position he coveted, that of headman looking after all the publicly owned bowling and putting greens within the city boundaries.

After he retired many a creaking sportsman would comment, 'Ah, the greens are not the same,' and in due course those lounge carpet surfaces would become known as Harry's Greens.

Harry met Bethan Jones when they were both twenty in the Dringo Tearooms at Penmaenmawr while he enjoyed a hiking, rambling, easy climbing holiday, which was apt, as Dringo was Welsh for climbing. Bethan was kitted out in a cute black-and-white uniform as she served Welsh cream teas, something that Harry feasted on during the week. He couldn't keep away from the place and was soon bewitched by her porcelain white Welsh skin, her sparkling blue eyes and easy smile, while Bethan was entranced by his huge bear-like paws. She had never seen hands the like of them before, and his neat English haircut.

She had taken the summer holiday job at Dringo to earn a little money and to get out from under her domineering mother, Phyllis's, feet, and if a nice young man came along, well, that would be a summer bonus to remember.

The Jones family lived in the hills above Mostyn where they could glare down on the English across the water on their flat Wirral peninsula, conspiring to subjugate Wales, or so they imagined. The Jones's had been long-time supporters of the Welsh National Party, Plaid Cymru, long before it was trendy and hip to be so, and even more fervent supporters of the Welsh Language Society, insisting that only Welsh was ever spoken in the Jones' household. Bethan was six before she mastered the masters' tongue. Fact was, that over the years the extended Jones family did a fair bit of glaring over the estuary whenever there was any anti English sentiment in the media, or round the hilltop villages where they lived, and they would laugh at anyone mentioning the Investiture of the English Prince of Wales.

'You can't marry 'im, ee's English,' said Phyllis in her sing song voice, forgetting herself and slipping into English, meaning Harry of course, the phrase spilling out almost as if it were one long word, youcan'tmarryimeesenglish, as if it were a Welsh place name belonging on some narrow gauge mountain railway.

Bethan would marry who the heck she darn well pleased, and she did.

Harry was high Church of England, Bethan, Welsh Chapel, where all the hymns and sermons were conducted in Europe's most ancient language. Seventy-eight people attended the service in the grey stone chapel, and not all of them could find a seat. On that one solemn occasion the chapel hierarchy made an exception and allowed a modicum of English to be uttered, but just the once, though not too much, and not too loudly.

Three weeks before the wedding, to his intense relief, Harry landed the job with the Chester Parks and Gardens department, and Bethan bit her tongue, swallowed her pride, and agreed to move across the border, to England.

They bought a rambling and crumbling redbrick terraced house at a discount price in Alfred Street beside the Chester City Walls, a house the estate agent described as needing work, a property Harry and Bethan could only afford because Harry's father, a bank clerk, put up most of the deposit, and arranged the mortgage on preferential terms.

Before they moved in, Harry and Bethan enjoyed a spectacular honeymoon in the Llaethlyd Lleuad Guesthouse, roughly translated as the Milky Moon, on the coast at Aberystwyth. Harry would always enquire as to the meaning of Welsh words. He was determined to learn the lingo, as he described it, but after three months of trying, gave up. It was too difficult for an Englishman to master, he said, and he wasn't the first to utter the phrase.

Bethan wasn't disappointed, because she could still curse him in her native tongue whenever they fell out, knowing that he wouldn't have a clue what she was chuntering about, something that happened, but never for long, and anyway, the making up after an anghytuno'n chwyrn, a disagreement bordering on the violent, was always the best bit.

During the honeymoon beside the seaside the sun shone every day, as the balmy onshore summer breeze blanched their locks. Bethan turned red and burned; Harry an attractive dark brown, for this was long before Factor Eight or Factor anything else had been invented.

Afterwards, they would spend all of Harry's working life in that rambling house where he, in his spare time, would turn it into a desirable residence, adding bathrooms, a spectacular kitchen, and a large nursery that would soon be full to overflowing.

Four big boys grew up in 17 Alfred Street, and in time fledged the nest and scattered across the globe to Australia, Canada, New Zealand, and Tegucigalpa, wherever the heck that was. Glyn had always been the odd one out, the rebellious child who opted for the most difficult decision, or the weirdest choice available.

Bethan and Harry enjoyed ten grandchildren they seldom saw.

The day after he collected his gold watch, Harry drove Bethan along the North Wales coast. They were bungalow hunting. He thought that as she had allowed herself to be taken to England for so long, the least he could do was to repatriate her to Wales, and spend their retirement in her beloved Cymru. Bethan was coming home and her heart sang at the prospect.

They found a beautiful but ancient, grey stone bungalow, with its original Welsh slate roof still intact, set high in the hills, not five minutes drive from where she grew up, and yes, she would still glare across the Dee estuary far below at the Saeson, the English, on the far side.

Despite her forty-five years living amongst them, she retained some hostility toward them for what they had done, though perhaps they weren't as bad as she had imagined. Three of her sons were confirmed Saeson, and that remained a deep regret for Bethan, though dearest Glyn remained stubbornly Welsh, and the only one who had mastered his mother's tongue.

Harry and Bethan shed a tear when Jones & Sons, Removals and Storage, a distant cousin of Bethan's, loaded up the blue and white pantechnicon, slammed the rear doors on their possessions, fired up the smelly diesel engine, and rolled away from Alfred Street for the last time.

The bungalow was heavenly. The fresh air bracing, the sound of the lambs somehow comforting, the large sloping lawn soon trimmed and lined and weeded to Harry's exacting standards.

Eighteen days after they moved to Wales, Bethan announced she would that night go to bed early, not only that, but she would sleep alone in the spare room, something she hadn't done since nursing the boys all those years before.

Harry put it down to the slight cold she had. He'd noticed she had taken two glasses of Spanish red wine with her dinner, or tea, as she still preferred to call it, when one at most was all she would take. She had been irritable too, he'd noted that, and that was unlike her, but he imagined she would be better in the morning.

She wasn't.

Harry found her lying on her back, like Sleeping Beauty, the covers pulled down and straight across her waist, her porcelain white Welsh skin still almost unlined, and as beautiful as the day he first set eyes on her in the Dringo tearooms. Her eyes were closed and her hands were clasped together before her, with no hint of pain on her death mask. She reminded him of some of the life-size marble memorials in the cathedral.

Eighteen days at home, eighteen precious days.

Bethan had always been a private lady. She often kept her feelings and innermost thoughts to herself; something that Harry had occasionally cause to chastise her over. There were some things she insisted she did in private and dying was one of them. She had never wanted any fuss. Bethan would do it in her own way, alone, and bravely, and that was what she did.

She had returned home to die.

Harry understood that now, as he kissed her dry lips and knelt down beside the bed in the spare room, wearing only his blue and white striped pyjamas, as he spoke aloud a prayer for his beloved Bethan, ending with one of the few Welsh phrases he could ever recall, rwy'n dy garu di, Bethan Jones. I love you Bethan Jones, and after that, he cried, and after that still, he went to the telephone and rang the Right Reverend James Kingston.

13

Chapter Four

The Right Reverend James Kingston had been seconded to Chester Cathedral from Lichfield. He regarded it as promotion and both he and his accountant wife, Sybil, were delighted to discover the fine red sandstone house close by the cathedral that came with the appointment.

Tradition demanded the new Right Reverend should hold his house-warming meeting and greeting party within one month of taking office, a busy affair where most of the people who helped and ran the cathedral would be invited. That included Harry and Bethan Wilkinson, who soon became close friends of the Kingstons. Harry was a regular worshipper in the cathedral and would donate his spare time to overseeing and cutting the fine lawns and grounds surrounding Saint Werbergh's, as the cathedral was sometimes known.

The party began at noon and ran until four o'clock in the afternoon, during which time legions of helpers would pop in, some briefly, and shake the hand of the upright fellow who had joined them. Some, but not all, took advantage of the chilled white wine Sybil had chosen from Waitrose's extensive catalogue. James enjoyed a glass or two, though paced himself, knowing it would be a long day. Even their only son, Michael, had put in an appearance, a tall and handsome twenty-something, studying tropical medicine at Liverpool University, a young man who charmed the ladies, young and old alike.

At close of play two elderly sisters, Amy and Harriet Bull, who provided many of the cathedral flowers, had become stranded. The arrangement had been their even older brother, Robert, would collect them in his Jaguar. Robert had fallen in the garden that afternoon while pruning roses, and had broken two fingers, and could not oblige.

The Right Reverend James, eager to please on his public debut, jumped into the conversation and volunteered to run them back the seven miles to Parkgate on the west Wirral coast.

'You've had a few drinks,' warned Sybil.

'No! Don't worry, darling. Only a couple spread over the whole of the afternoon, and I've had plenty to eat. I'll be fine.'

'Well, if you're sure.'

'Course I am. I wouldn't take a risk on something like that.'

The Bull sisters eased into the back seat of the Right Reverend's four-year-old blue BMW and zipped along the Chester High Road, northward to Parkgate, and home for the now tiring and yawning ladies.

'Thank you so much,' they said at the house, 'Are you sure you won't come in for a coffee?'

'Thank you but no, perhaps another time, it's been so nice to meet you, give my love and best wishes to Robert, and tell him I shall meet him another day,' and with that, minutes later James was heading south again... too quickly.

The police shot out of a quiet turnoff and were on him like an angry hornet on a wasp.

The first police officer stepped from the blue light-flashing car and headed toward the Beemer.

'Do you know what speed you were travelling at, sir?'

'Just on seventy,' mumbled James.

The officer shook his head and revealed the handheld device that displayed 82mph.

'Really?' said James. 'That much? It must be this car. I am so sorry.' And he added, 'I am the new vicar attached to the cathedral; I am on my way back there now.'

The police officer had clocked the white collar, and that was, to the best of his knowledge, a first, a speeding priest... with humming breath.

'Have you been drinking, sir?'

'No-ooo, well yes, just the one. It was my inauguration party today, and I had to take a couple of elderly ladies home.'

'Would you mind blowing into this device?'

James appeared crestfallen. He'd already guessed the result, and he was right.

The new Right Reverend at Chester Cathedral was prosecuted for driving whilst under the influence of drink, found guilty, one and a half times over the legal limit, and fined four hundred and fifty pounds, no exceptions for anyone, and especially for someone like you, said the magistrate. You should have known better, and worse still, James lost his driving licence for eighteen months.

The press had a field day.

The London redtops screamed CANNED VICAR BANNED, and RIGHT REVEREND WRONG, while the more conservative Chester Chronicle contented itself with: New Right Reverend Will Not Be Giving Lifts.

There was something of a public outcry, especially amongst the teetotalling temperance mob who had been campaigning for drink to be banned from all areas of the city centre for years, and to think that our new Vicar has behaved like that!

Harry and Bethan, who weren't above a glass or two themselves, supported James through and through, and that strengthened their burgeoning friendship. Despite that, feelings ran high. There was a weighty faction demanding the new man and his simpering wife be packed off to Lichfield on the first available train. It was rumoured the final decision went to the Bishop himself, who in the spirit of forgiveness, came down on the side of James and Sybil Kingston. James would take his punishment like a man, carry on with his duties, and be required to apologise as part of his next public address.

Come the day in question, the paparazzi camped on the green outside the cathedral, watching, listening and hoping for more juicy church gossip.

The Bishop intimated that James Kingston would be expected to never again be seen with an alcoholic drink in his hand, a stipulation that, though bothersome, mattered little when put into context of the wonderful house they enjoyed. He could do what he liked behind closed doors and did.

The telephone rang at half-past nine in the morning.

Sybil answered. She was working at home that day.

'It's Harry Wilkinson,' she hissed to James, 'and he sounds awfully upset.'

An hour later James found himself on the stopping train loping along the North Wales coast, heading for Mostyn station where Harry would collect him in the car. James would much have preferred to have driven there, but didn't dare.

16

He spent a good chunk of the day in the ancient bungalow praying with, and comforting his friend, before Harry drove him back down the hill to the station before the trains grew busy.

The driver had planned the day with great care. A quiet railway station where expresses rushed through. A small or non-existent staff. A lack of CCTV, and a trial run that had uncovered no unforeseen problems. Today would be the day. Mostyn would be the place.

Chapter Five

James Kingston was still thinking of Harry and poor Bethan, as he crossed the railway bridge and strolled on to the platform that would take him eastward back toward Chester, the line that followed the soft muddy, sandy coast.

Harry volunteered to stay with him until the unreliable stopping train arrived, but James sent Harry on his way with, 'You have so much to think about and arrange, you get on home,' and anyway there was an express due through, and James came from an age when little boys were hypnotised by railway trains. He was looking forward to it and reprimanded himself for not bringing his digital camera.

The driver sat in the car watching. There was one person on the platform, but you only need one. One cold soul, peering up the track, seeking trains, hoping one would arrive soon.

The driver stepped from the car. Headed for the platform entrance, specially chosen padded trainers enabling silent movement. The man on the platform still stared along the track. A vague rumbling, then the lines sang, an audible hum, the sound of bogies on steel rail, crossing the junction, over the points, louder now, approaching, exciting, exhilarating.

Most people step back from the platform edge when a train rushes through, especially when it's an express that will not slow or stop. James was keener for a better look. He stepped forward. The diesel loco pulling ten carriages was entering the station, hurtling toward him, acceleration, the Llandudno Junction to London Euston Express, stopping at Chester and Crewe and nowhere else. Yellow and red, raw power. How impressive a beast she was.

The car driver stepped forward too. No one about. Why would there be? This was a quiet unmanned station, the rush hour had yet to begin, and this train wasn't stopping.

Hand up. Palm open. Small of the back. The gentlest of prods. Falling forward, over the edge, into the abyss. Disappeared. Dispatched. A split second look of panic and terror on the engine driver's face as the train flashed by. The cold soul had disappeared.

Mangled beneath hundreds of tonnes of thrashing iron and steel. No one could survive that. What had been his final thoughts? Pondered the pusher. Maybe he uttered a prayer. Who knows? Who cares?

100 Ways to Kill People.

Push them under a train.

The driver grinned and turned about and headed back toward the car. It had been more enjoyable than before, and that was a surprise. Perhaps it was because last time it was a spur-of-the-moment thing. This time it was meticulously planned.

Desi had perished that way.

It was only right.

It was only a surprise it had taken so long for the idea to germ.

Desi was avenged, or at least partly.

Desi would never be forgotten.

Back in the car. Engine on. Left trainer pressing C. Right trainer pressing A. Acceleration. Away from the station. Away from Mostyn, and away from Wales.

But what about next time? What then?

There would always be a next time.

Walter arrived late at the police station. He had been to the dentist. His left cheek was puffier than usual. Karen was already there, gabbling on the telephone. He gawped at her and she set the phone down and smiled across at him.

'I've been to the dentist,' he snuffled.

'I can see that.'

'Anything happening?'

'There is. Another suspicious death,' she said, 'over the border in Wales.'

'How suspicious?'

'A middle-aged man fell beneath the London express at Mostyn.'

'Suicide?'

'Maybe, but get this, he was a preacher.'

'That is interesting. Any witnesses?'

'None that we know of, though the driver glimpsed something. He's very cut up about it.'

'Perhaps cut up is not the best phrase in the circumstances.'

19

'Sorry, but get this, Guv, the dead guy was well known.'

'In what way?'

'Remember that vicar from the cathedral, the one traffic did for drink driving and the papers got hold of it. It's him.'

'I remember. RIGHT REVEREND WRONG.'

'That's the one.'

'What was he doing in Mostyn?'

'I have no idea.'

'Do you know where the engine driver lives?'

'Yep. Nantwich.'

'That's handy, on our patch. He'll be taking leave for sure.'

'He is. I've just spoken to him; he's in all day.'

'I think we should see him.'

'OK Guv, I'll arrange a car.'

'One other thing, Karen, did you dig up anything weird on Marian Rivers?'

'Nope. Nothing at all. I don't think she's involved.'

Walter sighed and waddled toward the coffee machine.

'We'll go in half an hour, do you want a coffee?'

'Nope, bad for you, ruin my diet,' and she grabbed and sucked hard on her bottle of flavoured water.

It took less than half an hour to drive to Nantwich, Karen keeping within the speed limit most of the time. The driver's name was Bill Brambles, and he lived in a typical railwayman's terraced cottage that hadn't changed in a hundred years. It was two minutes walk from the station, handy for work. They heard a passing two-carriage passenger train as they walked up the short path.

There was no bell, just a big brass knocker. Karen thumped it twice, and the door opened a moment later. She smiled at the red-faced guy, short, stubby, maybe forty-five, thinning black hair, unshaven, bags under his eyes. He hadn't been sleeping well.

'Mr Brambles?' she said.

The guy nodded.

'I'm Sergeant Karen Greenwood, we spoke earlier.'

'Yeah.'

'This is Inspector Darriteau.'

20

The guy nodded at Walter, and Walter nodded back.

'Come on in.'

They went through to a small back kitchen and sat at a table and chairs, yellow topped; the kind of thing you can buy in a charity shop for next to nothing.

'Wanna cuppa tea?'

'No ta,' said Walter. Karen shook her head.

'I'd just like you to tell us in your own words what happened,' said Walter.

'I've already told the Railway Police.'

'Yes, we know that, but we'd like to hear it from your own lips.'

Bill Brambles glanced up at the unshaded bulb and back at the cops.

'We were just coming into the station…'

'We?' asked Karen.

'Me and the loco,' grinned Brambles, 'a hundred and thirty tonnes of raw power, ten carriages, perhaps thirty people a carriage, and the crew too, maybe three hundred people, I was hardly alone.'

'I see,' said Walter, 'so what happened?'

'We entered the station. It was very quiet. I noticed that because I thought there was only one guy on the platform. A tall bloke.'

'The unfortunate one?' said Karen.

Brambles nodded.

Walter gave her a look as if to tell her to stop interrupting.

'He stepped toward the edge, but not in a threatening way. It all happened so fast, more like a spotter, an enthusiast, as if he were about to take our picture, but he didn't seem to have a camera.'

'He was alone?' asked Walter.

'No! No, he wasn't, that's the funny thing. As he stepped forward I glimpsed another figure behind, he or she stepped forward too, always standing behind the main man. I couldn't see the other person; I never did, not properly.'

'What happened then?'

'We were travelling 65mph, maybe 70mph, that's pretty quick through a station. There are so many things to monitor. The last thing you want to see is an unattended pram, or buggy rolling toward the edge.'

'I can imagine,' said Karen.

21

'As we approached, the main guy was close to the edge, too close, and in the next moment he fell, almost dived, in front of Dodo.'

'Dodo?' said Walter.

Brambles childishly smiled. 'We call the engine Dodo.'

'I see,' said Walter, pondering for a second the absurdity of it.

'I slammed on the brakes, an automatic reaction, but a total waste of time.'

'Did you see the other person on the platform?' asked Karen.

'No. We were well past by then. Not even a glimpse. It was just a blur. You can't imagine how quick it happened.'

'Did the main man jump, or was he pushed?' asked Walter.

'Hard to say, it could have been either, but the second figure was very close, right behind, out of vision.'

'As if they were hiding from you?' suggested Karen.

Brambles pondered on that and pulled a face. 'Maybe.'

'What's your gut feeling?' asked Walter.

'My gut feeling is… he was pushed.'

'Why do you say that?'

'If you are going to jump in front of a train you would have planned it, wouldn't you? You would have gone to that station knowing what you were about to do.'

'You'd still be terrified at the prospect,' said Karen.

Again Walter shot her a look.

'Yeah maybe, but the look on this guy's face was not so much one of terror, more one of surprise, not that I got that much of a look, it all happened in a split second. One instant he's there, the next he isn't, the next I'm past him and out of there. All done, in the blink of an eye. Not pleasant, I can tell you. I wouldn't mind, but this is my second one this year.'

'Oh?' said Walter.

'Yeah, just before the Woodhead tunnel in January. No doubt about that one. He jumped on the track and walked straight toward me, grinning.'

'Oh, geez,' said Karen.

'Yeah, exactly. Why can't these cranks take a pot of pills or summat? What have we ever done to deserve this kind of trauma?'

'Maybe the guy at Mostyn wasn't a crank,' suggested Walter.

22

'Maybe you're right,' said Brambles, 'but we'll never know, will we?'

'Is there anything else you can tell us?'

'Not really. As I say, it all happened in an instant.'

Walter sighed and Karen stood up.

'Thanks, Mr Brambles, you've been most helpful,' said Walter, standing and offering his hand.

Brambles took it and shook it; and Karen's too, and a moment later the officers were outside in the car.

'Well?' said Karen. 'Back to the station?'

'No. Not yet. Take me to Audlem, it's near here, there's a pub I know. We'll have a drink and a think, and a chat.'

Chapter Six

The Shroppie Fly was located on the canal bank. Walter had discovered it when one of his former girlfriends, Audrey from the mission, had persuaded him to take a boating holiday with her. The one evening they spent in the Fly was the highlight of the week, so far as he was concerned.

There were three or four painted metal tables and chairs outside overlooking the brown water. A group of mallard ducks were squabbling on the far side.

'Grab a table,' said Walter. 'I'll get the drinks,' and he disappeared inside.

'White wine for me,' she said, smirking.

Walter harrumphed.

Karen sat down on one of the cold chairs and looked out across the canal. There were four narrowboats berthed there. They didn't look as if they had moved since the previous summer, long multi coloured craft with large names painted on their sides. Genevieve, London. RickySue, Skipton. The Blue Goose, Ilkeston, and Sir Winkalot, Chester. Two more barges were coming down the canal in line astern, heading for the locks that would take them down toward Chester. The first one had four guys onboard. They saw the slim blonde sitting there on her own-some and waved and smiled and shouted, 'Need some company, love?'

But before she could answer, a big black bloke came out of the pub carrying drinks, and sat beside her.

Karen waved them away, and the guys waved back and shouted 'Another time maybe!' and then they were gone.

'Friends of yours?'

'Not yet,' she grinned.

He passed her an orange juice. His was a large pint of foaming real ale, two inches already missing, in a straight glass, most important, 'and here's your lunch,' he said, 'on me,' tossing a packet of salt and vinegar crisps across the table.

'Diet,' she said, pushing them back.

He didn't mind. He could manage two.

'So,' he said. 'What have we got, exactly?'

'We have two deaths that could be accident or suicide, in which case there is no case to investigate.'

'True, but we also have two cases that could be murders, in which case there is one, and possibly two murderers out there, and that needs investigating.'

'We can rule Marian out of the railway death, she was at her solicitors,' said Karen. 'Let's assume for a moment we have two murders, and they're linked, are we looking for a man or a woman?'

'Could be either,' said Walter.

'I think it's a man.'

'Why?'

'Just a feeling.'

'Keep feelings out of it,' said Walter, gulping his drink, 'stick to the evidence.'

'Ooh, that's rich coming from you. You thought Marian did it.'

'No I didn't. I just didn't want to rule her out too soon.'

There was a short silence as if they were thinking on different lines and Walter said, 'What is the motive?'

'Good question. They were both preachers. Someone with a grudge against vicars, perhaps? Maybe they buggered up a wedding.'

Walter snorted. 'Hardly a good enough reason to kill.'

'It's been done for less,' she said, echoing his earlier words, and then she said, 'Could this be more sinister than we think?'

'How do you mean?'

'An Islamist thing. You know, someone messing with a fundamentalist's brain? Putting ideas into their heads.'

'Going round murdering Christian preachers? Well, it's possible I suppose, though unlikely, but everything about this case looks unlikely. One thing's for sure; we rule nothing out until we know different. More to the point, did the victims know one another?'

'That's a good place to start.'

'It is,' said Walter. 'When we get back to Chester you make that your number one line of enquiry. If you can show they knew each other, there might be a common friend or acquaintance, and then we could be getting somewhere. My worry is these are random killings.'

'What makes you say that?'

'How did the killer know that Colin Rivers would cross that road at that time? How did the killer know that James Kingston would be at Mostyn station standing on the platform at that time? I don't see a connection. I don't think he knew either. I think it's random.'

'You said he.'

'He or she.'

'If they are random killings, we'll have our work cut out,' said Karen.

'Random killings are the hardest to solve. No motive at all, other than personal satisfaction.'

'In that case let's hope it's the preacher thing. Do you think we should go public and warn all preachers to be on their guard?'

'I've been thinking about that. It won't be long before the press gets hold of this. I wondered if we should call a press conference before they go off at a tangent.'

'That'll create mayhem.'

'Yeah it will, but it might flush our little bunny out.'

'It's your call.'

'Yeah, I'll have another drink and mull it over,' said Walter, and he went back into the pub. When he came out he said, 'And another thing I need you to do. Check out recent releases, prisoners with previous, and the mentally unstable, care in the community, all that crap. Find out if the authorities have recently foisted on us some head-the-balls who should never have been released.'

'Good point; I'll check that out first. Erm, where's my drink?'

'Oh sorry, did you want one?'

'Nah, only teasing.'

The driver lay on the bed, hands behind head, staring at the ceiling. In ten minutes it would be time to get up and prepare for work.

100 Ways to Kill People.

It wasn't as easy as you might think, not if you wanted to be creative about it, and that was the whole point. Anyone could wander down the high street and pull out a carving knife and ease it into someone's back, but what was the point in that? Where was the challenge? No, that wouldn't do.

Time for thinking caps on.

They'd be surprised at the next one.

And why hadn't there been much publicity?

God, the coppers were slow. They hadn't put two and two together. They didn't appear to realise they had two murders on their hands. If they didn't buck up their ideas a letter to the press might bring them to their senses.

The driver stood and went through to the spare room. Four articles displayed. Much more interesting. Two on the highway, two on the railway. A little speculation by bored journalists, but not much. Had the whole world gone one-eyed? Even the dopey press hadn't picked up on it. That would have to change. They would all have to change, or maybe, just maybe, they should be next.

Ha, hah!

Would the casino be busy tonight? Probably not. There wasn't the spare cash about, other than with people who shouldn't have the money in the first place, and there would always be plenty of those.

Time to get ready. Must look nice.

No more bets, ladies and gentlemen. No more bets!

Twenty black! Vingt noir.

Chapter Seven

William Camber had always been a loner; leastways he had for the past twenty years, ever since he and Lorraine split. He had been a late developer so far as women were concerned. An only child, a domineering mother, a father in the merchant navy who went away for ten months at a stretch, and was drunk for most of the time when he came home. Perhaps it wasn't surprising William found it hard to relate to other people, and especially women.

He always struggled with the five-hurdle handicap.

To meet a nice girl.

To ask her out.

To have his invitation accepted.

To go on a date.

To take it further.

He'd get past one, or two, or maybe three, but by the time the fourth hurdle reared up in front of him, he'd normally have stumbled.

Then he met Lorraine Bickerstaffe.

She worked on the till in the convenience store on the corner. Lorraine was no kid, but that was fine because William was thirty-nine. She had smiled at him in that special way. She felt a little sorry for him. He always came in alone, and seemed lonely. He wasn't bad looking, and polite too, and she had been out with a lot worse, though she didn't care for the whippet he always tied up outside the shop, before setting foot in the store.

The next time he came in she could tell he was nervous. It was quiet that day and that was possibly part of the plan. Perhaps he'd been waiting outside. He'd had a shave and applied aftershave too, and she could tell what was on his mind, though she guessed he wouldn't have the balls, the guts, to ask her out.

He bought a couple of items and ambled to the till. No one else about. Just the two of them. It would be now or never. He made small talk. Nice spring day. Quiet in here. Been busy? See the Queen's under the weather.

He wasn't going to ask her, she just knew it.

He liked the dark blue skirt and the light blue blouse she wore. Fit her like a glove, they did, and she had a great figure. Was it company uniform, or her own clothes? He had no idea.

He heard Topsy outside yelping his displeasure at being abandoned.

'So glad I'm finishing in ten minutes,' she said, blowing out air.

She'd recently retouched her perfume. The aroma crossed the counter and attached itself to William's jacket.

'It's been a long day and I'm parched,' she wheezed, wiping her forehead with the back of her hand.

He still wasn't going to ask her. The bloody wimp!

She didn't want to go home to an empty house, and sometimes with daft horses you had to lead them to the trough.

'Can't wait to get into the Crown & Anchor, get a few drinks down my neck,' she said.

'You going to the Crown?'

Hallelujah! At last, the penny's dropped.

'Yep, thinking about it,' she said, smiling at him again.

'I might see you in there,' he stammered.

'Yeah, maybe. What's your name?'

'William. William Camber.'

'William, that's a nice name.'

'You think so?'

'Yeah. Like that young Prince William.'

'Yeah. What's yours?'

'Lorraine Bickerstaffe.'

Bickerstaffe? The name was familiar. He used to be taught by a Bickerstaffe. Maurice Bickerstaffe, that was it, and he was a right bastard. Maybe she was related. Maybe she was his daughter. Heaven forbid.

'I might see you later,' he said.

'Not if I see you first,' she said, grinning, to show it was a joke.

William wasn't sure about that, but went outside and hurried Topsy home for his tea. After that, went to the bathroom, combed his hair, cleaned his teeth, splashed some cologne on his face and inside his shirt, checked he had sufficient funds, and headed back toward the Crown.

He congratulated himself on how easy it had been. Asking her out, bet that surprised her, being accepted, and he put it down to his charm and attractiveness, and wondered why he had fretted about it beforehand. He should have had more belief in himself, just as his dead mother always reminded him. They couldn't resist him, could they; the women, and an attractive woman too. She fancied him, didn't she, course she did. It had been so easy, but deep down he always knew it would be.

She wasn't there.

The bitch!

She wasn't there.

He couldn't believe it.

Leading him on like that.

Standing him up.

Next time he went into that Expresso store he would give her a piece of his mind. He bought a drink, whisky, though he didn't much like whisky, and went and bunged some change in the fruit machine. Lost it in five minutes flat. Bugger!

Strolled back toward the padded bench seat. Sat down, sipped the drink. Glanced round. Four old blokes, two sitting together, two alone, minding their own business, looking miserable, a little like him. If he wasn't careful he'd morph into one of those old geezers before he knew it.

God, how shit life was when you're alone, when you're lonely.

Five minutes later she came in and the whole place came alight. It was as if someone had opened the double doors and allowed in the sunshine. The landlady smiled at the newcomer and asked, 'What can I get you, darling?'

The four old guys gave the newcomer the once over.

She had a lovely backside; you could make out her knickers beneath her tight blue skirt. The two guys sitting together elbowed one another and stared. The other two sipped their drink and glanced at her, and thought about what might have been, or perhaps about something from long ago.

She bought a white wine, turned about; saw the four old guys and William, sitting there, admiring her. She liked that, being admired;

and smiled at each one of them, and they all smiled back as she strolled across the bar like a catwalk model and said, 'Ah, there you are,' and sat down beside William, close beside.

He smelt her perfume.

He felt the warmth of her body next to his.

He felt like a million quid.

The old guys took a sniffy look at William to see what was so special about him, then sat back and glanced down at their well read red-topped newspapers, and waited for the next one to come in.

William and Lorraine dated for eight months. It might have been the best eight months of his entire life, and it would have been too, but for the way she finished it.

She wrote him a letter.

Said she'd met someone else, and she didn't want to see William again. Sorry, but there it is.

That was partly true. She was seeing someone else, that was honest enough, but she omitted to mention that she had been dating Joe O'Burn all the while she was seeing William.

She'd been trialling the pair of them, couldn't decide between the two. The truth was she liked them both. Joe for his manliness and wildness, quickness of temper, though he wasn't so bright. He was a redhead and what do expect from a redheaded man?

William for his conversation and gentleness and unthreatening company, won hands down on the more cerebral things of life. She was always far more relaxed in Will's company, for he was so easy to be with, but he was no wildcat that was for sure. Her lovers seemed to dovetail perfectly. Between them they provided her with everything she needed, but why couldn't one of them possess the attributes of both?

She'd grown tired of lying, covering her tracks, always having to remember what she'd said to the other, and what she hadn't. In an off guarded moment she'd actually called Joe "Bill", and she'd only got away with it because he chose that exact moment to turn up some heavy metal rock band on the television. He'd have gone mad if he'd heard what she'd said.

It hadn't been an easy choice when she chose Joe. Truth was, the sex was better, not that it wasn't nice with Bill, it was, but with Joe, well, that was something else, and good sex meant a lot to Lorraine Bickerstaffe. Sorry Bill, but there you are, out you go; thanks for the good time; you'll soon find someone new. But he didn't.

He had been a late developer so far as women were concerned, and an early finisher.

It took him ages to get over Lorraine, and that mean-spirited letter she'd sent. Truth was he would never get over it. He didn't want to get over it. If he was suspicious of women before, now he was positively hostile. He would never ask a woman for a date again, and neither would a woman ask him, unless you counted Marjorie Bates. She was an eccentric lady at the otherwise all male angling club, who made it her business to bed as many of her fish hunting colleagues as she could manage, before time ran out.

Bill wasn't interested in Marjorie Bates and told her so in no uncertain terms. The second sharp word he uttered was off.

He went prematurely grey before he was fifty, looking like everyone's favourite granddad. He stopped drinking, no bad thing, but the pubs had offered him something else, companionship, and he missed that dreadfully. He denied himself that pleasure, retreated to his flat and relied on his fishing; accompanied by whatever whippet he was homing at the time. He stopped eating properly, and what little weight he possessed deserted him. He wasn't looking after himself. His grubby shirt collars would flap around his neck like a scarf. He didn't clean the flat. What was the point? After a while the dust never got any deeper. He didn't care about his appearance and lost his job because of it, and worse still, he stepped up the smoking, emptying two packs a day, sometimes more, and it wasn't long before he had a permanent cough.

William Camber was stuck in a tailspin he wasn't even aware of, and there was little chance he would pull out of it. He had no friends or relations to tell him otherwise. He had become a bum.

Despite the passing of the years Lorraine Bickerstaffe was never far from his mind, though he had no idea what happened to her. He never saw her again. How is it the ones who hurt you the most are the ones who never leave the head?

It's crazy.

Lorraine came to regret her decision. She married Joe and presented him with a bawling ginger boy, though even before the birth she had become all too acquainted with Joe's freckled fists. William had never hit her; he'd never even dreamed of doing such a thing.

There would soon be another screaming baby on the way, while Joe admired other women in the boozer. Perhaps he was doing more than admiring, though she wasn't sure about that.

Lorraine felt trapped, by the kids, by him, by her choice, by everything in her life, but she was stuck with it. She'd made her own bed and look where it had brought her. She regretted it, of course she did. She didn't even like the boys that much. They were too much like their father, aggressive and hot tempered.

In her quiet moments she often thought of William.

She'd like another chance, to go back and retrace her steps, but she knew that was impossible. Life wasn't like that. It wasn't cricket. You don't get a second innings. You don't realise the consequences of decisions made in earlier life.

Sorry William, I made a mistake.

William was now sixty. His only pleasure was fishing, and the whippet.

His favourite beat was quite remote and hard to get to. He liked it for that very reason, because few people went there.

He hated human beings, and more than that, he thought he always had.

Nowadays he only fishes on the New Cut.

Tomorrow, at first light, he would be there.

Chapter Eight

Bird watching is a fine hobby to have, and the New Cut was the perfect place to pursue it. It was a birding crossroads where the town met the country, and the country met the estuary. Seabirds on the exposed mudflats at low tide, wildfowl lower down on the marshes, swans, Barnacle and Canada geese on the canal, starlings roosting on the nearby pylons, songbirds nesting in the scrubby vegetation, and all would attract the birds of prey, the marsh harriers, kestrels and buzzards.

The driver had a longstanding interest in birding, nothing too serious, no special equipment, other than a pocket book of birds, and a tiny pair of binoculars. It was relaxing, it was diverting, enjoyable.

The canal was at its best in the late spring sunshine, wide and deep after the heavy rain that had fallen in the night, boosted by the incoming spring tide. Before the afternoon was through, the banks would be tested to destruction.

It was a wonderful place to walk; quiet and peaceful, even if the paths were muddy, the perfect place to think, and plan. The new season grass glistened in the sunshine as the driver ambled along. There was a lot to think about, plans to formulate, ideas to test, but before that, there was some serious thinking to be done about the casino.

Last night had been hell.

It was expected to be quiet, but the place was packed out. A stag night gang of loudmouthed twenty, thirty somethings, who had been on the drink all night. A bunch of Chinese who couldn't speak English, but gambling is an international language, no words ever necessary. A ladies' night out, maybe nine or ten women doing their best sex in the city impression, and a team of professional gamblers intent on mischief… and winning.

Word flew round the staff that high rollers were attacking the pontoon tables. Big bets were placed, earnest whispered conversations amongst the punters, even a calculator appeared, though that wouldn't be welcomed. Long before midnight everyone in the place knew the house was losing. Something was going down, and it was more than the staff's Christmas bonus.

Extra sentries were placed; watchers sent out, croupiers in civvies, pretending to gamble, pretending to be on the other side. To the driver, they stood out a mile, and if the driver could see it, the serious gamblers could see it too? Whispers grew that innovatory cheating methods were involved, but where, and how, and by whom, and worst of all, how much was it going to cost?

The driver was glad that French roulette was the preferred station. Pontoon was a game to be avoided, and the bosses wouldn't be impressed by any croupier who lost a packet. Losers disappeared. Those playing roulette couldn't help but glance enviously at the card schools packed round the tables, couldn't fail to hear the raucous shouts of Yes! And Get in there! And feel the lucky winning mentality in the air, as heavy chips flowed across the table, toward the punters. The tide was running out, for the house.

The driver would not like to admit it, but maybe, just maybe, the eyes had been diverted for one split second, long enough to miss who placed the big bet on 16.

The winning big bet on 16.

Twenty-five ten-pound chips paying thirty-five to one.

£8,750!

God almighty!

A decent win in anyone's language, a great pay day for a mere ten second's work.

The problem came when two competing punters claimed the bet. The croupier hadn't noticed, couldn't rule, no one had noticed, such was the excitement flowing over from the card tables.

One claimant was Chinese and spoke no English, the other, a quiet, gay man, who had been a member of the Argosy Club for over twenty years. He wasn't quiet any longer, and neither was he weak. What began as a heated argument degenerated into a pushing and shoving match, and threatened to boil over into an all-out brawl.

'Gentlemen, gentlemen, please!' called the croupier, trying to bring them to order. It would never happen, because neither of them was prepared to back down, as the Chinese spat out filthy rhetoric that no one but his friends could understand. The management came running to mediate, and that annoyed them too, for they had their hands full watching the cards.

The croupier wasn't alone in wondering if this roulette charade was a diversionary tactic, but if it was, it was hard to see how. If it was, it was sure as hell clever, and had paid a big dividend.

The floor manager stared at the driver and asked: 'Whose bet was it?'

A shake of the head and the downcast look spoke volumes.

The driver didn't know; failed a basic instruction: always be aware of whose bets are whose; and especially big bets like this. The house took the men to one side, invited them into the private rooms for champagne and crepes, while pretty girls with reddened, pouting lips hung about in the background. Were they on offer too? A touch of compensation? Might they help settle the dispute?

Not much of an incentive for poor Derek.

After a further hour of furious argument the two claimants agreed to split the winnings, though both claimed total dissatisfaction at the outcome. It would leave one of them smiling and elated, and the other feeling robbed, and swearing never to attend the Argosy again.

It had been a dreadful night for everyone, the croupier, the owners and management, and for once the house was delighted to cut their losses and close the doors at 2am. The croupier couldn't get out of there quick enough, but on the way to the door, that same floor manager, Teddy Helms, called out, 'Sam, can you spare a minute, I need a word.'

Sam pulled a face and stepped into the private office.

'Take a seat.'

Sam sat down.

'You weren't on your game tonight.'

Was that a question? Sam pulled a face, but didn't reply.

'It's not like you. Is there something on your mind? You seemed distant from the start.'

'Everything's fine, Mister Helms.'

'You couldn't have picked a worse night to have a mare.'

'I'm sorry, Mr Helms, it won't happen again.'

'It bloody well better not! You get my meaning?'

Sam nodded.

Helms nodded toward the door, and as Sam stepped out, Helms shouted, 'Last warning, Sam. Last chance!'

No reply, just a nod, and a quickening of the feet to get out of there.

Mr Helms should watch his step or he might find himself in the crosshairs. A shaking of the head, a quickening of the step, a squelching of the trainers in the mud, a deep breath, forget about him, forget all about the Argosy and the black arts of gambling, forget about everything, other than the important things in life.

It was a beautiful day, cold but bright with a brisk wind that reminded God's creatures everything was well with the world.

It was a solitary place, the New Cut, far away from the main road. It needed a good walk to get there, and you'd only come if you knew of its existence, and that was why few people found their way to the waterside.

But there was someone there, away to the right, beyond some low struggling willows. A man, an old grey-haired man, slight and skinny, fishing, concentrating, standing on the edge of the cold, deep water.

It wasn't as the driver had planned.

It wasn't perfect.

But it was interesting.

A picture of Desi filled the mind for a second, interrupting the train of thought.

Unexpected opportunities must be taken.

Stood perfectly still. Glanced around. No one in sight. Not a sound, other than the freshening wind, bird song and territorial wild fowl, and the gentle hum of traffic on some distant busy road. An aeroplane came over the brow of the green hills, an executive jet, losing height, coming in to land at Hawarden airport. The skinny fisherman glanced up at the plane and back at the water, flexed the rod, peered at the surface, hoping for evidence of prey. He set the rod on the rest and stood with hands on hips, breathing hard, dying for a cigarette. He would have another in a second, peered up at the watery sun. It hurt his eyes.

Sam went on tiptoe. Closed on the prey. Crept forward. One last look around. The old man hadn't heard a thing. Perhaps he was going deaf. No one on the far bank. No boats on the Cut. Not another soul in sight. They had the world to themselves.

Hand up. Palm forward. Small of the back. Hefty shove.

The old man went in head first.

SPLOSH!

He didn't utter a word.

The water was freezing.

William Camber panicked and began thrashing around. His heart rate exploded. He was desperate to cough. His arms and shoulders and chest were freezing. He was desperate to breathe. He had never been a swimmer, swimming was for the fishes, he used to say. The tidal current swept him further out. He slipped beneath the surface and smacked the water with open hands, searching for air, but which way was up?

A sudden updraught brought him back to the surface. His head popped up like a cork. He gasped for breath, coughed and spat. He was facing the bank where his fishing rod stood. No whippet. Why hadn't he brought the damned dog with him? He couldn't remember. Safety was a long way off, and standing beside his fishing gear was a slight, grinning figure. Baseball cap pulled down over its round face, skinny jeans, and nondescript woollen jacket.

'What did you do that for?' William yelled.

The figure waved him goodbye.

The effort of shouting spent energy William could ill afford.

The current swept him into the centre of the canal, the deepest, coldest area. His legs lost all feeling. He could no longer kick. His arms were weak and feeble. They were going the same way. He grimaced in agony.

His head slipped beneath the surface. There was no sign of him. He'd gone. The driver felt elated. It had been so easy.

100 Ways to Kill People.

Push them in the Cut.

A hand broke the surface. He wasn't dead.

It wouldn't be long in coming.

William's white arm rose into the sky. The fist clenched like some communist black and white propaganda movie from the fifties. It shook at the figure on the bank, at the world in general, at all the people who had ignored him, hurt and belittled him. It retreated into the water, and was gone and would soon be forgotten.

Sam grinned and turned about. Pulled out the book of birds and strolled away along the bank. What species could be recorded today? Barnacle goose, yes, tick, Canada goose, yes, another tick, kestrel, yes, mute swan, yes, lots of ticks; it had been a good day. It had been a wonderful day.

Chapter Nine

The gaunt figure was washed up the following morning, downstream beyond the new road bridge, below the power station at Connah's Quay, dumped by the retreating tide. One hand was missing, essential foodstuff for three hungry fox cubs.

Two power workers had noticed the figure. They thought it was a mannequin, probably chucked into the water by a local band of mischievous kids. It didn't once move; it must be a mannequin. One of the engineers wasn't convinced and clambered down to take a closer look.

He was right. It wasn't a mannequin.

The body was in Wales, nothing to do with the English, well beyond Walter's jurisdiction. There, the Heddlu Gogledd Cymru ruled, the North Wales Police Service, but Walter had a pal in Prestatyn by the name of Dai Williams, and they would regularly speak and exchange intelligence and gossip. Dai was aware of Walter's interest in the unexplained death at Mostyn station, hence one of his first calls was to him.

'No ID yet, Walter,' he said, in his happy singsong Welsh voice. 'No one has been reported missing who fits the description, white man, difficult to age, we are saying between fifty and eighty, cause of death, drowning, no obvious injuries other than one nibbled paw.'

Three hours later the police patrols found the rod and bag and eventual identification. The dead man was one William Camber from Chester, aged sixty, no known relatives, and William Camber left behind one last mystery.

Was it suicide, accident, or murder?

Walter and Karen knew the answer to that. They couldn't prove it, they had precious little evidence, they simply knew.

They were no longer seeking a double murderer, but a triple, and that was a rarity, and there was something else of interest. William Camber was an atheist. He had never shown any interest in churches

40

or religion. The vicar murdering Islamist theory could be put to bed. They were looking for a serial killer; and a random striker at that.

Random killers were always the hardest to catch.

One of the telephones rang.

Karen snatched it up.

Walter heard her say, 'Yes, he's here, sure, I'll send him in.'

'What is it?' Walter snapped, though he had a good idea who it was.

'Mrs West wants to see you, right away.'

Walter cursed aloud.

Mrs West, known behind her back as John, was Walter's superior officer. Her name was Joan West, and she was ten years younger than Walter. She would often use the telephone to speak to her staff, even if they were sitting in the office right next door, preferring to keep her door closed whenever she could. It wasn't how the book suggested a station was run, but she didn't care about that. It had served her well in the past and she wasn't about to change.

Walter stood up and waddled across the office mumbling, 'That's all I bloody need.'

He knocked and went inside.

'Sit down, Walter.'

'You wanted to see me, ma'am?'

'Yes. I think you need help.'

'Help with what?'

'On this serial killer we have on the loose.'

'We don't know we have such a thing.'

'You said you did, and I believe you.'

'What kind of help?'

'A profiler.'

Walter grimaced. He'd feared the worst. 'Is that necessary?'

'I think it is. We need to catch this bugger before it gets out of hand.'

'Who?'

'The killer of course.'

'No, I mean which profiler?'

'Cresta Raddish.'

Walter grimaced. 'Not her, she's a menace.'

'She's very good. I've arranged for her to arrive tomorrow.'

41

'That must cost you a fortune.'

'Money is not an issue; the only thing that matters here is...'

Walter interrupted. 'Yes, I know, the safety of the public.'

'Quite. Make her welcome, Walter, and that's an order.'

'If you say so, ma'am.'

'I do say, and please remember this is happening on my watch. It's my neck on the block, not yours.'

'It won't come to that.'

'It better not!'

Cresta Raddish had made her name three years before by pointing the police at the Yorkshire killer operating in Sheffield, Hull, and Doncaster. She'd had further success helping to uncover the schoolteacher murderer flitting between Swansea and Cardiff. The team at Chester was intrigued and on parade to greet her the following morning.

Mrs West led the welcome, mwa-mwahing Cresta in full view of the team. Walter was next up, though he wasn't really a mwa-mwahing kind of guy. Cresta made a beeline for him, grasping his shoulders, depositing mauve lipstick on his cheeks, whispering in his ear, 'I am so glad to meet you at last, Mister Darriteau, I've heard so much about you and your fabulous work. It'll be a pleasure to work with you.'

'Call me Walter,' he said, though he wasn't sure about the working with her, but at least she'd made a decent start.

She had a strange aroma about her, Walter noticed that. Not perfume exactly, and certainly not BO, more of the new age palaver, or dare one think it, hints of satanic worship, that same aroma that always hangs around those crazy colour filled shops that flog that kind of rubbish.

Karen stood on the sidelines awaiting her turn. It seemed Cresta was crazy about purple, or was it mauve? Skirt, blouse, scarf, shoes, eye shadow, and lipstick, all a pronounced shade of mauve. She was a buxom woman, not fat, more rounded, and Karen couldn't help notice as Walter and Cresta embraced, they made a handsome couple, though he was a good twenty years older than she.

Karen wouldn't forget that. There had to be a good ribbing in there somewhere. She was looking forward to working with Cresta Raddish. Karen kept an open mind, and if Cresta had helped to bring serial killers to justice in the past, it had to be worth having her onboard.

Walter introduced Karen; and the rest of the team, and in the next moment Cresta clasped her hands together and said, 'Right, let's make a start shall we, there is no time to lose,' and Walter appreciated the sentiment, if not her determination to lead.

'Walter,' she said, 'could you bring us up to speed?'

He nodded and glanced round the room. Twenty people assembled there, Mrs John West at the rear, grinning, imagined Walter, at her minor triumph in inflicting this weirdo on the rest of them, on him.

'We have three unsolved deaths. A road kill, a fall or push in front of an express train, and most recently, a man seemingly tumbling to his death, drowning in the New Cut. It seems they are unrelated, but the fact we've had three in a short period is suspicious. We are treating all three as murder, and the suggestion is the same person is responsible. At this stage we don't know if we are looking for a man or a woman. The only description we have is of a short, slight person observed at the scene of the railway death. It could be either.'

'I think that is an important point,' interrupted Cresta. 'On the face of it you could be forgiven for assuming this is the work of a man. After all most serial killers are men, and most female serial killers conduct their work in the medical sector, hospitals, care homes, and the like. But we must not be swayed by that. This could be a pioneering female serial killer revelling in that very fact, that she is a pioneer, so to speak. I read up on the notes last night. There is nothing here to suggest this is a man.'

'Or a woman,' butted in Karen.

'Quite so, so we keep an open mind. I see that the press haven't cottoned on to this yet. I suggest that should be the first move.'

She glanced at Walter.

He nodded his approval and Cresta continued. 'Arrange a press conference for tomorrow. This person is dying to be recognised in the public domain for his or her actions. They are craving fame. Let us grant them that wish.'

'With what aim in mind?' asked Karen.

'Three aims. First, we are looking for leads of any kind from the public. Second, we are seeking to put pressure on the perpetrator, to stampede them into further action...'

'Isn't that dangerous?' asked Karen.

'Of course it is, but it is far more likely that he or she will make a mistake if we hassle them into early action. Far better than to sit back and wait for the next well-planned and neatly executed, forgive the pun, tragedy.'

'And third?' asked Walter.

'Thirdly, Walter, is the best reason of all. I believe this he-she creature will contact us, and more accurately, you Walter, once they see your handsome face filling the plasma screens over teatime, pleading for help.'

Everyone laughed.

Walter pulled a face.

'I take it nothing came of your research into recent prison releases?'

Everyone glanced at Karen. 'There was one candidate,' she said, 'but he was away on a dungeons and dragons event in Birmingham at the time of the New Cut death.'

'I am not surprised,' said Cresta. 'This isn't someone who has been in the system before. This is a newbie, a pioneer.'

'I agree with that,' said Walter.

'Anything else I should know?' asked Cresta.

There was nothing of consequence, so Cresta leant over and whispered in Walter's ear, 'Perhaps we could have a quiet word in private.'

'Sure,' he said. 'Now?'

'No time like the present.'

Walter led her away down the corridor to a quiet comfortable room set aside for such heart-to-hearts.

Cresta sat down and crossed her legs. Walter sniffed the air.

'I don't want you to feel I am taking over. I am not.'

44

'I know that.'

'Good. I'd like to make a few suggestions for the press conference.'

'Fine by me. They have never been my favourite aspect of police work.'

'Excellent. Here's what I'd like you to do.'

Chapter Ten

Sam lay back on the bed, propped up against four pillows, nibbling a pre-prepared tuna salad, watching the old-fashioned spare television parked on the chest of drawers. The national news came on. Nothing. Not a thing. What was wrong with these people? What did Sam have to do to gain their attention?

The local news came on, that oh so irritating music. The dumpy, dusky girl with the nasal voice. She was gabbling on about a party of local scouts who were flying to Tanzania to walk, or was it climb; up Mount Kilimanjaro. They still needed additional sponsorship, if anyone was interested. But three quarters of the way through, she interrupted what she was saying and said: 'We're going over now live to Chester Police Headquarters for a news conference,' there was an excited frisson in her voice, as if something different was about to happen.

Sam sat up straight and paid attention, slipped the salad on the bedside table.

Could they have woken up at last?

They had!

Sam's mouth fell open. Blue eyes widened.

The small room filling the tiny screen was packed. The moving camera switched from showing the chatting journalists seated in rows, to the bank of desks at the front. There were three officers behind the desks, a fat black guy who looked due for retirement, a slim blonde who looked as if she had stepped straight in from the gymnasium, and a middle-aged white guy, introduced as Bernie Porter, the Police Press Officer.

He opened the meeting, introduced the players.

'Inspector Walter Darriteau.'

Sam grabbed a pad and a pen and began making notes. Darriteau? What kind of name was that? Hardly a Cheshire man, was he? Sergeant Karen Greenwood. She was a pretty kid, maybe mid twenties, but there was a hardness about her. The kind of veneer a prostitute develops, thought Sam, though only in a good way. It was difficult to describe, kind of the reverse side of the coin. She looked fit, her unblemished skin pulled tight over her unmarked face, like a kid playing games with a balloon.

The black guy was doing all the talking. Was there a slight West Indian accent there? Or maybe Sam was imagining it. Bet he's a cricket fan.

Darriteau had spoken about the man on the highway and had progressed to the death at Mostyn Station. He was appealing for witnesses, someone must have seen the incident, the police were putting up a substantial reward, gee whiz, mumbled Sam, from zilch to this in a few minutes. This was more like it, and Darriteau moved on to another unexplained death on the New Cut, where a sixty-year-old man had died in mysterious circumstances.

Were you there?

Did you see anything?

I might have been, grinned Sam. I might have done.

Anyone walking in the vicinity was advised, instructed, pleaded, it was difficult to tell which, to come forward. 'We need your help,' said the guy, staring into the camera. 'I need your help.'

He glanced at Karen as if for approval and she half smiled and nodded. All the while a strapline was streaming across the foot of the screen, black letters on a yellow background, telephone numbers direct to the twenty-four-hour manned hotline in the Chester Incident Room.

Then the guy turned to the side and faced a new camera.

A much closer close-up, as close as could be, if they went any nearer they'd cut off his considerable thatch of grey hair. Walter's lugubrious face dominated the screen, huge dark, satanic eyes, Sam thought, like a nightmare big brother figure, staring into a million living rooms, putting people off their dinner.

'I want you to know I am coming to get you, and I shall find you wherever you are. I want you to think about that, and I want you to show courage. I want you to give yourself up, to hand yourself in at any police station, because you know that is the right thing to do, because you know I will catch you in the end, nothing is more certain, and that day is coming, and remember this, you and I will meet soon, so think about that. Hand yourself in and save yourself further anguish. The victims do not deserve their fate. You know it's right. I know it's right. I believe you are a clever person, and deep down you want to bring this to an early end. Think about it, and do the right thing.'

Walter nodded and turned back to the front.

He had made it personal.

In cases like this, he always did.

The camera cut back to Bernie Porter. He thanked Inspector Darriteau; he thanked the sergeant, said they would not be taking questions. It didn't stop journalists trying their luck and firing a barrage of questions at the panel. Bernie Porter threw up his hands and repeated, 'No questions!' and wound up the meeting.

The TV Company switched back to the studio. Nasal nose pulled an impressed face, and in the next moment they were showing library pictures of the summit of Mount Kilimanjaro.

Sam sat still, staring ahead. Biting lips. Whispered, 'Walter Darriteau, Inspector Walter Darriteau, you and I will meet soon, yeah, right.'

Walter returned to the Incident Room and was greeted by a sporadic round of applause. He smiled and half waved and bobbed his head and sat down.

Cresta came bubbling across the room.

'Perfect!' she cooed. 'Just perfect,' as she closed on him, and patted him on the back. 'You're wasted here. You should be on the stage.'

Sam pointed the remote and flicked off the telly. No doubt it would be on the news again later, be at work by then, must set the recorder.

A fat black detective. Who would have believed it? Sam wished Desi was here to share the moment.

He'd laid down a challenge, this Darriteau person. Sam hurried into the other room and booted up the Internet. Typed in "Walter Darriteau", not expecting much. One hundred and eight pages of entries about the guy. Geez, he even had his own entry on Interpedia, the online encyclopaedia, and that was interesting because anyone could update that. The mind pondered on opportunities, as Sam surfed the sites and devoured the data.

Details of his cases, his press conferences, his history, his disciplinary matters. God, don't you just love the Internet, a nosey parker's whole new way of life!

I want you to know I am coming to get you.

Bloody nerve, there should be a law against public threats like that.

It was an infringement of Sam's human rights.

I shall find you wherever you are.

Not if I find you first.

You know I will catch you in the end, nothing is more certain.

Well come on big boy, let's see you try!

That day is coming soon.

Says who? A bad actor like you, Walter, Wally, what a Wally you are, and Sam sniggered. Wally Darri, what a prick!

Remember this, you and I will meet soon.

Yeah, just for once, you might be right.

Chapter Eleven

Maggie O'Brien came from a big family. They were all dead. Ten assorted brothers and sisters, twelve uncles and aunts, two sons, all dead. Michael, her first son, had struggled through childhood. He never suggested he would make it, and he didn't. Leukaemia. What a bugger.

At least Liam had reached forty. Dead now though, killed in a car crash while drink driving in the outback, knocked over and killed a king kangaroo, and himself. Not such a surprise, for all the O'Briens could worry the liquor bottles when roused.

All dead, every one of them.

True, there were fifty nieces and nephews and heaven knows how many grand nieces and grand nephews, but none of them were in the slightest bit interested in Maggie O'Brien, not since she'd grown old, become forgetful; began repeating things every five minutes. At the beginning that had been funny, but it soon became a fatal irritant.

The modern kids weren't interested. They didn't see the point of the lonely old lady that none of them knew. It wasn't as if she was any of their mothers or fathers. They didn't owe her a damned thing.

Maggie had one close friend, Floria Beech, who had been in and out of hospital for the previous two years. Heart trouble, poor girl, Maggie always called her girl because she was quite young at seventy-nine. She was in dry dock again, the Countess of Chester Hospital, on the north side of the city.

Maggie visited her whenever she could, but she had fallen into a bad habit. She kept missing the bus. If anyone was watching they would have noticed that. Maggie came puffing and panting round the corner to see the maroon and cream bus pulling away. She put it down to her sciatica playing up, and the Meniere's disease that kept her awake at nights, when it was down to plain forgetfulness. The bus left the end of her bungalowed road at ten past seven, not quarter past, and that five minutes made all the difference.

She did it again.

Stupid woman! She cursed aloud. What am I like?

The single decker pulled away. There were two young children on the back seat with their mother. The kids put their fingers in their mouths, widened their gobs, stared at Maggie through the dirty glass, pulled a face and nodded their heads.

Cheeky beggars! What was the world coming to? Even their mother glanced over her shoulder, back through the window, stared at the old woman standing forlornly at the bus stop, a tiny bunch of daffodils wrapped in a damp copy of last week's Chester Chronicle, in her rheumatoid hands. The woman on the bus stuck her nose in the air and turned back to the front.

I blame the parents, said Maggie aloud, but there was no one there to hear.

A shiny dark car pulled up at the bus stop. The nearside window buzzed down. A kind voice said, 'Have you missed your bus? Do you want the hospital? I am going that way.'

It was hard to hear. The stereogram, or whatever they call it these days, was on loud, thumping pop music; bang, bang, bang, rat music, was it? Was that what it's called?

Maggie bent down and peered inside.

'Were you talking to me?'

The doctor nodded.

'Sure. I am going to the Countess if you wanna lift.'

Lovely car, nice clean person, and you can always trust a doctor in a white coat.

'Well, if you're sure, I'll pay for the petrol.'

The doctor laughed and reached across and opened the door and said, 'Jump in.'

Maggie O'Brien's jumping days were long behind her.

She grasped the headrest and made to enter, but had forgotten which foot to begin with. She thrust in her left, but that didn't seem quite right, but she was already half in, and in the next second she fell into the red sports seat. It had been nine years since she had last sat in a car. It took a moment to get her breath.

'Can you close the door?' said the doctor.

'What!'

'The door, we can't go far with the door wide open.'

Maggie stared at the open door. It seemed so far off. She wasn't sure with her dickey shoulder if she could reach it, but the nice doctor must have gathered that, because in the next second the doc jumped out, ran round, and closed the door, ensuring that Maggie's coat was tucked inside, and in the next moment the doctor was back in the car, starting the engine.

'What's you name?'

'Maggie O'Brien. What's yours?'

'Doctor Finlay.'

'Really?'

The doc smiled ever so nicely. 'Honest.'

'I used to love that programme.'

The car moved off, quicker than Maggie would have liked, as the dreadful music seemed to get louder. The doc was pumping up the sound with fingertip controls on the steering wheel.

Maggie had a dreadful headache. It had been there since she first staggered out of bed at half-past nine. The music was unbearable, like something from a nightmare.

'I've got a terrible headache,' she uttered. 'Could you turn the music down?'

The doctor glanced across at her. Maggie had turned inwards, displaying that soft, old, pleading face. She didn't look well.

'Sorry, yeah, sure, course,' and the doc reached forward and turned the music off. 'Tell you what I'll do; I'll pull into the petrol station. I need petrol and I'll give you something for that head.'

'Oh, there's no need.'

'I have to stop, anyway. Need the juice,' and in the next second the doc drove onto the forecourt and turned off the engine. Reached across and opened the glove compartment, took out a brown bottle labelled, Headaches and Flu, in big black letters. Opened it, which was as well because it had that awkward anti child top that Maggie always struggled with. Took out two tablets and slipped them into Maggie's trembling hand.

'What are they?'

'Ordinary headache pills, I use them all the time, get them from the hospital, they're great, here take them with this,' and the doc reached under the seat and pulled out a small half full bottle of water.

52

That was another thing Maggie didn't understand about the modern world. Why do young people walk round carrying bottles of water? Are they expecting a drought? We never did.

'It's not what you know, it's who you know, eh?' said Maggie grinning, throwing the pills into her mouth.

The doctor smiled, ever so charming like, and said, 'That's it Maggie, it's who you know that counts,' and jumped out of the car and began loading up the petrol.

Then they were back on the road, Maggie delighted the doc hadn't put the music back on, and maybe the pills were working. She yawned.

'Oh sorry,' she mumbled, bringing a hand to her mouth.

The doc yawned too.

'Look what you've made me do,' the doc said, grinning across at her, still yawning.

Maggie's face was on her shoulder, facing inwards, facing the nice doctor. She could get used to this, being driven to see Floria by her own personal physician. Sometimes it was good to miss the bus.

The doc drove into the car park at the Countess, took ages to find a space, and by then Maggie was fast asleep, deep breathing, a contented look set on her face, as if she had enjoyed a fabulous luncheon.

The doc ripped off the stethoscope and threw it in the back.

Started the car and pointed it toward Delamere Forest.

Floria would remain alone and miserable that night, wondering where her friend had gone.

Temazepam, two 10mg tablets, that's all it took. The doc correctly guessed that Maggie would have been on a cocktail of drugs. The Temazepam was the final straw. She wouldn't wake for hours. The doc turned the music back on, loud, it wouldn't make any difference.

Sam had been to Delamere many times before, often used to go there with Desi, walking. They both liked the isolated places best, for in desolate places people can get up to all kinds of mischief. Desi certainly did. Sam made a habit of returning often, if only to revisit memories.

Took that same track down toward the little lake known as Victoria's Pool. Some crazy story ran that the old queen had stopped there once, a place where Sam and Desi used to picnic. There was an old wooden and concrete seat there, overlooking the brackish water, and Sam parked the car, facing the bench, maybe ten yards away. With any luck there would be no one about at night, maybe the odd courting couple, but it was already raining and dark, and there was no one there at all.

Sam jumped out and opened the hatchback. Took out the length of corrugated piping. It was part of an old vacuum cleaner that had become surplus to requirements when they had gone bagless two years before. It had been Desi's idea to keep it, though God knows why. It fit over the exhaust perfectly; Sam had checked that a week earlier, fed it through the back window. Jumped in the car, blocked up the space where the tube entered with an old Chester City Football Club scarf, took one last look at Maggie. She was sleeping deeply, a contented look on her face, as if this was the best sleep she had ever had. Turned on the engine, closed the door, quietly, though it still sounded like thunder, and walked away.

The rain had stopped, though large drips were still sploshing from the pine trees. An owl hooted for its mate. The car motor ticked over. Sam squelched around the small lake, as they used to do, hand-in-hand, three circuits should do it. No, maybe one more for luck, plenty of petrol, the engine would not stop.

Back to the car. Opened the back. Filthy smoke flew out into the night. Took out the yellow rubber gloves. Slipped them on. Opened the door, more fumes rushed out, flushing up Sam's nose. Bloody terrible! Coughed loudly. Wafted the hands. Turned off the engine. Grabbed Maggie's body, she'd long since departed this world. Her black handbag fell to the muddy ground, carried her to the park seat. She weighed next to nothing, sat her down, set her up straight, hurried back for the handbag, wiped it clean, leaving her money intact, no need to pay for the lift, Maggie dear, no robbery here. Hooked the bag over her wrist, crossed and folded her arms, straightened her hat, closed her eyes, upturned her lips, geez she looked happy, probably happier than she had been in years.

Quick look around. Nothing dropped. Nothing left behind. No one about. Sam would never come this way again. The car stank.

Removed the gloves. Took off the white coat, chucked it on the back seat, switched on the headlights, full beam. Maggie O'Brien was bathed in light. She looked as if she was on the stage; hogging the spotlight, the woman in black, as if she were about to open her eyes and deliver a monologue. I have a story to tell, you won't believe, but it really happened. The beginning of a play, a murder mystery, perhaps, and Maggie O'Brien was the star, and the only person who knew how it would end, except she didn't.

Sam winked at Maggie.

Started the engine, buzzed down the windows.

Left designer trainer to C, select gear, right trainer to A. Acceleration! Not too quick, pulled the car round, made it without any reversing. The rain had returned, heavier than before, and that was no bad thing, it would wash away the evil spirits.

Maggie O'Brien was going to get wet.

Sorry Maggie, dear.

100 Ways to Kill People.

Carbon monoxide poisoning.

You hear of it all the time.

Most popular way to commit suicide, so they say.

Surprised it wasn't used more often.

During the quick trip back to Chester Sam reflected on the innovative use of props. The stethoscope bought in the Oxfam shop in Frodsham high street for a fiver, the use of one of Desi's white coats that Sam had recently considered binning.

They had worked like a dream, and no one would ever know.

There were lessons there to be learned, the value of good props. Sam closed the windows; the flushing chilly night air had cleaned the interior.

That should give them something to think about, those dopey coppers, those loopy press people.

Over to you, Walter. Wall. Wally.

Prick!

Sam laughed aloud.

This was fun, and it was getting better.

Chapter Twelve

Stevie discovered the body. The old lady was still sitting on the bench as if she had been waiting for the hospital bus and had fallen asleep. There was dew on her hat and shoulders and the end of her nose, and her dark coat was soaked through. The handbag was untouched, still containing the pension she had collected the day before.

An enormous spider's web stretched from her earring to the corner of the bench. The spider had scarpered when Steve arrived on the scene, sniffing around Maggie's feet.

Stevie was a red setter.

It was ten minutes to eight on a moist morning and Maggie would always be asleep at that time. She was asleep still, enjoying the start of the big one.

Two minutes later Stevie's owner showed up, panting like the dog, Mr Milkins, sixty-nine, retired solicitor. He fired up the mobile phone his granddaughter Sara had bought him for his birthday, and tried to remember how the damned thing worked. Figured it out, and zapped 999.

The Incident Room was packed; everyone was in early to sift through the results of the televised broadcast. The phones had been red hot for four hours following the initial showing; and again later when the feature was repeated on the bedtime roundup. Every loony and attention seeker in the county had called, or so it seemed to Karen.

It was me I did it, stabbed the guy; kicked him in the river.

No, you didn't. Go away! Stop wasting police time.

The phones were still busy the following morning, though the initial rush of idiots had abated.

One or two interesting things had come in. But nothing concrete; and nothing seemingly from the perpetrator.

Walter half expected that. He sniffed and sat back in his chair, and clasped his hands behind his head. One or two thoughts had come to him during the six fitful hours of sleep he had grabbed. It was hard to think in the Incident Room with all the kafuffle going on. He might take some time out and sit in one of the private offices. One of the young WPC's came in and set a mug of coffee on his desk. He hadn't asked for it, but was happy to accept.

'Thanks, err…' realising that he did not know the kid's name.

'Thompson, sir,' said the girl smiling. 'Jenny Thompson.'

'Thanks Jenny Thompson,' and he smiled, and she pulled a pleasant face and hurried away to begin data entry on the latest computer program that supposedly aided finding the killer. Maybe it did, but it was not something that interested Walter much.

He glanced across at Cresta. Still in purple, though different shades today. She'd combed her straight, dyed hair differently, and there was a purple clip in it to keep it just so. She was writing fast, longhand, and she was an immaculate writer, standard forward sloping style, each individual letter almost identical, like you see in American universities, which may not have been so daft, for she had studied at Stanford for three years. The Americans were the best at profiling, miles ahead of anyone else, leastways Cresta believed that, and she might have been right.

Some of the younger guys had suggested she was spending her time writing a crime novel at Chester Police expense, building in the realistic atmosphere she witnessed, which might not have been such a ludicrous idea, judging by the pile of completed papers she had turned over.

'How are you doing?' asked Walter.

'Fine, Walter,' and she stopped writing and looked up, 'I have nearly finished my initial report. I have a few ideas.'

'Me too,' he said, 'though I can't think straight in here.'

He called to Karen. She looked away from the latest data on the screen.

'I want a small meeting, just you, me, and Cresta. Organise a room, drinks and toast would be nice.'

'Maybe we should include Mrs West,' suggested Karen, looking back over her shoulder toward the private office that bore the boss's name, a door that remained closed.

'You think?'

Karen nodded.

Walter sighed and said none too enthusiastically, 'OK, you tell her, will you?'

Karen made to walk that way but came to a halt as soon as WPC Jenny Thompson stood up, still holding the phone, and shouted, 'We have another one, another suspicious death!'

The room fell silent, Jenny conscious of all eyes upon her.

'Where?' said Walter and Karen and Cresta almost in unison.

'Delamere Forest.'

'Who?'

'A woman, an elderly lady, a Chester woman by the name of Margaret O'Brien. Some retired solicitor found her. He's still there now; the local police are on the scene.'

'Tell them not to move a thing. Nothing! We are on our way. Come on, Karen.'

'I'm coming too,' announced Cresta, getting up in a hurry and dragging her purple coat from the back of her chair.

Walter and Karen shared a look. They weren't used to having passengers riding when they were on a case, but what could they do?

Karen drove, Walter sat in the front with Cresta behind him. Karen had grabbed a marked car, a powerful BMW, one of her favourites. It didn't take long to get there, not the way she drove. She adored seeing the traffic scuttling from their path like panicking beetles, and when they delayed her, she didn't hesitate to use the blue lights and wailing siren to sweep them out of the way.

Cresta held on tight. Walter closed his eyes.

They found the place, radioed in by their man on the spot. It was a remote location, way off the main road, down a re-laid gravel track. Two local police officers were there, and a doctor, and the old solicitor, and Stevie, and they all glanced up as the shark-like car pulled into the small car park.

Walter stepped out to be confronted by the older man.

'Are you in charge?'

'I am.'

'I've given your man a statement; I am getting very cold and not a little irritated, and I need to go home.'

'I'm getting cold and not a little irritated too,' said Walter, striding toward the bench.

The man huffed and puffed and followed.

'Give me five minutes,' Walter said, 'after that we'll have a quick chat and then you can go.'

Milkins pursed his lips and nodded his head and led the dog to the water for a drink.

'Well?' said Walter. 'What's the score?'

The doctor looked away from the dead woman and said, 'Estimated time of death between half eight and half-past ten last night. There are no obvious injuries.'

'Cause of death?'

'Too early to say. You'll have my full report before close of play today.'

'And if you had to guess?'

'I am not a guessing man.'

'Try! Please.'

'If I had to guess, I'd say carbon monoxide poisoning.'

'Why do you say that?'

'Colour. Look at the skin. Hypopigmentation, a common sign.'

'Mmm,' said Walter, peering at the corpse. 'Not natural causes?'

'Oh no, I'd be surprised at that.'

Walter nodded. 'Ring me, will you, when you're done?'

The doctor nodded, and they all turned and watched the ambulance bouncing down the track toward them.

'Karen.'

'Guv?'

'Have a word with the solicitor guy. Ask him if he saw anyone else. Tell him we'll need his fingerprints to eliminate him. Tell him to go with the local boys and get that done and then he can go home.'

'Sure, Guv.'

Walter peered across the lake and pictured the scene when the killer was there. Was the murder carried out on site, or elsewhere, and the victim brought here? It was a quiet place. It could have been done on site, in which case what was the killer doing while it was going on? Standing by, watching? Maybe. A killer would not be squeamish. But if not, pound to a penny Walter would wager the killer would have wandered off, a quick stroll round the lake, perhaps. Maybe a good place to find footprints in the mud, especially if the path was rarely used.

59

He called the local officer over and instructed him to make certain that SOCO took casts and photographs of all footprints in the vicinity, and especially those on the far side of the lake.

'Don't let me down,' said Walter, staring into the young kid's eyes.

'I won't,' he replied, and he wouldn't because this was the most important thing he had ever done.

'Cresta?' called Walter.

'That's me.'

'What do you make of it?'

'Much as I would have expected. A remote place the killer has previously visited. That's how the he-she thing knows it's here. Probably been here before with a partner, maybe more than once, maybe with more than one partner, a scene of happy memories, I'd say.'

'Memories?'

'Yes, the partner's gone now, departed, maybe voluntarily, maybe died...'

'Maybe murdered,' added Walter.

'Could be.'

'What sparked everything off?'

'Loss of the partner, I would say.'

'Yeah, that's what I was thinking. But how long ago?'

'Within the last twelve months. Not recent, I suspect. It's been festering in the back of the brain, gradually building. At first they imagined they could cope with it.'

'When all the while they couldn't?'

'You've got it.'

'How many people have been through a broken relationship in the last twelve months?'

Cresta pulled a face that said it all.

'Another random killing?' said Walter.

'Looks that way.'

'The he-she thing is either incredibly lucky or incredibly clever.'

'Why lucky?' asked Cresta.

'The track has been freshly gravelled so no traceable tyre marks, and the heavy rain has washed away any footprints.'

'That looks like luck.'

'That's what I think, and if the he-she's had all the luck up to now, it's about time their luck ran out.'

Cresta nodded.

'Man or woman?' asked Walter, as Karen came back.

'I can't tell,' said Cresta.

'Man for me,' said Karen.

'Me too,' said Walter, 'course it's a man.'

'Let's wrap it up here and get back to Chester.'

Returning in the car Karen said, 'Was the press conference such a success?'

'I think so,' said Cresta.

Walter said nothing.

'We now have a dead old lady on our hands,' said Karen.

'That would have happened anyway,' said Cresta.

'You think? Is this not his response to our baiting?'

'He or she, are in this for the long-term. It, for want of a better word, will keep on killing until you catch them.'

'I think Maggie O'Brien would still be alive if we hadn't done the broadcast,' said Karen.

'Rubbish!' said Cresta.

'We'll never know,' said Walter, 'but we now have more to go on, more evidence, more leads, so from that point of view, the broadcast was an undoubted success. In the end the evidence will trap him.'

'Or her,' added Cresta.

'Yeah, that too.'

Chapter Thirteen

They hadn't been back in the office more than twenty minutes when Karen took a call from Prestatyn. 'Dai Williams for you,' she said. Walter grabbed the phone. 'Hi, Dai.'

'Saw you on the telly.'

Walter laughed. 'That was the idea.'

'I never knew you were so good looking.'

Walter guffawed. 'I'll take your word for that.'

'You are going to owe me one huge drink.'

'Why's that?'

'I've found a witness for you.'

'For the Mostyn death?'

'Yes.'

'Go on.'

'A schoolgirl, though she doesn't look like a schoolgirl, as you will see when you meet her. Her name is Chloe Evans; she's fourteen but looks twenty. She says she saw the whole thing.'

'Where is she now?'

'At school I should think.'

'Could you have her there at half four?'

'I don't see why not.'

'Prestatyn station?'

'Yep.'

'We'll be there, oh and Dai, I owe you one.'

'Yep, and I know you won't forget.'

Walter rang off and told Karen to organise a car for quarter to four. Told her to keep it to herself, they'd go alone.

Mrs West made a rare appearance and stood in the centre of the room and said, 'About this meeting?'

'I'm ready,' said Cresta.

Karen nodded and Walter couldn't avoid being rounded up by the three women, and a couple of minutes later the meeting got underway.

'Who wants to start?' said Mrs West, sitting at the head of the polished mahogany table.

Cresta glanced at Walter, as if seeking his permission. Walter nodded her on, and she began.

'We are looking for a loner...'

'Aren't we always?' mumbled Karen.

Cresta forced a smile and continued. 'Aged between thirty and forty, is my best guess...'

There's that word again, thought Walter. Guess, which was all it was, and couldn't anyone guess? You didn't have to go to some fancy Yankee university to do that.

'We could be looking for a man or woman, and I want to stress that. There is still no evidence this is the work of a man. Margaret O'Brien was a slight lady; anyone could have picked her up and carried her. We are looking for someone who was in a meaningful relationship, probably the most meaningful relationship of their entire life, maybe their only relationship, a relationship that went horribly wrong. I suspect they had a ferocious row and split. Maybe they fought, physically; perhaps the other party simply upped and left, walked out, abandoned their lover, or maybe they were murdered by the person we are seeking. Whatever it is, the perpetrator felt dirty and damaged when it all came tumbling down.'

'So we could have five unexplained deaths, not four?' said Mrs West.

'That's quite possible,' said Walter.

Cresta resumed. 'They are a car owner, a driver, with a nice car, in full-time employment, a well paid job, maybe living alone...'

Another worthless word, thought Walter. Maybe. Maybe this, maybe that. Maybe I'm a Chinaman. Was it all guesses and maybes? Is that what we are paying for?

'The killer will go on killing until he or she is caught. I expect them to become more brazen, take more risks, seek more publicity, and most interesting of all, I suspect they may try to attack you.'

With the "you", she glanced at Walter. They all did.

And just in case anyone hadn't understood her meaning, Cresta said, 'To kill you.'

'That's comforting,' he joked.

'I am serious.'

'I agree,' said Karen.

'So do I,' said Mrs West. 'You must be on your guard, Walter. Try not to go out alone, especially at night; try not to be alone.'

What wonderful words they were, he pondered.

Try not to be alone.

He had been trying not to be alone for over thirty years and had failed miserably.

'If any of you three ladies wish to come and sleep with me, you are all most welcome… in the spare room, I assure you.'

Karen laughed aloud.

Cresta grinned.

Mrs West looked shocked, before realising he was joking, when she said, 'You are a fool, Walter.'

Cresta began again. She sure as heck liked the sound of her own voice.

'I suspect he or she will contact us direct.'

'With what aim in mind?' asked Karen.

'To bait us, of course.'

'I agree with that,' said Walter. 'It will give him pleasure.'

'Women like pleasure, too,' grinned Cresta.

No one was going to argue with that.

'When is the PM due on Mrs O'Brien?' asked Mrs West.

'This afternoon, ma'am,' said Karen.

'You said earlier you might have some thoughts,' Cresta said to Walter.

'Yes, I do.'

'Well, let's hear them,' said Mrs West.

'We think this person is in full-time employment, but two of the deaths occurred in the middle of the afternoon; and another in the early hours of the morning. That suggests if they are employed it isn't in any ordinary day job. But not nights either, as if they start in the evening and go through to the early hours.'

'Yeah, like a barman or a nightclub bouncer, that would fit the bill,' said Karen.

'It would,' said Walter, 'though there are any number of jobs that fit the bill. Taxi drivers for example, transport ready to hand, the public trust taxi drivers and never think twice about jumping into a cab when they would never get into a stranger's car. Or hospital porters on the four till midnight shift or whatever it is they work, bus drivers, train drivers, supermarket stockists, there are many jobs that fit these odd hours.'

'I like nightclub bouncers,' said Mrs West.

'I'll bet you do,' whispered Gibbons.

'I don't,' said Cresta.

Mrs West shot her a look over her glasses. 'Oh? And why is that?'

'There is positive ID, the person responsible is slight. Have you ever seen a slight bouncer?'

'Fair point.'

'I know who's slight and works in nightclubs,' said Karen.

'Who?' said Mrs West.

'Pole dancers and strippers.'

Not all pole dancers and strippers are slight, thought Walter, though he didn't say.

Cresta's face lit up.

'That would work perfectly. Maybe someone who had a grudge against the punters. Did any of the dead men have any history of attending strip clubs?'

'Not that we know of,' said Walter, 'but anything's possible. Karen, can you look into that?'

'Don't forget two of them were preachers,' said Karen.

'Makes no difference. Preachers ogle too,' said Walter. He was going to say perv, but stopped himself in time.

'The thing I don't understand is this latest death,' said Karen. 'It doesn't fit with anything else. It buggers up the work times for a start.'

'Everyone has a day off,' said Walter.

'And it's an old lady too, all the others were men.'

'As I said before,' said Cresta, 'the he-she thing is getting bolder.'

'So what do we expect next time, if God forbid there is going to be a next time?' said Mrs West.

'Impossible to predict,' said Cresta. 'Random killers do exactly that, kill randomly.'

'Just so long as it isn't a child,' said Walter.

'Oh, God help us, not that,' said Mrs West. 'That's not what you think, is it?'

'It's not what I think, it's what I fear.'

65

There was a brief silence as they pondered on that dreadful possibility, and then Mrs West asked, 'Anything else?'

No one had.

Meeting over.

At half-past three Walter whispered to Karen, 'Where's purple haze?'

'Gone to freshen up,' said Karen, grinning.

'Good. Come on, let's go, I know a cracking tea bar on the way.'

They crept from the office and five minutes later they were negotiating the inner city ring road in a brand new unmarked white Jag, heading for Queensferry.

Chapter Fourteen

They took the A55 expressway, a four-lane highway known as the top road that ran over the hills, always going up, or always going down. On one of the down stretches, away to the left, set on the hill, was a spectacular bungalow. In the sunshine, a man was mowing the grass. Harry Wilkinson couldn't stop himself; in time he would cut that grass on the day he died.

Walter said, 'When I retire I am going to buy a bungalow like that, and raise chickens.'

Memories from long ago of those spectacular bantams back in Jamaica filled his head, and the yellow yoked eggs they produced.

'And when will that be?' asked Karen, giggling.

'Ages yet,' said Walter. 'Why? Are you after my job?'

'Course I am, thought you knew that.'

They shared a look as the bungalow slid away over Walter's left shoulder and out of sight.

Half way to Prestatyn, Walter ordered Karen to pull into a packed lay-by. There was a portable café there called Jock's Trap. It was run by Jocky Smith; a man Walter had arrested ten years before for aggravated burglary. Since then they'd become loose friends and Jock had pretty much gone straight ever since. He was known for his strong, sweet tea and toasted bacon sandwiches.

'We've plenty of time, pull in for a snack,' Walter said. 'Fancy a bacon butty?'

'Nope,' said Karen, 'diet.'

'Don't you ever eat?'

'Yes, at mealtimes.'

Walter pulled a face.

He stepped from the car and Karen shouted after him, 'I'll have an orange juice.'

Ten minutes later they were back on the road, Walter trying hard not to belch, sucking peppermints, as they took the Prestatyn turnoff and dropped down toward the coast.

The main police station was large for a smallish town, on the sea side of the main road. Karen pulled into the car park and cut the engine. The Jag was a pleasure to drive; she'd grab it again when the opportunity arose. Inside, Dai Williams came out to meet Walter, who introduced Karen.

Dai was typically Welsh built, short and stocky, with trimmed straight sandy hair, and he wore round-framed glasses that seemed out of place.

'Is the girl here?' asked Walter.

'She is, interview room three, follow me. If you need anything, don't hesitate to ask.'

Walter said, 'Ta,' and Karen smiled at the guy and nodded.

Walter took off his raincoat and set it on a chair outside, opened the door and stepped inside.

The girl was standing with her back to Walter, staring at a notice board. When the door opened she turned round and smiled at the guy, an automatic smile. She was the kind of girl who would smile at any man. Her mother was sitting at the table wearing creased jeans. She didn't stand up, didn't say anything, just half smiled at the newcomers.

'Chloe Evans, I believe?' said Walter.

'That's me,' said the girl, still smiling at the guy who looked a little younger in the flesh.

She was tall and pretty, well developed, tumbling auburn hair; didn't look fourteen at all. She was wearing a short blue skirt, tailored school uniform, far too short, no more than twelve inches from waist to hem, black tights, light blue blouse and a tiny neatly knotted blue and yellow striped tie, probably a clip-on.

'You must be Walter,' she said, too forward for Karen's liking, 'I saw you on the telly.'

'Yes, Inspector Walter Darriteau, and this is Sergeant Karen Greenwood.'

Karen bobbed her head and took a seat.

The mother didn't speak.

'Take a seat, Chloe,' said Walter, as he sat down.

Chloe pulled a seat back from the table and sat down and crossed her legs, displaying her knickers. Walter couldn't help but notice. The mother saw the look on Walter's face as he averted his eyes.

'Pull your chair in and put your feet on the floor and sit up straight!' said the mother, and the girl did as she was told.

68

'So,' said Walter, 'you saw something at Mostyn station?'

'Yep,' she said, smiling and bobbing her head.

'Tell us what you saw,' said Karen.

Chloe glanced at Karen. She didn't want to talk to the female officer; it was Walter she liked talking to.

'Well, I saw him do it, didn't I.'

'Him?' said Karen.

'Yeah, course; it was a man... wasn't it? Now you come to mention it, I'm not sure it was.'

'Tell us what you saw,' said Walter, 'start at the beginning.'

The girl nodded again and took a deep breath.

'We were coming out of the Mobri.'

'The Mobri?' said Karen.

'Yeah, the old Mostyn Brick Company; it's derelict now, disused, lots of the kids use it, it's a safe place to go, quiet like.'

'Who's we?' asked Walter.

'Me and Lee, my boyfriend.'

'What time was this?'

'I dunno, don't have a watch, probably about three, something like that. He gets off early, see, starts early, finishes early.'

She spoke in that strange North Wales coastal accent, short clipped flat words, hurriedly delivered, occasionally quite difficult to comprehend to the English ear, inner city Welsh, as Walter described it.

'What were you doing there?' asked Walter.

Chloe's eyes widened, panic style. She pulled a face. 'Do I have to say? What do ya think? I don't want to get Lee into trouble or anything.'

'Why were you sagging off school?' asked Karen.

'To see Lee, of course, 'cos I can't see him at night, can I.'

'Why not?'

'Didn't they tell you anything about me?'

'Why not, Chloe?' persisted Walter.

She extended her bottom lip, shook her head, and said nothing.

'Because he's tagged,' said the mother. 'He has to be in the house by seven.'

'Why's he tagged?' asked Karen.

Chloe shook her head. 'I dunno.'

'Burglary,' said the mother.

'He's not a burglar!' insisted Chloe.

'He was caught ransacking the bedroom drawers in the vicarage,' said the mother, becoming exasperated, dying for a fag.

'So tell us, after you and Lee came out of the brickworks, what happened then?'

'We was walking along the road up toward the station. I could see the platform through the railings, and the two guys, well I think they were guys, standing on the station. One was a big guy, really tall, in a suit, businessman type thing. The other one was much shorter, and he was standing behind the big one. Some way off to begin with. But as the train came in, he kind of crept up behind the tall guy. I thought they might have been mates, you know, and then I saw the little one reach up and push the big one in the middle of the back, just a gentle shove, and over he went, off the platform, in front of the big train that was thundering through, not stopping like.'

'And you are certain the little guy pushed the big guy off the platform?' asked Karen.

'Course I am, just said so, didn't I.'

'What happened next?' asked Walter.

'Nothing, I was just so gobsmacked, I said to Lee, did you see that? That little guy pushed the big guy under the train.'

'He was too busy trying to neck me, you know, he still had his arm round me, he was trying to give me a big thank you kiss, you know how it is,' she said, addressing Karen, knowing she would understand.

'What happened after that?' asked Walter.

'Lee said to me, "What small bloke?" And when we looked back he'd vamoosed, the titchy fella, gone right down the platform and out the station.'

'Did you see him again?' asked Karen.

'Nope.'

'Did you see him drive away?' asked Walter.

'Nope, though now you mention it a nice car came by, dark and shiny, I didn't see who was inside. I think the sun must have been shining on the windows, it could have been him.'

'What sort of car was it?'

'Oh, I dunno, I'm not very good with cars, maybe Japanese, hatchback perhaps, yeah, I think it was probably a Japaneser.'

There was a short silence and then Walter said, 'I want you to think very hard. Please describe the man to us.'

'The titch?'

'Yeah.'

'Well, he was small, wearing jeans, I noticed that, tight blue jeans, designer ones I'd say. They fit him like a dream, he had a nice bum I can tell you that, and a sweatshirt, grey I think it was, and a blue baseball cap, but it looked too big for him, kind of pulled down over his face.'

'Anything else?' said Walter.

'Yeah, he had expensive trainers, designer ones, German I think, new, blue and white, those with the three white lines down the side.'

'Adidas,' suggested Karen.

'Yeah,' smiled the girl. 'That's the one.'

'What else?' asked Walter.

'That's about it.'

'Was he a white man?'

'Oh yeah, definitely.'

'Hundred percent certain?'

'Deffo.'

'Would you recognise him if you saw him again?'

She shook her head. 'I don't think so; it all happened so quick; I didn't see that much, and not much of his face.'

'Think carefully,' said Walter, 'was it a man, or was it a woman?'

'Before you said, like, I was sure it was a man, never occurred to me it might not have been. But now that you say different, well I'll tell you this, there're loads of girls at school who'd kill for a bum like that. It could have been a bitch, it really could.'

Walter glanced across at Karen.

She frowned and shook her head, evidently nothing to ask.

'What did you do then?' asked Walter.

'Lee took me home in his old banger.'

'You didn't think to tell the police?'

'I wanted to. I said to Lee, I think we should tell the police, but he said he didn't see anything, he thought I was making it up, he thinks I am a bit scatty as it is, and he said it was best not to get involved with the cops. So I didn't, and then I saw you on the telly, like, and I said to me mum what I'd seen, and she said we should get in touch.'

They all looked at mum, and mum nodded and looked pleased with herself.

'Will you excuse me a moment, I need the Gents,' said Walter, and he left the room.

He went and found Dai.

'This Lee character, what's he like?'

'A complete waste of space.'

'Would you mind if I had a chat with him, put a bit of pressure on him?'

'Be my guest. You'd be doing me a favour. Do you want me to pick him up?'

'That would be perfect, oh, and can you make sure the girl doesn't see him?'

'Sure.'

Walter went back inside.

The girl was examining her painted nails. The mother was yawning. Karen was checking her text messages.

'Thought of anything else?' Walter asked the girl.

'Yeah,' she said, pulling herself across the desk, looking Walter straight in the eye. 'Is there a reward? You said on the telly there was a reward.'

Karen grinned and said, 'If your evidence results in someone being prosecuted, you may be entitled to a proportion of any reward. But it's unlikely, don't hold your breath. But if you could give us a name…'

'How am I supposed to do that?' said the girl, sitting back in her chair, folding her arms, disappointed.

'That's life,' said Karen.

'Can we go now?' said the mother.

'Sure,' said Walter. 'We'll be in touch if there's anything else.'

'Are you gonna run us home,' said the girl.

Karen shook her head. 'Sorry no, we're too busy; we don't run a taxi service.'

'Typical,' muttered the mother as she ambled out. 'We try to help and this is all we get.'

'Bye, Walter,' grinned the girl, as she followed her mother out.

When they'd gone Karen said, 'PM's in on Maggie O'Brien. Carbon monoxide poisoning confirmed cause of death.'

'Not a surprise.'

'Are we off then?'

'Not just yet.'

'Well, that was a complete waste of time.'

'You think so?'

'She was a right little madam. I wouldn't trust anything she said; and asking for a reward, well...'

'It wasn't a complete waste of time. We now know for sure we are looking for a white he-she thing, we also know it was no accident, it was indeed murder, and we know what it was wearing, and best of all, we know it has a nice bum.' Walter chuckled at his summation.

Karen grinned too and said, 'And what proportion of the population possess a nice bum?'

'Not as many as they used to.'

'Too true.'

'We have someone else to interview,' said Walter.

'We do?'

'Lee Davies, he should be here in a mo.'

'When did you fix that up?'

'Visit to Gents. Just one thing, I might ask you to step outside for a minute.'

There was a short silence as Karen pondered on what Walter had in mind.

'Don't do anything rash,' she said.

'Me?' he said, pointing to his chest. 'As if.'

He went outside and a minute later returned with Lee Davies. Karen gave him the once over. About twenty, wiry build, short mousy hair, blotchy white skin, drawn face, as if he was not unacquainted with illegal substances. He glanced at the girl. Half smiled; she was all right, for a copper.

'Sit down, Lee,' said Walter.

The guy sullenly sat and Walter joined Karen opposite.

'What's this all about?' he said.

'You were in Mostyn at the time of a murder.'

'Was I?'

'You were with Chloe Evans.'

73

'Was I?'

'We don't want to know anything about that,' said Karen. 'We are only interested in the murder.'

Lee shifted in his chair, wondered what to say.

The black fella began talking again.

'Chloe witnessed the murder.'

'Did she?'

'Don't mess with me!' said Walter. 'You are in enough trouble as it is!'

'Didn't see nottin'.'

'You saw nothing at all?' clarified Karen.

'S'wot I said.'

Karen and Walter glanced at one another. Walter nodded her away, and she stood and left the room.

'What's all this caper, then? Fancy your chances, do ya?' said the lad.

Walter stood up and went round the other side of the desk, bent down and whispered in the guy's ear.

'I've got something to say to you.'

'Really?'

'Don't you lay your hands on that girl again.'

'Oh yeah? Fancy her yourself, do ya?'

Walter drew his big hand back and cuffed the guy over the ear. There was an audible slap. Karen heard it sitting outside.

'Hey! What the hell! You can't do that to me!'

'I just did. Just making my point.'

'She's my girlfriend.'

'She's fourteen.'

'Have you seen her?'

'That has nothing to do with it. She's a child, and it's what's in here that counts,' and he tapped the guy's head with his middle finger.

'And if I don't?'

'I will make it my business to put you away for five years, and the place you will go offers special treatment for people like you. When you come out your bum hole will feel like it has had a red-hot poker permanently rammed up it! Understand me?'

Lee shrugged, never said a word.

'Understand?'

Lee nodded.

'I'll be watching you, Lee Davies. Now get out of here before I change my mind.'

Karen watched the door burst open and Lee galloped out.

'He's mad, your friggin' boss!' he shouted, and he hurried away through the doors.

Walter came out, rubbing his hands together.

'What was that all about?'

'I was just giving him a little parental advice.'

Karen cocked her head and peered over her non-existent spectacles.

'Now then,' he said, grabbing his raincoat, 'time to head home, I wonder if Jock's place will still be open.'

'God, I hope not.'

Chapter Fifteen

In the morning Walter was again late in the office. By the time he ambled in, it was obvious the refresh meeting was about to start. Mrs West peered at him and said, 'Been sleeping slow again?'

'Sorry I'm late, ma'am, I've been to a funeral.'

'Sorry to hear that. No one close, I hope?'

'Colin Rivers' funeral.'

'You thought the murderer might have attended?' said Karen.

'It's possible, it's not unknown.'

'Were there many there?' asked Mrs West.

'About a hundred.'

'Did you know anyone?' asked Karen.

'Only Marian, and the daughters. They were in bits.'

'Anyone suspicious?' asked Mrs West.

'The murderer wasn't there.'

'How do you know?'

'There were no pert bums on display, outside of the Rivers' family.'

Karen grinned.

Cresta said, 'Is this a private joke or can anyone join in?'

'It will become clear when Karen gives her update.'

Everyone turned to Karen.

'Away you go, K,' said Walter.

Karen glanced at her notes and began.

'We have a description of the railway killer. Height between five foot four and five foot seven, short for a man, tallish for a woman, slight build, pert bum,' and she grinned, as one of the young guys shouted, 'Wha-hey!'

'Shut up,' scowled Walter.

'Rules you out, Thompson,' another of the young blokes whispered to Jenny who turned and pulled a face.

Karen continued, 'The killer is white and was wearing tight designer blue jeans, grey sweatshirt, overlarge baseball cap, and new

76

blue and white Adidas trainers. I need to stress that our eye witness could not confirm whether the suspect was male or female.'

Cresta couldn't wait to jump in, blurted, 'I am becoming more convinced it's female!'

'There's your pert bum,' said the same guy from earlier.

Walter shot him a look and mouthed, 'Sorry, Guv.'

'A smart new black or dark hatchback was seen driving away.'

Walter added, 'It may well have blackened windows, hence the witness could not ID the driver.'

Karen nodded and said, 'It's possibly a Japanese hatchback, but we can't be certain. The PM report on Maggie O'Brien confirms she died of carbon monoxide poisoning. The usual location for such deaths is of course in cars, most notably suicide, but Maggie did not commit suicide. The car in which she died will continue to show traces of carbon monoxide, regardless of how well it has been cleaned. Find the car; find the murderer, simple as that. Look out too when searching vehicles for any suspicious piping that could have been used to introduce gas. At the crime scene in Delamere the heavy rain had washed most of the footprints away, but on the far side of the lake we found footprints in the heavier mud. The prints had been blurred and fuzzed by the rain, but were still of sufficient standard to show they were Adidas trainers, size six if they were men's, size eight, if they were women's. The size on the bottom of the sole is blurred beyond ID,' Karen waved to Jenny and she flashed up the latest photos, enlarged and enhanced on the big screen fixed to the wall. Footprints in the mud, four of them, differing quality; ranging from vaguely useful to totally useless. Footprints left by a murderer? It was possible.

Everyone peered at the pics and back at Karen.

'Of course we don't know for certain these are the killer's feet, but there must be a good chance. They are small feet for a man, and big feet for a woman, in either case, rarer than your average punter. The killer, if he is a man, probably has size six feet, is of slight build, possesses a pert bum, and we believe, is aged early thirties.'

Karen looked up and saw Walter nodding, and then he said, 'We think the suspect is in full-time employment, working slightly odd hours. Perhaps seven in the evening till two in the morning, or maybe an hour either side. Anyone got anything they want to add?'

He observed a sea of puzzled faces, people pursing lips, glancing at their neighbours, hoping the spotlight wouldn't fall on them.

'Come on, no budding Sherlock Holmes's amongst you? OK, but I want you to think hard about it. Are we missing something here? We probably are. It could save someone's life. If you think of anything, no matter how tenuous, come and see me or speak to Karen.'

Cresta followed on. 'The perpetrator is attractive, likeable, easy to talk to, the kind of person you would want to know, someone you would trust, the kind of person you could easily let your guard down against. One day that might be important.'

'That is excellent advice,' added Walter. 'Right, OK, moving on, black or dark Japanese hatchbacks. Find out how many there are in the area, find out who owns them, and if need be, we'll check them all, one by one.'

'Great,' muttered the young guy, and the team trudged back to work.

Chapter Sixteen

Armitage Shelbourne was a precious child in more ways than one. His mother suffered four miscarriages before Armitage struggled into the light. Kay had been warned by the family doctor this must be her last stab at motherhood. It was taking its toll. The doctor told the father, Donald, another such event could take the mother too. Don and Kay doted on Armitage.

They wrapped him in cotton wool. Even the slightest sniffle or spot would be treated as a medical emergency in the Shelbourne household. Whenever they could, they kept him away from other children, no kindergarten or Sunday school for Armitage, and they dreaded his fifth birthday when the law demanded he must attend the local primary school, and mix with other children, including that tough and dirty lot off the council estate. Kay dreaded the thought.

Don had worries of his own.

Before starting school, Armitage would play at home, spending the sunny summer days running and hiding in the big back garden, as his mother called, 'I'm coming to get you!' as the oldest game of all, hide and seek, got under way.

When Kay found him, she would grab his wrist and swing him in the air as Armitage screeched with delight.

'Again, mummy, again!'

'Come along, Army,' she said, as she always preferred to call him. 'It's time for tea.'

Armitage wanted for nothing, except the company of creatures of his own age. He was treated like a prince, while his mother dressed him and bathed him as if he were a baby.

Kay need not have fretted about the oncoming business of school, because she would never live to see it. She had never fully recovered from the ordeal of bearing a child, of producing the son and heir that Donald craved.

She had always been on the frail side; it was one of the reasons Donald found her attractive, her slightness and femininity, and an overwhelming sense of vulnerability. It attracted many a man into her sphere. Donald wanted to protect her, to look after and provide for her, to marry her, and he did.

Kay lacked confidence, and when a handsome man like Donald courted her, it meant a lot. Though whether she really loved him, only Kay knew the answer to that. He asked her to marry him, and so politely too, and she did, for that very noble reason, because he had asked.

Donald had won the race because he had been the first to show an interest, the most persistent, he would not go away, wouldn't disappear even when she had several flings with rivals. He would always be there, hanging about outside her house, waiting to pick up the pieces, and most of all, he won the race because Donald possessed an impressive car.

She couldn't have told you what make it was, but it was so comforting, big and shiny, you couldn't miss it. The kind of thing that people in the street would stop and stare at. Humber, Bentley, Jaguar, Rolls Royce, it was one of those big jobs for sure, old British iconic makes, that guzzled petrol and boasted fragrant calf leather seats, spacious and comfortable on the back seat too.

Donald overspent himself, and lavished the biggest local wedding of the year when he married Kay in the village church just beyond the city boundaries, a wedding that took place before hundreds of guests, some of whom the happy couple barely knew. By the time Kay returned from their Cretan honeymoon she was already expecting the first of those agonising miscarriages.

He made his living through his own business, The Shelbourne Motor Company. For some time he craved changing the name to Shelbourne and Son, Motor Dealers, or better still, Sons, but he would have to wait for that. He had another target too, to land a main dealership with one of the prestigious manufacturers; one of the self-selling brands that would make his fortune.

He was unlucky in that.

Perhaps it was because of his lack of finance, or maybe, as he suspected, his lack of connections. But for whatever reason, whenever he was interviewed and vetted by the big boys, they would always turn him down.

Thank you for your application but we regret on this occasion we cannot offer you a dealership. But please try again in another year or two. In the meantime, we wish you well and shall bear you in mind.

They never did, or at least if they did, they never advised Donald Shelbourne of their interest, or their reasons for his rejection.

He was forced into marketing marques that few people had heard of, and even fewer people wanted to buy. He stumbled from one useless foreign supplier to the next, damaging his reputation, because of his inability to make any of the franchises work. The major manufacturers hated that, to see a dealer flitting from one to another. They revelled in long-term loyalty, and Mr Shelbourne, with his sales site at the bottom of the high street in the small town just outside the city, had showed repeatedly that he could not be relied on.

The Shelbourne Motor Company stumbled on, making a living by selling other peoples' second-hand cars, not so different from the one man bands that proliferated everywhere, and stuck their wares up for sale on the greens in front of the council estate, gaudy handwritten price notices tossed in the front window.

When the economy was good, Shelbourne would do well enough to treat his family to exciting holidays in Barcelona, Tuscany or Sicily. In the poor years when few people were buying, they would pile into the big car, take to the road, and spend the week in rainy Newquay, not that Armitage cared about that. He could find pleasure and mischief wherever he went.

Four months after Kay's death, Donald moved Donna into the house. She was a flighty woman, painted and over fragrant, who had been employed by the Shelbourne Motor Company to keep the books. That was another of Donald's weaknesses. Accounting and bookkeeping skills were not high on his list of priorities, a fact that more than one German manufacturer had noted when inspecting the finances. How could they work hand in glove with a person, a company, that could not produce accurate records?

It was unthinkable!

There was more to Donna than met the eye.

She realised that Donald relied on her. True, the accounts were annually audited, but only by old Fotheringay from the village. His eyes were not what they once were, and things had moved on since he had done his training forty years before. Donna knew what he checked and what he didn't. She knew his weak spots and where to set up the dummy company, Laddon Motor Supplies. She imagined she was being ridiculously clever because Laddon was an anagram of Donald. She created several fictitious identities, bought an accommodation address service in London, had some striking green and yellow letterheaded invoices produced well away from the district, and Laddon Motor Supplies was in business, and sending bills to the Shelbourne Motor Company, a regular monthly invoice of inventory, not too large to invite investigation, not too hefty to cause Shelbourne financial difficulty.

Donna paid the invoices on the nail.

Donald signed the cheques. He never looked at them twice.

Donna treated Shelbourne as a cash cow, her own personal savings bank. She had never possessed any real money of her own, and she would milk it, not wanting to weaken it so that it ailed and died. She was good at it too. No one suspected a thing, and each month she would draw the looted money from Laddon's bank account in cash, jump on the train, head to London, travelling first class in her best frock, where she would pay it in over the counter of the Geneva & Zurich Bank. The funds would be zipped to Switzerland, well away from prying eyes. No one in Britain would ever know it was there.

Donna's little nest egg grew and grew.

Armitage detested Donna the instant he set eyes on her. Who was this loud painted lady who sat in his mother's seat at the dinner table, and worse still, slept in her bed? Who was this brazen cow who would hug and kiss his father in public, in the garden, in the car, in the house, every blinking where, in front of Armitage, passionate and longing kisses that had no business being displayed before an infant?

Donald encouraged her to play hide and seek with the boy, seeing as he knew his son enjoyed that pastime with his mother. Donna wasn't keen, but once let herself be persuaded. Armitage led her to the far corner of the garden, beyond the viburnum bushes where he knew a wasp's nest festered. It was a blazing hot day, Donna, stumbling in new high heels in the unkempt grass, lost her footing, threw her hand up for support, set it through the nest that was still in the early stages of construction.

The wasps went crazy.

Stinging Donna twenty times.

Her face wouldn't look the same for weeks.

She shrieked and screamed and ran for the house, searching for a shoulder to cry on, and more gin. Armitage hid in the long grass, grinning, and thinking of his mother. He could still hear Donna wailing in the house. 'Donald, Donald, do something for God's sake!'

Armitage laughed to himself and tried to catch a big red butterfly. It had been one of the better days, so far as he was concerned.

When he was five, his father began taking him to the garage on Saturday mornings. He thought the boy would be interested in the cars and the engines. Armitage detested the idea. He hated the smell of petrol, diesel and oil. He disliked engines, the sharp edges underneath the vehicles, and the frightening noise as the mechanics went about their work. He had no interest in science or engineering in any form. He would take his teddy bear along for company and would ignore the cars and customers and find a quiet corner, and content himself by playing with his only pal.

The second Saturday that Donald took him was busier than usual. Donald lost track of his son. He was far too busy for parental supervision, Armitage wandered outside, up the high street, and in the first shop he came to.

Greenaway's Florists.

A magical place full of multi coloured blooms and a scent that reminded him of his mother.

'That's a fine bear,' said Mrs Greenaway, who owned and ran the shop. She'd noticed the little boy standing in the doorway. He'd been there for some time.

'What's his name?'

The boy said nothing.

'Would you like to help me arrange the flowers?'

The boy nodded.

'Come here, then.'

The boy ambled across the little shop.

'Set your teddy down there, and we'll begin.'

Armitage liked Mrs Greenaway from the first moment and soon came to adore her. She smelt of soap and cleanliness and warmth and scent. Perhaps it was working with blooms all day, he imagined, she smelt like his much missed mother. She was always smiling and producing chocolate fingers from her pinny, and once they grew to know each other, she would put her arms around his tiny shoulders, or pat his freckled forearms, encouraging him in, advising which flowers went best with which, which blooms to select, as Porridge the bear sat contentedly before them, observing, amongst the vases of multi coloured tulips, happy that his friend Armitage was in good company, and in high spirits. The bear hadn't seen that in ages.

Armitage had been in the shop for well over an hour before his panicking father burst in.

'There you are, you naughty boy! I've been looking all over for you!'

Mrs Greenaway knew her business neighbour well enough. She knew Kay as a friend. Kay had been a regular customer, always buying flowers for the house and the showroom, and in latter times she shared confidences. Mrs Greenaway knew Donna too, and of her reputation, though she was too polite to say anything about that.

'Don't shout at him,' she said. 'He's been helping me with the flowers. He's very good at it, and he's most welcome,' and as if to prove the point, she slipped a heavy silver coin into the boy's hand. It was the first time anyone outside of the family had ever given him money, and he would remember it forever.

'Would you like to come back next week?' She asked the boy.

Armitage nodded. He still hadn't spoken a word.

Mrs Greenaway stared at Donald, as if challenging him to refuse.

He thought about it for a second and nodded and said, 'All right, if it's what the boy wants.'

Armitage smiled sweetly.

Mrs Greenaway did too and said, 'Good, that's settled. I must get along, I have a wedding at three.'

Army picked up Porridge and waved the lovely lady goodbye, as his father took his hand and dragged him back to the smelly and noisy garage.

Armitage knew well enough where he preferred to be.

Chapter Seventeen

Samantha was getting dressed. She'd slipped into the pink skirt and jacket. She glanced in the mirror. Cocked her head from side to side. Her neat blonde bob-cut hair looked fab. Red lips, hint of mascara, not too much makeup for it was a lunchtime meet. She slipped on the designer white sling backs she'd bought with Desi in Manchester, and the ivory pigskin gloves. Desi had bought them. A special present for a special person.

They made a point of going to Manchester once a month for a big spend up. Always returned with far more merchandise than necessary, but that was half the fun, the naughtiness of it. Sam missed the trips to Cottonopolis, with Des. She'd tried it once by herself but it wasn't the same, but there was nothing that could be done about that now.

Samantha had a date.

A blind date; and blind dates were always the most exciting. She'd found him on the Internet. You can buy anything you want on the Internet these days. It had usurped the Young Conservatives as the easiest place to locate a new squeeze. She had done it by the book.

They suggested, the website owners, that to begin with you met at lunchtime in a very busy place. Safety in numbers. You can never be too careful. There are millions of weird people out there. Sam wasn't taking any chances.

They agreed to take lunch in the Hunting Rooms of the Royal Hotel in the Grosvenor precinct. They would meet outside the main entrance at one o'clock. She glanced at her watch. 12.15. Time to go.

Jago Cripps cleaned his glasses. He had a date with something of a mystery girl. She said he would not be disappointed. He'd soon see. He had no idea what she looked like. She said she was too shy to upload her picture. She would recognise him, because he would carry a bunch of daffodils. Jago had never bought flowers for a woman before, and the weird thing was, he had no way of recognising her. She'd insisted it be that way, and that made him nervous, but he was always nervous.

Jago was an accounts' manager at one of the American credit card companies that had opened for business on the expanding business parks south of the city. Chester was becoming a thriving financial centre, though that was the last thing on his mind as he backed out the car. He earned good money, though his masters took their full pennyworth in return. He also spent good money, up the ladder, down the snake. He hoped that Lena's lack of a picture wasn't because she was so dog god-awful.

Sam had chosen him because he looked wild. Long wavy dark hair, black-framed glasses, straight prominent nose, white skin, two red spots. He said he was twenty-nine but he looked younger. He'd written a biog that came over as if it had been written by a fifteen-year-old school kid on one of the wackier social networking sites.

Hobbies and interests: Getting pissed, taking drugs, acting wild, screwing, and hanging out with cool dudes.

In Sam's eyes the hobbies and the photos didn't match, and that was another reason she had selected him.

She saw him standing there, looking nervous, smoking a cigarette, a bunch of damp daffs in his hand, and she walked away. She would make him wait. Come back in ten minutes, no, fifteen, see if he was still there.

He was still there, in his vile blue trousers, and even viler green jacket, shirt and tie, probably his effort at looking smart. Or had he come straight from work? She didn't care. She ambled along the busy corridor, passed him; he barely offered her a second glance. Why not? Men usually did. Did he think she was too good to be true? Or did he think she wasn't coming?

She turned round and wandered back. He was still there. He was facing away and feeling the inside of the back of his shirt collar, as if he had been sweating, and it chafed.

'Jago?' she said, in her best sexy voice.

The guy swivelled round. Almost fell over. His face lit up at the perfect blonde before him. He liked her hair; and the pink suit. He liked her face and figure; he liked the red lipstick and bright green eyes, and the classy ivory gloves. Geez, he adored everything about her. She was perfect.

'Lena?' he said.

Sam nodded.

'You're late,' he said.

'Sorry,' she said, as if she enjoyed being admonished. 'The bus broke down.'

'No worries. You are here now.' He glanced down at the soppy daffies, 'These are for you.'

'Thanks,' she said, and gave them to an ancient woman who was shuffling by. She took one disdainful look at them and dumped them in the nearest bin.

Jago actually looked disappointed, then said, 'Shall we go in?'

'If you want to.'

'Oh yeah, so long as you do.'

'I'm hungry,' she said.

'Come on,' he said, as he strode toward the door and held it open.

Once seated at the corner table in the Hunting Rooms restaurant, they sat and studied the vast menu.

'It's very expensive,' muttered Jago.

'Not too much for you?'

'No, No! Not at all.'

He just wanted to make sure she had noticed, that she appreciated how much of his hard-earned cash he was about to lavish on her. Not to put too fine a point on it, was she worth it? She'd better be.

Sam chose her meal, not the most expensive items on offer, but not far off, and then she said, 'I always like champagne at lunchtimes, don't you?'

Jago hid the grimace and said, 'Yeah, of course, anything you say.'

They talked about this and that, and something and nothing, and then surprisingly, the plates were empty; the glasses were empty; the bottles were empty; and the meal was over.

She had never once removed her gloves.

He teased her by referring to her as the glovely lady, giggled at his own witticism, a joke that Sam, or was it Lena, forced herself to share.

The foreign waiter presented the bill. Jago squinted at it and tried to banish the figure from his mind. He hoped Lena might volunteer a contribution, but none was forthcoming. He took out his credit card, manufactured by his employers, and realised that with this meal he'd be maxed out.

He forced a smile across the table. Lena smiled back. She had gorgeous teeth, far better than his. He'd like those teeth down his pants. He paid the bill with that thought in mind, and could contain himself no longer.

'Well,' he said, 'Do you want to go out again?'

'Maybe,' she said, fiddling with her glove.

'Tomorrow night?'

She pulled a face. 'I might be able to do that.'

She was playing hard to get. He didn't care. He wanted to date her again; he wanted her back at his place; he wanted...

'What time did you have in mind?' she said.

'Eight o'clock OK with you?'

She bobbed her head.

'We could go for a meal, in some country pub.'

Lena nodded, didn't say anything.

'Where do you want to meet?'

'Outside the swimming baths.'

'OK,' he said, 'I can do that, you're on.'

Lena nodded and stood up and made to go but paused and said, 'Thanks for the meal, Jago,' and she walked off and left him sitting at the table.

He made no effort to follow, and that was cool.

Chapter Eighteen

Armitage looked forward to his visits to the garage, but only because he could slip away and run around the corner to the shop where the bell at the top of the door announced his arrival. Mrs Greenaway treated him like the son she never had. She'd raised three daughters, all now married and away. Army soon developed a deep interest in flowers. His imagination would fire as he matched the red tulips, roses, and geraniums.

Within a month he was filling the shop window with his selections, within a year he was creating displays far beyond anything Mrs Greenaway could match, and within two years people were coming from far and wide to have their arrangement made up by the handsome boy with the artistic touch.

He had a following.

He had an artistry.

At school, his interests were clearly defined between the things he loved and the things he couldn't abide. He adored art and drawing, anything creative, English composition, and stories. He detested science, physical education, and all sports. That went without saying. Sport was for the smellies.

His father was a keen rugby and football fan. He tried in vain to fire an interest in his young son in sport, as he rolled and kicked a wide selection of balls toward him in the back garden. Armitage would cry and run away. He wanted Mrs Greenaway; he wanted Porridge; he wanted the flowers, and his painting books, and most of all he wanted his mother.

Right there, in that garden, he didn't want his father at all.

After two years of trying, his father gave up. He even reconsidered the idea of changing the name of the business to Shelbourne and Son, so disappointed was he in his only offspring.

The following year Army discovered another interest. Classical music and singing. Mrs Greenaway would often have the radio on in the shop, always tuned to the station that only broadcast classical music. It was never on loud, though sometimes if a piece that Army knew came on, or when the shop was quiet, Army would ask for the volume to be increased, 'Louder Mrs Greeny,' he would shout, 'Louder!'

She would glance at his little face and couldn't refuse.

At school too he was introduced to classical music, when the children would be encouraged to dance.

'Dance to the music, children, dance!' the elderly lady would trill, often to The Dance of The Sugar Plum Fairy.

Many of the girls held dreams of becoming ballerinas and would dance like courting swans. They were old hands at seven. They knew the ropes, and how to impress. Armitage had never heard of ballet, and had no idea what the girls were doing, but that didn't stop him. He threw himself into it, holding the centre of the floor, dancing moves that bemused everyone. They seemed to seep out of his soul. The girls were fascinated and flocked to him, all desperate to dance with the crazy boy with the imagination of a rattlesnake.

The boys thought him a Nancy and shunned him still further. The girls weren't sure, but they were curious. He was different.

The biggest love of his life was singing.

He had a voice that could induce tingles to the spine, though no one outside of school knew that, until one day in the flower shop, a piece of music came on the radio they had been learning.

The shop was busy; it was coming up Saint Valentine's, and there was standing room only between the remaining blooms. Without a thought, Armitage burst into song. He was working in one corner, facing away from the others, building a bouquet of fragrant lilies. In the next second the shop was filled with his treble voice, pure as crystal snow.

Mrs Greenaway imagined the angelic voice was coming through her tinny speaker, but no, it was Armitage. The seven or eight customers present fell silent and stared. Mrs Greenaway's mouth fell open. There wasn't a sound in the shop but for the radio, and Armitage's soaring voice, as the old single-decker bus came rumbling up the high street.

At the end of the song, the adults burst into applause. Army was aghast, caught out, as if he had been doing something naughty. He turned and smiled at them, flushed beetroot red, felt even more uncomfortable, and ran outside and skipped back to the garage.

The following week Mrs Greenaway said, 'You're a wonderful singer, Army.'

'Thank you, Mrs Greenaway.'

'Where did you learn to sing like that?'

'At school.'

'Would you like to sing in a choir?'

'Don't know.'

'Would you like me to take you to the choir?'

'Dad wouldn't like it.'

'Would you come if I asked your dad?'

Army nodded and thought nothing more of it.

That night after Army had gone to bed, Mrs Greenaway called at the Shelbourne's mock Tudor detached house. She wasn't initially welcomed because Don and Donna had been canoodling on the settee. Donna was still adjusting her dress when Don brought Mrs G into the sitting room.

'What can I do for you, Mrs G? What has my son been up to now?'

'Your son is a very well-mannered boy.'

'If you say so.'

Mrs G explained she was in the choir at Saint Andrew's church, and that Armitage was a fabulous singer. She wanted him to go to the church for a trial to join the choir, and Army had expressed a wish to be given the opportunity.

'Has he now?' said Donald, a little miffed that this woman knew more about his son's interests than he did.

Donna said, 'Are you sure you're not mixing him up with someone else?'

Mrs G gave her a look that said everything.

'Let me sleep on it,' said Donald, and he did, and give him his due, the next day he popped into the florists and told Mrs G that Army could take the trial, if he wanted to.

Mrs G said, 'You won't regret it,' and rang the choirmaster and fixed an audition.

The choirmaster's name was Mr Davis, and he had a spiky reputation for strict discipline. If the boys couldn't turn up on time and behave themselves, they needn't bother coming. If the boys couldn't attend every single practice session, they needn't bother

91

coming either. Most of the boys were keen enough, because they would receive a small payment when they attended special services like weddings and christenings, while the lead singer would receive a handsome bonus. The competition to be top dog was hot.

The vicar was there that evening too, pottering about, mulling in his mind the coming Sunday's sermon. Mr Davis was well used to pushy parents who believed their little Johnny was something special, if not the best thing since Aled Jones, better even. He would not suffer fools and regularly dismissed triallists by asking one of the better singers to sing after they had finished, thus showing how things could and should be done, and how woeful little Johnny was. He was in that frame of mind when he called Armitage forward. Army stepped up, his throat dry.

The entire choir were there, hundreds of them, it seemed to him. He could never remember being so nervous. He glanced around as if for comfort, and saw Mrs Greeny on the back row of the ladies' section. She smiled and nodded him on.

'Well?' Davies said, far too abruptly for a young child, thought many of the ladies gathered there. 'Don't waste my time, boy. Sing if you are going to.'

Armitage took one last look round, grabbed a big breath, and launched into Jesu Joy of Man's Desiring.

His voice filled the church. Soaring into the void of the steeple. Filling people's heads. Mr Davis closed his eyes. He had never heard a triallist sing like it, and one so young. It beggared belief.

As Army finished, the ladies' choir burst into spontaneous applause. Even the vicar had crept closer for a better look to see who it was who had captivated everyone. The boys' choir applauded too, though not as enthusiastically. Perhaps one or two of the soloists had already realised their one-off fees might be in danger.

Armitage Shelbourne had arrived.

Donald and Donna were invited too. They hadn't intended to go; it wasn't their thing, but something deep inside Donald brought him there, and he dragged along Donna for company. Perhaps it was because he knew Kay would have wanted him to attend. Donna bitched about it all the way there. She hadn't been inside a church for fifteen years, and wasn't looking forward to it. Eastenders was on the television, for gawd's sake.

Like everyone else, Donald and Donna were captivated.

How could it be that from one so young, and so slight, a voice could emanate that filled that vast church, and moved people to tears?

'Who taught the little bugga to do that?' she whispered.

'I have no idea,' said Donald, feeling guilty that it had taken others to show him what a talented son he possessed.

He would never underestimate Armitage again.

Chapter Nineteen

Samantha was standing upstairs in the swimming baths, staring from the huge windows that afforded a great view of the car park and the forecourt below. Jago was down there, biting his nails, sitting in his ten-year-old family sized hatchback. At least he'd washed it and polished the silver wheels. Sam had been in far worse cars. He'd been waiting there for ten minutes. She would make him wait a little longer.

Jago saw Lena come out of the main entrance to the pool. He hadn't expected her to come that way, but that didn't matter, the only thing that mattered was that she was here. He reached over and flipped open the door.

'Hi,' she said, as she jumped in.

'Hi,' he responded, as she settled in the seat beside him.

He started the car and pulled out on to the inner ring road.

'Where are we going?' she asked.

'A country pub, I know,' he said. 'On the Frodsham road.'

He had chosen it with great care. They served a decent carvery for next to nothing, for he had next to no money. Tonight, if she asked for champagne, she would be disappointed. She was wearing a black two-piece suit, skirt and jacket and slinky leather gloves, and as he drove, he stole glances at her pert knees and breasts, and neat but understated makeup. She was as he remembered, sweet, sexy, and desirable, and later on, after he'd slipped her a tab or two, she would be his.

The pub was OK, and the meal acceptable. Jago bought them each a glass of wine, saying that he had two expensive bottles in his fridge at home, and because he was driving, he didn't want to drink too much while they were out.

'That's cool,' she said, and it was cool too, for she didn't fancy riding with Jago if he was drunk.

During a break in conversation, she asked him if he ever experimented with drugs. She'd asked it as bold as that, not even bothering to lower her voice, as if she didn't care who heard.

'Didn't you read my biog?' he said, grinning like an ape.

94

'I did, but I thought you might be exaggerating.'

'Nope!' he said. 'No way! I'm up for anything, me. You only live once. Bring it on, sister.'

Lena smiled wickedly and said, 'That's great Jago, because I'm really into all that stuff. Tell you the truth, it's the only thing I really like, the only thing that truly excites me.'

'Yeah?'

'Yeah, sure. Have you got any gear back at the flat?'

He was about to say, sure thing, when a weird thought crossed his mind. He didn't really know this babe from Adam. She could be a copper for all he knew, a drugs' undercover officer. He'd read about such things in the National Inquirer, police stings on unsuspecting punters.

'You're not a cop, are you?'

As if she would tell him if she was.

'Me? Course not. Don't be stupid. I told you I work in the booking office at the racetrack,' and as if to prove the point she brought out the new Chester racetrack diary, the expensive green leather-bound edition with the gold logo on the front cover, and the slogan: England's Oldest Racecourse. 'You can have it if you want,' she said, 'I can get hundreds of them.'

'Yeah, ta, I will,' and he took it from her be-gloved hand and slipped it in his inside pocket. It seemed to do the trick for there were no more questions as to whether she was a copper or not. What a ridiculous suggestion.

Then he said, and he lowered his voice, 'If you must know, I've just taken delivery of some wicked skunk, and I keep a selection of tabs in, for the weekend, like, or any other day come to that,' and he laughed. He saw Lena smiling her approval across the table and said, 'The two go well together, talk about a trip...'

She smiled crazily and said, 'I like you Jago, you're cool, I can't wait to get back to your place and give it a whirl. Have you finished here? Shall we go, come on... the tabs are calling,' and she stood up and headed for the door.

What a crazy bitch, he thought, am I lucky or what? This could be a night to remember, maybe above all others, and he jumped up and followed her out.

She was standing by the car, coquettish look on her face, waiting for him to open up. He pointed the key and fired, but nothing happened, key battery dead. Jago cursed and slipped the key in the lock and opened up.

She fixed her seatbelt, but he did not. Stared at her instead, waiting for her to turn and look at him, for he knew this was the point where he could land a kiss.

She knew what he was after, and saw him coming, swaying across the cabin toward her, eyes closed, lips puckered, glasses steaming. Yuck! Yuck! Yuck! At the last moment, she turned her head and allowed him to kiss her on the cheek.

'Later, Jago, later,' she whispered in a come on a voice. 'Let's get back to your place.'

'Sure, babe,' he said, struggling to keep the disappointment from his voice as he started the car.

Jago Cripps lived in a modern second-floor flat on the northern side of the city, next to a huge new health and fitness club that many of the block residents used. When he'd moved in, he checked out the fitness palace, saw the huge annual membership fee, and declined. Jago had never been much of a health and fitness fiend, so what was the point in starting now?

The flat boasted a fair sized living room, a sweet smell throughout, noted Sam, a modern kitchen and bathroom, and two bedrooms, one boasting a king-size bed where Jago did his thing. In the other bedroom he threw his junk and closed the door and hoped it would disappear. The apartment was exactly the same as ten million others that had sprouted up throughout the kingdom. In the sitting room was a huge flatscreen telly, bought on the credit card, and a soft white sofa, also paid for by Jago's employers. It was only eighteen months old and already growing grubby.

'Drinky first,' he said, going to the kitchen.

Lena nodded her approval, and Jago smiled.

He ran into the kitchen; he seemed to run everywhere, and she heard the pop of a bottle of wine being opened. Perhaps it was a good bottle after all, no screw tops for him.

He grabbed two large glasses from the cupboard, and held them to the neon light. They were cleanish, but to hell with it, clean enough, and he emptied the bottle, half in each.

Then he was back in the sitting room. She was ensconced on the sofa. He handed her the wine, put his on the low table, and disappeared into his bedroom, saying, 'I'll get the business.'

She grabbed the glass and scurried to the kitchen, dumped half of it, and skipped back to the settee.

He came back, grinning, sat beside her, but not too close, clocked the half empty glass and said, 'The wine all right?'

'Fab, Jago,' she said, kicking off her shoes and tucking her feet beneath her like a young deer.

Jago nodded, two or three times, as if he had a tick. Took an almighty glug from his glass, and set a neat, square box on the table, and a pouch from which he produced a spliff. A moment later, a disposable lighter in hand, he flicked a huge flame to life and began puffing, as Sam made a big show of taking another mouthful of German white.

Jago took in several breaths of burning skunk, held the thing toward her. Lena grinned and reached across and took it, brought it to her mouth, feigned to take in a big swallow, in reality took in a little, not too much, for she wasn't that keen on weed, and passed it back to him. Pink lipstick on the butt. He noticed that, and he liked it too. It was the closest he'd been to it yet, though the night was young, as he sucked the lipstick away, drawing heavily in. Lena reached down and emptied her glass and set it on the table.

God, she could drink, this bitch, he thought, following suit, and retreating to the kitchen for an early refill.

When he returned, she had a strange look on her face. She looked out of it already. That was cool. The more out of it she was, the better.

Then she said, 'Tabs I like,' and she giggled, as if there could be rewards on offer.

'Yeah?' he said, unable to suppress the grin from his spotty face. 'You're in luck, just you wait and see what I have in here,' and he opened his dinky box of treasure.

It was packed with pills. At least four different types.

He glanced wide-eyed into the box, and peered across at her, over the top of his specs, a manic look creeping over his face.

'Ecstasy?' she said.

'Among others,' he said, in a superior way. 'These,' he said, holding a large white tablet up at the side his face, 'Are supercharged babies. Unbelievable!'

'Fantabiosa,' she said, pretending to drink more wine. 'And,' she added, 'Seeing as you have been such a good boy, or a bad boy, in this case, I have not come to the party without contributing.'

'Yeah?' he said, grinning.

She grabbed her bag and flipped it open. Took out her purse, opened it, removed a long silver strip of sweeties, and set them on the table next to his precious box.

He gazed down at them as if they were diamonds. Then picked them up and brought them closer to his glasses. 'What are they?'

'Te-maz-e-pam!!' she said with a flourish, an exclamation that reminded him of the American superhero comics he adored.

'Te-maz-e-pam!!' he repeated, 'Bang, bang, bang, baby!'

She almost burst into laughter. The guy was away with the mixer. A parody of any regular drug user. She wondered if he had only recently begun to experiment, and pondered if his tabs were real. Maybe the klutz had paid through the nose for a hangover cure. She was having doubts.

'How many?' he said in a rush.

'I take four, with the E.'

'Yeah?' he said, unsure of the number.

He watched Lena bend forward and empty them all from their silver covered bays. They bounced on to the table.

'I like to crunch one first,' she said, and she slipped one in her mouth and made a point of crunching the tiny thing like a horse with a mint.

Jago's mouth fell open. This bird was crazy. Up for anything. He grabbed a tab and threw it in. Crunched it and grimaced.

'Awful!' he said, swigging his mouth clean.

'It's not the taste, it's the feeling,' she said. 'Give us an E.'

He couldn't pass her one quick enough. All the success he'd ever had with women came through E.

She took it, picked up the glass, made a big show of presenting it to her mouth, took a gulp of wine, in reality a sip, threw the tab in her mouth and drank and swallowed.

'Yeah, baby!' he screamed, grabbing an E and flushing it down.

'Chase her with Te-maz-e-pam!' Lena screamed.

'Yeah, yeah,' and he swept a handful of the remaining pills from the table and in they went.

His glass was almost empty.

'Have you got any more drink?' she asked.

'Yeah, but not as good as the others.'

'Don't care! If it's alcoholic, I like it,' she said.

He made to stand up.

'No, you're all right. I'll get it.'

'It's in the fridge,' he yelled as she hit the kitchen.

She reached up the back of her jacket and pulled up her blouse. The tab fell into her hand. She'd been practicing that sleight of hand, drink before the face, throw in the tab, seemingly into the mouth, in reality down the neck of her blouse. It had worked better than she'd ever dreamed. He never had a clue. Flushed it down the sink.

'Find it?' he shouted.

'Yeah, just coming,' and then she was back, setting the screw top bottle on the table.

He was yawning.

She sat beside him, more sure than ever that he was a drugs novice. All talk and no experience. He was game though, she'd give him that. But he didn't even know that E and alcohol should not be mixed. He was looking nervous, more nervous than usual, and that was something. The E was kicking in. He flexed his jaws, there was tightening there, his heart was speeding, he began to sweat, nothing new in that either with Jago, but it was more pronounced. He felt sick and thought it was the wine. It wasn't. It was the E taking over. He was coming up. The E was making him hyperactive, fighting the Temazepam that was trying to put him to sleep.

'There's something bugging me,' he slurred.

'Yeah, babe? What's that?'

'The glovely lady hasn't once removed her gloves.'

99

He watched Lena smile at him. 'I do sometimes,' she said coyly, leaving the thought in the air.

'Yeah? Like when?'

'Like… in the bedroom.'

'Yeah? Do you wanna go the bedroom?'

He watched her slowly nod.

'More temaz first, though,' she said.

He threw out his tongue and waggled it like a snake in anticipation of a kill. She grabbed more pills and fed him, gave him another big drink, pretended to take more tabs herself, threw them behind the sofa.

Jago yawned, but said, 'Come on, baby!'

She sat there, playing for time. He stood up, unsteady on his feet. 'Come on!' he repeated.

Lena stood up as Jago put his arm around her and led her toward his room, steadying himself as he went. He fell on the bed, on to his back, and laughed.

'Come and join me,' he said, yawning again, and patting the mattress.

She lay down beside him. Let him slip his arm around her.

'Take those bloody gloves off!'

'Take your shirt off first!' she said, propping herself up on her elbow, her green eyes wide and ablaze. He had never seen eyes like them, not on a human being. They were like the eyes of a black mountain lion he had once seen in a California Zoo, an amazing holiday he had taken with his cousin Jeff, the first extravagance that had started all the trouble with the damned credit card. He'd been unable to stop himself using it ever since.

'Yeah?' he said to her invitation to remove his shirt.

Lena was gazing down at him, like a nurse in some alco-druggy clinic, persuading him to take medication, nodding encouragingly. He began removing his shirt. It was a big effort but he was free. He lay back. She stared down at him. His skin was white and spotty. In the centre of his chest were five straggly hairs. His nipples were pink and childlike, his arms thin and weak. He yawned again, deeper than before.

The Temazepam was winning the war.

'Take those bloody gloves off,' he slurred.

100

She sat up straight, high above him, as if she were on the top of a mountain, he thought, and he, so far below, on the shores of the Dead Sea. She took hold of her left glove with her right hand and pretended to tug.

Jago's eyelids fluttered and closed.

Victory to the Temaz.

She eased herself from the bed. Jago didn't stir.

She retreated to the living room. Took her glass to the kitchen, washed it thoroughly, taking great care to remove every hint of lipstick, dried it and put it away. Picked up the spliff butt from the ashtray, took it to the bathroom, closed the door to keep the noise inside, flushed it down the loo, standing and waiting and making sure it had gone.

Took a look round the kitchen and living room. No fingerprints, of course. Was there any other evidence she had ever been there, other than the microscopic fibres from her jacket and skirt, and she'd deal with that little connection later. No footmarks on the hall floor, it had been a dry night; she hadn't left a trace.

She returned to the bedroom.

Jago was snoring, already in a deep sleep.

The E might have wanted him to dance the night away, but the Temazepam was boss, and thought different, and the Temazepam had allies, the drink, the spliff, and Jago's weak and neglected body.

She glared down at him.

He might already have taken enough to kill himself, and she considered leaving him to his fate. But on second thoughts she wouldn't. What was the point in that? She wouldn't take any chances. She opened her bag and removed the steel craft knife.

Gently seized his left wrist and sliced into it, just above the hand. The iconic place for suicide. The blood gushed and flowed down to the white sheet, spreading like wet ink on blotting paper. She knew two leakages were always better than one, as in opening a can, or anything else come to that, two holes increased the flow threefold. She slipped the knife into his right wrist. It was easy.

Serves you right, Jago, for drugging and raping unsuspecting girls, if indeed that is what you have done. She didn't care about that. She didn't care about Jago; didn't care about anything, not since her precious Desi had left this world. She wiped the blade clean on the sheet and slipped it into her bag.

100 ways to Kill People.

Drink and drugs, and invite their wrists to taste the fresh air.

Not clean, but pretty effective. There was no way of coming back from that, not for Jago Cripps. He was on his one-way trip to oblivion.

Samantha laughed.

It had been a good day.

She took a last look at him. He looked so peaceful.

His mother would be proud.

She picked up Jago's car keys; left the room, opened the front door, and left the flat.

Chapter Twenty

Armitage woke in a sweat. Porridge slumbered on beside him. His father and Donna were downstairs, arguing. Their loud voices had woken him. In the darkness, Armitage sat up and glanced at his Toy Town clock. It ticked on merrily, oblivious to the boy's worries. The luminous hands signalled their message. The small man was pointing towards the twelve, the big man toward the three. Armitage yawned.

Still, they yelled at one another downstairs. He couldn't make out what they were saying; hearing only the muffled rumbling discontent floating up through the plaster, floorboards, and the carpet. It sounded spiteful. It sounded frightening. In the darkness, Armitage grimaced. They had been arguing more often, sometimes every night, disturbing the boy's sleep and dreams. He boasted black rings around his eyes, though he was unaware of that, he hadn't noticed. But the teachers at school had, and so had Mrs Greenaway.

As the days and weeks and months slipped away, so his hatred for Donna Deary increased. It was mutual; that dislike, for she had taken to slapping him when his father was missing, or in another part of the house. She'd admonish Army and clip his ear for the slightest misdemeanour, real or imaginary. Afterwards she would say, 'And don't go running and whining to your father! He's not interested, and if you do, I'll take that wooden ruler of yours and thrash your legs to shreds!'

Armitage valued his legs, and whether the threat was real or bluster, he didn't know, but he wasn't about to test it. She frightened him, and he remained silent. His father never noticed a thing. He had troubles of his own.

A moment later Armitage made out what they were saying. They must have stepped up the volume; perhaps the dispute was reaching a climax.

She yelled: 'If you don't take me to see the pyramids this year, we're finished, understand? Finished! You promised to take me, and you can bloody well take me!'

'Why can't you understand I don't have the bloody cash!' his father screamed back.

'Then sell something! What about that money you've put aside for the kid? You could use some of that! He's not interested in money. You only have to look at him to tell that. Use that if you have to!'

'I will not touch Armitage's inheritance. That's Kay's money. She set it aside for him.'

'Wake up and open your bloody eyes! Kay's dead, you barmpot! In case you haven't noticed, it's me you should be looking after. You're not living in the real world, you useless article!'

'We can't use that money and that's final!'

'Use what you bloody well like, but you understand this, Donald Shelbourne, if you don't take me to Egypt this year as you promised, we are finished. Understand me? Finished!'

'We are not going to Egypt!'

'We'll see about that! And another thing, you can sleep in the spare room tonight. I don't want you anywhere near me! You give me the creeps!'

After that, Armitage heard a heavy slap, echoing through the house, magnified by the after midnight stillness.

Then silence returned.

In his mind Army imagined she had slapped him, for his father would never slap anyone, and certainly not a lady. Though thinking about it later, perhaps it might do her some good. Armitage would admit that sometimes he imagined slapping her himself, if only he could find the courage. Perhaps his father felt the same way.

If only she would disappear.

Army turned over, pulled the pillow over his head, kissed the bear, hugged the creature to his shaking chest, closed his eyes, and tried to sleep. Tomorrow was dancing day. It was important there was a spring in his step. There wouldn't be, if he didn't sleep.

Throughout the following week, rows and fights disturbed his nights. During mealtimes they would glare at one another and say almost nothing. They'd glare at Army too and bite his head off over any tiny thing. Living in the house was hell. He couldn't help comparing it to how it was when his angelic mother ruled the roost.

Unbeknown to Armitage, the economy had taken a hefty lurch away from prosperity. People were no longer buying cars, worse still;

104

they were selling them, chasing the cash like everyone else. The Shelbourne Motor Company had been in financial trouble for some time. Everyone worked hard but there was never any money in the bank, and the situation had become critical.

For one moment Donna considered using a small proportion of her Swiss bank savings to help the business over the lean times. Perhaps £10,000, that would help, and it wouldn't make too much of a dent in her £180,000 nest egg. Recently she had stepped up Laddon's invoices, keen as she was to break the £200,000 barrier, and her greediness had worsened Shelbourne's plight.

She decided against it, of helping anyone, and especially Donald Shelbourne, after he had actually hit her. Slapped her across the face, the cheeky git. She could still feel the stinging sensation on the cheek. No, she wouldn't help a living soul, not Donald, not that hopeless queer son of his, nor the floundering company. They could all take a run and jump. She would not touch any of her savings.

The following day when Donald was at work, Armitage at school, she had a dental appointment. Afterwards, she hurried home, packed two cases, wrote a hurried note: Sorry Donald, it is obvious we have come to the end of the road, you clearly don't love me, and please don't follow me. I am out of here, Donna.

She called a cab and ordered it to the railway station and boarded a train for Bristol. Sitting waiting in the hairdressers, she had read grand things of the West Country. She would visit all the big towns, Bath, Cheltenham, Bristol, Gloucester, Wells, Taunton, Exeter, and settle in the one that suited her best. She was a lady of means, though she had no intention of squandering her hard earned wealth.

No, she would find another man. She was still young and desirable, so she told herself, so she witnessed, as she stared into the mirror, painting. She would take up golf, act the damsel in distress, book some lessons, seek new company, a rich widower would be perfect, a handsome golf pro on the side, anyone who could show her the ropes, take her into their circle, provide her with everything she desired, just so long as he was a decent-looking man, and solvent.

Donna knew how to foster interest, how to find a patron, and there must be thousands of businesses in the West Country looking for a good bookkeeper.

She might change her name too. Donna Trowbridge, she decided after staring at the map for an hour; she had never liked Deary, What's up, Deary? She was young and carefree, with no ties to restrict her. More than that, she was a great catch for someone, and already she had visions of handsome beaus from Bath to Bristol begging for her hand.

Donald and the squirt could go to hell.

Armitage was thrilled at the news.

He slept better; began dancing better; and looked better; and Mrs Greenaway could guess the reason when she heard the welcome news that Donna Deary had fled the town. 'Not before time,' she muttered, 'not before time.'

This newfound sense of wellbeing did not spread to his father. Things lurched from bad to worse. The Shelbourne Motor Company failed to pay for the latest batch of cars. The wholesalers were furious and descended on the forecourt and repossessed everything that hadn't been paid for. The Shelbourne Motor Company had entered its death throes. Donald wasn't thinking straight. He had even used Armitage's inheritance, Kay's money; that she had earmarked for her only son. He hated doing it, and Armitage would never see a penny.

One week later, the business went bust. It owed just shy of a million pounds. An Official Receiver was appointed to wind up the company's affairs. Donald was out of a job. He was broke, and broken.

Armitage did not understand what all that meant. He had always hated the garage and the cars and the filthy mechanics and the stink. He was elated to see it go, and pleased to be free of going there every Saturday morning. He could go straight to the florists and for a short while life was heaven.

But it hit home when the house went up for sale. Donald had mortgaged everything. The equity had fled as quickly as Donna. His father told him they would be moving out.

'Where are we going to live?' moped Army.

He adored the house, his room, and the garden where his mother had chased and played and laughed with him. Such happy, sunny days and beautiful memories that seemed so long ago, days that would never return.

106

'I have found a little flat for us,' said his father. 'On Kenneally Drive.'

'On Kenneally Drive?' said Army, imagining he was hearing things.

'Yes. We are moving there on Saturday.'

'But that's…'

'Yes, I know… it's on the council estate.'

Armitage pulled a face and said: 'Will I be able to take Porridge?'

'Yes, son, of course, Porridge is coming too.'

So they moved into a small two-bedroom flat on the second floor at number 39 Kenneally Drive on the same council estate that Donald had been so sniffy about. As it turned out, the residents were friendly, even to the dancing freak with the plummy voice.

Donald soon made friends. It was as if a mighty weight had been chipped from his shoulders. He met a young widow by the name of Janet Everrit who lived in the house on the corner. She had taken a shine to the upright, well-dressed bloke who'd moved in up the road.

Donald and Army began taking tea there. Donald fixed up her old car and he would drive them all to the supermarket on Saturday morning to buy provisions. It sure as hell was better than taking the public bus. They began spending evenings at the Everrit house, and the following week they even had a sleepover. Armitage was forced to share a room with Smelly Everrit. He had never shared a room with anyone before, other than Porridge. He didn't like it much, but his dad seemed happy.

Chapter Twenty-One

It had gone two in the morning by the time Samantha left Jago's flat. It was dark and quiet and cloudy, looking like rain, as she opened his car and adjusted the seat, jumped inside, clicked open her bag, dragged out a folded baseball cap, and pulled it down over her face. She started the car and rolled from the car park and headed across town for the swimming pool, just as fine rain began tumbling down.

Her own car was still there, alone and safe and unmolested. She pulled Jago's car skew-whiff into a bay some way off, glanced round, no one about, and stepped into the miserable night. Checked she'd left nothing behind, closed the door, took Jago's keys with her to her own car, opened up, jumped in and drove away.

Sam's flat was on the south side of the city. It was one of four apartments in a redbrick Victorian detached house. Two flats to the left, ground floor and first, and two mirroring flats to the right. Sam's was the ground floor right. She'd lived there on and off for five years, and she liked it. The other residents were single and quiet and past fifty. They kept themselves to themselves, immersed in their work and studies and books. They would say hello in passing, but that was about it. At least two of them were shortsighted, and another was going deaf. She had rarely been in any of the other flats, and they had never been in hers, and that suited Sam just fine.

As she crossed the river on the Grosvenor Bridge, she buzzed down the passenger window and hurled Jago's keys over the handrail. They turned over in the air several times and splashed into the river. On the still night air she imagined she heard the plop, though she might have been mistaken.

There was no one about at the flats. Iona House was asleep.

The other three residents, two guys and a woman; were strict timekeepers. They all went to bed between half-past ten and eleven o'clock, and they didn't hear the car cruise into the small car park, and they didn't see or hear Sam get out of the car and hurry inside.

Each of the flats possessed a wood-burning stove that provided hot water and heating. Sam would keep it burning all year round, except for the hottest summer months. She stood before the stove and undressed. Took off her jacket and skirt, opened the stove, as the iron metallic clunk echoed through the old house. That couldn't be helped, as she tossed the clothing inside. Blouse? Yeah, that too. Slipped it off and in it went. Three minutes later and the clothing didn't exist. The last item she would remove that night would be the gloves. The glovely lady, she said aloud, mimicking Jago's idiotic voice. I am the glovely lady. She giggled. Would she burn those too? Of course not, that was unthinkable. Desi had bought them special. She'd wash them in the morning.

Sam smiled and yawned. It had been a good day. It had been a good night too. She went to bed, slept well; didn't think of Jago Cripps once. He was a rapist and woman molester, a drug addict and a wastrel. The world would not miss the likes of him, and there was no reason for Sam to waste precious time thinking about the guy.

In the morning Sam rose at ten. Turned on the radio. Nothing new. No murders in the city. Turned on the Internet. Nothing special. Big fuss over some oil leak off Africa, but that was nothing new either. Navigated to the word processor, settled on the kooky AR Delaney font, and wrote a letter. It had been coming for a few days. Today it would be written and posted, and after that, the next night's clothes needed attention. Yesterday had been an off day; but tonight it was back to the casino. Work could not be avoided. The bills had to be paid; the mortgage on Flat 2 Iona House wouldn't pay itself.

Walter knew there was something weird about the letter the moment Jenny Thompson handed it to him. One large A4 manila envelope, one solitary sheet inside judging by the skinny feel of it, one self adhesive first class stamp, one postmark reading Chester City, 2.30pm from yesterday. It was the address that grabbed Walter's attention. A homemade label, black print on white paper, ink jetted letters, unusual font, taped to the envelope.

Private and Personnel
Inspector Wally Darrito

Two spelling mistakes in eleven words. Walter opened his desk drawer and took out a pair of latex gloves and slipped them on, grabbed the letter opener from the centre of the desk, eased it inside the flap, and carefully opened. He had been right. A single sheet of unfolded A4 paper. Same inkjet printing, same strange font.

Wally,

We thought you was clever. Perhaps you should retire, sod off back to Jamaca. You ain't up to the job, mate. Its past your retirement. You said we'd be meeting soon. It hasn't happened. It ain't going to happen. Your thick, but we like you. Keep smiling, that's what fool's do.

The Chester Mollesters

Walter read the message three times. Counted the spelling mistakes, five to add to the two on the address label, six if you included the missing apostrophe in "its". Poor grammar too, was, aint, really clunky, and written by an ill-educated person, or maybe that was what the writer intended. The big question was, was it from the killer, or was it some sick hoax from someone desperate for attention?

He held the paper to the light. No watermark, standard supermarket issue copy paper if he had to guess. Untraceable. He slipped it into a clear plastic sleeve and ambled to the photocopy machine, made four copies, returned to his desk, placed the original and the envelope into his drawer, and closed and locked it. Ambled across the office, taking the copies with him, pondering as he went as to any hidden meaning in the signature: The Chester Mollesters. It wasn't something he'd ever come across before.

He tapped on Mrs West's door.

'Come,' she said, glancing up and removing her spectacles.

'I've had a letter, ma'am.'

'From the killer?'

'Maybe.'

'Come in, shut the door, sit down.'

They talked about the letter. He showed her a copy; assured her the original was untouched and would be sent to forensics for fingerprinting and DNA tests. She asked him if the phrase Chester Mollesters meant anything to him, and he said it didn't. She asked him what he thought the letter meant. He said he thought the killer had already struck again. Mrs West grimaced and rolled her eyes and said, 'Not the child you mentioned? God forbid.'

'Let's hope not, ma'am.'

'Bring Karen and Cresta in. Let's see what they think,' and in the next minute they were all around the table staring at Walter's copies.

'You said he'd be in touch,' said Mrs West to Cresta, 'And he has.'

Cresta glowed and then added, 'Could be a woman, Mrs West.'

Karen said, 'How does the killer know about Jamaica?'

'I think we can blame the worldwide web for that,' sighed Walter.

'The he-she thing is baiting you,' said Cresta.

'I know that,' said Walter, and then he said, 'There are two things that interest me, the spelling mistakes for a start.'

'And me,' said Karen.

'Is the person poorly educated, or is it a con?'

'I think it's a con,' said Cresta. 'It's too obvious. Jamaca looks so wrong.'

'I agree,' said Walter. 'So we might assume the person is well educated.'

'For sure,' said Cresta. 'Uni wouldn't surprise me.'

'Chester Mollesters?' said Karen.

'Means nothing to me,' said Walter. 'Dreadful expression, not the kind of words you would associate with adult murders.'

'You said there were two things?' said Mrs West.

Walter bobbed his head. 'Why does the note refer to we? Surely there isn't a team of the buggers.'

'More likely the royal we,' said Cresta, 'Didn't Mrs Thatcher once say: We have a grandson? I don't believe there is more than one person involved for a minute. Split personality, yes, two different people, unlikely.'

'Yet it's as if the killer is part of a couple,' said Karen.

'In his or her mind they still are, except, as we have discussed before, I believe the partner is no longer there. Gone but not forgotten. The killer can't get the memory of being part of a couple out of their mind.'

'Do you think they will contact us again?' asked Mrs West.

'Yes,' said Cresta.

'I agree with that,' said Walter.

'So what are we doing now?' asked Mrs West, just about keeping the natural tetchiness from her voice.

'We'll see if there is anything on the letter, the paper itself, maybe even in the ink, or the envelope, or the stamp, but I doubt there is,' said Walter.

'And the checking of cars?'

They all glanced at Karen.

'We have so far checked the owners of and searched three hundred and eight cars that match the vague description. We haven't found anything unusual except some weed in one, quite unrelated.'

'I hate to say it,' Mrs West said, 'but we seem to be stalling. Are we waiting for another murder to kick-start things?'

'I am going to stay late, go through everything again, right from the beginning,' said Walter. 'I think we are missing something.'

'I'll help you,' said Karen.

Walter nodded his appreciation.

They checked out purple Cresta, hoping for inspiration.

She sensed her moment and threw out the first thought that came into her head. 'The he-she thing will kill again' she said, 'for sure.'

'Great,' muttered Mrs West. 'That's all I need.'

'I'll be late in the morning,' said Walter. 'Funeral, I'll be at the cathedral, Right Reverend James Kingston.'

They all nodded and went back to work.

Chapter Twenty-Two

Samuel was getting dressed. He slipped on a fresh blue shirt and red tie. He glanced in the mirror. Cocked his head from side to side. His neat, short blond hair looked at its best. Man moisturiser, he couldn't get enough of it, kept the crow's feet at bay. It surprised him more men didn't swallow their pride and use it. He had a lunchtime meet and was looking forward to it. He slipped on the black casual shoes he'd bought with Desi in Manchester, and the gold tiepin Desi adored.

They made a point of going to Manchester once a month for a big spend up. Always came back with far more merchandise than they needed, but that was half the fun, the naughtiness of it. Samuel missed his trips to Cottonopolis with Desi. Afterwards he tried it once by himself, but it wasn't the same. Never mind, there was nothing that could be done about that now.

Samuel had a date.

A blind date; and blind dates were always the most exciting. He'd found her on the Internet. You can buy anything you want on the Internet these days. It had usurped the Young Conservatives as the easiest place to locate a new squeeze. He had done it by the book.

They suggested, the website owners, that to begin with you met at lunchtime in a busy place. Safety in numbers. You can never be too careful. There are millions of weird people out there. Samuel wasn't taking any chances.

They'd agreed to take lunch in the Hunting Rooms of the Royal Hotel in the Grosvenor precinct. They would meet outside the main entrance at one o'clock. He glanced at his watch. 12.15. Time to go.

Sally Beauchamp was looking forward to the date, even if he was a mystery man. He assured her she would not be disappointed. She'd soon see. She had no idea what he looked like. He said he was too shy to upload his picture on the Internet. He would recognise her, because she would carry a bunch of daffodils. Make sure you do! Sally felt stupid, standing there with a bunch of yellow flowers.

Flowers weren't her thing, and the weird thing was, she had no way of recognising him. He'd insisted it be that way, and that made her nervous, and she'd almost called the whole idea off, but then again, she was up for adventure, always had been.

Sally came from a good family and had trained as an accountant, but the pay had been lousy and her progress slow, and one day when a client had been in town, he'd asked her to go for a drink after work. He was pretty old, at least forty-five, but as her mother would have said, well preserved, and his greying hair suited him, and she had nothing better to do, so she agreed.

He took her for a wonderful meal and with the coffee afterwards he said he was going to make her a proposition. Yeah? She'd said, expecting some kind of pass to be made, and in a way it was, though not as she had imagined. I'll give you £500 cash now to spend the night with me, here at the hotel. He'd said it just like that, bold as brass, not even bothering to lower his voice.

Sally had taken a fair bit to drink, and the guy was quite handsome, more so through booze, and £500 was £500. She'd smiled and said, 'OK,' and that was that.

It was a good night; and a very profitable one too. Michael had been a man of his word, and in the morning they parted, smiling at one another, a few aching bones on either side, the roll of used tenners sleeping in her handbag.

It was her ticket into prostitution.

She'd never planned it, she told herself; she had never even considered the idea, the career move, as she later came to refer to it. It had just happened as if by accident, and she had never regretted it.

That had been ten years before, and now in her mid-thirties she was a woman of means and was looking to settle down. She was hoping to retire. She was on the lookout for a husband, maybe even start a family, it was not too late, and something about this guy intrigued her.

Tristram, his name was, and she had never known a Tristram before. It sounded kind of cute, sexy even, Trist...ram, and his brief biog said: Writer and Broadcaster seeks an attractive lady with a view to marriage and hopefully, children. Interests include foreign travel, lino cuttings, and fashion.

How could any woman not be intrigued by a man who listed his interests as lino cutting and fashion? Not to mention the Writer and Broadcaster bit that carried hints of glamour.

She'd donned the good navy blue suit; she could still squeeze into it despite the few extra pounds that had crept up on her almost unnoticed over the previous two years. Sally left her city centre loft apartment, buzzed open the garage door, jumped into her Audi sports, and drove the short distance into town. She had fallen into the habit of driving everywhere. She knew it was lazy, but what the hell. There were other, more important things to spend her precious energy on.

She hoped Tristram's lack of a picture wasn't because he was so dog god awful, and an image of a short fat bald man who had trimmed his age by ten years filtered into her mind. You could never tell with men. So many of the bastards were out-and-out liars, and through her career she felt as if she'd met every one of them. Just so long as she had never met Tristram before. Sally shivered at the thought.

Samuel had chosen her because she was short. He could look down on her, and he liked that, and more so, imagined that women did too, being looked down on by their partner, and also because she looked tarty. It was difficult to say why. Her clothes appeared expensive, and the locket around her neck had cost a pretty penny. Her straight auburn hair curled under her chin and had been expensively coiffured, and though she may have been a few pounds overweight, no one was perfect.

She said she was thirty, but he thought you could add five years to that. Human beings were born liars. In Samuel's world everyone lied; everyone except Desi, of course. Sally had written a biog that came over as if she were a founder member of the Women's Institute, listing cake and jam making as some of her hobbies. Samuel doubted that. She looked far more of a good-time girl to him. He could see it in her eyes, and he doubted if she had ever baked a cake in her life.

He saw her standing there, looking nervous, smoking a cigarette, a bunch of damp daffs in her hand, and he walked away. He would make her wait. Come back in ten minutes, no, fifteen, see if she was still there.

She was still there, in her businesswoman's dark suit, a little like the women in the Building Society opposite. She didn't have an ID badge pinned to her lapel, but he wouldn't have been surprised if she had. Come to think of it, he didn't know what she did for a living. Maybe she had come straight from work, maybe she did work in a building society or bank. He didn't care. He ambled along the busy corridor, passed her by; she barely offered him a second glance. Why not? Women often did. Did she think he was too good to be true? Or did she think he wasn't coming?

He turned round and wandered back. She was still standing there, facing away from him and staring down at the daffodils, as if they had somehow failed her.

'Sally?' he said, in his smoothest sexy voice.

The girl started and swivelled round. Almost fell over. Her face lit up at the sight of the neat blond gentleman before her. He was a little on the short side, but that didn't matter, still taller than her. She liked his neatly trimmed hair; and the dark suit. She liked his kind face and trim figure; she liked his bright blue eyes, and the neat gold tiepin. Geez, she liked everything about him. To her, he appeared to be perfect husband material. She could imagine herself being married to this guy, having his children. It was quite perfect, this might be her lucky day.

'Tristram?' she said, smiling, all hint of discomfort gone.

Samuel nodded.

'You're late.'

'Sorry,' he said, smiling at the slight admonishment. 'I had to take my mother to the hospital.'

'Nothing serious, I hope?'

'No, it was her monthly check-up, I forgot all about it.'

'You are here now, that's the main thing.'

He glanced down at the soppy daffies and slipped them from her hand. She seemed happy to be rid of them, and a moment later he gave them to an ancient woman who was shuffling by.

Samuel said, 'Shall we go in?'

'If you want to.'

'Oh yeah, so long as you do.'

'I'm hungry,' she said.

'Me to. Come on,' and he strode toward the door and held it open.

Good old-fashioned manners, and she liked that too.

Once seated at the corner table in the Hunting Rooms restaurant, they sat and studied the vast menu.

'It's very expensive,' grinned Sally, all the while thinking, is this guy going to splash this much cash on me? Or did he expect her to go Dutch?

'Not too expensive for us,' said Samuel, 'My invite, my treat.'

Sally smiled across the table. If she hadn't been impressed before, she was now.

Samuel chose his meal, not the most expensive items on offer, but not far off, and then he said, 'I always fancy champagne at lunchtimes, don't you?'

Sally smiled at that too. The date was getting better and better. If she drank too much, she could always leave the car and walk home, and then she said, 'Yeah, course anything you say.'

They talked about this and that, and something and nothing, and then surprisingly, the plates were empty; the glasses were empty; the bottles were empty; and the meal was over.

She had never once asked him about his home or his work. There didn't seem the time. The foreign waiter presented the bill. Sam took one look at it, brought a roll of cash from his top pocket, peeled off the necessary and a big tip, and the waiter grinned at the pair of them, grabbed the money and ran.

'Are you sure I can't contribute?' she asked.

She'd come well equipped, plenty of cash in her bag for emergencies, he'd be surprised. One thing that Sally Beauchamp had in abundance was money. Her chosen career path had always paid well, and she had never once been forced to edge downmarket, or take a lower price. Discount was a word that didn't exist in her language, premium prices, more like. Top of the range is top of the range, she told herself, and people would always pay through the nose for top product.

'No,' answered Tristram, 'but thanks for offering. I appreciate it.'

He had a gentle smile, and a gentle way about him, almost slow, though that wasn't the right word, relaxed, that was nearer the mark, and she felt relaxed in his company, and she'd felt that way long before she'd dispatched a quantity of vintage Champagne.

'Well,' he said, 'Do you want to go out again?'

117

Too bloody right! She wanted to blurt, but remembered herself in time. 'Maybe,' she said, sucking her finger.

'Tomorrow night?'

She pulled a face. 'I could do that.'

She was playing hard to get. He didn't care. He wanted to date her again; he wanted to see what she was made of; he wanted her back at his place; he wanted...

'What time did you have in mind?' she asked.

'Eight o'clock OK?'

She bobbed her head and said yes.

'We could go for a meal in some country pub.'

Sally nodded, feeling more secure after she'd secured a second date.

'Where do you want to meet?' he asked.

'Outside the library, by the old picture house.'

'OK,' he said, 'I can do that, I'll see you there.'

Sam nodded and stood up, and she did too. She didn't think she was incapable of driving, and the car wasn't far away, and neither was her apartment, and she hated walking.

'Thanks for the meal, Tristram,' she said, as they headed back toward the Audi.

He had insisted on escorting her, and she liked that too.

It was cool.

He was cool.

Sally's mind lurched into overdrive.

She could see her entire future mapped out before her.

'Don't be late,' she said, as they parted.

'Don't be cheeky,' he muttered, as he strode away, leaving her to watch him go.

He never once looked back.

Chapter Twenty-Three

Donald Shelbourne was putting his life back together. He had given up the tiny flat he shared with Armitage and they moved in with the widow, Mrs Everrit. Six months later they bought their council house under the government's right to buy scheme, and from somewhere, raked together sufficient cash to add a small extension to the side of the house.

Armitage had his own bedroom again, and if all was not exactly right with the world, it was a heck of a lot better.

Donald was keen to make the arrangement more permanent and married the widow at the earliest opportunity. Smelly Everrit was now Armitage's stepbrother. That didn't bother Armitage much. He was too busy with his singing and dancing and flower arranging. Smelly played rugby and football and went fishing in the upper reaches of the River Dee. Came home stinking like a dead crab, even worse than usual, and their paths rarely crossed.

Armitage was ten and due to go to the big school in the city, probably Chester's most famous school, King's. They had accepted him under a longstanding scholarship arrangement. Kay, ever mindful of the importance of planning ahead, had put his name down two weeks after his birth, and though the parent's situation had radically changed, Mrs Kay Shelbourne was long deceased; the school honoured the arrangement, and went further, by waiving the fees.

They might have thought it odd that the Curzon Park address had morphed into Kenneally Council Estate, but if they noticed, they said nothing, and didn't change a thing.

They had been persuaded of the boy's potential when glimpsing Armitage's outstanding dance class reports; and on hearing him sing, as had been suggested they do, in the cathedral choir, where he was one of the four chosen soloists. The King's School ran a choir of their own, and Armitage would be a useful addition. The boy was something special, everyone said so, and King's was ready and willing to waive fees for exceptional boys whose parents could no longer foot the bill.

Army was impressed with the school and the tutors, who promised him individual after Hours attention, should he desire it. Armitage did desire, ever eager to learn, eager to improve the skills in his chosen paths.

He was looking forward to the day when he would first set foot in the establishment as a bona fide pupil. For Armitage, it couldn't come soon enough.

During the summer holidays, before he was due to start at senior school, a top motor racing festival featured at Oulton Park. His father was going, taking the new wife; and Smelly too, and they tried hard to persuade Armitage to go along.

'I'm not interested in cars, dad, you know that.'

'I know, son, but I thought it would be nice to have a day out all together as a family.'

'I'd be bored to tears, and anyway, I have promised to help Mrs Greenaway. She has four weddings to do; I can't let her down now.'

'Perhaps another time, eh?'

'If you want to take me out, dad, you could take me to the Shrewsbury Flower Show.'

'But we are not interested in flowers.'

'And I am not interested in cars!'

His father, his new wife, and Smelly, piled into the ancient German hatchback that Donald had been servicing all week, together with a huge picnic, and they set off eastbound on the Nantwich road.

On a fast straight stretch Donald put his foot down.

'Doesn't she go? Terrific engine,' he exclaimed, happy that his work had paid such dividends.

'Not so fast,' said the widow, 'you're frightening me.'

'Go on, Mister Shelbourne,' yelled Smelly from the back seat. 'Faster!'

It was all the encouragement Donald needed, as he gently pressed the accelerator. The car surged forward. Began vibrating. Didn't feel right at all.

The back axle cracked, nearside, close to the wheel.

The weight of the load and the velocity of the vehicle stressed it to breaking point. The rear nearside wheel fell alarmingly to the left and flattened.

'What the?' screamed Donald, glancing at the dash. 70mph.

'Don!' yelled the widow. 'What's going on?'

'I don't like the look of this,' snorted Smelly.

The car bucked and reared up and veered across the oncoming lane.

Up ahead, one of Midge Ridge's maroon grain wagons, a brand new bulk tipper, was speeding westwards. It was late, hauling a delivery of heavy milling wheat, bound for Rank Hovis McDougall at Birkenhead. The driver was under pressure to deliver. The truck was speeding, and the two vehicles were closing at more than 150mph.

Donald wrestled with the non-responding steering wheel. The truck driver was distracted by his newly installed mobile phone trilling through the cabin. He knew it would be the same old demand: Where the hell are you?

The trucker cursed, caught between answering and paying attention to the road. When he glanced up and ahead he saw the old red hatchback, out of control, crossing the centre line, coming toward him on the stretch where there was only one lane in each direction.

The trucker emergency braked.

In the hatchback Donald was braking too, not that it was having much effect. He grabbed the handbrake.

The car fishtailed and continued its course along the oncoming lane.

'Donald!' shrieked the widow, staring forward. 'Donald! Donald! Look out!'

'Bloody hell!' yelled Smelly.

Donald didn't say a word.

His eyes grew wide, his hands sweaty, as he gripped and twisted the wheel ever tighter.

Too late.

SMASH!

The car struck the centre of the maroon cab unit.

Glass shattered, hurling high-speed shards of death through the air.

The trucker swore and closed his eyes.

Pieces of hatchback flew in all directions.

Pieces of the passengers followed.

Pieces of the picnic rained down.

The truck tipped over.

Ran along the highway on its side, clipped two more oncoming cars. The noise was deafening. The trailer deposited twenty-five tonnes of best heavy English milling wheat along the highway, as it slithered along the tarmac, one long trail of high protein corn, spitting sparks as it went.

The hatchback fuel tank exploded.

The remains of the passengers began to fry.

A sweet aroma of roasting meat and wheat filled the sunny country air.

The truck rumbled to a standstill.

The trucker clambered out, his head bleeding, his hands shaking, his shirt torn, his voice silent, his phone obliterated. He staggered to the front of the cab. Remnants of the hatchback, and the passengers, and the picnic, were all ablaze, half jammed beneath and between the upturned front wheels. He turned round and vomited over the cheerful dandelioned verge, then turned back toward the truck.

Fire was licking around the front tyres.

He remembered he'd taken on a full load of diesel.

It could go up any minute.

He ran for his life, forgetting his wounds, forgetting everything, away from the truck, along the highway, toward Chester.

The truck exploded.

Blew the trucker into the air.

He somersaulted three times before landing face down in some bordering gorse bushes, their long and spiteful needles happy to impale a stranger.

Somewhere close by, people were screaming.

122

People came running.

Cars arrived from nowhere.

Mobile phones burst into life.

Far too late for Donald and the widow, and Smelly Everrit.

The trucker groaned and rolled over and fell from the hedge and landed face down in a fresh cowpat.

Ten minutes later sirens were heard, echoing through the green Cheshire countryside, and then the rumbling sounds of stressed diesel engines, huffing and puffing toward the carnage.

It was half-past three before the police arrived at the flower shop. They had been to the house and had found a neighbour who knew where the boy worked.

Mrs Greenaway and Army were jubilant. The shop had enjoyed its best ever day thanks to Mrs Greenaway's reputation, and Armitage's burgeoning skills. Some of the wedding bouquets that went out were better than Mrs Greenaway had ever seen. The till had been singing, and Army knew he would rack up a decent bonus. Mrs Greenaway was a sensible woman, and fair too. She recognised the raw talent she had on her hands, and she wasn't about to let him slip through her fingers by paying him buttons.

Armitage was the best paid boy in his school.

He was still keeping busy, crouched down amongst the remaining blooms.

They had finished all that day's special orders; he was using the time to prepare an eye-catching new display that would sit in the centre of the small window. He saw the police officers enter the shop, but that wasn't unusual. Officers were always dropping in on the traders in the town, ensuring that everything was just so.

Mrs Greenaway smiled a greeting, and they forced a smile back. Army thought nothing of it and carried on caressing the delphiniums. One officer whispered something in her ear. Army watched on. The cheerfulness on Mrs Greenaway's face and the bonhomie in her body language vanished, replaced by one of shock.

She'd known Donald Shelbourne. True, she hadn't got on with him as well as she had with Kay, but she'd known him for a dozen years at least.

How dreadful.

What could be the matter? thought Army. Perhaps one of the complicated wedding displays had collapsed.

She came over and said they had terrible news.

His father's car had been involved in an accident on the way to Oulton Park. His father, his father's second wife, and her son, had all been killed. She was most dreadfully sorry. There was nothing more she could say.

The police officers stood in the background, their hats in hand; their faces sorrowful. They were used to the drama of death, but this was the pits.

Perhaps it hadn't sunk in.

Children do not think of death as adults do.

Perhaps it seemed to Armitage like playing dead in the playground. One minute you're down and out, the next, you're up and grinning and running again, smiling at the non-existent camera of life, as if nothing had happened.

Adults' deaths are different.

One officer came over and said, 'Now then young man, you are going to have to be brave. I'm afraid you won't be able to go home tonight.'

Perhaps at that point Armitage experienced something of the difficulties he was about to face.

'That's all right,' he said, trying to cope, 'I shall live with Mrs Greenaway, won't I?' and he glanced across at her and smiled.

Mrs Greenaway didn't smile.

'Oh, but you can't do that,' she said. 'I only have a small cottage, just the one bedroom, there isn't the room, and anyway, I can't possibly look after a small boy.'

It was Army's turn to appear downcast.

What was happening to the world?

Why couldn't Mrs Greenaway look after him?

What would become of him now?

Where would he sleep?

Where would he go?

Who would feed him and wash his clothes?

The second officer stepped forward, for he thought the boy was about to cry, and said, 'Now, now, you're not to worry about a thing, you hear me? Everything will be fine; we'll look after you. You can be sure of that. You can come with us. We will take you into care.'

Chapter Twenty-Four

It was four days before Jago Cripps's body was discovered. He had taken occasional unscheduled periods off work before; he had never been considered the reliable type, but after four days of absence, the credit card company grew angry and rang the emergency number they had on file, his mother's.

She possessed a spare key for the flat, and with great trepidation she set out to visit. Horrific thoughts rushed through her head as she drove the twenty-minute journey across town. She slipped the key in the door, and let herself in, seeing the general untidiness and empty wine bottles, smelling the dreadful odour, crossing the flat to push open the main bedroom door, seeing the corpse of her only son, and all that dried blood, so much of it. A sight never to be forgotten.

Jago's mother's hands went to her mouth.

She bent over as if she were about to vomit.

Nothing came, other than a hideous wail from the far-flung reaches of her cold soul. It wasn't like her Jago to commit suicide. Not at all. What had gone so horrifyingly wrong?

The wailing went on for some time.

Three people in the block of flats heard it.

No one came running.

It was ten minutes before she had gathered herself. She had retreated to the sitting room and had sat and cried, alone in the stink, and the silence.

Her eyes alighted on the landline phone. Who should she call first, her estranged husband, or the police?

The police. It had to be the police.

She grabbed the phone and poked in 999, dead slow because of shaking hands, and she didn't want to miss a number.

Karen was the first in the Incident Room to connect things together. She called to Walter, 'We may have another one, suspected suicide, maybe, maybe,' and the look of doubt on her face alerted him.

'Where?'

'Harberry House, close to the new gym.'

'Get a car, we'll check it out.'

Ten minutes is all it took. Some paramedics were already there. One of them was standing in the bedroom doorway, peering down at the mess; the other was comforting the mother whose blood pressure had skyrocketed. Walter sent the medics on their way, explaining that as it was a crime scene, nothing was to be touched. The body was not going anywhere. They could take the mother away though, ostensibly for a check-up. Walter explained he would see her later, he would deal with everything, and she wasn't to worry.

Some hope.

After they'd gone, Karen summoned reinforcements. SOCO, and the doctor, and sufficient manpower, person-power, to search the grounds and interview everyone who lived in, or had recently visited the block. Walter removed his raincoat and hung it in the hallway, slipped on rubber gloves. Karen was already gloved up.

'This is the crime, the killing, that will nail this bastard,' muttered Walter.

'I bloody hope so.'

'He's crossed the Rubicon.'

'How do you mean?'

'Pushing people under a train, into the canal, running them down, even gassing them in the car is one thing, but here, here we have actual physical assault. The bastard's growing bolder. It's the first time the killer has done the killing. One car, one train, one drowning, one gassed, but here the killer stared down at the breathing body of a live human being, looked directly into that crazy face, and attacked him with the single intention of ending his life. This is quite different. It's a big step up.'

'And it can't be suicide?'

'Not unless the victim went to the window and threw the knife outside afterwards, closed the window, and lay down to die.'

'He could have hidden it,' said Karen, still not ruling out suicide.

Rule nothing out until the evidence tells you to. She recalled her college CID training.

'With what purpose in mind?' asked Walter. 'If you are going to kill yourself, why hide the bloody weapon? No, the killer brought the weapon with him, and took it away again; I'd stake my pension on that. How many flats are there in this block?'

'Fifty, ten on each floor, five floors.'

'How do you know?'

'Rodney used to live here, top floor, number forty-one.'

Ah yes, thought Walter, the rakish Rodney, he'd almost forgotten about him.

'He doesn't live here now?'

'Nope, been gone a year, when we split up.'

Walter pulled a face.

'I want every occupier interviewed, and any recent visitors logged, I want detailed descriptions of any strangers that have been seen in or near these flats in the last week, and that includes delivery people and estate agents, I want to know who Jago Cripps has been fraternising with, been seen with, and I want to know every Goddamn thing about this unfortunate young man.'

'Got you, Guv.'

'Seal the block off, no one comes in or goes out.'

'There're loads of people living here.'

'I know that! No one comes or goes until we have interviewed them.'

Karen nodded and said, 'You still think it's a man?'

'Course it's a man!'

'Not a he-she thing?'

'If I knew what a he-she thing was, I might be more amenable to the idea.'

There was a knock at the door, the doctor, with SOCO close behind and behind them, Walter's eager foot soldiers, waiting for direction, awaiting their tasks.

'Find out if the guy's got a car. Find out where it is,' rattled off Walter.

'Got you, Guv,' muttered Karen, gabbling into her mobile.

Moments later she said, 'It's a blue Vauxhall, ten years old, I've sent someone down to check the garage.'

Walter was in the kitchen, looking in the cupboards, glancing at empty glasses, lined up, gleaming, silent witnesses. He could feel a presence there. Imagined wine bottles being opened, happy pouring into clean glasses, laughing and joking, and all the while one of the two had murder in mind.

'Guv?' Karen called.

Walter returned to the sitting room.

'What?'

'Found this, nice little box of sweeties.'

Walter peered inside.

'Quite a collection, E's, uppers, downers, and God knows what else.'

'And this,' she said, pointing to spent silver strips of Temazepam.

'That's a weird one. Quite a party.'

'I wonder if the neighbours heard anything.'

'Find out!'

'Yes, Guv.'

'There must be fingerprints here, no one could be so careful as to wipe them all, unless...'

'Unless what?'

'They were wearing gloves.'

'What? All the time, seems unlikely, and another thing, Guv, who's more likely to wear gloves, a man or a woman, woman for sure, and a woman could get away with never taking them off, don't think a man could.'

Maybe she had a point.

A foot soldier came in and said, 'The garage is empty, the car's not in the car park either.'

'Find the bloody car!' said Walter.

'Yes, Guv.'

They found it in six minutes flat, parked outside the swimming pool. Traced there by the four overstay parking tickets, flagged up and already logged into the system.

'No one's to touch the car, no one, you hear me? SOCO, that's your next job.'

A couple of guys grunted and bobbed their heads; annoyed they would be working late again. The sooner they caught this bugger the better.

'So how did the car get there?' said Karen.

'Let's see,' said Walter, attempting to imagine the sequence of events. 'Jago here went out to meet someone, a friend maybe. They had a few drinks, a meal perhaps, then Jago drove them back here with promises of a nightcap, or drugs, or sex, or all three, only to be murdered by our killing fiend. The killer then jumped in the car and drove back to the swimming pool and dumped it. Maybe his car was already there. Doing a switch over. Find out if there is any CCTV by the pool and get someone on the CCTV coverage on the ring road. If the car went from here to there, there must be some coverage somewhere. With any luck, we might have a pretty pic of the perpetrator just waiting to be viewed. And another thing...'

'Yes, Guv?'

'As soon as we have a definite time of death, find out if Jago was seen about town that evening, dining, and if so, with whom?'

'Yeah, Guv, I'm on to that,' said Karen. 'I've thought of something else too.'

'Yeah, like what?'

'Was the guy gay?'

Walter gave her a look.

'How the hell would I know?'

'Well, whether he was or not, he could use the Internet to line up dates. There might be records of who contacted him.'

'You think he might use the Internet?' said Walter, well out of his comfort zone.

'Could be, looks the type. Everyone's doing it these days.'

'OK, good, find out, and get someone to check his computer over, it's in the bedroom. Read his emails, check the sites he's been visiting, there must be any number of leads and clues there, and while we are discussing technology, where the bloody hell is his mobile phone?'

'There, Guv,' shouted back one of the SOCO guys, pointing to the windowsill, and the modern expensive phone that looked as if it had been abandoned to fend for itself.

'Good,' said Walter. 'If we can't mine a bucket load of information from this scene, we don't deserve to be paid. None of you, that is!' he shouted, and everyone knew that Walter Darriteau was angry.

This time the killer had made mistakes; he must have made mistakes.

130

'And another thing,' shouted Walter.

'Yes, Guv?' she said, trying to listen, while doing three things at once.

'Get his phone records. I want to know who he's been ringing, and who's been ringing him.'

'Yes, Guv, I'm on it,' and Karen grinned at him as the adrenalin pumped through her body, reminding her of why she enjoyed her job so much, and why she enjoyed working with him.

'Has he got an answering machine?'

'Can't see one, Guv.'

'Mmm, well we can't have everything,' mumbled Walter, thinking of other things. Was Jago gay? Homosexual? Were the preachers closet homosexuals? The lonely fisherman too? Could be. Maggie O'Brien certainly wasn't. The preachers had kids, not that that meant anything. No, it didn't stack up. There must be something more. Why and where had the killer found Jago Cripps, and more pertinently, why had he ended his life?

He wondered what Cresta Raddish would make of this mess. She had said he would kill again, except she was stuck in the he-she thing nonsense, but she'd been right about the killing.

There was one tiny consolation, too late for the unfortunate Jago. At least it hadn't been a child. But what about next time? What then? They had to catch him before that. They had to. Walter didn't want a child killing on his hands. He had to catch him before that, and at that moment he knew there would be another ill spelt letter winging its way through the mail.

The gloating season was about to re-open.

'And another thing, Karen.'

'Yes, Guv. What?'

'Find out if he had money worries.'

'Sure, Guv.'

'And another thing…'

Karen shook her head and half smiled and shared a look with a dishy SOCO guy and said, 'Yes, Guv?'

'I'll tell you in a minute.'

Chapter Twenty-Five

Desiree Holloway came from an archetypal English middle class family, brought up in the green hills above Lancaster. Her father was a bank manager at the local branch of a Hong Kong-based bank. It was a steady job that paid well, and Desiree and her elder sister Louise wanted for nothing. Both of Desiree's parents adored books, indeed dabbled with writing themselves, and both read stories to Desiree and Louise as soon as the infants were old enough to pay attention.

By the time they went to primary school, the sisters were competent readers and capable writers. It gave them a head start they would maintain all the way to university, and beyond. Louise became a maths teacher at the best school in Lancashire, while Desiree majored in the sciences in which she excelled.

When Desiree was fifteen, she discovered boys, and by the time she was sixteen, she'd discovered sex. When she was seventeen, she ran two passionate affairs, one with the nineteen-year-old head boy from the same high school, and the other with a twenty-three-year-old local builder who specialised in lowering the colours of the local fifth and sixth form young women.

Desiree wanted them for one thing.

Sex, and if they weren't good at that, she'd cut them dead.

She was not a beautiful girl in the classical sense, but was comfortable with her striking looks. Her straight shiny black hair, parted in the centre, worn below her shoulders, and red tinged skin gave her an appearance of a native American. She rarely applied lipstick, she didn't need to, indeed behind her back some of the more unkind pupils referred to her as Marcus's squaw, Marcus being the blond tanned head boy who had a following all of his own.

Desiree didn't waste a moment's thought or sleep over spiteful gossip. There were far more important things to think about, and for so long as Marcus continued to cut the mustard, she would visit him after school at his house, where he would remove her school uniform before his parents came home.

In the previous two years she had discovered a great deal about herself, most of which had been enlightening, educational, and pleasurable, though one discovery troubled her, something that she could never discuss with anyone.

When she was nineteen, she walked through the school gates for the last time, never to return, and headed for university where she could be free. Marcus offered to write. Desiree declined, and wished him well in the future, and boarded the train out of town, armed with her straight A's in Chemistry, Physics, Biology and Mathematics, and headed south for Liverpool, and the famous university there that majored in the subjects that were Desiree's true loves.

She excelled at university in all things.

Bedded several of her contemporaries, and two tutors for good measure, but never once let her affairs and outside interests, few though they were, interfere with her work. Desiree Holloway was a high flier. Everyone knew that, including an aging professor by the name of Jack Robertson. He had been recruited as a talent scout way back by some faceless London organisation.

Jack recommended her, gave her his full five star rating, something he'd only ever awarded twice before. Once, years ago to a future prime minister, and once, more recently, to a highly-strung young man who turned round and murdered his lover, Julian, in a dispute over a darts score in The Eagle & Child.

In the mundane London office that peered out through dusty windows over the grey Thames, Jack Robertson's recommendations were always treated seriously. A missionary was dispatched to the far away territories of the Duke of Lancaster, one Mrs Bloemfontein, a woman who bred roses and black Labradors, whose family had returned a generation before from the South African town that was famous for roses, and happened to share the family name. Mrs Bloemfontein had devoured all the reports and couldn't wait to interview Desiree Holloway.

Their meeting did not start well.

The young and headstrong Desiree couldn't figure out what the freckled, greying woman wanted. The weird interloper seemed to talk in abstracts and vague possibilities. Desiree struggled to grasp the bigger picture. Yet by the time the second meeting came round,

(Mrs Bloemfontein was staying three days in the Swindley Hotel, and longer if necessary), a clear promise had been made, or at least Desiree thought it clear, that all her tuition fees, and indeed more than that, additional extra curriculum courses at the best colleges, would all be covered. She would never have to pay a penny again, nor her father, not a bean.

Things were looking up.

When she told her father the news, he burst into tears.

'Go for it, girl, grab it while you can!'

Desiree remained suspicious.

At the third meeting, the fog cleared.

Mrs Bloemfontein was offering Desiree a job once she had finished her studies on the banks of the murky Mersey. Perhaps Desiree had been a little slow on the uptake, for she had never conversed with anyone quite like Mrs Bloemfontein before, a woman who weighed up every syllable before it spilled from her thin lips.

The job would be well paid, guaranteed by contract for ten years, everything written and signed by both parties, one hundred percent legal and watertight. Desiree was encouraged to seek legal advice over the contract, should she have any doubts.

In addition, after her five year study programme was completed, she would be invited to attend exclusive and intensive courses at crammers yet to be agreed, and more than that, the hefty salary mentioned would be paid on the forthcoming January 1st, regardless.

How cool was that?

From paying fat tuition fees to landing a weighty salary in a matter of months. It seemed an amazing transformation. It seemed too good to be true. Things like this didn't happen in the real world, in Desiree's world. Nagging doubts continued to bounce into her head. Somehow she kept them at bay.

There were, however, several conditions.

First, she must not discuss the arrangement with her fellow students. It wouldn't be fair or right if her colleagues discovered that while they were struggling to pay their way through uni, she was being paid well for the privilege. She was required to sign a secrecy agreement, but that seemed a small price to pay.

She would do it.

Second, it was vital she maintained her studies and followed clear research programmes, some suggested by Mrs Bloemfontein. That startled Desiree. She couldn't agree to research into things that didn't interest her. But when Mrs Bloemfontein produced a four-page document from her black briefcase that mirrored the fields that fascinated her, the objection was dropped.

Third, and last, Desiree would be required to travel overseas during the summer breaks to meet like-minded individuals researching into fields similar to her own.

'Where would I be going?' she asked.

'Japan, Australia, Germany, the US, everything paid for, five-star hotels, first class air travel, and full expenses too. You'll enjoy it.'

'OK,' she said. 'That seems fair enough.'

What was that phrase, beware of Greeks bearing gifts? She thought more than once. Mrs Bloemfontein was clearly not Greek.

Then Desiree asked, 'But why me?'

Mrs Bloemfontein thought about that for a moment.

'Because you come recommended. Your initial work is groundbreaking, your tutors are enraptured by your work, and frankly, my dear, we want to work with you, because we believe you are heading for higher things. You are quite brilliant. We need the very best young brains, the best talent available. You are a shooting star, my girl; we have such high hopes for you.'

Desiree's face cracked into a wide smile. She shook her head as if bemused, a little like Mrs Bloemfontein's favourite dog, as Desi's long hair danced about her like a black halo, dark eyes shining, her large teeth highlighted by her glowing rouge skin.

No one had ever been as complimentary to her before. How could she not be impressed? And more to the point, how could she turn the woman down?

Mrs Bloemfontein set the contracts on the desk.

'You have a month to read them and sign them and return them to me,' she said, in the same businesslike tone, adding, 'There's my telephone number,' slipping a plain white card bearing a name and two numbers into Desiree's hand. 'If you have any queries, contact me at any time of day or night. If you haven't signed within the month, the offer's lapsed.'

Desiree took the card and the contracts back to her room and read every word three times over. There was nothing there she couldn't live with. Her mind was in a whirl. She had to keep reminding herself it had really happened.

Afterwards, she respected Mrs Bloemfontein's wishes and didn't tell a soul of the meetings, or of the employment contract offered, not even her sister.

Three days later, she signed it.

The following morning she posted the papers to London.

As far as the Inland Revenue was concerned, Desiree Holloway was now officially employed.

On the following thirtieth of January the first instalment of her hefty salary dumped into her bank account. She had never possessed so much money before. She arranged a party, paying for everything herself, explaining that one of the premium bonds her grandmother had bought for her eighteenth birthday, had scrambled from the heap and paid a healthy dividend.

ERNIE was paying for the bash.

It was all a lie, but somehow to Desiree, that made it more exciting. They all stood in her room together, drinks in hand, grinning at one another, toasting the Lytham St Annes' premium bond computer.

Much later, the memorable night ended with Desiree shovelling the hangers-on out through the door, everyone except her latest pleasure provider, Toby Malone.

Chapter Twenty-Six

Walter glanced again at Jago Cripps's post-mortem report. He stood up and said, 'Right! Listen up, everyone. Pay attention!' They were all there, just as Walter had ordered, crammed into the main Incident Room, Karen sitting opposite, Purple Pamela, as some of the younger ones referred to Cresta Raddish, sitting at the end, Mrs West, standing in the doorway to her office, embracing a fat manila file, as if she hadn't seen it in months.

'Jago Cripps was drugged to the eyeballs, a cocktail of drugs, but it was not the drugs that killed him. The killer slit his wrists with either a razor blade or a craft knife. My guess is it was a craft knife. Razor blades are too fiddly to handle, and you can easily cut yourself, so will all those on car searching duties be on the lookout for craft knives. How is that going, by the way?'

'Up to last night we have searched four hundred and eighteen suspect vehicles,' said Karen.

'Without any result, I presume,' said Walter.

Karen pursed her lips and shook her head.

Walter resumed, 'Of the fifty flats in the block, two are empty and unlived in, the keys are with the agents, thirty-six are owner occupied, and twelve are rented. Of the forty-eight occupied flats, thirty house a single person, and the other eighteen, a couple. Of course, that is what we are told, it doesn't mean there aren't visitors and dossers and sharers, who may well be breaking lease clauses, living and kipping in the building unbeknown to the landlords, so bear that in mind. How many of these people have been interviewed?'

DC Gibbons, the young guy who was always larking around, answered. 'All bar six, Guv.'

'Why is that?'

Gibbons glanced at his papers.

'Three are out of the country on holiday, due back at the weekend, one is in hospital, appendicitis, one is working in Bristol, the local police haven't found him yet, but they are still looking, and one is due to be seen this morning. He's been in Glasgow, back at lunchtime.'

Walter nodded and said, 'And how many of them saw the killer?'

There was a noticeable hush.

The he-she killer's luck had remained with him, or her, or so it seemed.

'None of them?' said Walter.

'None that we can find,' said Gibbons.

Walter sighed and said, 'CCTV? Over to you.'

Another guy started talking. 'Yeah, we have CCTV of the Vauxhall on the ring road twice, once heading toward the flat,' and he flashed up a blurred black and white blow up on the big screen. The only clear feature on the image was the superimposed time and date. 11.16pm. It showed the shadows of two figures sitting in the front seats of the car, but they were unrecognisable. 'And here it is going back, 2.12am, one person in the car, large baseball cap, face unrecognisable, that's the last sighting we have. That person sitting there, driving that car without a care in the world, is, or so it would seem, a mass murderer.'

'Thank you,' said Walter. 'What about the CCTV at the swimming pool?'

'Knocked out,' said the same guy. 'Some kids stoned it. Should be fixed some time next month, so the council bods say.'

Walter pulled a face and gave Mrs West a look, as if to say: This is what we have to cope with. Can't you give them a nudge? She understood and smiled and nodded back.

Walter resumed. 'We have not located the murder weapon which the killer may still possess, and nor have we found the car keys, which we must assume the killer has dumped, maybe in the river. How are enquiries progressing on the dating business? How did the killer get to know Jago?'

Karen answered. 'So far, we have found his details on four dating sites, heterosexual, all of them. We have no evidence he was gay.'

'Bet you enjoyed trawling through that lot,' said Gibbons, grinning at his neighbours.

'Shut up, Gibbons!' yelled Karen. 'We are trying to catch a serial killer here, you prat!'

138

'Sorry, sarge,' he said, and he caught the look of contempt on Walter's face and that was not a good sign.

Walter sighed and said, 'Carry on Karen.'

'Two of the four sites are paid subscription, you have to log all your details, and two are free. The killer had open access to the free sites, anyone can. We've looked at Jago's emails and found the initial contact messages. They were sent anonymously to Jago via a Polish run Internet café in the town. It's a pay as you go place, no ID required; anyone can just go in and buy fifteen minutes. It's a very busy place too, doing well, with transient people coming and going all the time, foreign workers, that kind of thing, many of whom can't speak English. We have no way of checking which of their clients was our boy,' and Karen made eye contact with Cresta and added, 'or girl.'

Cresta nodded her appreciation.

'So Jago's straight, and was dating a woman on the night he died. You think?' said Walter as he stared around the room.

'It would seem that way,' said Karen.

'Maybe it's a tranny,' said Gibbons, unable to stop himself laughing.

A few of the others tittered too.

'No!' said Walter. 'This time he may have a point. It could be a transvestite. Why not? Trannies get angry too. There's nothing to say a killer couldn't be a tranny. Where would you go in Chester to meet a tranny, I mean, is there such a thing as a tranny directory, Pink Pages maybe, help me here, I am out of my comfort zone.'

'There are three clubs in town that are known tranny/fanny/manny places,' said Gibbons, still grinning.

'Trust you to know that,' said Karen.

'It would fit with our earlier idea of a late night worker,' said Jenny Thompson, still a little backward at contributing to such packed meetings.

'It would,' agreed Walter. 'Thanks, Jenny. Gibbons, tonight I want you to work the tranny joints, oh, and take someone with you. Have a few discreet words, if that's possible. Spread the word that one of their pals could be a killer, see what comes back.'

'I think he should dress the part,' said Karen.

'Oh, yeah,' said Gibbons.

'What do you think, Cresta? You've been quiet.'

'Just waiting to be invited, Walter, that's all. I don't know why you are sidetracking on trannies. I have said all along that the killer could be a woman. What little we have to go on supports that fact. Jago met this girl, he seemed convinced she was a bona fide woman otherwise he'd have binned her from the off. This killer is comfortable in her own skin. She appears as a woman and probably is a woman. If any of you are thinking of finding an obvious man dressed as a woman, with ridiculous clothes, a deep voice, heavy make-up, and a bristly chin, think again. The killer is, to all intents and purposes, a woman. If you are looking for something different, you are looking in the wrong place.'

Walter nodded. He couldn't argue with any of that, and said, 'How did the checking of restaurants go on the night Jago died?' He already knew the answer to this, asking for the benefit of everyone else.

Another guy joined in. 'We have a probable sighting, Guv, a possible ID.'

'We do?' said Walter.

Everyone paid closer attention. This was the news they wanted to hear.

'Where?'

The guy glanced down at his notes.

'The Black Horse on the Frodsham road. A guy there, a Bulgarian waiter cum barman, he doesn't speak much English; he said he thought he recognised Jago's photo. He remembered him coming in for a meal; he didn't leave a tip, but he remembers a little about the girl he was with. Said she was blonde, but that wasn't what he remembered about her. It was her eyes; bright green they were, so he says. It was the only thing he remembered. He couldn't make up an e-fit; it was only the eyes that made an impression.'

'Bright green eyes, eh?' said Walter. 'How many people here have bright green eyes, not many, I'll bet. I don't.' A couple of people giggled at that. 'Go on, tell me. How many people are here right now? Maybe forty of us. How many of us can boast bright green eyes?'

'Mine are greenish,' said Gibbons.

Everyone peered at the bloke.

140

'Yes, they are, but they are not what I would describe as bright green. It's a rare thing. Don't underestimate it. We can rule out maybe ninety percent of the population, perhaps more, on this alone. This could be important; the killer may have bright green eyes. Keep an eye out for that, if you pardon the pun. What's next?'

'Were there any fingerprints in the flat?' asked Jenny.

'Good question,' said Karen. 'The only prints we could find in the flat were Jago's, and his mother's, so what does that tell us?'

'He was a sad and lonely bastard,' quipped Gibbons.

'It also tells us the killer wore gloves,' said Cresta, 'and women wear gloves much more than men, especially on a dinner date. I mean, have you ever seen a man wear gloves on a dinner date?'

No one had.

'Anything on his phone and finance records?' asked another WPC who had never spoken before.

'The guy had minor money worries, but who doesn't in twenty-first century Britain. He was keeping his head above water, just about,' said Karen.

'What about the drugs, where did they come from?' asked the same girl, emboldened by her first question.

'Now there we have a result,' said Karen. 'When we interviewed Jago's work colleagues we found one guy who popped up as known to us. Small-time drug dealer. It didn't take much pressure to get him to cough, threatened him with a murder trial if he didn't. He supplied Jago with everything in his toy box, except the Temazepam.'

'So where did he get that?' asked Walter.

'Not from his doctor,' said Karen, 'I checked.'

'You can buy it on the internet,' said Gibbons, 'I checked.'

Gibbons and Karen shared a look, and a faint smile.

'You can buy just about anything on the Internet,' added Mrs West.

'Too true.' Walter nodded and sighed. The Internet had a lot to answer for. 'Anything else?'

At that moment, no one had.

'So to recap,' he said. 'The killer is around five feet five inches tall, of slim and sexy build, pert bum, sometimes blonde, definite green eyes, personable, attractive, pleasant, wears designer trainers, just the

141

kind of person you would never believe to be a killer. They could be male or female or transvestite, I suspect we shall never know the answer to that until we take the he-she thing's pants down and take a look.'

Mrs West and Cresta exchanged a look and a grimace. Walter was still talking. 'They have a fondness for craft knives, wearing gloves, a lucky person in some respects, they have been lucky so far, probably drives a dark Japanese hatchback car, aged around thirty, maybe a bit more, so why the hell can't we find him, she, or it?'

'Because they are ordinary,' said Mrs West.

'Yes,' agreed Cresta.

'The typical girl next door,' added Karen.

'Or boy,' said Walter. 'Let us not forget that. And there is something else that we should not forget. This killer is killing people, five so far, killing at random, and we believe it is because they are alone, broken up, spurned, lost their partner, binned, single, finished with, call it what you will. This person lives alone, yes?' and he glanced at Cresta.

'Most likely,' she said.

One day Purple Pamela will say something for definite, he thought, but didn't say.

'We keep looking, we keep checking cars, and bars, we check out the tranny clubs and all the nightclubs, too.'

'What about casinos?' suggested Jenny.

'Yeah, them too, good point.'

'Might I make a suggestion?' said Cresta.

'It's what you are here for.'

'I think you should do another televised press conference. Say you are closing in, say you have fresh evidence, say it is only a matter of time, ratchet up the pressure on the....' and even she hesitated, fighting to find the right word.

'Swine,' suggested Jenny.

'Twat!' said Gibbons.

Karen said, 'Oh please.'

'Let's stick with killer, eh,' said Walter. 'Or murderer.'

'I agree with that,' said Mrs West. 'About doing another press conference. I'll speak to the TV company.'

It wasn't Walter's favoured strategy, but he wasn't going to disagree.

'I want everyone on their toes, think green eyes, craft knife, attractive personality, blonde, Jap car, gloves, slim build, it's all there for you. This person will be out and about tomorrow and one of you will walk right past him or her, so keep your eyes open and find the bugger!'

Walter sat down and grabbed the telephone, while Gibbons went about picking his partner for their night-time trawl through the lowlifes' bars.

There was no shortage of volunteers.

Chapter Twenty-Seven

Samuel was inside the library, glancing at the newspapers. He was surprised to find they had introduced evening openings, and that was good. It fitted with his plans. From there he could see outside, the hustle bustle of people going on dates, couples arm in arm, singletons rushing to get there on time, people hurrying to meet their lovers outside the old cinema.

Sally Beauchamp had arrived five minutes before. She was standing outside with her back to him, glancing at her expensive watch. She was wearing a smart suit; skirt and jacket, maroon, and Sam correctly guessed it had cost a pretty penny. It might be a special purchase for the occasion. She was trying to impress. How sweet.

He turned back and read a long article on photography in one of the broadsheets, before making his way outside.

'Hi, Sally,' he said from behind her.

She swivelled round and half smiled. 'Tristram! There you are, I thought you weren't coming.'

'Sorry, I had to pay a quick visit to the bathroom.'

'Yeah?' she said, as if she didn't believe him. 'You're here now, that's the important thing.'

She gave him the once over. He was as neat and tidy as she remembered. and she liked the dark, almost black suit he wore, and fresh red tie and white shirt.

'Shall we go?' he said, offering his arm.

She linked him without hesitation, and he led her along the high street to where he had parked his car. He produced the key, pointed and fired, and the doors unlocked with an audible click.

'Like your car,' she said. 'The new Cayton Cerisa, isn't it?'

'Yep,' he said, getting in.

She joined him, and in the next minute they were easing through the city streets, heading for the inner ring road.

'Where are we going?' she asked.

'The Road to Jerusalem.'

'Pardon.'

'The Road to Jerusalem,' he repeated. 'It's a pub on the Wrexham road.'

'Don't know it,' she said.

'They do lovely meals.'

Sally smiled, relaxed in his company.

They crossed the river and headed south, passing Iona House as they went. Sam glimpsed the lights on in three flats, only his remained in darkness. He didn't say a thing.

The Road, as the regulars knew it, was busy, a testament to the new chef they'd attracted from one of Chester's top hotels. Sam had booked a table in Tristram's name, and they were soon settled and munching their way through the expanded menu.

'Tell me about this writer and broadcaster thing?' she said, barbecue chicken wing sauce smudging her bright red lipstick.

He told her all about the articles he wrote on photography for several newspapers that were syndicated across the south of England, all true, and the broadcasts he made for the BBC at Manchester on the Cheshire life of the socialites, all a complete fabrication.

She swallowed it whole, fascinated by his tittle-tattle stories of minor celebs he made up as he went along. A good bottle of wine enabled a relaxed girl to believe almost anything, and the dapper Tristram was so believable. Why should she doubt him?

The longer the meal progressed, the more convinced she became he was the right man for her. He was single and had no children, or so he said, while she had sufficient breeding time left. She could offer him something that no previous woman had managed, a family, as she alluded to, when painting a picture of a tribe of little Tristrams running about his feet. Hadn't he ever yearned for such a thing? Of course he had, but not and never with Sally Beauchamp.

Afterwards he suggested she go back to his place for coffee. Sally was used to going back to men's places afterwards; it was part of the arrangement, where the business would take place, cash transaction first, sweaty transaction second. She would return with Tristram, but no transactions would take place that night, for she didn't want to appear easy. She knew that wasn't the way to catch a good man, though she would drop a hint that so long as he continued to court her, for that is what she imagined he was doing, anything was possible, and soon, too.

Tristram paid the bill in cash, and a moment later the Road to Jerusalem was retreating fast in the Cayton's wing mirrors.

By the time they arrived back at Iona House, the place was in darkness. He pulled on to the small drive that ran to the right of the house, around to the back where there was a small car park. The usual two cars were sleeping there; an old rusting Jaguar that when running you could hear a mile off, and the green Ford saloon that badly needed a wash. Mrs Hymas didn't possess a car, hence the extra spare space. Tristram backed in, toward his rear door. Being a ground-floor apartment he boasted front and back entrances, and in the next minute they were out of the car, and he was opening the door and lighting up.

'I like your flat,' she said, taking a peek round.

Apartment, he preferred, though he didn't say.

It was old-fashioned, his stuff, but clean and in good condition and she correctly guessed, expensive. A big modern TV, and on the coffee table was a fat green book entitled How to Cheat and Win at Roulette. It was the latest block-busting tome on the subject, quite revolutionary in its way, and essential reading for all croupiers. Sam had forgotten he'd left it there. Sally saw it and said, 'You're interested in gambling, are you?' It was the first downer of the night. She'd met too many hopeless gamblers in her life and she didn't rate them, and wouldn't want one for a husband.

'No, course not,' he said, picking it up and taking it away. Out of sight, out of mind. 'A friend of mine had this crazy idea of driving down to Monaco,' said Tristram, thinking on his feet, 'and trying to beat the casino. I told him it was a rubbish idea and he could go by himself. We never went. I'll give him the book back tomorrow.'

'Gambling's for mugs.'

'I know. I work hard enough for my money; I'm not about to throw it away. Coffee?'

'Yeah, sure. Thanks, Tristram.'

It seemed to placate her and after glancing at a couple of his wall mounted pictures, black and white photographs, she sat on the leather chesterfield and crossed her legs and waited for him to join her. He wasn't long, carefully setting the percolated coffee on the

146

table. You can tell a lot about a man from his coffee, she thought, and it was only as she imagined. Tristram Fellows was clearly a man of high standards, and she liked that too.

He sat beside her and she linked his arm and pulled herself closer. The evening was going well, she thought, and she pondered whether to invite him to her flat for dinner at the weekend. She was an excellent cook, or so she told herself, and it would be a big step forward, to have him there, with her.

'Tell me about your mum and dad,' she said, eager to know everything about him. So Tristram rambled on about his parents and his childhood, some of which was true and some not. It made her laugh though, the stories he could tell, relaxed too, and in the next instant she was staring into his mesmeric blue eyes.

He knew it was the moment.

She expected him to kiss her, and he didn't want to introduce any moment that might sour things, might set her on edge, might have her grab her bag and demand to be taken home. He didn't want to kiss her, he didn't want to kiss anyone, other than Desi, though that was impossible, so he steeled himself, tried not to show it on his face, closed his eyes, thought of absent friends, and closed on her. She shut her eyes too, and they kissed; her freshly applied lipstick now on his lips, she noticed that as they came apart, and she liked that too, as if it were a sign of ownership.

Once apart he said, 'Look at me, forgetting myself, I didn't think to ask, would you like a nightcap, malt whisky, brandy, coffee liqueur?'

The thing she most would have liked was another lingering kiss, better still, a thorough necking session stretched out on the chesterfield. But the night was young, and she was in no hurry to head home, despite her wish not to appear cheap. He could kiss her as often as he liked. She wished he would. He was a good kisser, but he was offering her alcohol, and as he brought the thought to mind, the idea had some merit.

'I'd love a brandy,' she said.

Tristram smiled and stood. 'Anything in it?'

'Nope,' she grinned, 'just as it comes.'

147

He smiled and bobbed his head and headed for the kitchen. He took out a brandy glass, ensured it was clean, opened the bottle, his earlier words coming back to him. Anything in it?

Nope, she'd said.

Tough luck, darling.

In went a good slug of flunitrazepam.

Large measure of best brandy on the top.

A thorough swill around, no trace of smell, no trace of anything, just perfect. Back to the sitting room. She heard him coming and turned and glanced up toward the door, smiled at him. Geez, he was cute. He handed her the drink.

'Aren't you having one?'

'No, better not, driving and all that.'

Ah, that was sweet too, she thought. She linked his arm and sipped the drink. She wouldn't confess it to a soul, but it had been the best day in her life in ages. It was the first time she had been out with a man in yonks who hadn't paid for her company, and stuff, and it made a big difference. She didn't want the money; she wanted to be wanted for herself. Sally was relaxed in his company, relaxed in his flat, relaxed in his arms. He was such a gentleman, was Tristram Fellows. He didn't push it, and she liked that. She couldn't wait to tell her only friend Sonia all about him.

It had been a hectic couple of days. Perhaps dating without payment was more tiring than she remembered. It was certainly more enjoyable, and she yawned.

'Oh, sorry,' she said, 'I don't know where that came from.'

Tristram yawned too. He had such lovely teeth.

'You wouldn't mind,' she said, 'if I had a little doze.'

'Course not,' soothed Tristram, 'be my guest, you sleep for as long as you want.'

Then she was gone, out of it, and yet her eyes hadn't closed.

Sam smiled to himself. Part one accomplished. The stupid bitch had never once suspected a thing. How gullible some women were. Part two was coming soon, and he laughed and retreated to the kitchen, opened the cupboard where he kept the hardware items, light bulbs, matches, lavvy rolls, fly killer, and brown tape. He grabbed a fresh roll of tape, slipped on the yellow rubber gloves and returned to the sitting room.

She hadn't moved a muscle. Her breathing was long and slow, but her eyes were wide open. He drew his palms across her face, no blinking, no recognition, nothing. His neat nails found the beginning of the tape and pulled the end free. It shrieked as it rolled out. He stuck it to her cheek, rolled it across her face, across her smudged mouth, around the back of her head, imprisoning her hair, covering her ears, across the face again, slightly higher, upper lips, around again, nose, around again, more firmly across the nose. Sally jerked, fighting for air, round again, covered the eyes that still stared at Tristram, and he wondered if those drugged eyes could see. He thought no, not that it mattered. Could Sally Beauchamp see Tristram Fellows, as she believed him to be, as he was murdering her in his front room?

He'd never know. He didn't care.

It wasn't Sally Beauchamp he was murdering, she had stumbled into his path, it could have been anyone, he didn't have any beef with her. In another life he might have quite liked her, but he would not lose any sleep over that.

He had set out on a deliberate course, coldly chosen it, and he would not stop now, round and round and round the tape went, covering her hair covering the neck, the jerking had long since ceased, until her face resembled a brown mummy, the entire head covered like a model in some hat shop window. It was strangely attractive, like a piece of modern art, smooth and clean and shiny. Perhaps he could display it at the library, enter it into some wacky art exhibition, and he laughed again at his own ridiculous thinking, tugging the tape round one last time. The entire roll was spent. Job done.

100 Ways to Kill People.

Cover their heads in brown tape.

Easy peasy. Anyone could do it.

That person who wrote the original article should do a follow up.

100 Ways to Dispose of the Body.

That was the hardest part, but Sam had no worries about that. He'd already planned it. He already knew. Sam would wait until the small hours when the world was fast asleep, and then he would act. Before that, he took the brandy glass through to the kitchen and washed it. Dried it and put it away.

Returned to the sitting room.

Brownhead was sleeping, dead.

Its handbag was on the floor. Sam grabbed and opened it.

In the back compartment he found condoms, a huge roll of them; fifty, God, the girl had been expecting an exciting night.

A fat, well thumbed black diary. Sam flipped it open.

It was full of men's names and telephone numbers.

Ronnie (Ginger bastard) Phelps and then a number.

Richard (Bad breath) Bettinson.

Harry (Big tipper) Wilson.

Donald (Shortarse) Smith.

Peter (Spotty) Wignall.

Jerry (Frightening) Herridge, and so it went on.

Alan (Donkey) Harris.

Grahame (Creepy) Willis.

Dozens and dozens of them.

It seemed she remembered them more through their nicknames than their actual names, or the names they had fed her.

Sam wondered what she might write about him.

Tristram (Top man) Fellows perhaps, or was he being vain?

Tristram (Tight tape) Fellows more like, and he laughed aloud.

In the date sections were assignations.

Saturday. Ginger bastard. Royal, Bristol.

Monday. Bad Breath. Argosy, Bournemouth.

Wednesday. Starey Eyes. Regency, Southampton.

He had been right all along. She was a tart, touring the country, servicing Ginger bastard, Bad Breath, Big tipper, Shortarse, Spotty, Frightening, Starey Eyes, and the rest, and to think, I kissed that.

Sam felt sick, went to the bathroom, washed his face, cleaned his teeth, applied fresh deodorant, felt a hell of a lot better. Returned to the sitting room. Brownhead unmoved. It was time to begin.

He went into the bedroom and grabbed the wheeled suitcase he had bought in a Chester department store, especially for the purpose. Pushed it through to the sitting room. It was huge, or at least he thought so, but when he parked it in front of Brownhead, he was having second thoughts.

He laid it flat and opened it. Grabbed Brownhead and presented it to the case. No way, not a chance.

There must be a way. Folded up the knees. Brought the head down, squeezed and pushed and squeezed and pushed and re-presented to the case. It might just work. A couple of cuffing blows to the shoulders like spanking steaks before they are grilled. It helped a little. More waggling, and pushing, hitting, standing on, and prodding and pulling, and then it was in. Still standing proud of the edges, but in.

Sam forced the top closed.

A hand fell out.

'Shit!' he yelled; then reprimanded himself.

Didn't want to wake the co-sharers of Iona House. Must keep quiet.

Closed the lid, forced it down; sat on it, the fastener almost caught. More effort, more pressure. Down, you bugger! There! Done! Shut it at last. Flicked the right fastener. It closed with a satisfying click. Weight on the left side. Click!

Job done.

Brownhead had disappeared.

The only thing that remained was to dispose of the case, and Sam knew how to do that.

He grabbed the handle and wheeled it toward the back door. It ran like a dream. You would never have guessed there was a nine stone woman inside, or whatever it was.

Parked it there, ready. He would leave in an hour.

Returned to the sitting room. Picked up the handbag. Emptied the contents on the low table. Cosmetics, ladies tools, eyebrow plucker, nail file, nail clippers, two more that he didn't recognise; women's toiletry things, only to be expected, and a bulging purse.

He flipped it open and emptied the cash on the table.

A huge roll of notes.

Sam was used to seeing banknotes; working in the casino, someone would always have a fat wad, and the desire to show it off to the world, every night, though more often on the way in than the way out.

This roll could compete.

One thousand seven hundred pounds. Geez! He was in the wrong business. Maybe she should have paid for the meal after all; maybe she should have paid him for his company.

151

He held the open bag to the table and swept everything inside, purse, change, condoms, the whole bloody lot. Clicked it shut. Went to the wood-burning stove. Flipped it open, threw it inside. Real leather it was, expensive too, a pity really, and the cash as well, but he couldn't take any chances. It had to be destroyed. It was all going, burning cheerfully, brightening up the apartment, not entirely useless; spreading its warmth into the room.

Sam went to the kitchen. Made a corned beef sandwich, dash of English mustard. Ate it in a hurry. Pretty good. He returned to the back door. Opened up, went outside. Glanced up at the Victorian façade. No lights on. The building fast asleep. Went inside, through to the front door, crept outside, on to the small spongy lawn. Glanced up again. No lights, no sleepless nights, everyone asleep. He heard a single car chugging along the road, diesel engine, old model, rattly exhaust. Ducked into the porch. It was a taxi, maybe the last fare of the night, the driver hurrying home to a cold bed. Then it was gone and silence returned.

Sam went back inside and locked the front door. Through the house to the back. Went outside again. Opened up the hatchback that he'd earlier reversed as close as he could to the door.

Manoeuvred the case over the threshold, it bounced down on to the gravel path. Shush! Damnation, it was heavy. Presented it to the car's backside. He knew it would go in; he'd brought it home that way. It must go in. Tried to lift it. Couldn't get the leverage. It wouldn't budge. Changed his position. Tried again, all his strength, up it came and over the rim, and clunked into the back. Wouldn't like to do that again. Never will, that's the main thing.

Closed the hatch, almost silently. It was one reason he liked the Cayton Cerisa. All the doors closed with the softest of clunks.

Went back inside. The fire was still burning. He glimpsed curling twenty-pound notes, blackening, catching fire, turning to ash, worthless things, worthless trash.

Glanced round the sitting room.

She had never been there. No trace.

Maybe the odd fingerprint, but he would go to work on that in the morning. He'd have to make an early start because he was back at work tomorrow evening.

One last look round.

For now, it would do.

Turned off the lights. Went out the back. Locked the door and crept into the car. Started the engine. It was real quiet, yet sounded like thunder. Pulled the car round the side of the house and out on to the road, headed for Queensferry.

There was almost no traffic about, the occasional police car, he noticed that. He stayed inside the speed limits, not too slow to attract attention, not too fast to warrant a speeding ticket. He was the model citizen. Always had been. Always will be. It wasn't his fault everything had gone so terrifyingly wrong. It could have happened to anyone.

He crossed the River Dee, slinking into Wales.

Away to the left he glimpsed the New Cut shining under the sodium light, the black water far below, drifts of mist forming, the same stretch where William Camber, the fisherman, had met his tragic accident.

Sam eased off the dual carriageway at the first exit and headed left up the hill toward Hawarden village. Then left and straight right, before turning on to the A5104, and the quiet rural road signposted for Llandegla and Corwen.

The road was rising, the cottages thinning out, and soon he was travelling through unfenced moorland. It was misty, and the wipers were working overtime.

He'd been this way many times before, mostly long ago, though once recently, to check out it was still as he remembered. He passed the old pub, the last watering hole before Corwen. It was blacked out, the owners and guests hunkering down after a busy night.

The mist worsened.

The headlights on full beam.

The Cayton Cerisa motored happily on.

No traffic at all, nothing coming, nothing behind.

He passed an abandoned white delivery van, dumped at the roadside, tyres missing, burned out at the front. It hadn't been there last week.

Up ahead there was something else on the road.

Sam slowed, and the big case in the boot slithered toward him.

It was a ewe, standing in the centre of the road, quite unperturbed, a nervous lamb to either side. Sam edged forward. The ewe didn't

153

move a muscle. Sam cursed aloud. There was no way past. Edged forward again. The ewe dug in its heels, imagining it was protecting its young.

'Ba-aaa,' it cried, as if she could stare him down.

He jumped from the car and crept to one side of the stubborn animal and slapped its rump.

'Ba-aaa, ba-aaa,' it complained, and ambled away into the heather, the lambs giving him one final worried look, before disappearing after their mother into the darkness.

Back in the car, not far to go.

He was almost at the turning.

Then he saw it, the short gravel track to the right. He turned off the road and bounced along the track, the full beams dancing from jagged grey rocks and heather and scrub, making weird shapes and patterns on the mottled stone, and then he saw the signs.

Llandegla Quarry. Disused. Dangerous, Keep Out. Keep Away. Steep Drop.

He pulled the car to a stop and got out. Looked around. Silence, but for the wind. No birdcall, no traffic, no aeroplanes in the sky, nothing. He had the world to himself. He grabbed the torch and went to the back and opened up. Set the torch on the roof and heaved out the case.

It hadn't got any lighter.

Collected the torch and pulled the trunk toward the quarry. The plastic wheels were amazing. Worked incredibly well, even on rough ground. Then he was standing by the last of the Danger signs. Peering over the edge. Shining the torch down. Maybe a hundred feet. The beam bounced back from the black water below. The winter and spring rains had gathered there. In high summer it was bone dry. You could walk on the bed. He had done that many times when he used to visit with the unofficial camera club, taking more meaningful black and white arty-farty shots. They thought they were so clever. He still had some on his bedroom wall, striking they were too, and that reminded him, he must get rid of those, into the fires. A pity, but there we are.

He glanced back at the case. Thought of Brownhead inside. Brownhead would not be missed, not by him.

Wheeled it to the edge.

154

Pushed it over.

It fell in silence, cartwheeling in the air, the torch beam following it all the way down.

SPLASH!

Reached its destination.

The water was shallow. The case was vertical, jammed in the thin layer of mud beneath, perhaps two-thirds standing proud of the water, like the first standing stone in some elaborate plan.

He chuckled and turned about and hurried back and jumped into the car. Reversed back to the main road, the car making that brutal reversing noise. Why do cars do that?

Headed back toward Chester.

Job done.

Number six.

100 Ways to Dispose of the Body.

Case them and hurl them into a disused quarry.

Anyone could do it.

He buzzed down the windows to keep awake, and headed home to bed and brandy, and a sound night's sleep.

It had been fun.

He had enjoyed it.

Chapter Twenty-Eight

Following his father's death, they took Armitage to the police station to await collection. It had gone five o'clock before the on-call social worker arrived. He was a tall slim guy who said little, as he signed the papers, and led Army away to the car.

'Where are we going?' asked Army.

'Saint Edmond's, on the Wirral.'

That didn't mean anything to the boy.

'What's Saint Edmond's?'

'You'll see.'

Saint Edmond's was a vast Victorian orphanage that stood in its own grounds. It had altered little in the hundred and forty years since the day it opened. On the first day it intimidated the boys, and was still doing that when Army jumped from the car and stared up at the vast building. To anyone it was overwhelming; to a little boy, it was the stuff of nightmares.

The social worker met the bursar who introduced them to an under manager named Hancock. He led them away through a maze of corridors, to a small musty office where the handover documentation would be checked and signed. Everything in order, done by the book. Everything at Saint Edmond's was done by the book, and Armitage Shelbourne's welfare belonged to Saint Edmond's Orphanage.

'You're in luck, you haven't missed tea,' said Hancock.

'I won't be staying here long, will I?'

'Well, Master Shelbourne, we will have to see about that. It depends on whether anyone takes a shine to you, you know, likes the look of your face. Foster parents will always take the children they like the look of the most, the ones who laugh and smile. You take a tip from me, young man, if you want to find a suitable home, when the foster parents come calling looking at children, smile, be happy. No one wants a misery guts.'

Armitage didn't feel like smiling at all.

He thought he might never smile again.

At that moment, a scruffy boy came running down the corridor.

'Ah, Swallow, just the tyke I was looking for, and haven't you learnt yet not to run in the corridor? How many times have I told you about that?'

'Sorry, sir.'

'Never mind about that now. This is Shelbourne. Take him with you to tea, make sure there is an extra place laid. Look after him, boy.'

Swallow glanced at the skinny new arrival. He was about a year younger than himself. He nodded at the kid and said, 'Come on, mate,' and when they were out of earshot he said, 'What's your name.'

'Armitage.'

'No, I mean your first name.'

'That is my first name.'

The boy pulled a face and said, 'Bit of a wanker's name, ain't it?'

'Is it? They call me Army for short.'

'Yeah, Army,' he said. 'That's much better. We'll call you Army. Mine's Dennis. Come on, we'd better hurry or we'll miss tea.'

Army followed Dennis through the dim corridors. Dennis was still talking, babbling away about rules and regulations, and he spoke real fast, imparting advice that was meaningless to Armitage.

'The one you need to watch out for is Mister Gilligan, he's a bastard.'

'Will you point him out to me?'

'I won't need to; you'll know him when you see him.'

They came to a pair of half glazed doors, and the faintest whiff of well-boiled cabbage. Through the glass they could see hundreds of boys, all ages, standing at their tables, waiting for permission to sit.

'Follow me,' said Dennis, and he pushed through the free-swinging doors. scooted around to the right, across to the far side of the hall, to a long table where two empty places remained at the bottom end.

'Stand there,' he said, 'opposite me, and wait.'

Army stood at the table and waited. He was different to all the others, wearing his own clothes. Everyone else was decked out in navy trousers and thick grey shirts. They all craned their necks to

157

inspect the skinny new kid. Nothing special about him. Looked a bit of a weed to most eyes, an easy touch, maybe, easy prey. Two of the older ones turned back to the front and grinned at one another. The kid would have to grow up fast or they would eat him alive.

Three adults entered the hall, pompous men, noses in the air, one wearing a black gown, the flankers in mismatched jackets with leather patches over the elbows, and cord trousers. They stepped on to the raised platform at the end of the hall, ambled to their table, chatting amongst themselves, not in any hurry, as if they hadn't noticed six hundred ravenous boys waiting on their every word. The men stood behind their chairs and stared out over the gathered throng.

'Quiet!' yelled the fatter of the jacketed ones.

The gowned one raised his head and said grace, speaking in a rush. It almost came out as one long word.

'Forwhatweareabouttoreceivemaythelordmakeustrulythankful, Amen!'

'Amen!' bellowed the boys as one, pulling out the long benches and sitting down to thunderous noise.

Tea was about to begin.

Brown Windsor soup.

Thick, gooey, and vaguely warm, though it didn't taste of much. Some kids said it was the leftovers of yesterday's gravy, and they were probably right.

'Who's your new mate,' said one of the bigger boys to Dennis.

'His name's Army.'

'Oooh Army! Get him. Hard are ya? You and whose army?' said the other one opposite.

'What happened to your parents, eh? Got tired of you? Chucked you out? Couldn't wait to see the back of you?'

'They're dead,' said Army.

'So are mine, so what?' said the big boy. 'Expect us to feel sorry for you?'

Army pulled a face but said nothing.

'I never had none,' said Dennis. 'You're better off without them.'

'You must have had parents, dickhead!' said the big one.

'Yeah, they took one look at him and threw up. Chucked him in the canal as a baby, I shouldn't wonder.'

158

Dennis flushed; then pulled himself together.

'Shut your fat face, Robinson. At least I'm not in here 'cos my parents can't stand the bloody sight of me.'

That shut the big one up, for a while.

The soup had vanished, not a drop remained. A boy came running down the line like a sprinter grabbing the baton for the relay race, collected all the soup plates, and disappeared.

Another kid rolled up a double-decker steel trolley, began unloading dinner plates, and set a meal down before each boy. Dennis and Army were at the end of the table, the bottom of the heap. They received their food last, and it would be the smallest and least appetising portions.

Army peered down at it. One thin slice of curling cheese. One browned pickled onion. One slice of margarined bread. One red apple. One tiny scone containing two dried sultanas, and all scattered on a warm heatproof olive green plate.

Army glanced across at Dennis.

His head was down, and he was eating fast like a dog. Occasionally he glanced up, as if imagining one of the bigger beasts might steal his tea. He didn't say a word; none of them did, not while they were eating. Army ate his meal in silence. Left the pickled onion. He noticed he wasn't the only one to do that.

Dennis had already finished.

'Don't you want that?' he said, staring across the table, glaring at the unwanted food.

'No,' said Army. 'I don't.'

Dennis's hand shot across the table and scooped up the foul smelling article. Threw it in his mouth like a gobstopper. Chewed it hard through an open mouth. Grinned and breathed across the table. The stench was vile. Army turned to his right and glanced up the table. He counted twenty boys on either side. Forty identical empty olive green plates. Not a morsel remained. Even the ripe onions had gone. It had taken less than ten minutes.

'Is that it?' said Army.

'Yep,' said Dennis, 'Nothing else till breakfast, 'cept the cocoa of course, but don't drink that if you wet the bed. Gilligan goes crazy if you wet the bed.'

159

'Are you a bed wetter?' scowled Robinson, eager to get involved again. 'You look like a bed wetter to me.'

'No,' said Army, 'are you?'

Robinson flushed.

Dennis giggled behind his hand.

Mr Hancock appeared at the end of the table, his hands in the pockets of his brown corduroy trousers. He smelt of stale adult, swayed back and forth a couple of times and said, 'Ah, there you are, Shelbourne.'

'Ooh, Shelbourne, is it?' said Robinson. 'Born in a shell, were we? Come to think of it you look like a crab.'

Several of the others laughed. Even Mr Hancock smirked.

Dennis didn't laugh.

Then Mr Hancock said, 'All right, all right, Robinson, that's enough of the jocularity. Have you finished your tea?'

The boys glanced at their clean plates.

'Looks that way,' said Robinson.

Two others tittered.

'Yes, well, if you have, Shelbourne, follow me, I need to talk to you about one or two things.'

Army slipped from the end of the bench and stood up and made to follow Mr Hancock, then glanced back at the table. The boy opposite Robinson was staring at him, grinning stupidly, making gestures with his fingers, one hand, finger and thumb making a circle, the other hand, index finger, pushed in out of the circle, time and again. Army had no idea what that meant.

He didn't want to know either.

They skipped up the stone stairs to the third floor to Mr Hancock's office, a small room with a tiny window that looked out over the back gardens, with a fine view of the bins and the waste food receptacles. The window was open, introducing an aroma of stale bin. Hancock didn't appear to notice.

'Sit down,' he said.

Army sat in the plain dining chair set before the desk.

'You won't be going to King's, you know that, don't you?'

'Oh, but…'

160

'No buts, Armitage. We can't lay on transport for one boy to travel to Chester and back every day.'

Army linked his fingers in front of him and stared down at his hands.

'I will arrange for you to go to the local comprehensive. You'll be with all the others. It's for the best.'

Army said nothing.

'And erm, I have another disappointment for you, the dancing classes will have to be cancelled.'

Army said nothing. Pulled his fingers tighter and tighter, as if trying to pull them from their sockets.

'Don't do that, boy!'

Army stopped.

Said nothing.

Pouted and looked up and across the desk.

'I have one bit of good news for you,' said Hancock. 'I understand you are a bit of a singer?'

Army said nothing and nodded.

'Good, well, I've arranged for you to join the choir at the local parish church. You'll find out all about that come Sunday.'

Army still said nothing, just nodded again.

'Any questions?'

Army shook his head.

'Good, that's the spirit. Well, run along and find Swallow; he'll show you where you sleep.'

Army said nothing.

Stood up and ran outside.

The dormitory housed eighty boys; it was one section of the juniors, the normals, as they were known. The non-normals slept on the floor upstairs, which was a nuisance because when they were at their most agitated at full moon, they would leap around and scream and keep the normals awake.

The dorm was a long narrow room with forty beds on either side, the beds having large numbers affixed to the top of the metal headboard, in case anyone forgot who they were, and where they slept. The numbers were more necessary upstairs. Dennis was

161

docked in eighteen, Army given the only vacant berth, twenty, halfway along the line.

At half-past eight they were herded into a line of open communal showers. It was a tough moment for Army. He had never been naked before in company, and the others guessed it, and teased him. What's that pimple between yer legs, Barmy? All the new jerks were the same on their first strip. Walking through the dorm and across the corridor and into the showers, he had no idea where to put his hands.

'Bed wetter,' whispered Robinson in his ear as they left the dorm.

'Ignore him,' said Dennis. 'He's an idiot.'

Robinson glared at Dennis and Army.

Army said nothing.

Tried to ignore him. Tried to ignore everything.

It was like being in hell.

The dorm lights were switched off at half-past nine. The room was in darkness, except for a moon-like nightlight set high on the beams above Army's bed. Every half an hour Hancock would come in and wander down the dorm, slow noisy footsteps on the polished wooden floor, ensuring that every boy was in their own bed; no talking or larking around. No one dared.

Army wiggled and wriggled down the bed, pulled the covers over his head, locking himself inside, away from the weird world in which he found himself, and cried.

Not blaring wails, nor gasping for breath jerky sobs, just a still, silent cry, as the tears slipped down his fair face, dampening the sheets. He was crying for his long dead mother whose memories were fading; and his father too, who had been ripped from him. Army was crying because he could not go to King's. He was crying because of the loss of the dancing lessons he adored, but most of all, he was crying for himself.

He hated the place, and everyone in it, except perhaps Dennis Swallow, and he wondered what tomorrow might bring. He didn't care. Perhaps the world would end that night. Maybe he would fall asleep and never wake.

He prayed he would.

Chapter Twenty-Nine

Toby Malone hurt Desiree Holloway. He hurt her mentally. He hurt her physically. He hurt her when they made love. And when they didn't.

It was all a novel experience for Desi. She had become used to calling the shots, to having men and boys chase her, doing her bidding, wooing her, desperate to impress. She had known nothing different.

With Toby Malone, everything was different.

She couldn't comprehend why he should treat her that way. He made her cry, worse still; he appeared to glean enjoyment through making her cry. She should have cut him dead.

But she didn't.

Because she couldn't.

Like a moth drawn toward the brightest fire, Desi Holloway was entranced. It unnerved her. It made her ill.

For the first time since she was four, her education went backwards. That alarmed her, and it alarmed her tutors and sponsors even more.

Her senior tutor, Professor Jack Robertson, wrote a re-appraisal and dispatched it to London, so concerned was he at the retrenchment that had set in. That alarmed Mrs Bloemfontein, and her superiors too. Discussions took place outlining how the watertight contract could be terminated.

Desi was unaware of that, and even if she had known, it wouldn't have made any difference. She couldn't think of anything else. She went off her food, lost weight, and for a short time the incredible sparkle that was never far from her dark eyes, dimmed and died.

Her friends feared for her.

Their advice was rejected.

Her tutors cajoled her.

She seemed not to notice.

Professor Robertson feared for his reputation after Toby Malone took an interest in Desi Holloway.

Toby was studying aeronautical design. He wanted to be a jet fighter designer and already had a lucrative contract lined up with British Aerospace up at Preston. That interested Desi too, and she encouraged him to follow his dreams, just as she was determined to do.

He was due to escort her to the Autumn College Dinner Dance. It had been a longstanding date, carved in the diary for months. Everyone was going. Everyone was looking forward to it, a chance to dress up and flaunt one's success, one's outfit, and one's partner.

Toby didn't show, leaving Desi to sit shamefaced across the table from an empty chair, while all those around laughed and joked and felt sorry for Desi Holloway, the girl who could not hold on to a man. They pitied her, and some behind her back, laughed. How the mighty are fallen. The shooting star with unending supplies of cash had crashed to earth.

Desi had never experienced a setback before, in anything. She did not know how to deal with it, and imagined that things couldn't get any worse.

They did.

Toby Malone arrived at the dance with an impossibly beautiful willowy girl on his arm named Fiona Gilkes-Wood. Fiona's father was the chairman of the second largest Scottish bank. Loaded, they said, multi-millionaire. Whoever married her would be made for life. Fiona Gilkes-Wood had everything, and now she had Toby Malone too.

How could Desi compete with that?

She couldn't and didn't.

Diners and dancers pinched surreptitious glances at her when they imagined she wasn't looking. She sat alone, picking at her food, unblinking, sipping wine in silence, as if an icy embryo enclosed her. She spoke to no one, and saw no one, not a soul after that appalling moment when she spied Toby striding into the hall with the elated Fiona Gilkes-Wood on his arm.

Desi could cope with the violence, the kinky sex, and his ever-stranger demands, but she could not cope with public humiliation.

It would never happen again.

She would never let it happen again.

She finished her meal in silence, grabbed her things together, and slipped away into the night.

Some of the more aware people breathed a sigh of relief and whispered: How embarrassing was that? She did the right thing, getting out of there when she did, though she should have gone sooner. Poor Desiree. That Toby Malone was a bastard, but didn't everyone know that already?

It seemed not. Or if she did, Desi could not accept it.

The mesmerised moth was damaged.

She returned to her room alone, took two co-codamol painkillers, and blotted out the world.

In the days that followed, Toby beat a path to her door.

Apologised profusely.

Sent flowers.

A crate of Desiree's favourite red wine.

Letters.

Love letters.

Sex letters.

Pleading letters.

Letters detailing how pathetic Fiona was in bed, nothing compared to the passionate Desiree Holloway, and how she must take him back, because he knew she wanted him more than he wanted her.

Whether that was true was immaterial.

It was too late.

The clock had ticked on.

Ticked forward.

Desiree Holloway had rediscovered her first love.

Science.

She was brilliant at it too, everyone said so.

A shooting star.

Destined for heavenly things.

Everyone knew that.

She shut herself away from the world; away from everything, except her work. It was as if Toby Malone had never existed. She would never date at university again. She would never allow any man to touch her, vowed solemnly against it, and she maintained that vow for years.

Professor Robertson wrote a hasty re-appraisal re-appraisal and sent it by special courier. Collective sighs of relief were heard from the Thames to the Mersey.

Toby Malone had hurt Desiree Holloway. That was undeniable.

He didn't any more.

He couldn't.

She wouldn't allow it.

At the end of her five-year course she passed out with a double first in Mathematics and Chemistry, with honours, and everyone attended her graduation in Liverpool. Her father and mother, sister Louise, Professor Robertson, and even Mrs Bloemfontein jumped a train, ostensibly to support her protégé, when in reality she possessed Desiree's instructions as to where she should go, and what she should do next. Desi explained Mrs Bloemfontein's presence away with flippant remarks, saying she was an advanced careers advisor, which in a strange kind of way, she was.

Toby Malone didn't attend. He couldn't.

He'd long since disappeared, though he would never be forgotten. They found him dead one balmy summer's morning, bound in fuse wire, secured to his bed, wearing black lace knickers, an orange in his mouth, a ligature around his neck, and three small neat cuts across his hairy chest. They were not deep, just bloody. The cuts hadn't killed him. The ligature had. No one ever discovered who shared his final tryst, or who tightened that rope. Merseyside Police were still looking into it and the file remained open.

It had nothing to do with Desiree, or so she said.

The morning after her graduation, she was busy packing her things away prior to vacating her room. Mrs Bloemfontein appeared at the door. Desi was expecting her and nodded away a neighbour of hers, a distraught young woman who had flunked her exams, with a flick of the head and a whispered: 'I'll see you later.'

Mrs Bloemfontein sat at the desk without waiting to be invited.

Desi perched on the bed and said, 'So? What now?'

166

Mrs Bloemfontein produced a single unmarked brown envelope from her bag. Handed it across to Desi.

'It's a beautiful morning,' she said, 'I'm going for a walk. I'll be back in half an hour. Have your questions ready,' and she let herself out.

Desi slipped her finger beneath the flap of the envelope and eased it open. The front sheet was a congratulatory letter from the Scientific Research Organisation. It didn't say what they did, just an address and telephone number in London.

The next page instructed her to attend Billington Hall near Ludlow in Shropshire when the summer holidays were over. Desi guessed it was one of the crammer colleges that Mrs Bloemfontein had mentioned a while ago. Before that, they instructed her to fly to Tokyo where she should meet a Professor Takanato at Tokyo University, and after that, on to Canberra where an appointment was arranged to see a Professor Jim McClaine.

The tickets, further instructions, and authorization documents would be with her within the week. There was a telephone number she should contact if she had any queries. She recognised it; it was the same number Mrs Bloemfontein had given her before, and a firm written reminder that everything regarding her employment was covered by the secrecy clause she had signed. The last letter informed her she had qualified for a pay increase, fifty percent, starting the day she flew to Tokyo.

She read it a second time in case she'd missed anything; in case she'd imagined it all, before replacing the papers back in the envelope.

Mrs Bloemfontein returned ten minutes later.

'Well?' she said. 'How did you get on?'

'Seems clear enough.'

'Good. So glad.'

'It didn't say what I will be doing.'

'No, it wouldn't. But you can be sure it will extend the pioneering work you have been studying. I can't say any more right now, other than it will be hard, and difficult. You will need to steel yourself. It won't be easy.'

'I'd rather guessed that.'

'Yes, I hoped you had. Any further questions?'

'No, none.'

'That's good.'

Mrs Bloemfontein glanced at her watch.

'What's the best way to get back to Lime Street station?'

'Taxi.'

'Do you know the number?'

'In the hall downstairs.'

Mrs Bloemfontein smiled and bobbed her head and offered her hand.

Desi took it and shook it, and a moment later Mrs B was gone.

Chapter Thirty

On the morning of Walter's second televised press conference, the script had to be hurriedly amended. As expected, he had received a second letter. Same inkjet production, same wacky font, same forced inadequate spelling and grammar.

Well Wally,

Even we didn't think you was so stoopid. You are no nearer to finding us, are ya? You need help pal.

Here's a little conundrum for you.

CRJKWCMOJCSB??

Get it? The magnificent six, and guess what Wal, the seventh will be a lot closer to home, know what I mean?

You should have retired long ago, while you still could. Maybe it ain't too late. Maybe it is.

See you soon.
The Chester Mollesters

He slipped the letter into a clear plastic sleeve and showed it to Karen. She whistled through her teeth.
  'What are the letters?'

'The initials of the dead.'

Her eyes widened as she recalled them, 'Colin Rivers, James Kingston, William Camber, Maggie O'Brien, Jago Cripps,' she recited, reeling them off, thinking of each corpse and the set of sorry remains she'd witnessed. 'So who is SB?'

'Good question. No idea, but by the look of it, the he-she killer has struck again. Go through the list of recent missing persons. See if you can find anyone who fits the bill. Top priority.'

'Sure, Guv,' and then she said, 'so who's the seventh? The question marks?'

'I think that's meant for me.'

She thought about that for a moment and said, 'So do I.'

The press conference followed the same path as before. In the can by lunchtime, so the TV Company could broadcast their latest hot news at one o'clock, six o'clock, and half-past ten.

Across the city Sam lay on the bed, grinning at the screen.

The Darriteau guy looked more tired than before. Weather-beaten. Nervous. Perhaps he wasn't sleeping. The blonde looked well enough, though. It would take more than a few murders to deprive her of sleep. She didn't say a lot, just supported the Darriteau character, nudging his arm, passed him an occasional message, the slightest of encouraging smiles, and sly prompts, his rock, that's how she came across. Perhaps he was plugging her, mused Sam, when no one else was about. Maybe in the cop shop, late at night, Sam could imagine that, in the stationery cupboard, across the desk, it must happen all the time, it happens everywhere else.

Darriteau was talking again, making a pathetic plea for more information about SB. Was there an SB missing? Who is SB? Had SB been murdered, and if so, where is SB's body? Darriteau demanded proof.

'Find it yourself, you moron!' Sam yelled at the screen. 'Do you expect me to do everything for you?'

The black copper continued with the same vacuous threats.

I'm coming for you. We'll be meeting soon. Your time is almost up.

Yeah, sure thing, granddad.

You should be retired, put out to pasture, it should have happened years ago. It had taken Sam to bring that little fact to the public's attention. Walter Darriteau was a waste of space, a spent force, a man promoted beyond his ability. Truth was, Walter Darriteau was an embarrassment.

The broadcast ended, and Sam flicked off the telly and went through to the other bedroom. Unlocked the door, went inside.

Wally's Wall was covered in articles and features. Newspaper pictures of Walter in the field, looking dishevelled. Pictures of the pair of them answering impromptu questions outside the cop shop. Sam had been there that morning, hidden in the crowd, inwardly giggling and gloating, outwardly looking as concerned as all the rest.

Where would the Chester Mollesters strike next?

The same question was on everyone's lips.

Some idiot from the Incident Room had leaked the name Chester Mollesters to the press for five hundred pounds in used notes. Mrs West and Walter were livid when that happened and were determined to locate the leak, though that could wait for another day. It must have been a genuine leak too, not some inspired or lucky guessing journalism, because the newspapers were even spelling it correctly, Chester Mollesters, or incorrectly, as it was.

People were becoming wary of going out at night in a pretty city like Chester. It was unthinkable; it was unheard of, and what were the police doing about it? Not a lot, judging by their complete inability to apprehend the perpetrator, or was it perpetrators?

Ridiculous rumours flashed around. A mad priest was responsible, it was a crazy doctor; it was all to do with drugs, Jago was a drug dealer, everyone knew that, it had to be, drug assassinations, and even, it was one of their own, a disaffected police officer, passed over for promotion.

Sam glanced over the displayed articles. There would be another fresh batch tomorrow and that was pleasing.

Within twenty minutes of the press conference ending a potential match popped out of the police computer, a local missing person

171

with the initials SB. Sally Beauchamp, aged thirty-four, marital status, single, occupation unknown.

Walter sent Karen and Gibbons to interview the parents, leaving the officers with his final thoughts. 'Find out where she lives. Find out where she works. Find out what she does, or is it did, for a living.'

Hugh and Cerys Roberts were keen amateur birdwatchers. They would venture out first thing in the morning, often when the ground hugging mist had yet to clear. That morning it had. Hugh was scanning the skies for red kites using the new American binoculars his wife had bought him for his recent sixty-fifth birthday. Cerys preferred waterfowl, as she swept her glasses low across the shallow water of the quarry.

'What's that, Hugh?'

'What? Where?'

'In the water, see, there, away to the left.'

Hugh scanned and focused.

'See what you mean. Looks like a case. New looking, too. I've never noticed it before.'

'Me neither.'

'I'll pop back to the car for the wellies.'

When he returned, they made their way down to the quarry floor. Hugh slipped on the Wellington boots and waded out. It was easy enough; the bottom was flat and stable, and the water shallow.

'It's a case.'

'Can you bring it back?'

Hugh tried to lift it.

'It's very heavy.'

'Will it open?'

'Don't know. The fasteners are visible. I'll try.'

Hugh unclipped the fasteners.

The end of the case popped open.

Enough for Hugh to see, and smell.

'Oh God!'

'What is it?'

'Ring the police. Now!'

'Why, what is it?'

'It's the body of a woman.'

Cerys pulled out her iPhone and pumped in 999.

Back in the Incident Room Karen took a call from Prestatyn.

'Hi Karen, it's Dai Williams. Is Walter about?'

'Sure Dai, just a sec. Walter, Dai Williams for you.'

'Hi Dai, what's up, man?'

'I believe you've lost another body.'

'Saw me on the telly again?'

'I did, but more than that, Walter, I've found a body, and I thought of you.'

'No! Where?'

'In a suitcase in a quarry, over at Llandegla.'

'A woman?'

'Yep. Thirties, I'd say, and get this Walter, the head was buried in brown parcel tape, from the base of the neck to the tips of her hair. None of us have ever seen anything like it. Bound tight like a mummy.'

'Oh, geez.'

'You've a nutter on your hands.'

'We know that, doesn't make him any easier to find.'

'I'll wire you over the PM report as soon as I have it.'

'Thanks, Dai. I owe you one.

'Two, I think.'

'Yeah, let's hope there's no more, eh?'

'Be in touch.'

Chapter Thirty-One

Armitage had been at the orphanage five years. Things had improved. The food was better and there was more of it. The staff improved through better training and adopting a more enlightened attitude, and every boy incarcerated there breathed easier when the predatory Mr Gilligan was disciplined and removed. But as there was no concrete evidence against him, he escaped prosecution and kept his pension. The boys cared little about that; they were too busy celebrating his demise.

To everyone's relief the non-normals were moved too, taken to a brand new redbrick facility at Willaston, where only four boys would share a room, where hot individual showers were always on tap, and where any hint of bullying and intimidation from the so-called normals was eradicated. Some of the non-normals knew that some normals were in the wrong classification, and vice versa. But those non-normals who had been evacuated were now delighted to be wrongly classified and away.

Those remaining at Saint Edmond's slept better. The crazy night-time shrieking upstairs soon became a thing of memory and folklore. The new jerks were told horrific stories of how it used to be, and how lucky they were, and the confused new arrivals didn't know what to believe.

In all that time, no one had ever come for Dennis Swallow.

They had looked at him right enough, considered him, those potential foster parents, countless times, like people inspecting dogs on dog death row. But always he would be rejected because of his darting untrustworthy eyes, so reported back more than one middle class Wirral family, or maybe it was his rat-like looks. Dennis was sixteen and on the brink of leaving school, searching for employment, and finding somewhere to live outside the system.

Dennis had never lived anywhere else other than at Saint Edmond's. He didn't know what a family home was like. He didn't know anything better. The idea of him going out into the big wide world alone was terrifying, yet exciting too. Dennis cherished his dreams, holding them close to his chest, like all the rest.

Armitage was still stuck in Saint Edmond's too.

Even more potential fosterers had considered him, yet there was something about him that put people off. His limbs appeared to develop at different rates, like a yearling colt where one end grows faster than the other, and the creature never looks quite right. He didn't look natural, the finished article, and this weird appearance resulted in those same people staring at him, and smiling down, and grimacing, shaking their heads, and muttering, 'Maybe not,' and often in Armitage's presence.

All the kids were relieved when they changed the viewing system. They didn't do that anymore. Reject them on the spot, in full view of the rejected. Thank God for that. It was just a wonder it took them so long to figure out that constant and obvious rejection could lead to more problems, and more of the same.

When the vicar of Saint Jude's, the local parish church, first heard Armitage sing at eleven, he was transfixed. It was a case of love at first sound. The vicar fell head over heels. There was nothing he would not do for Armitage, so long as Armitage felt the same way.

Armitage did not.

Not that the Reverend Christian de Wyk would be put off by that, and nor did he block or hinder Armitage's singing. He didn't, and he couldn't, because he adored it so, the magical treble voice that soared through Saint Jude's church, filling the place with joy. Despite the rebuffs he would keep Armitage in the choir because he, Christian, was ambitious. The Saint Jude's choir had been widely talked about and admired once in the past, but that was ten years back, long before Christian de Wyk took up his post.

Christian intended to return it to how it once was, and backed by the Bishop of Chester, who was a friend of his; he was determined to achieve it.

Armitage remained on the front row of the choir.

He didn't know what the vicar wanted; but he knew he didn't. It came from his deepest instincts that this God fearing man the parishioners so adored was dangerous. Army shared his thoughts

175

with Dennis, who couldn't sing for coal-scuttles. Army told him all about it. Of his doubts and fears, and the creeping feeling of cold discomfort that came over him whenever the vicar called him to his private rooms, and how he couldn't wait to get away, and the numbness he felt when Christian would stand close behind him at choir practice, his hands alive on Armitage's slight shoulders, as Christian's raucous baritone echoed into Army's ears, through the hearty never-ending renditions of All People That On Earth Do Dwell and Onward Christian Soldiers, a favourite of the vicar's.

Dennis explained in graphic detail, and would never forget the look of horror and disbelief on his friend's boyish face, as the penny dropped.

'You can't be serious!'

Dennis nodded his head, unable to keep the likeable smirk from his rodential face.

Armitage had avoided being alone with the vicar. After that enlightenment he refused to attend the vicar's private rooms under any circumstances, risking any punishment or banishment.

A year later Christian de Wyk disappeared.

Amongst the adults, wicked rumours circulated, not that any of those filtered through the thick walls of Saint Edmond's. Armitage was delighted he was gone, as were all the choirboys, especially the prettier ones.

He was replaced by the Reverend Blair McGowan, who, as his name suggested, was very Scottish and mighty proud of it. He was happily married with four mini McGowans, three boys and all would sing in the choir, two would later become ordained, and one shy girl, Machara, who didn't sing a note, but stood on the front row of the congregation with her mother. A position from where the older boys would inspect her, as they concentrated on pronouncing their vowels Dwell, Hallelujah, and Praise, as in Praise Him! Praise Him! gazing across at Machara with a mixture of curiosity and excitement, pondering on those naturally pink lips, as she silently mouthed her words, the boys wondering what she might wear beneath that thick tartan skirt, and wondering too where that might lead.

After the coming of the McGowans the choirboys relaxed.

They came to adore Blair McGowan who, with his three sons, would play football with them on the green, pretend matches between his beloved Raith Rovers, and Everton or Liverpool, or their own local Rovers, Tranmere. But more importantly, for the choirboys, on Sunday afternoons before evensong, he would invite some of them home for tea, ensuring that through the course of a term, each boy took his turn. It was an invitation no one refused.

Armitage's opportunity arrived one hot sunny June day. Fresh strawberries and cream were served in fancy blue glass dishes, the boys eyeing them through wide eyes, the berries picked by Machara's fair hand, from the extensive fruit patch at the rear of the vicarage. Red salmon sandwiches made from real tinned salmon, and best English butter, not scrimped with either, the sandwiches cut neatly into fours, the faint aroma of a woman's perfume upon them, as if they had been cut and prepared by Mrs McGowan, or better still, Machara.

'The crusts cut off!' exclaimed Armitage. 'Can you believe that?' as he later told Dennis about it. 'All the crusts cut off!'

Armitage wasn't alone in wondering what happened to those crusts. He'd liked to have taken them back to Saint Edmond's, but he still hadn't finished his gleeful descriptions.

Homemade sugar topped fruit scones with raspberry jam, and more cream, and gallons of hot steaming tea, served in cups and saucers, the good stuff too, Typhoo. Not the dishwater muck we have to drink, with a large bowl of sugar lumps parked in the centre of the table where the boys were encouraged to take as many lumps as they liked.

'Sugar isn't rationed here, you know,' grinned the Reverend Blair, 'not in this house,' through his jovial red face, remembering as he did his own childhood from long ago when sugar was worth more than gold.

The boys took him at his word, and every week the bowl was picked clean, many of them secreting extra lumps into their pockets to eat later as sweeties.

'And afterwards he put on the record player and played records,' recalled Army, perhaps getting a little carried away at the beauty and warmth of it all, of being in someone else's happy home, something that Armitage remembered all too well, but something that Dennis could not relate to. It might as well have been in far off Hollywood, for all he knew.

177

Dennis was interested in the descriptions of the food and drink; and envious too, that went without saying. The mere mention of it made his mouth water and his stomach rumble, but there was something else that interested him far more.

'Tell me about Machara!'

'Well,' said Armitage, thinking about her, and trying to remember what she wore and what she said and did. He hadn't paid that much attention. 'Well, she's very clean, and quiet, and pink, and smells of scented soap, with black shiny hair in a helmet sort of style, and she was wearing a white top, and a green tartan skirt with a large silver pin in it, and long green tartan socks.'

'Yeah, that's all good, but would you fuck her?'

Armitage flushed.

He had never considered such an outrageous idea. It had never entered his head. He had been far too preoccupied with the strawberries and cream. He was about to stammer out a no idea reply, only to halt himself as he remembered how the other boys always acted when they talked dirty, and he copied them.

'Yeah, yeah, course I would!'

'I knew it,' said Dennis, leering, 'I bloody knew it! You dirty bugger!'

'I saw her knickers,' said Armitage.

'What! Did ya? When? How?'

'When she sat down on the settee, when she took her strawberries to eat, after she'd made sure we all had ours, as guests, as her dad had asked her to do. They were green.'

'Were they? Yeah? Green?'

'I only saw them for a second before I looked away.'

'Looked away?' asked Dennis, not believing what Army had said. 'What did you do that for, ya limpet?'

'It's rude to look up women's skirts.'

'Is it? I don't think it is. I look up women's skirts all the time, it's only natural, not that I get much opportunity.'

Armitage glanced across at him, thinking him a little weird, though he didn't say, for Dennis was the only genuine friend he had in the whole world.

Saint Jude's church choir had built up a fine reputation. While church attendances across the country were plummeting, Saint Jude's was packing them in. It wasn't unusual for the place to be full. Word went round the Wirral and beyond. There was a singer there, a treble who was better than those celebrity singers you heard on the TV at Christmastime. Far better! I kid you not. Well better, as the local boys might have said. You should listen to him. See and hear for yourself while you have the chance.

People did. Hundreds of them.

Saint Jude's was a chunky red stone church with a straight and skinny steeple. It continued to sell out, not that they ever charged anyone to attend. Though Blair McGowan with his Scottish roots, had considered doing so when he saw the queues of excited people hurrying through the lichgate, talking excitedly as if they were going to a music concert at the Liverpool Philharmonic Hall.

Blair resisted the temptation to charge, contenting himself with a Please Give Generously plea, at the end of his brief sermon. He realised many folks had not come to hear him, as the mauve velvet collection bags were sent out. Saint Jude's had never collected so much cash, including, as the choirboys would witness afterwards, when the donations were emptied into a rusty red Crawford's biscuit tin, banknotes amongst the haul.

'I mean,' said Army, meeting Dennis afterwards on the way back to Saint Edmond's, 'what kind of person puts notes in a collection bag? They must half be loaded.'

Dennis shook his head in disbelief and returned to thinking of Machara and her green kilt and long socks and matching green knickers.

After the service, the Reverend McGowan stood on the steps and pressed the flesh of people he had never met before. He heard worshippers muttering in amazement as they made their way home. Snatches of conversation permeated his hairy ears. 'What did you think of the boy? Amazing, wasn't he? Well better than that bloke off the telly. Unique, truly unique.'

'Well better,' nodded the others, in that slight Merseyside accent that intrigued Blair and Machara so.

179

Someone informed the local radio station. It featured on one of the radio phone-ins that dominated the schedules. Radio Merseyside sent a scout to the next service. She returned with excited tales of packed churches and electric atmospheres, and people coming from all over. The boy is amazing! We must cover it!

The broadcasting truck rolled up on Thursday, and for the next two days technicians pulled and prodded their wires and mics into place.

House full notices went up outside the church!

A loudspeaker relay was set up outside to feed the overspill crowd. Armitage was fifteen and a seasoned performer. He was due to solo two of his favourite pieces and aimed to be note perfect. After he had finished final practice Machara came into the church, seeking her father, but she made a beeline for Armitage, thrusting a rabbit's foot into his hand, whispering in her gentle Scottish lilt, 'All the best for tomorra, Armitage, aye,' and her father arrived and they turned and hustled away.

Armitage didn't answer, not even a mumbled thanks.

Crazy talk of a record company executive being spotted in the car park circulated, though how anyone would recognise such a person was never explained.

'You're going to be a star,' someone said, not that Armitage heard.

In the Saint Jude's choir, Armitage Shelbourne was already a star.

He had been from the first day he'd arrived.

On the Saturday night before the concert he'd gargled his throat, went to bed in the same long dormitory; pulled himself down his narrow bed, and said a silent prayer for his mother. He caressed the rabbit's foot, thought of Machara and the concert, and his singing, and fell asleep.

He enjoyed a good night's sleep and woke early… with a sore throat.

He coughed hard to clear the phlegm.

There wasn't any.

He sat up and stared across at Dennis. He was sitting on the side of his bed scratching his mousy head.

'Hey, Dennis, I've got a sore throat.'

Dennis beamed and jumped up and walked over to Army's bed.

'You haven't got a sore throat, you prick! Your voice has broken, and about time! We were thinking you were a right one. We thought it might never happen!'

That couldn't be right, not on his big day. Surely to God, not today. Dennis was talking rubbish. He often did. Army took a deep breath and launched into Mozart's The Violet and Alleluia. The croaking that followed sounded like rusty barbed wire being dragged across dusty glass.

'You're knackered, mate!' grinned Dennis. 'You'd better get used to it. You're a man now! It's taken long enough for your sprouts to hit the deck!'

Army rushed to the church. The technicians were hustling about, completing final preparations.

He hurried to the reverend's private rooms at the back. Blair was standing before a full-length mirror, practising his speech. It was his big day too, live on local radio, the chance to put his thoughts across to millions, well thousands, maybe. His words would be broadcast across the region, and he had plenty to say. Machara was there too, sitting at the back, reading her red leather bound New Testament.

'Sorry, vicar, my voice has gone,' croaked Army.

Machara glanced up.

Blair stifled three seconds of disappointment, smiled and said, 'Your voice has broken, that's all, it's God's work, it happens to everyone. It's natural. Perhaps there is a reason behind it. Jimmy Wilson will take your place. He can manage, don't you worry.'

'But I was so looking forward to it.'

Machara grinned at the rough sounds escaping his mouth and returned to the book of Luke. He sounded ridiculous, as if someone was strangling him, yet oddly endearing.

Blair McGowan said, 'Don't ye worry about a thing. You'll soon mature into a great tenor, bass, or baritone. It's all there for you.'

Armitage doubted that.

'But, but…' he said.

'But nothing,' said the vicar, and resumed his rehearsal, as Armitage stared at the floor and sauntered away.

The concert went ahead as planned, Armitage scowling at the back, not daring to inflict his ear wrenching contribution on a packed house.

181

The nervous Jimmy Wilson struggled throughout, missing top notes, and forgetting words. He had never imagined he would have to perform live on the radio. Afterwards the crowds melted away, a feeling of disappointment and anticlimax in the air.

They all heard the comments as the congregation melted away.

Nowhere near as good as usual.

The lads in our local church could have done better.

The occasion got the better of them.

If only I'd known I'd have stayed away.

What a waste of time.

What was all the fuss about?

How disappointing!

Armitage returned to Saint Edmond's with a heavy heart. That night he lay awake into the early hours, thinking of what might have been.

Through the following months, he waited for his voice to set. He was desperate sing again. But his voice stubbornly refused to settle. He continued to blare out a ragged mess of uncoordinated clatter and never found an authentic voice again.

He was on the brink of adult life and had no idea what he would do next.

There was talk of him leaving, going into a halfway house betwixt the orphanage and the great beyond. Dennis's leaving date was already in the diary. They found him a job making soup for a huge multinational American corporation. Monday, tomato. Tuesday, vegetable. Wednesday, oxtail. Thursday, chicken. Friday, mushroom. Saturday morning, service and clean the machinery, and away. Dennis couldn't wait to leave the orphanage, start work, and earn some money.

Armitage was confused. Whatever the world held in store, one thing was certain, he would never become a soup maker. There had to be more to life than that.

Chapter Thirty-Two

Two days after Desiree Holloway returned from Japan and Australia, she made her way by rail to Ludlow, and then by taxi the five miles into the border country to Billington Hall. It was a large and attractive redbrick house, formerly the residence of a minor aristocrat who had returned from the First World War, minus his four sons, and his mind.

The gentleman never recovered, and in exchange for his ongoing lifetime medical care, the government requisitioned the property. There was no one else who wanted it, and it had fallen into a state of disrepair. The locals were happy to see it brought back to its former glory, though some wondered where the lavish amounts of money being spent came from.

It had remained in government hands ever since. Signalling station during World War Two, interrogation centre afterwards for suspected war criminals, intelligence briefing centre during the cold war, monitoring station during the Irish troubles, and then a crammer college specialising in politically sensitive fields.

It was a rambling place, three times extended since the government took possession, and comfortable. Desiree would live there for the week.

She adored Japan.

The countryside, the warmth and vibrancy of the people, the food, and the crazy technology that was everywhere. She was impressed with Professor Takanato at Tokyo University. He was open about his work, allowing her to sit in on his experiments and classes. Took her to dinner too and gave her his telephone numbers, should she ever need his advice.

Australia was different. Professor Jim McClaine was standoffish, as if concerned she might borrow his work and pass it off as her own. The country was going through one of its periodic droughts. The sun blazed down every day, and temperatures soared. Patience frayed, and though they parted on amicable terms, she hadn't enjoyed her trip down under.

In Britain, she returned to the classroom, staring at the same old revolving, reusable blackboards bearing traces of scrubbed former lessons. There were only four people in the class, two men and two women, all under thirty, with three tutors, all under forty. They did most of the talking. The pupils listened and noted and wrote. The days were long; starting at eight and finishing at seven, and by the time they had dined and updated their notes, it was time for bed.

Much of the one-sided discussions involved coping with the testing work that lay ahead. On the second last day, they were advised of some significant changes. The Scientific Research Organization was being wound up. The government was going through one of its budget crazy routines to cut national debt. The SRO was being sold off, but because of the sensitive nature of the work, there would be no public share offering. Five entities would take equal shares in the new PLC, disguised companies belonging to the governments of Japan, Australia, the United States, Germany, and Britain.

The Scientific Research Organisation changed its name overnight to Trencherman Research PLC, Desiree's new employers.

On the last day, Desiree was summoned to a private office on the top floor, a room looking out over rear lawns and away to the Welsh hills. The room was Spartanly furnished, a plain table set before the window with a basic chair on either side. On the table was a recording machine, and there was no one else in the room.

Desiree glanced through the window. Two local guys were mowing the lawns. To the left, on the grass, behind a tall wire fence, was a bank of five impressive radio aerials, and two supersats, large white dishes pointing at the sky. Beyond another wire fence, fifty sheep grazed.

The door opened and Mrs Bloemfontein breezed in.

She smiled her distant smile and asked Desiree to sit.

'How are you?' she said.

'I'm well, and you?'

'I'm good.'

'I am recording this meeting; it saves the bother of taking notes. It will go on your file. Every word uttered. Any objections?'

Desiree shook her head.

'Please answer aloud.'

184

'I have no objections,' said Desiree.

'This is your last opportunity to withdraw from the programme. Do you understand?'

'Yes.'

'Do you wish to do that?'

'No.'

'Good. You will know we now have new masters.'

'So I heard. Trencherman Research.'

'Yes, they are our new paymasters, we must get used to it. I am assured nothing will change.'

'It's all new to me.'

'Quite. No doubt you will want to know where you are going next.'

'Yes, of course.'

'Nowhere romantic, I'm afraid. You'll be going to the Eden Leys complex.'

'Which is where?'

'Not so far from here, south of Whitchurch, north of Shrewsbury.'

Desiree would be lying if she hadn't imagined an exciting posting to California or Kobe or Bavaria, but once in a laboratory it didn't matter where one worked. All labs were the same, and she didn't stare through windows, admiring scenery. Shropshire was cool. She could get home to her parents easy enough, though she would have to pass her driving test first.

'Here are your accreditation documents, your security, and your tags. They must be worn at all times on site.'

Mrs Bloemfontein pulled an envelope from her bag, removed the items she had mentioned, and slipped them across the table.

'Desiree Holloway is taking possession of her documents,' she said to the machine. Desi picked up her security tags and admired the startled picture of her face, a colour photograph she couldn't remember being taken.

'Nice picture,' she said.

'Not bad, you should see mine.'

The women shared a nervous laugh

'When do I start?'

'Monday.'

'And where do I sleep?'

'There is accommodation booked for you on the base. It is an enormous site; you will want for nothing there, supermarket, cinema, bowling facilities, swimming pool. I doubt you will leave that often.'

'I see.'

'You will report to a Professor Mary Craigieson, got that?'

'Mary Craigieson,' Desiree repeated.

Mrs Bloemfontein nodded and said, 'Any questions?'

'No, none.'

'If you think of any later, you have my number. That concludes this meeting. Good luck. I am sure you will do well.'

Mrs Bloemfontein stood, switched off the device and offered her hand. Desi took it and shook it, the same cold handshake, and an awkward moment as Desi stood her ground, only to be nodded away. Desi was dismissed. Time for someone new. She bobbed her head and left the room.

In the morning a black BMW took the same four students back to Ludlow railway station, where they boarded separate trains and headed home. Desiree would never see Billington Hall again.

Chapter Thirty-Three

The PM report on Sally Beauchamp was in. Walter mulled it over in his mind. Death by asphyxiation, but a considerable amount of flunitrazepam evident in the body, Rohypnol by any other name, the date rape drug. Where does one acquire flunitrazepam? In the past, there may have been a lead there, tracking the supply chain, but now? No chance.

It came from the Internet, where else? Log on, type prescription drug supply into the browser and away you go. The Internet was a wonderful invention, but it had a lot to answer for, and policing it was impossible.

The suppliers were likely to be in Latvia, Ukraine, Nigeria, Jamaica or Belize. A hopeless task and what about quality control? Who knows what substandard product might be delivered, if anything ever came, when one went online and paid through the nose for prescription drugs bought without a prescription?

Death by asphyxiation.

What kind of person could do that? Walter put himself in the killer's shoes, tried to imagine what was going through his, or her sick mind, as they wound a whole roll of sticky tape around someone's face. What was the point in that, when a couple of feet would have done the job? No fingerprints on the roll either, not a surprise. Walter hadn't expected any.

He wondered if the killer enjoyed it, the drawn-out act of murdering a fellow human being. It wasn't like a single gunshot or stab wound, over in a second. No, this must have gone on for minutes. Hadn't it worried them? Were they happy in their work? Smiling, grinning, chuckling, what? Were they talking too, as they went about their murderous work, winding round and round, perhaps talking dirty as if frantically making love. What was in the killer's mind? Would he ever know?

He was sitting in John's office, Mrs West's, and Cresta was rabbiting on about something. He glanced across at her. What was this? A primrose blouse, unbelievable, that was different. The purple garb must have been in the wash. It still left purple skirt, eye

187

shadow, nails, hair, and lips. Darting lips, spouting forth her latest theory. Not that he heard a word. They were a nightmare, those purple salivating lips.

He pondered on whether Cresta was someone's squeeze. She had never mentioned anyone. No rings that day, either. If she had worn any, they would have contained purple stones. A nightmarish thought flashed through his head. Him waking on a Sunday morning, finding Cresta there in the bed, purple from toenails to hair, some kind of weird purple alien, talking, talking, talking, spewing out verbiage through those restless lips, expounding new thinking, fresh from the killer's mind.

Sounded good, meant nothing.

Walter had been in the game long enough to know that no matter how well you knew someone, whatever they said, did, wrote, or intimated, you never knew what was in the dark recesses of the human mind. You couldn't imagine what complicated thought processes were going on in there, because human beings didn't want you to know, because they were too scared, frightened, and ashamed of their real thoughts, and of other people knowing them.

Cresta Raddish had been a useful addition to the team, he would admit that. When any bunch of human beings met and mulled over a complicated case, there was always the chance someone might throw a new thought into the communal pot. It hadn't happened yet, but it didn't mean it couldn't happen. But neither did it mean profilers were the answer to all their problems and thank God for that.

Cresta Raddish contributed nothing toward the killer's arrest, but no one had, because the killer was still at large. Free to murder again, something Walter was convinced he, she, or it, would do, and sooner rather than later. Or maybe they had already. At least they knew the Chester Mollester was the killer. Any idea of a crazy hoaxer was out. The last missive named the latest victim's initials, SB. Long before a body was discovered, before any murder was known about.

Death by asphyxiation, the latest in a long and differing line, death by asphyxiation, by slitting wrists, carbon monoxide poisoning, drowning, being flattened by a train, by being run down by a car. What next? Where does The Chester Mollester go after that? Was

188

there any pattern to it? There was a build-up in the ferocity of the personal violence inflicted on the victims, but where and when and what was to come? If Walter had to guess, he would plump for firearms. But could the he-she thing gain access to a gun? The Internet again. Could anyone buy a firearm online? Probably, if you looked hard enough.

Cresta's lips ceased flexing like a rubber puppet's. Thank heaven for that. She had run out of words, for now.

Earlier, Mrs West had called him into her private sanctum for a one-to-one. She explained she was under enormous pressure. Weren't we all, Walter wanted to add, but didn't, and he could imagine the daily strained telephone calls from her superiors that must have wriggled into her business-like head.

He didn't envy her that, one more reason he had never sought the top dog job. He would remain in the field for as long as he could. The idea of him sitting in his run down Edwardian detached house, flicking through daytime TV channels, alone, with his Police magazines and newsletters and Racing Post, was one too dreadful to contemplate.

'It's coming to crunch time,' she said.

He knew what that meant, but she explained it in more detail.

'The Met will be brought in. We'll lose control of the case. Lapdogs, that's what we'll become, lapdogs to the mountain lion, do you want that?'

There had been a time when he was the mountain lion, as she described it. He'd enjoyed it too, being parachuted in, taking charge of complicated murder cases from Cornwall to Norfolk, from Northumbria to the south coast, annoying the local plod, detecting errors, pointing out their provincial mistakes, and getting up everyone's nose. But he would produce a result by identifying the killer, making an arrest, prosecuting the criminal, securing a conviction, witnessing the satisfying moment of sentence, and seeing the devil being taken down. So why couldn't he do that again?

'It will be a huge stain on my curriculum vitae...' she said, 'and yours too.'

He knew that, about his record being stained, but was too old to worry about failure. It wasn't the stain on his record that concerned him; it was failing to bring the culprit to justice that irked him. He

189

had never failed to track down and prosecute a serial killer, and he wasn't going to spoil that record.

'Let's get Karen and Cresta in and go over everything again,' she said, and the four-way meeting began.

'We are missing something,' said Joan West. 'Missing something!'

Of course we are missing something, thought Walter. Six bloody deaths and we still don't have a prime suspect. But what?

'How is the car search business going?' he asked, though he was thinking of something else.

'Almost finished,' said Karen, 'only about twenty to do.'

'Maybe that will turn something up,' mumbled Walter.

'Let's hope so,' said Mrs West, becoming more impatient.

It wouldn't turn anything up because it couldn't, because unbeknown to them, the killer had already been checked and passed and eliminated from their enquiries. It had happened the previous Saturday afternoon. Two rookie police officers had called at Iona House, as Samantha was preparing to go out.

'Sorry to bother you, ma'am,' said the first, as the second checked out the slender, classy woman. 'Just routine enquiries, but we want to look over your car?'

'Sure,' she said, in that gentle way of hers, producing the keys from her designer bag, and leading them across the small car park to her gleaming Cayton Cerisa. She didn't need to go near the car, she could have stood on the doorstep and pointed and fired, but that seemed bad manners, so she followed them toward it before opening up.

'Is it OK to go inside?' said the handsome younger bloke.

'Course,' she said, nodding, her blonde bob cut shivering in the breeze.

He opened the boot.

Empty, nothing there at all, pristinely clean, like the lady herself. You could always tell. Not a hair out of place, perfect make-up, everything immaculate.

He opened the doors and climbed inside. Glanced in the glove compartment, under the seats, in the side panels, in the cash box nestling beneath the handbrake, in the CD holder secreted up toward the roof to fool potential car thieves, nothing on the parcel shelf, nothing in the pouches on the back of the front seats except

190

for an old and outdated UK road atlas, once common. Now redundant through satnav.

No craft knives or rolls of brown tape, no railway timetables with details of services along the North Wales coast, no hose-piping to introduce gas, no lingering smell or sign of gas either, no bumps or scratches on the front of the vehicle, no syringes, or signs of drugs of any kind, not even a blessed aspirin. Clean as a fresh penny whistle.

They tried to engage her in casual conversation. Samantha knew that. Perhaps they were hoping she would invite them into the flat. There was no chance of that. Hell would freeze over first. Perhaps they were hoping for a relaxing coffee and a sit down on her leather chesterfield, even a free sandwich. It was never going to happen.

'Will you be much longer?' she asked. 'It's just I have a date, and William goes crazy if I'm late.'

The two guys shared a look. Lucky William.

'No, miss, I think we are finished here.'

'Excellent,' she said, locking the back door and getting into the car, making ready to drive away.

They smiled at her again and she smiled back.

They would never forget that smile.

Jumped in the police car and drove away.

Before they had gone twenty yards one of them said, 'Before you say anything, I most definitely would.'

'Me too, no doubt about it.'

'You're married.'

'Don't care.'

'It couldn't have been her anyway,' said cop number two. 'The killer has green eyes, so Cresta Raddish said. Did you see her blue eyes?'

'Of course I did. You couldn't miss 'em.'

'Don't think I've ever seen such blue eyes.'

'William goes crazy,' cop number one mimicked her words.

'I'll bet he does,' said the other.

'He probably gives her a right thrashing.'

'I'd give her a good thrashing if I had the chance,' said the other, and as they were thinking about that, driving concentration waned.

191

Neither was the young woman concentrating as she stepped out into the road, pushing a buggy containing two gurgling toddlers.

The cop braked at the last moment, throwing up smoke, depositing rubber on the tired tarmac; blowing a loud squeal into the air. Stopped in time, no sweat, only just, though, as the dizzy young thing grinned into the car and mouthed: Sorry, as if it had been her fault.

After that, the policemen forgot about the fragrant woman. They were thinking of their next five appointments, all in Handbridge. They were nearly finished, and because flashy Japanese hatchback owners were likely to be owned by young and attractive career girls, with any luck, they might find the lady of their dreams. There was more chance of that than finding the killer.

Cresta Raddish was saying something about a female serial killer in Arkansas she had studied who had cut off her victims' fingers and fed them to her dog. It didn't go anywhere, and Walter wondered if it was to fill in time, or perhaps to demonstrate how well qualified and experienced in her field she was.

A sharp rap came to the door.

Mrs West harrumphed.

She had given strict orders they were not to be disturbed.

'Get that, Karen,' she snapped.

Karen opened the door.

It was Jenny Thompson, a satisfied smirk on her face; none of them could miss.

'Sorry to interrupt, ma'am, but Walter's had another letter, I mean Inspector Darriteau,' and she produced another skinny manila envelope. 'Same wacky print,' she said, holding it up for all to see.

Walter leapt from his chair, surprising everyone, including himself, at how quickly he moved. Took the envelope between finger and thumbnails like some old-fashioned fairground machine trying to grasp a prize.

'Thanks, Jen,' he muttered.

Karen nodded at the WPC and closed the door in her face.

He set the envelope on the desk before them.

Mrs West handed him a metal letter opener and a pair of tweezers, and retrieved a clear plastic sleeve from her drawer.

Walter drew out the sheet of paper and set it on the desk.

192

All three women were standing behind him, staring down at communiqué number three.

Well Wally,

You need help man.
You'll never catch us at this rate.
Lady's Day. We'll see you there.
We have so much to talk about.
Can't weight.
Can you?

The Chester Mollesters.

PS: Make sure your life insurance is paid up.

The same font, same inkjet production, same obvious bad spelling, same weird use of the plural, as in we'll, not I'll, when everyone was convinced they were looking for one person, one man or one woman. Perhaps that was where the "we" came into it, the he-she thing was so confused it believed it was two people, split personality gone crazy. We are murdering. We are a murderer. We can't be caught. We are laughing.

'What does he mean there?' said Cresta, revealing that even she thought it might be a man, 'When he says Lady's Day.'

'Chester races,' said Karen.

'Biggest day of the year,' said Walter, recalling several carefree days spent on the tight but cute track, admiring the tiny but cute visitors, and especially on Ladies' day, as it should have been spelt.

'When is it?' asked Cresta.

'Day after tomorrow,' said Mrs West.

'It doesn't give us much time,' said Karen.

'Time enough,' said Walter.

193

'I don't think you should go anywhere near the track,' said Mrs West, back in her chair, glancing at Walter.

'I'm going, ma'am. I have to.'

'Am I missing something, or has the killer not made a direct threat against you? Make sure your life insurance is paid up.'

'Maybe, ma'am,' said Karen, 'but if he doesn't go, the killer may walk away. Walter will have to be there, and be high profile too, so the killer can see him; and when and if the he-she thing makes its move, we strike.'

'I agree with that,' said Cresta. 'Hundred percent. I mean, what's the he-she thing going to do, gun him down in broad daylight before thousands of witnesses? Unlikely, don't you think?'

'Hope not,' muttered Walter.

It may have been unlikely, but the image of it was powerful.

'We'll flood the place, thirty, forty, fifty, how many officers do you think you'll need?' Mrs West asked Walter.

'Thirty is more than enough. We don't want the killer frightened off by hundreds of suspicious looking police officers lumping around, not interested in racing.'

'They'll all have to look their best,' said Karen. 'They'll stick out like sore thumbs otherwise. Best party wedding day frocks, jackets, pressed trousers, ties, neat shirts, and buttonholes for the boys.'

Great! Thought Walter, but when necessary he could dress up, when the occasion demanded, and this time it did.

Mrs West asked Karen, 'Have you renewed your firearms licence?'

'Yes, ma'am, recently done.'

'Good. Go fully armed; and you too, Walter.'

Walter nodded; he always intended to do that.

'You don't think this could be a bluff, do you?' said Karen.

'How do you mean?' asked Mrs West.

'A diversionary tactic? While we are concentrating on the racecourse, the killer strikes somewhere else.'

'The world is a big place,' said Walter. 'We can't be in hundreds of locations at the same time. If it's a diversion, so be it, but I don't think it is.'

'Neither do I,' said Cresta in a rush.

'Get on to the racecourse right now,' said Mrs West to Karen. 'We want thirty of the most expensive tickets, access all areas, we don't want police staff flicking IDs every five minutes, and we are not paying either, and it's to remain most secret, and don't take no for an answer. I don't care if they have been sold out for months. No, on second thoughts, we can do better than that. It's only just across the road. Go down there right now, see them in person, throw your weight around if you have to, and take that Gibbons bloke with you for added muscle. He always seems to have time on his hands.'

Karen grinned and glanced at Walter.

He nodded the briefest of nods.

She frowned, flicked a smile and headed for the door.

Cresta was thinking of what to wear. She had bought a beautiful tight fitting purple frock in New York the last time she attended the International Profiler's Conference. That should do.

'You better call everyone together,' said Mrs West to Walter. 'Explain what we want. Everyone is to look as if they are attending their favourite brother's wedding. I'll organise the buttonholes. If anyone lets me down, they will have me to answer to. Oh, and remind the girls they will need to wear a hat. If they don't have anything suitable, come and see me; I have a cupboard full of fancy items. I'll want everyone dressed and ready and on parade by nine o'clock Thursday for final briefing, remind everyone there are big prizes to be won for the best turned out people.'

'Yes, ma'am,' said Walter, standing and ambling outside.

They shouldn't be thinking of winning bloody prizes.

He might forget to mention that incentive.

They should be thinking of arresting a serial killer, someone who had murdered six people to date, and was still running amok; someone who had the impudence to suggest that he update his life insurance.

There was no point in doing that. He didn't have any.

What was the need?

After he'd gone Cresta asked: 'So what do you think the he-she thing is going to do now?'

'I have no idea,' said Mrs West. 'You?'

Cresta pursed her lips, pulled a face, shook her head and regretted asking the question.

Chapter Thirty-Four

Armitage celebrated his eighteenth birthday sitting alone in the Dublin Packet public house, set on the square opposite the picture house in Chester city centre. He was staring at a barely touched pint of lager, a folded newspaper, the Liverpool Echo, on the table, a brown paper parcel at his side. He was looking for a new job, but there was nothing suitable in the paper.

Saint Edmond's fixed him up with a job selling shoes in a branch of a multiple in Frodsham Street. To say he detested it was an understatement. He was amazed at the number of people who arrived with stinking, sweaty feet and ragged socks. Armitage paid attention to his appearance, both what you could see, and what you couldn't, and was surprised so many people did not.

Many of the lads from Saint Edmond's had found jobs as waiters or barmen where the punters regularly tipped. Some of the young guys made more money on tips than they did on wages, and Armitage liked the sound of that. When did you last hear of anyone tipping a shoe salesman, he would mutter to Dennis.

Answer, no one, and never!

He was waiting for Dennis, who had left the halfway house, Bellingfield, where Armitage now lived. Bellingfield was the Ritz Hotel compared to Saint Edmond's. A maximum of two boys per room, unlimited showers, and usually they were hot, plus decent food and no lack of it. It was the closest thing Armitage had experienced to a proper home for longer than he cared to remember.

Dennis had done well at the soup factory. He was coming up twenty and had already been promoted twice. Seven trainees worked for him, at his beck and call, and at least three of them had arrived from Saint Edmond's, so he knew what they would be like.

He worked hard, saved a little money, and put down a deposit on a small third-floor flat in Hoole. The flat had been cobbled together in the eaves, but he didn't care about that. Too busy was he in revelling in having his own home. A place where on his days off he could get up whenever he chose, where he could bathe in hot water any time of the day or night, where he could eat what he wanted, and when he wanted, drink whatever he liked, though that freedom had turned him away from binge drinking. A safe place where he could watch television when he chose, and the channel he preferred, every time, and there was never anyone to tell him different. Dennis was like a pig in muck. He had never been happier.

His happiness was complete when in a greasy spoon café he met the mousy Jillian. She followed him everywhere and linked his arm at every opportunity, as if frightened someone might steal him from her. Dennis came into the Packet with Jillian, bought two halves of lager, and joined Army at the table.

'How are you doing?' asked Dennis.

'Fine. You?'

'Yeah, great,' he said, 'never been better,' smiling at Jillian, who blushed.

Armitage glanced across at her. They were the perfect match. Dennis looked more like a rodent with each passing month, his long pointed nose and narrow face, truly rat-like, while Jillian boasted mousy hair, and a mouse like appearance bordering on the cute animals you could see in any American cartoon in the local picture house.

Sitting together on that bench seat, she linked Dennis's arm, pulled herself closer, and squeaked, 'Are we going to the pics, or what?'

'Yeah, when I've finished my drink. Bought you this,' Dennis said, sliding a wrapped present across the table.

'Ta,' said an embarrassed Armitage.

It would be the only birthday present he would receive.

'It's not much,' said Dennis, 'Jillian chose it.'

Jillian smiled awkwardly.

'Ta,' said Army again, 'I'll open it later.'

Jillian didn't like Armitage. Perhaps she saw him as a threat to her future happiness, but she put up with him because she didn't have any choice. Dennis had been on at her to find a girlfriend for Army for weeks, and she had fixed him up with three dates. Two of the girls didn't repeat the performance, while the third lasted a month before binning Army.

197

'They don't like his attitude,' explained Jillian, as she and Dennis were alone in bed at the top of the oddly named Charwell Mansions. 'He's too sarcastic.'

'That's only his way,' Dennis explained.

'That's as may be, but girls don't like being compared to animals. He told Shania she looked like a wild boar, and Lesley said he began calling her my favourite giraffe.'

Dennis laughed. He could see the logic in Army's thinking. Lesley was giraffe-like.

'And when he said to Sharon, she reminded him of a meerkat, and did that silly nat-nat-nat impression, I could have died. She was furious. No wonder she didn't want to see him again.'

'He'll grow out of it,' said Dennis, trying to excuse his friend's awkwardness with women.

'That's as may be, but my friends won't wait until he does.'

Dennis and Jillian finished their drinks and stood up to go. Dennis, at the last moment, turned and asked Army if he'd like to go with them to the pics. Armitage saw the horrified look that Jillian flashed Dennis.

'No,' he said, 'you go on, I've got things to do.'

Dennis grinned and bobbed his head, and the pair of them left. After they had gone Army picked up the paper and folded it and stuffed it in his back trouser pocket, collected his present; and the brown bagged parcel, glanced at the beer, realised that he didn't like lager, and left it on the table.

He would walk around the complete city walls. It was something he did to relax. He enjoyed the history of it, and it had become a new interest for him, and as he walked around that vast clockwise circle, it enabled him to think things through, to work things out.

He was aware he was at a crossroads in his life.

The actions he took and the decisions he made would affect the rest of his days, and if those thoughts were unusual in an eighteen-year-old on the brink of adulthood, perhaps it was understandable, given the turbulent years he had endured.

Losing his mother, losing his home, losing his father, all before the age of eleven, losing the happy days at the flower shop, the scholarship to King's, the dance classes, losing his voice and the mini stardom and adulation that it brought through his angelic singing, and living in the rough house that Saint Edmond's was back then, open to bullying, harassment and predation, both physical and sexual, by pupils and staff alike. Perhaps it wasn't surprising Armitage was not like other eighteen-year-olds.

Little wonder he could be sarcastic.

He had learned tough lessons.

He had learned that the only person who would ever do anything for him was himself. When he returned to Bellingfield, he ripped the paper from his present. It was a pack of three string vests. He hated string vests. Jillian had chosen them. Yep, that would be right.

Armitage still attended Saint Jude's church, though he never went near the choir stalls. All the McGowan boys were away at college, and Machara had gained entry to Saint Andrews University, studying medicine, which thrilled her parents because the reverend had studied at that fine university.

Blair McGowan noticed the hangdog look that sat on Armitage's face, and the general sense of gloom that cloaked him. One Sunday, standing on the steps after the service, shaking hands and smiling at parishioners as they left, Blair said, 'Is everything all right, Armitage?'

Army nodded unconvincingly, and the reverend asked him to stay behind for a chat. Armitage had nothing better to do and agreed.

When everyone had gone, he followed Blair through the church to his private rooms at the back. Seated in that same musty office where Chris de Wyk had first touched him brought back dreadful memories, that he thought of getting up and leaving, when the reverend spoke.

'I can't help noticing that something is troubling you.'

Army took some time to reply.

'I don't seem to be making any headway in life. I can't seem to get a steady girlfriend, I have a hateful job I despise, while everyone else seems to be getting on with their lives, I am stuck in a stinking rut.'

'It will come, Armitage. Don't be in such a rush, don't force it, relax and try to enjoy life.'

'That is easier said than done.'

Blair said something that surprised Army.

'Have you ever felt the calling?'

'The calling?'

'Yes, to God, of course. You believe in God, don't you?'

'Well, yes, I suppose so.'

'The thing is, Armitage; I have always thought you would make a fine vicar.'

Armitage smiled. It made a change for anyone to think he would make a fine anything.

'Don't you have to have qualifications, and stuff?'

'Yes, you do, but you have plenty of time. You're a clever lad; if you worked hard, I am sure you could get there. Why don't you think about it, and if you are interested, I have dozens of books you could borrow from my old seminary. I could give you some lessons if you wanted?'

Armitage bobbed his head and promised he would think it over.

When he told Dennis, he laughed like a drain.

'It could be worse,' Dennis said, still guffawing, 'at least you're C of E; imagine if you were a catholic, you wouldn't even be allowed nookie!'

'I think if you wanted nookie you'd get it, regardless of whether you were a priest or not.'

'True. You're probably right.'

Army didn't know what nookie was, or more accurately, he knew what it was, but not how and where to get it.

The following Sunday, Armitage told Blair McGowan that he was interested in taking things further. Blair smiled a satisfied smile, produced some books that he had brought with him in case of that eventuality, handed them to Armitage, who took them home and started out on the long road to becoming a Church of England vicar.

While he studied, it took him four years to find a new job, an employer who would take him seriously, by offering a post that he deemed acceptable. He raised his standards and rejected supermarket shelf stacking, bar work, waiting on table, telephone selling for commission only, loan sharking around the council estates on behalf of minor criminals, and not so minor drug dealers, (good pay, short life expectancy). He rejected retailing of any kind; his days of pandering to the ungrateful and smelly public were behind him.

Rejected agricultural labouring too, picking swedes in the rain, for God's sake, backbreaking work where the pay was lousy, and none of his colleagues would speak English. He didn't try it. He didn't try any of them, he wanted something better, and was determined to find it.

The day the letter came from the Inland Revenue offering him a clerking job in their brand new offices at the bottom of Northgate Street was a day he would never forget. It gave him huge satisfaction when he handed in his notice at the stinking feet farm, as he referred to Mawdsley's Shoes.

What had broken him was not the sweaty feet, nor the holey socks, not the lack of tips, nor the poor money, or the complete lack of a career structure, no, the thing that had annoyed him the most was the arrogant and cold way so many of the Great British public treated shop assistants.

Boy, can we try the size nines? Boy?

These are awful, get something else!

I said tens, for God's sake! Are you stupid?

Haven't you anything better than this?

Pay attention when I'm speaking to you!

Wilsons up the road are much cheaper than you.

Go to bloody Wilsons then!

It wasn't as if the customers were anything special. If they had been, they wouldn't have been seen dead in Mawdsley's. They were jumped up middle class pricks, most of them, who imagined that was the way to speak to servants like him.

When he left the store for the last time he vowed he would never look down on shop assistants, never treat them like dog dirt, and the next time he bought a pair of shoes, he would tip the assistant.

He did too. The young hard faced woman into whose hand he slipped the fiver; looked at him in disgust, imagining and wondering what he was offering her money for.

'Bugger off!' she yelled, thrusting the fiver back in his direction, a scruffy old note that fell to the maroon carpeted floor.

201

Armitage didn't wait to retrieve it, but turned and left after noticing the heavy brigade coming to the girl's assistance. Though it didn't put him off being polite to shop staff.

In the beginning he enjoyed working for the taxman. After a while he was doing what everyone else did, what they were told not to do. When no one was looking he would log on to the central computer and inspect the tax returns of all the people he knew, and illuminating they were.

How much money they earned; how much tax they paid, how much money they didn't declare, though you had to know them personally and be able to read between the lines to calculate that. Mrs Greenaway in the flower shop, under declared by forty percent, he estimated. Armitage felt guilty at prying into Dennis's financial affairs, but it had to be done, and it was only in fun. It turned out he didn't earn anywhere near as much as he said. Jillian the mouse; she was doing well, typing away in a big insurance company, running round and round and round the corporate wheel. She was earning more than Dennis, though he would swear blind that was not the case. No wonder they were planning to buy a house and get married, with all that money plopping into the communal pot.

As for Reverend Blair McGowan, Army had no idea vicars were paid so well, or were so wealthy. Look at the share dividends for God's sake; are you listening and watching, dear God? And income from property too, let out in Scotland. The parishioners would be surprised to learn about that. Even Hancock at Saint Edmond's, and his manager at Mawdsley's, just about everyone he had ever known who was still alive and employed, all fascinating stuff, and contrary to his current terms and conditions of employment.

The Inland Revenue management were becoming extra keen on team bonding. It built a more efficient office and added to the happiness and contentment of staff, so the mantra said. There had been an alarming increase in people becoming bored and jumping ship, though Armitage did not mind that, because he landed two promotions through it, and two pay increases too, enabling him to take over Dennis's flat, when the happy couple bought a dinky house down at Saltney, at not too many feet above sea level.

It took him a long time to get used to living alone.

No matter what hour he arrived back at Bellingfield there would always be someone there to share a pot of tea and a chat. Returning to his deathly quiet flat stuck high in the gods was a depressing experience.

Dennis and his mousy spouse took what little furniture they possessed to dinky town, and after paying rent and deposit and insurance on the flat, there was precious little left for Armitage to spend on luxuries... like furniture.

He visited the Salvation Army centre for wayward boys and girls, who supplied him with a clean single bed, he was single, so single was all he qualified for, one small stained settee, one tiny yellow plastic topped dining table with two rickety chairs, and a filthy set of pans he tossed in the dustbin.

It was a start.

It was home.

It was his home.

But it was damned depressing.

The latest wheeze of team bonding was bound to terrify all but the boldest of staff. Parachute jumping, or skydiving, as they preferred to call it.

When it was first announced many of the team mouthed 'Oh yeah? Not me, pal,' but over the days that followed it became a test of one's bravery or lily-liveredness, indeed one's cowardice.

Who was up for it, and who was not?

Armitage was not the boldest young man there, but neither was he the weakest. But when Alan Steadman, the guy who'd always been considered the office wet, said he was looking forward to it and would jump, and declared that anyone who didn't was a "fucking weed", it became harder to refuse.

The date was set, engraved into the diary, logged up on the brand new office notice board as: Who's a Yellow Bastard Day?

It was a Saturday morning.

203

The scruffy hired coach set off from outside the tax office at nine o'clock sharp. Anyone not there would be nominated an "utter weed" by none other than Alan Steadman.

Somehow, Armitage dragged himself from his single bed, threw on a jumper and jeans, staggered down the stairs, and set off for the office, determined to hide his shaking legs.

The coach was packed with nervous sweaty-palmed tax collectors, as it headed west toward Hawarden airport, and the Glendower Aero Club. The rattled tax team would be taken up in groups of six and hurled from the Skyvan plane, yelling some ancient Indian war cry as they plummeted to earth.

If there was a God, pondered Armitage, and he wasn't sure about that, this was as near as he was ever going to get to meet him.

The nerves kicked in as they ambled through the old tumbledown buildings that sufficed as reception centre and warming down rooms, trying to appear nonchalant.

The previous party of adrenaline fuelled lunatics were making their way back from the landing grounds, rolled up parachutes in hand, talking aloud, recapping their terrifying experiences, more than one saying, 'I was certain the chute would not open!'

Doesn't everyone think that?

The tax party was making ready to go, forced to listen to several barbed comments from the staff dishing out the gear: This party are tax inspectors; make sure they get the dodgy chutes, followed by strange laughs and weird looks. It was all in jest, wasn't it?

The previous party were coming back, many of them saying they couldn't wait to do it again; when everyone knew that once they were clear of the airfield, wild elephants would not drag them back.

Then it was Army's turn.

They could see the aeroplane. The Short Brothers' Skyvan, twin-engine turboprop, propellers stationary and waiting for the next gang of terrified pioneers.

The instructor turned up; assuring them there was nothing to it.

Piece of cake! Easy peasy! Come on! Let's do this! Let's go!

Armitage was no longer listening.

In an instant, he was miles away.

A million trillion miles above the earth, for the lights had switched on.

Chapter Thirty-Five

Ladies' Day dawned bright and clear; the perfect early May day. Samantha was up early, took a shower, wanted to be in plenty of time. She hated rushing; nothing good was ever created in a rush. Even God took seven days. She glanced at the expensive navy blue suit she'd bought on the last expedition to the expensive Manchester bazaars. No party frock for her, nothing flash and garish, but a businesswoman's suit, for Samantha was on business.

Breakfast. Crushed fresh orange juice, bran flakes, a slice of toasted low carbo bread, dry and crunchy, no butter, no margarine. She would eat nothing more than an apple before her seven o'clock dinner.

Brush those perfect teeth, brush, brush, brush, no one would flash better teeth on the Roodee today, 'cept perhaps the favourite for the big race. Desi had good teeth too, but much larger than Sam's. Some people might have thought they were too large, ugly even, but Sam didn't, and Desi was comfortable in her own skin. Didn't care a jot what anyone said or thought about her, and she was never short of admirers, lovers, that in her time Desi took full advantage of, until that hateful Toby Malone appeared and spoiled everything.

Sam took ages on the makeup. Foundation, a hint of blusher, perfect eyebrows, perfect lashes, understated lipstick. So many women looked tramps by going over the top, not Sam. Brilliant eyes. So blue. Unmissable. Desi said they were the brightest, bluest eyes she had ever seen. Sam had slept well. No need for chemical eye droplets to induce sparkle, not a hint of a bag. The eyes were alive with excitement as adrenaline rushed through her slender body.

Dressing. Stockings and suspenders. Very sexy. New bra and pants, not that anyone would ever see them, no one had, no one ever did, not since Desi went away. Perfect figure hugging suit, it was as if it had been tailored especially, fit her like a glove, and bound to attract wandering eyes. Many people went to the races to admire the punters. That was half the fun. To smile and chat and become better acquainted, and maybe, just maybe, collect a telephone number or two.

Sam could cope with that, being pursued, courted, quite enjoyed it if truth be told, and she'd dispense a telephone number if necessary. Not that it would be a real one, not one that could ever ring.

Ridiculously expensive black shoes, low heels, necessary because high heels could be such a drag, plus matching bag, and don't look at the price tag, also culled from Manchester. What would mother and father have made of that?

Black hair, bob cut, thick and shiny, healthy appearance, like the best mare favourite for the big race, black beauty, shiny coat, top condition. No wonder she had a big following.

All the cash would be laid down that day.

Pose before the long mirror. Pout, for there would be no more pouting later. Turn to the left, perfect, turn to the right, yes, all good. Does my bum look big in this? Of course not, don't be absurd; Samantha had the perfect, pert bum. Desi always said that after the eyes it was the first thing she noticed, though she must have had x-ray vision to see because Sam was facing Desi at the time.

Adjustment of the bra, adjustment of the breasts? Why in heaven's name? Young, upturned, unmoving, pert, not too big, not too small. What more could any woman ask?

Dandruff on the collar? Don't be ridiculous.

Red and gold member's pass, shaped like a shield, classy braided tie-ons, fitted neatly on the suit collar. They had kept their membership since they'd first gone to the Roodee. They didn't even have to apply for tickets, never missed a meeting, came automatically, bank account debited, tickets and tags in the mail, through the post box, on the mat, reliable as Christmas, just a pity one of them, Desi's, would remain unused.

Ah well, just have to make it a year to remember.

That was the aim.

A finger on the doorbell.

That would be the taxi, bang on time.

Good man.

Where to?

The races, of course.

206

The Incident Room resembled someone's front room prior to the wedding of the year. No one had turned in late; everyone had gone to great effort. Walter was amazed at how an attractive bunch they were. Such a change to the scruffy mob who normally lounged through the building.

Mrs West was flapping about like a nervous bride's mother, calling out: 'Everyone got their buttonholes?' and, 'is there anyone who still hasn't selected a hat?' Meaning the women, Walter imagined, for he had no desire to wear a spring bonnet.

He was becoming annoyed at the all-pervading party atmosphere. They shouldn't be thinking about hats and bonnets and bouquets. They should think of finding and arresting a serial killer, a cheeky wretch who'd had the nerve to threaten him, Inspector Walter Surprise Darriteau, the family joke was that he came as a complete surprise. Walter clacked his lips and glanced at the ceiling. Karen watched him do it and smiled to herself. She wondered what he was thinking about.

What an unusual man he was.

Walter's patience ran out.

He stood up and clapped his huge hands.

'Quiet! Settle down. It's time to focus, get your minds in gear. Remember why we are here today!'

The hustle bustle noise and frantic fiddling with dress abated.

They turned and stared at the man.

That's better, he thought, though said nothing. Took a beat.

'Today is the day,' he said, pointing at the ceiling, doing his best Churchillian impression, so he imagined, when in reality he came over more as a revivalist Christian minister. It wouldn't have been out-of-place if someone had chirped in with a big, 'Yeee-esss, A-men!'

At least he had their attention.

'Today is the day we are going to catch the bastard!'

This time there was a reaction.

Gibbons yelled, 'Yes sir! We bloody are!'

For once Walter enjoyed the interruption, nodded at the guy appreciatively, and said, 'Karen! Over to you. Update on description of the killer.'

That caught her off guard. She hadn't expected it.

Thanks, Guv. Thanks a lot.

'Yes, well,' she began, 'picking up the latest papers from her desk, re-gathering her thoughts. 'The killer is, we believe, around five feet five inches tall.'

'Could be taller in heels,' threw in Cresta, her of the tight fitting enticing purple frock, voluptuous breasts, or so they appeared, white spray of carnations strategically positioned, interesting backside, Gibbons wasn't the only one who looked at Cresta in a different light after seeing that dress.

Karen nodded and continued. 'Believed to be blonde, believed to have bright green eyes, slender, attractive, well dressed, but then most people will be today, I mean, look at you lot, you look as if you've stepped out of Brown's shop window.'

A few nervous giggles.

Walter gave her a gentle look that reminded her not to stray from the point.

'Drives a smart Japanese hatchback, though might not arrive by car today.'

Seeing as parking was at a premium anywhere near Chester city centre, and especially on race days, it was likely the car would be left at home, wherever that was.

Walter wasn't the only one to think the description was useless. Blonde hair, could be changed. Height, same applied, stick on bigger heels and away you go. Green eyes, maybe? Japanese hatchback, yeah, if indeed it came, it would be in good company with hundreds of identical others, slender, attractive, well-dressed people.

What on Chester Ladies' Day?

Are you kidding?

Have you any idea how many slender, attractive, well-dressed men and women would flaunt themselves on the Roodee today? No one did, because the answer would be thousands. No, the description was worthless.

What they had to look for was someone who was not at the races to watch the horses, not to bet, not to party, not to get drunk, not to

208

socialise, not to meet friends, not to cop off, and was probably alone. Someone not involved in press or TV, not catering, nor bookmaking, not pick-pocketing. No, this person was coming to the race meeting with one aim in mind, to murder him, and though no doubt the killer would carry the necessary props, binos, racecard, Racing Post, Member's badge, they would merely be that, props, and they shouldn't be distracted by them. This fiend was coming to divvy up death.

The only question was, how were they intending to do it?

Gunshot? In a public place, before thousands of other people? Seemed unlikely. It was feasible to gun someone down at close range, but how would they escape? And escaping was high on the killer's agenda, Walter was certain of that. He ruled out guns, he couldn't see it, but still encouraged his officers to search bags when the opportunity arose. The women officers on the entrance gates, making snap inspections of handbags under the guise of a random drugs search, the slim guys having their bino cases opened.

So if not guns, what then?

Poison? A la KGB. Poisoned tipped umbrella. Seemed far-fetched, but the killer had consistently showed imagination. Perhaps the idea wasn't so stupid, and you didn't need to carry an umbrella. A little scratch would do, so long as you had access to toxic poison. Walter wouldn't rule that out. He didn't rule anything out.

It only needed a little accident with a glass, a minor scratch to the cheek or neck or arm. It was easily done. He would have to watch out for that. Not bump into people, and not have people bumping into him, especially young and slender ones, though on a busy race day that was easier said than done.

Walter shared his thoughts with his captive audience, and plenty of other ideas too.

Karen said, 'Don't forget, this person, this he-she thing, is equally likely to be dressed as a man or as a woman.'

That was all they needed.

They were including every slim youngish person in attendance that day. What percentage was that? God knows. Pretty high, for sure. Just as well to know, though, to remember the young green-eyed guy standing at the bar next to you could be your potential nemesis.

So if guns were unlikely, and poison a possibility, what other crazed methods might the killer employ? What fiendish thinking was coursing through the maniac's mind?

Walter did what he always did. He put himself in the killer's shoes. If he were going to the races to kill someone, how would he do it?

An answer flashed into his mind.

He would wait. He would be patient. He would do it at the end of the day, when everyone's guard was down, when everyone imagined the killer had bottled it and fled, or not shown at all. Or maybe this had been a diversionary tactic as Karen had suggested. Maybe the he-she thing was busy murdering elsewhere, some unfortunate soul in the suburbs while the police were otherwise engaged and sidetracked. That couldn't be helped, but the end of day theory held water.

Walter envisaged that, as they made their way toward the exits at the end of an unsuccessful day, ambling out, muttering their disappointment, dispersing home, hands in pockets, eyes down, imagining the day had been wasted, but maybe not. Perhaps that was the exact moment the he-she thing was waiting for, and if so, how would the he-she thing strike?

Run him down as he came out through the gates?

Why not? He, or she, had done that before, though it didn't follow the established pattern.

It had always been something different.

It would be different this time too.

But how, and where, and when, and why?

There was only one way to find out.

Display the target and see who fired.

The police operation split into ten distinct groups, left the building at three-minute intervals, ambled down to the course, not speaking, not seeing their own kind, not thinking of racing, not hearing the clip clops on the cobblestones as the thoroughbreds began unloading, not admiring the pretty girls or handsome guys, though that was more difficult for some than others, some of them armed, some of them not.

All nervous, and some afraid.

Chapter Thirty-Six

A tall, dark gentleman bought her a glass of champagne. They were in one of the best bars at the back of the main grandstand. He knew Samantha, or at least remembered her from last year. Gerrard was his name, ran his own engineering business on the Wrexham Road Business Park, so he said, not that Sam was in the least bit interested in that.

She was glad to be in his company. A lone person at the races can look out of place. Who goes racing alone? Not many, especially on Ladies' Day. They made a handsome couple, jet black hair on the pair of them, the man instantly smitten, the classy lady looking demure and cooing, 'No-ooo, Gerrard, not today,' or similar nonsense.

He asked her for her telephone number.

She glanced at his wedding ring.

He watched the track of her eyes.

'Oh that,' he said, 'that's long finished, been over for years.'

Liar liar, pants on fire, Samantha wanted to scream, but didn't, stopped herself in time. Weren't all men so damned predictable, all spaffed the same nonsense, as she smiled and flicked her eyelashes, and made some excuse and went to freshen up.

It wasn't the first pass she had received that day, nor would it be the last. It was Ladies' Day after all; it was to be expected.

She had already clocked Walter.

It hadn't been that difficult.

Chester was still primarily a white city, and a big black man with a head of misbehaving grey hair was hard to miss. She had seen him twice. First, he had been standing in front of the rows of bookmakers before the first race, before it was too packed to move. He was talking to three others, two goonish blokes, and the same slim blonde, his rock, from the broadcasts. They had been talking, mumbling under their breath, glancing at their racecards and newspapers, binoculars slung around the goons' necks, pretending to be discussing the favourite's chances, when all along they were saying, 'Check out that character by the rails, could be him, or her,' or, 'Look at these two coming now, they fit the description.'

Samantha almost felt sorry for them.

They did not have a clue, literally.

And what was that bulge in Walter's trousers? Ah, Wally, do I excite you that much? Sam inwardly giggled, the thought of meeting his dream date, but ah, alas no, it wasn't Sam he was excited about; he wasn't excited at all, not in that way. It was a gun, a pistol. Naughty Walter, naughty boy, fancy coming tooled up, if you pardon the expression. What do you think I am going to do, blow you away in broad daylight before ten thousand people? God, give me strength, grant me a smidgeon of credit.

Did you think I was as unimaginative as that?

Samantha had identified twenty-two plods.

It wasn't difficult, and the racing hadn't even started. It was so easy. They were not enjoying themselves. They weren't checking out the talent, not as they should have been. Yes, they were inspecting people, but in a different way. They weren't laughing and joking, and meeting and greeting old friends in that hearty way you see at the races, at Wimbledon, and Henley and Cowes too, though Sam had never been there, though she was young and ambitious, and there was plenty of time.

They looked too earnest, as if they had the troubles of the world on their shoulders. As if one of their number might be in for a nasty surprise. Samantha giggled, aloud this time, enough to attract the attention of a passing Jockey Club steward, dressed in tweeds, hurrying away to his position, but not in too much of a hurry that he couldn't pause and doff his trilby before the stunning woman and say, 'So nice to see you here again this year,' whether he had met her before or not, and departing with, 'I'll be in the Grosvenor Bar later for a snifter if you fancy it?'

Sam smiled and bobbed her head and said she might be there, and the steward grinned and turned and hopped away, an additional spring in his aging step.

'Where's Karen?' grunted Walter.

'Gone to the ladies again,' said Jenny, 'had a bad curry last night, by all accounts, touch of the runs.'

212

That was more information than Walter needed. He rolled his eyes and swept them over the gathering throng. Was the murderer among them? Of course he was, and Walter still believed it was a man, despite Cresta's protestations otherwise. He found it difficult to believe there was a woman in Chester who was evil enough to murder six people, and attempt to murder him in broad daylight at the big May meeting. It was a man. It had to be a man. Of course it was a bloody man! He scanned the crowd again. But which man? Which one of these crazy bastards had come with murder in mind?

Karen came back. She looked awfully pale.

'You all right?'

She nodded. 'Touch of the squits, bloody curry.'

Again, too much information.

Walter slipped his hand in his pocket. Stroked his pistol.

Comforting, it was. Cold and menacing.

Glock 22, new issue, seven point three inches long, five point four inches tall, twenty-three ounces in weight, when empty. Walter's was fully packed, as was Karen's, forced into her black, shiny bag. The Glock 22, made by Glock GMBH in Austria. The American law enforcement officer's favourite handgun, and it wasn't hard to see why. Bet that annoyed the hell out of Smith and Wesson. Five hundred and fifty dollars' worth of protection, brand new, plus carriage and taxes, you must never forget the carriage and taxes.

At least Walter hadn't paid for the damned thing.

First race down. Favourite bolted up. Punters happy. Lots of smiling faces and fattening wallets. Early days.

Sam ambled to the Grosvenor Bar.

There was no hurry.

Gerrard was there, talking to three middle-aged fattening women. They looked like farmer's wives with ambitions to join the Cheshire set. He spied Samantha over one of their shoulders, and made his excuses and left them to their fizzy drinks, and nonchalantly ambled across, becoming bolder; the champagne working its magic.

'There you are,' he said, as if they had known each other for years. 'How about dinner tonight? Everything on me.'

'You are a persistent man, aren't you?' she said, scrawling a non-existent telephone number on his racecard, or maybe it really did exist, who knows? But certainly not hers. Random numbers that popped from her pretty head. Someone could be in for a cranky surprise call.

'You won't regret it,' he said.

'I hope not,' she smiled, 'I'll have to go, my friends will wonder where I am,' and she left him there to his imaginative thoughts, as she swayed away.

Second race over. Favourite number two wins by a nose, roared home by a jumping crowd. Bad day for the bookies. Good day for the gamblers and bars. Corks popped. Still early doors. A dangerous time. More ammunition to take on the bookies. Many punters bet too big when they have cash in hand. Lose big too.

That was when she saw Walter again, at the back of the main stand where the corridors went through to the bars and restaurants and toilets and corporate and private function rooms, where the hospitality was high, and the big money spent.

She was happy to see him there.

Closer to where she wanted him.

Walter was thinking his theory of a late strike when guards were down was most likely. Unobtrusive runners came to him with reports all afternoon. He reminded them of his earlier thinking. Don't let your guard down, stay alert, stay focussed, right till the end of the day. It wasn't over till it's over.

Race three.

One of the big ones.

The popular mare. Could she win again?

Who cares? Forget about the damned horses!

While everyone was heading for the expensive boxes and trackside bookies, and the rails, and saddling enclosure, anywhere to get a better look at the popular mare, Samantha was heading in the opposite direction.

Based on the theory that everyone needed the lavatory sometime, she was waiting, standing in the doorway to one of the hospitality suites, as if she had popped out to take a personal call, talking on a mobile phone to a non-existent lover. No one glanced at her twice.

A fat woman waddled by and went into the toilets.

A slim woman followed her in. *The* slim woman.

The broadcasting blonde. Walter's rock.

Time to move.

214

Time to go to work.

Samantha closed her phone, slipped it in her pocket and followed them inside.

The fat woman was washing her hands.

The blonde woman was locked in a cubicle. The big woman glanced at the smart woman with the bright blue eyes. Rolled her eyebrows in half recognition and said, 'Mustn't miss the big race.'

'You've got time; one of them's split a plate.'

'Really? Super, I fancy the favourite,' and she bustled away, time enough to get a big bet on the shiny black mare.

Samantha followed her toward the exit, through the narrow corridor toward the door. White-tiled walls from floor to ceiling. In the background the sound of dripping water, the chemical stench of disinfectant block. The door flapped closed. The big woman had gone. Sam opened her bag, took out a light chain, drew it across the entrance, fixed it to the walls with sticky tack, blocking admission, pulled out the homemade sign, bright red letters, Toilets Closed For Cleaning, not in wacky type, amazing what you could knock up on the computer, hung it on the chain, it wouldn't matter to desperate users, there were plenty of other facilities along the way.

Went back to the main room.

One cubicle door still closed.

Noises coming from within.

Plenty going on.

Samantha crept into the cubicle next door.

She'd left her bag open, no need to unclick.

Closed the pan lid. Stood gently on top.

Took the thin rope from the bag.

Set the bag on the window ledge.

Reached up to the top of the dividing wall.

Pulled herself up.

Outside, the crowd was going crazy, the racket flooding in through the open windows. The mare was leading, a hundred and fifty yards to go, the crammed stands had never been so raucous. Karen didn't hear Sam, couldn't hear a thing above the crowd.

Samantha peered over the top.

215

Blondie was down there, still busy; looking straight ahead, upset tum by the smell of things. Still hadn't heard a thing. Couldn't hear a thing.

Neatly tied, pre-prepared rope, brand new, white, almost silky, thin but strong, there would be only one chance. She had been practising at home on a large imported teddy bear. Had it off pat.

Lowered the noose.

'Go on Pandora! Go on!' yelled the crowd.

The colt was catching the mare.

The crowd was in ferment.

Quickly down, over the hair, around the porcelain neck, perfect, and PULL!

The knot tightened.

Karen's eyes almost popped from her skull.

What the bugger! She wanted to scream, but couldn't say a word.

Reached for her bag and the salvation of the Glock 22.

The bag was on the floor.

Karen was rising fast.

She grasped at thin air.

Samantha yanked the rope hard and fastened it to the strut of the open metal-framed window.

Karen's hands clutched at the rope, trying to slip her fingers inside the knot. Her weight dangling on the rope tightened the noose.

She couldn't breathe.

She couldn't shout.

She couldn't reach the gun.

She couldn't ease the knot.

She was turning purple.

She was dying.

Samantha smiled.

Seven up.

100 Ways to Kill People.

Hang them in the lavatory at the local racetrack.

That should give them something to think about.

That might make that arrogant bastard Darriteau think again. Serve him right for his negligence. Serve him bloody well right. He could pay this time. See how he liked it, to lose someone he cared for. And all the time he thought it was his turn today. Arrogant prick! Typical man. Couldn't see beyond his own importance. Couldn't see the end of his gigantic nose. Arrogance, a fatal flaw.

The colt pipped the mare on the line, spoiling Ladies' Day for many. The crowd grew quiet. Long faces. Wallets were being checked. How much are we down?

Samantha collected her bag and hopped down from the pan.

Choking sounds, soft dying gurgles, came from the cubicle next door, growing ever fainter. She made her way to the exit. Eased her way over the sign.

Two women were coming in after the race

'Closed for maintenance,' Sam said, smiling and pointing at the notice. 'There's another one just along there,' and she took them outside and showed them the way.

'Thanks a lot.'

'You're welcome.'

Samantha turned and hurried away toward the exits.

Job done.

Number seven.

Seven times over.

Mission accomplished.

There would be no more.

Now she was satisfied.

She would leave Walter alone to mull over forever his own inadequacies. To miss the one he loved. See how he liked it. See how he coped. He could stew in his own filthy juice. He'd probably get fired, which was what he deserved. He could spend the rest of his days mulling over how he let down his rock. How he had failed to detect the Chester Mollester. To reflect on what a useless piece of shit he was.

Karen blacked out.

No feeling, no sense.

Gently swinging on the end of the rope, her hands limp by her sides, knickers around her ankles, filthy muck oozing down the inside of her thighs, designer handbag and loaded Glock 22 still asleep and unemployed on the floor.

Ladies' Day at Chester races, in the Ladies.

217

The mare's in trouble.
Favourite downed.
Seven up.
Balmy breeze floating through the open window.
Swaying body. End of a rope.
Job done.
All over.

Chapter Thirty-Seven

The first time Desi saw Eden Leys, she went there by taxi. She made a mental note of the route for she was determined to pass the imminent driving test. She had been collected from the small railway station at Whitchurch, and they headed south on the A41, until the road forked at the big truck stop, left to Wolverhampton, right to Shrewsbury. She held on tight as the taxi swerved around the roundabout to the right, before turning left onto the Shrewsbury road.

'Not far now, miss,' said the cabby, in his gentle local accent. 'Coming up on the left.'

Desiree peered that way, at the gigantic former aircraft hangers that were used as grain stores, though the European grain mountain had long since vanished, flogged off to pay for the club.

Then a sharp left turn down a narrow straight road, a single square red sign on the left, TRENCHERMAN RESEARCH PLC - No Unauthorised Persons. The road continued onward, bisecting two vast grey neglected hangars. Up ahead she could see a guard post, red and white barrier across the road, tall wire fence topped with rolled barbed wire, winding away to the left and right as far as she could see.

Set back ten yards inside the wire were conifer plantations, thick enough to stop anyone on the outside seeing the interior.

Beyond the entrance was a two-story redbrick building, wide and flat-topped, that also blocked any view of what lay beyond. The cabby stopped at the gates, nodded to one of the security guards as if they were familiar, and completed a three-point turn, making ready to leave.

'That's twelve pounds, miss,' he said.

Desiree tugged fifteen from her purse and slipped it into his hand.

'Thanks miss,' he smiled. 'Do you want a hand with your bag?'

She had brought one large wheeled case.

'I'm fine, thanks,' she said, and stepped out into the sunshine.

'Good luck,' he called over his shoulder, and drove away.

Desiree turned and looked at the two guards who were eyeing her up. They wore dark blue uniforms with yellowy-gold flashes on their shoulders, badges on their left chest. When she was closer, she could read the gold writing: Trencherman Research – Security, that ran all the way around the outside of the badge in a circle.

She walked toward the guard hut and smiled.

'Desiree Holloway signing in.'

The guards nodded and one muttered, 'Let's see what we've got,' and began tapping on his laptop.

It must have checked out.

'Passes?' he said, holding out his hand.

She showed ID, and that was checked and entered.

Must have been OK.

'That's fine, ma'am,' and he turned and called another bloke forward who was sitting and reading a trashy tabloid.

'Tom, another one for Mary Craigieson,' he called, and Tom set his paper down and came forward and said, 'Right-ho.'

'He'll take you there, ma'am.'

Desiree nodded and in the next moment she was following Tom through the gate to a dark blue four by four parked on the inside of the fence. He took her case and set it in the back, started the vehicle, and drove around the redbrick building, left, right, right again, and then left again, and headed into the heart of Eden Leys.

'Are you busy?' she asked, making small talk.

'Always busy, ma'am, always,' and that was that. He didn't speak again until he was saying goodbye, after dropping her at a modern grey and glass structure somewhere in the centre of the complex.

She glanced up at the entrance. Terminal 19, it said, in big silver letters, grabbed her bag and wheeled it inside.

Professor Mary Craigieson showed Desiree her accommodation, modern, comfortable, but small, showed her where she would work, within Terminal 19, explained something of the work she would do, an area where most newcomers began, advised her that her four-day induction and basic training programme would begin at eight thirty the next morning. Then introduced her to another young woman named Sarah Sleepman, who would show her the facilities and explain the daily routine. Desiree Holloway was in, an accepted member of the Eden Leys Research team.

She was excited at the prospect of starting work, contributing, of using her skills and expertise, of pushing her research programmes further than she had ever been permitted before.

All the training, all that hard work, all the imaginative and creative ideas flowing through her head, all engendered through her total love of science, was coming to fruition. She couldn't wait to begin.

Not for nothing was Eden Leys known within the scientific community as the Porton Down of the north. Desiree had been expecting a large site. What was it Mrs Bloemfontein had said? It is huge, you will want for nothing, supermarket, cinema, bowling facilities, swimming pool, I doubt you will feel the need to leave.

She hadn't been wrong. The complex was far bigger than Desiree had ever imagined, mind boggling, like a mid-sized town, beavering away on countless research projects in dozens of modern buildings, all set behind the ring of impenetrable conifers and juniper trees that were set inside the ring of firs.

The other four countries involved possessed their own terminals within the site, more than one for the United States. They always had to be bigger, but all results and breakthroughs were shared, fed into the giant central computer system housed within Terminal 10.

Desiree was surprised to bump into Professor Jim McClaine, and he was surprised to see her. He explained he had never realised how qualified she was, how brilliant she was, now that he knew her pioneering work was gaining universal praise. Jim said he wished he could turn the clock back, have that time together in Australia again, where he admitted he had kept things from her.

He'd underrated the young woman, and he wasn't the first to do that. He couldn't believe that someone so young, from such an ordinary background, could be so talented, and he apologised, almost embarrassingly so. Afterwards they became friends, sharing an occasional coffee, joining the same bowling teams, for teamwork and extra curricula activities were encouraged at Eden Leys.

Experimenting on live animals had always been part of Desiree's brief. She had known that all along, since the early days at Liverpool University. It didn't bother her at all. She understood the best way to advance science, to find cures, to engineer scientific breakthroughs, to make genuine progress, advances that only a few years before would have been unthinkable, was experimentation on live and living tissue.

Started on mice, worked up through rats, guinea pigs, cats, dogs, to chimpanzees, that was the accepted ladder of progression. Most of the animals were bred on site; the breeding programme carried out in the single story green roofed Terminal 8. It saved a great deal of hassle. What people didn't know about, they couldn't crow about.

Working with mustard gas had long been one of Desiree's aims. She had written a dissertation on the Effects of Mustard Gas on Living Tissue, and was becoming an authority on the subject.

Introducing mustard gas to a chimp's arm took courage.

Desiree steeled herself. Once it was done the first time, it became easier. She was desperate to get onto the PLACAD programme and would do anything to achieve it.

Working on fresh human body parts was interesting too. They would arrive daily by dispatch rider from hospitals within a hundred-mile radius of Eden Leys. Most times they were young and healthy parts, maybe from patients who had died through accident, or other diseases, that had not contaminated the portions that arrived vacuum packed and ready to go. There was little difference between working on a human liver to that of a pig, lamb, or chimp, and freshness was everything.

Desiree wallowed in her work. She made rapid progress, enjoyed three pay increases in her first two years, and attended further crammer colleges in California and Bavaria. She had made new friends, had passed her driving test first time, had treated herself to the latest updated version of the Supa Cayton Cerisa, silver with a dashing maroon flash; that she drove home. Those visits became fewer and less often. There was little to leave the site for. All her requirements were catered for, and she rarely left.

222

She joined, and enjoyed the frantic social life, though never took a lover, despite the many overtures that came her way, including during one drunken night in the Red Caves Social Club, from Professor McClaine himself.

She was no longer interested in the squelchy business, or so she told herself, and afterwards an idea spread round the quarters that she was a lesbian, a rumour that returned to her like a boomerang, and one she laughed off in a millisecond.

Desiree was content.

It was what she was born to do.

But she had a problem, and one she couldn't share with anyone.

There were voices in her head.

Chapter Thirty-Eight

Samantha left the grandstand and made her way toward the exit. No hurry. No rush. No alarms. No intention of attracting attention. She skipped down the stairs and headed out across the forecourt toward the gates. Behind her, the crowd were still murmuring, wondering how they had lost so much cash. An elderly gent was manning the exits. He saw the classy young woman coming toward him, a gentle smile on her pretty face.

'Not going already?' he said.

'Lost on the first three races,' she said, 'that's enough for me.'

'Ah well, never mind. There's always next year, pity about Pandora, wasn't it?'

'Sure was.'

He held the door open for her and she smiled again, stepped through, and headed up the cobblestoned hill toward the city.

The old guy took a last look outside, at the opportunistic group of five or six rough looking youths gathered there, hoping to bunk in without paying. They could forget that, and he stared at them and frowned and closed the gate and fastened it shut.

Walter was busy doing his rounds. The favourite mare had been turned over, pipped on the line, much to the annoyance of the crowd. Almost everyone backed Pandora. The collective smile had returned to the bookies' faces.

Walter wasn't smiling.

He made his way to the back of the main stand. Gibbons was there, hanging about, hands in pockets, looking bored.

'Where's Karen?' asked Walter.

'Bog,' muttered Gibbons, nodding up at the Ladies sign.

'How long has she been in there?'

'Five minutes, maybe ten. She's got a touch of...'

'Yes, I know. Diarrhoea. Anyone else go in?'

'Nah. Two women came out. A fat gal and a black-haired woman.'

'What was she wearing?'

'Navy blue suit, black bag, black shoes.'

'Slim, slight, and attractive? Right?'

'Yeah,' said Gibbons, standing straighter, taking his hands from his pockets, pondering on what Walter had said.

Walter glanced at the Ladies sign. Ladies' Day. Ladies.

It wasn't him the bastard was after; it was the lady.

'Come on!' he yelled as he headed for the entrance.

By the time he was at the door, the younger Gibbons was ahead of him. He pushed through the door as if it didn't exit, ripped down the homemade sign that brought their instant nightmares home, and dashed into the room.

All stalls wide open, bar one.

Gibbons shouldered it. It didn't budge.

Went into the next cubicle.

Jumped on the closed lid.

Saw the rope tied to the window strut.

Pulled himself up.

Looked down.

'Oh, hell!'

'What is it?' yelled Walter.

'She's been hung, Guv.'

'Oh my God! Get her down! Now!'

Gibbons didn't need telling. He was busy working on the rope. Karen's weight had contributed to the cord being tied real tight. Gibbons broke his nails, wrestling it undone. He grabbed Karen's body as it fell toward the floor.

'Open the door!' yelled Walter.

One hand supporting her, one hand slid back the catch.

'Oh God!' shouted Walter when he saw her. 'Set her on the floor.'

Two women came in for a pee.

'Police!' screamed Gibbons. 'Out!'

They glanced down at the purple-faced unconscious young woman; and the terror etched on the two guys' faces and hurried away.

'I don't think she's breathing, Guv,' said Gibbons, 'I think she's gone.'

'There's a pulse,' said Walter, loosening her blouse, 'faint, but there. Ring for an ambulance. Quick!'

225

Walter crouched down and took a deep breath. Circled his lips around hers. Blew in. Came off her. Another big breath, down on her mouth again, and blow.

'There's an ambulance on the course,' said Gibbons. 'They say they'll be here in two minutes.'

Same thing again, breathe in; breathe out, into another human being.

'Come on, Karen! Come on!' yelled Gibbons.

The sound of the ambulance's beep-borp beep-borp filtered in through the open window.

Walter blew in again. Came off her.

Karen spluttered.

The men shared a look.

Two paramedics rushed in. Saw her. Knelt down. Asked what had happened.

'Been hung!' snapped Gibbons.

The medics took over. She was just about breathing. Her eyes revolving in their sockets, and foam on her blue lips.

'Stay with her,' bellowed Walter, 'and don't forget the bag... and the gun.'

'Where are you going?'

'After the bitch!'

'Be careful!'

Walter bumbled down the twenty-five steps. Headed toward the exit. The same old guy was there, surprised to see a big puffing black man coming his way.

Walter flashed ID.

'Have you seen a slim young woman come this way, navy blue suit, black hair?'

'Certainly have,' he smiled. 'A few minutes ago. You couldn't miss her. Why, do you know her?'

'You could say that. Which way did she go?'

'Straight up the hill toward the town.'

'Thanks,' said Walter, as the old guy opened and closed the gate behind him.

Walter puffed his way up the hill, pondering on where the killer might go next. If she'd parked her car close by she would be away and out of the city. But what if she hadn't come by car? What then? Where would she go? The railway station? That made sense. He jumped on his mobile, rang the train station, spoke to the railway police guy there and asked him to take a look. The bus station too? She didn't come across as a bus station kind of girl. No matter, he rang home base and ordered a car there.

Where else? Where have you gone, he-she thing?

Young, smart, trendy, personable, slender, where do you see people like that in the middle of a sunny May afternoon. Coffee bars, that's where. Not the old-fashioned milk bar places he preferred. No, the new American inspired trendy places, where people sat all day long with their mobile devices and laptop computers, half asleep over a cup of coffee or two, each cup costing more than a fiver, and don't dare ask the price of a calorie busting cake.

He'd been in one or two of those poncy dives; sometimes with Karen, for she adored the places, and sometimes by himself, and he wondered how Karen was now, as the ambulance dashed northward through the traffic toward the Countess Hospital.

He checked the coffee bars. No sign of the he-she thing, and no one fitting the description. Plenty of pretty women but dressed in worn out split jeans. He questioned the staff. Slim, black hair, navy blue suit? Seen anyone? No one fitting the description, sorry, Inspector. He checked four or five alcohol watering holes. The trendy places she might patronise. They were all packed, people crammed around television screens, watching the racing from down the road, spent and alive betting slips still on the bar, weighted down with full pints, and G & T's and pretty vodkas, discarded racing papers everywhere. Plenty of slim and attractive women in there too, but none that fitted the bill.

Where the hell are you, he-she thing?

Where have you gone?

Samantha had jumped on the first double-decker bus that came her way, took the four stops south, over the Grosvenor Bridge that afforded a splendid view of the packed racecourse. The horses were coming round the bend, the fourth race of the day under way; another favourite about to take an early bath.

By the time Walter had arrived in the first of the bars Samantha was already home, getting changed, planning a shower, reflecting on a satisfactory day's work, thinking of dinner, duck breast and Jersey Royals, very nice, the end of an adventure, seven was enough, seven times over, getting ready to go to work, there would be no more killing. None. It was all over and she could celebrate at last.

Walter jumped back on the phone. Rang base. Nothing at the railway station, nothing at the bus depot. Rang the hospital. Gibbons came to the phone.

'No news, Guv, she's in with the consultant now.'

Walter clicked off and headed back to the station. Perhaps the he-she thing didn't need to catch a bus or train. Maybe she lived bang in the centre of the city in any of the thousands of flats and houses crammed within the city walls. But where, he-she thing? Where?

They had missed her this time by a whisker, but they were getting closer, Walter knew that. They would nab her next time for sure; maybe Karen had seen her, might have some vital information, just so long as she was all right. Gibbons shouldn't have left her alone, none of us should. What were we thinking?

Walter wasn't to know the he-she thing had retired.

He hurried into the police station. Everyone was back at base, bar Gibbons and Karen.

The de-brief got underway.

Mrs West looked at Walter as if he'd blown his last chance. Said, 'We almost lost one of our own today.'

That brought it home.

Cresta stared through the window as if in a trance, trying to make sense of it, trying to come up with a nugget of thinking that no one else had stumbled on. Jenny Thompson brought Walter a cup of coffee and set it down with a supportive look.

'Thanks,' muttered Walter.

Jenny smiled without showing teeth and retreated.

Mrs West was talking again.

She had a harsh voice. Shrill and hard on the ear.

Walter had not noticed that before, and though she was still speaking, she didn't say a word, leastways not one that mattered.

Chapter Thirty-Nine

To be accepted on the secret PLACAD programme was the ultimate aim of all the ambitious scientists employed by Trencherman Research at Eden Leys. Desiree Holloway was no different. She was desperate to be included because it brought huge cachet, but far more than that, it was where she felt she belonged. It was where she knew she could make the greatest contribution.

PLACAD stood for Parkinson's, Leukaemia, Alzheimer's, Cancer And Dementia, and the ultimate aim of Eden Leys, aside from defence projects, was to find cures for the five devils, as some of the younger scientists christened them.

Trencherman Research had been set a target of producing results showing they could conquer these diseases within ten years. They were three years into the programme. It wasn't a matter of if they could produce satisfactory vaccines and cures, but when.

All the scientists believed that, and Desiree was no different.

One morning Desi was called to Professor Mary Craigieson's office where she was told to sit. There were two faceless gentlemen present who were not introduced and said little.

They asked her about her research; they quizzed her on her social life, though Desiree gained the distinct impression they knew the answers to the questions before they were issued. They asked for her views on PLACAD, and demanded to know where she could produce her weightiest contribution, and they asked about her own health, and in particular, her mental health.

Mental health issues had long been a major concern throughout the industry, stretching way back to 1917, when the serious work began. It was not everyone's cup of tea; spouted one of the grey suited gents, repeating facts that everyone already knew.

Desiree answered their questions, assuring them she was happy, which she was. She said she gleaned great satisfaction through her work, and that bred happiness. She was healthy, and appeared that way, shiny hair and glowing rouge skin, and confirmed all was well up top, as they described it.

No one knows if all is well up top until it is too late, as all four of them knew when they sat round that desk, and mulled over the question. But her affirmation that mental health was not and had not been a problem for Desiree, was comforting to her inquisitors, and it was on her record.

They asked her if she had any plans for marriage and motherhood. She replied she had no such thoughts and had no intention of ever bearing children. That reply was both satisfactory and unsatisfactory. Satisfactory because it meant that she could concentrate on her work at Trencherman without maternity interruptions, unsatisfactory because wasn't it normal for any woman to want to produce children? Could that lack of interest point to a slight problem up top?

Perhaps that should be investigated further.

They dismissed Desi from the room and told her to wait.

Professor Craigieson assured the gentlemen there were millions of women who did not wish to produce children, and that it would be ridiculous to deny her access to PLACAD on such flimsy grounds. The gents reluctantly concurred and PLACAD AUTHORISED was stamped on her record.

Desiree was called back and given the news, subject to her signing and agreeing to the new five way Security Secrets Agreement, drawn up by the CIA in far away Langley, Virginia, in cahoots with the British security services.

Desiree's face beamed like no other the panel had witnessed. The smile that broke across her face was amazing. Her large white teeth reflected the neon light back across the desk; her whole demeanour one of total elation. She would be included among the world elite in her field. She was determined, single handedly if necessary, to produce a cure for one of the five devils, and particularly Alzheimer's, which had afflicted her father.

Experiments on live human patients at Eden Leys were one of the key benefits of being accepted into PLACAD. Prior to that, Desiree was unaware such research work existed at Eden, or anywhere else.

231

But she understood the benefits.

Experimenting on chimpanzees was one thing, experimenting on live human beings was something else. The possibilities were endless.

Where the patients came from she did not know, or care. All of them were severe sufferers of that dreadful disease, and all died soon after the experiments were completed.

Afterwards they were issued with standard death certificates and taken to the on-site crematorium. She never saw a relative attend the brief ceremony in the all faiths chapel that sat alongside, and Desi attended every service whenever she could.

All too often, she was the only one there.

Why she began taking her work home, she could not explain. She had bought a smart maisonette in Chester that sat just above the weir, and the old stone bridge on the Handbridge bank of the river. During summer evenings she would sit on her balcony, alone with her thoughts, Singapore Sling in hand, gazing out toward the ancient city across the water, as the River Dee tumbled over the weir, the relaxing sound of constant dashing, crashing water, as it made its inevitable way toward the New Cut, and the wide estuary beyond.

Samples, blood, data, phials, all found their way to the office she had created in her spare bedroom. Security at Eden had become lax. There had never been a problem detected before, and that contributed to a lowering of standards. Vehicles were not properly checked, sometimes not at all. Security staff were poorly trained and badly managed. They did not know what was going on inside, and had little understanding of what they should look for. It was only a matter of time before it all blew up in someone's face.

In the meantime, Desi's collection of data and samples exploded. Sometimes she would sit and stare at them. Perhaps it gave her a feeling of power. After all, much of the data and samples were products of her pioneering work. Why shouldn't she bring some of it home? It was hers.

If the neighbours had known of the toxic substances and discarded body parts living on the other side of the thin walls, they would have been aghast. Perhaps she spirited them away as some form of unconscious protection from the voices that infected her head, though she would not have agreed with that.

Didn't everyone hear voices?

Didn't everyone steel themselves when necessary and say: Come on, you old fool, you must deal with this!

Didn't everyone do that?

Isn't that the same?

Voices in the head.

Desiree explained away her troubles in that way.

It wasn't a problem for her.

It wasn't anything she couldn't deal with.

It wasn't worth worrying about.

Live human tissue experimentation was producing results.

That was the only thing that mattered.

She was closing in on the ultimate prize.

Conquering one of the devils.

A huge breakthrough was expected any day.

One day Desiree Holloway would be feted.

One day her second bedroom trophies might include a Nobel Prize.

Chapter Forty

Walter was denied access to his sergeant for the whole of the day after she had been attacked. He tried to bully his way in by saying she was a vital witness in an ongoing murder hunt. He was rebuffed. She almost died, she's still ill; you can't see her today, go away; try again tomorrow.

Walter harrumphed and went home and sat up all night, thinking.

He stirred himself at first light, ran the electric shaver over his lined face, cleaned his aching teeth, applied deodorant, and left the house. The birds were singing as he ambled down the tree-lined road. Another fine day forecast. At the junction he jumped a bus the few stops into town. Went to the market, bought a bunch of seedless grapes from the surprised to see him sellers, who were just setting up.

Jumped a cab to the Countess Hospital.

They were surprised to see him there too.

He was asked to wait, perched on a padded bench at the end of the corridor. Breakfasts were being wheeled in. Sizzling bacon and eggs, porridge, orange juice, all came trundling by.

No one offered him any. He wasn't hungry.

He'd try to catch a sister's eye, a doctor's. But they would rush by without recognising his nod. When they did, he was told to wait. The patient was not ready to see visitors. He would have to continue waiting, or he could go home. It was his choice.

He waited, nibbling on the sourish grapes.

At gone eleven, a doctor appeared. A young Indian man, greasy parted hair, the demeanour of one who'd worked a twelve-hour shift.

'You're waiting to see Karen Greenwood?'

'Yes,' said Walter, getting to his feet.

'She's been very ill, a close call.'

'I realise that.'

'You can see her for five minutes, no more; then you must leave. Understand?'

'Sure.'

The doc bobbed his head and said, 'Follow me.'

She was in a room by herself. Sitting up, or propped up against a bank of pillows, hooked up to a drip.

She looked appalling.

The last time Walter saw her, she was purple. Now she was as white as milk, her blue eyes sunken in her head, like circles of lapis lazuli tossed into deep snow. Her usual vibrant blonde hair was lank, parted in the middle, and tied back revealing extensive bandaging around her neck.

Walter nodded down and pulled up a seat.

'How are you?'

A slight movement of the head, a forced smile, a croaked, 'OK.'

'I bought you these,' he said, setting the grapes on the side table.

She glanced at the browsed fruit, and wondered how long he'd been waiting. He couldn't have known she couldn't eat a thing.

Walter exhaled and checked out the room. There were so many things he wanted to ask, but it didn't seem the right moment.

'I didn't see him,' she said, her voice coming out in half whispered croaks.

'A him?'

Karen nodded and mumbled, 'Strong.'

Walter's turn to nod.

'I've been thinking,' he said, 'this person has a big grudge against us, against me. He tried to hurt me by taking you. He must have seen us together on the TV, in the papers; it's very personal for him. Who would have a beef like that?'

Karen pulled a face and shook her head. Whispered, 'Could be anyone, must be hundreds...' as her voice tailed away.

'Yeah, but this guy's got a bigger grudge than the usual nutters.'

She frowned and shook her head.

'Beats me,' he said, 'there must be something.'

He glanced into her face. Was there a hint of recognition? She tried to speak. An otherworldly breath escaped her lips. She turned to the bedside table, pointed to a pad and a blue pen. There was ample writing on the pad: need loo, need water, terrible headache, another pillow, hungry. He placed the pad in front of her and the pen in her right hand. She was cack handed, he'd forgotten, took it from the right, slipped it into the left. She half smiled, and began writing.

H…

'Harris?' he said.

Shook her head. O…

'Hooker?'

She shook her head.

He gave up trying to guess.

L…I…D…A…Y.

'Holiday, when I was on holiday?'

Karen bobbed her head.

Walter never took holidays. He hated going away. He hated leaving his station to come back to find other people sitting at his desk, other officers dealing with his cases, poking around. He hated missing the day-to-day things, tiny facts that could later build into a case, clues that once missed were gone forever, and you could miss so much in two long weeks. It took ages to get back up to speed afterwards. Holidays were for amateurs.

The spring before last Mrs West lost patience with him and ordered him away from the station for two weeks. She said he was tired, jaded, and not the Walter of old, all facts he decried. He'd gone home, where he'd sat alone for forty-eight hours, before ringing in and pleading to be allowed back.

'No!' she said, 'You come back and you collect your cards.'

Why he did what he did next, he couldn't explain. He jumped a train to London, then the express commuter to Heathrow, and caught the first plane to Kingston. Had to pay through the nose for a standby ticket and that annoyed him. He hadn't been back for twenty years and most of the people he knew were dead. His parents had been dead when he'd left the island as a nine-year-old, packed off all alone to see his Aunt Mimosa in Brixton. He thought he was on a holiday treat back then, only to discover he had a one-way ticket. Walter wouldn't be going back. He'd never gone back, not permanently. His Aunt Mimosa was his new mummy, the only person he had in the whole world. She was dead too.

Throughout the ten-day stay, he revisited all the haunts of his childhood. Reminiscing, seeing fleeting ghosts from his past, playing with his schoolboy pals in the fields and on the beach with Jackie

Nurse. Jackie had later gone to the States and fallen in with the wrong crowd. Got busted for car theft, drug running, and possessing an illegal weapon. He was sent to the FSP, the Florida State Prison in Bradford County.

And Wellworthy Griffiths, Welly, as everyone called him. Walter tried to find out what happened to Welly, but no one knew. They shrugged their shoulders and said, 'He's gone away,' as if he'd vanished. 'He's gone away,' no one knew where, no one knew when, hadn't been seen in years. No one seemed to care much either. Walter wondered what happened to his friend, the tall skinny happy kid who would bowl at him all day long, as Walter tried to copy the main man, Everton Weekes, Sir Everton DeCourcy Weekes, to give him his full title, the greatest batsman ever to pick up a cricket bat, according to Walter Darriteau, even if he was a Barbadian.

Maybe when Walter retired, he could return to Jamaica and use his detection skills to find out what really happened to Wellworthy Griffiths, though even as the thought occurred to him, he knew he wouldn't.

The holiday took ages to run its course, and when it was through, he was glad to be going home, for Britain was his home. It had been for fifty years, more than five sixths of his entire life. It was where he belonged, where his work was, where his friends were, where the he-she thing lived, where he wanted to be.

He glanced back at Karen.

'What happened when I was on holiday?'

Karen gulped, tried to speak. Pointed at the glass of water. Walter handed it to her. She noticed his hand shook. Took a big pull on the glass, emptied it. Walter refilled it. Set it on the table. Karen nodded her thanks. Started writing again.

D...E...A...

'Death?' he said, unable to stop himself.

Karen half smiled and nodded.

O...N

'Death on the Nile?'

Karen smirked and shook her head. Began again.

R...A...

'Radio? Range? Race? Rally?'

Karen shook her head, carried on.

237

I…L…

'Rail? Death on the railway?'

Karen stopped and nodded.

'Like at Mostyn?'

'Ya,' she said, one short, sharp syllable.

'Where?'

Karen shook her head.

'You can't remember? You don't know?'

She nodded.

'What about a death on the railway?'

She looked spent, close to tears, looked in need of a week's sleep.

'I need a name, Karen, I need a name.'

She closed her eyes, thinking, resting, sleeping, maybe.

Her blue eyes popped open again. Recognition, memory, fighting through whatever drugs they'd pumped into her. Began writing again.

H…O…L…L…O…

It took an age to write.

W…A…Y.

'Holloway,' he said aloud. It meant nothing to him, and yet, there was something there, but what? He couldn't remember. He wasn't even sure he'd ever known.

'What about Holloway?'

She shook her head, closed her eyes.

Walter noticed the doc hovering in the doorway. Glanced over his shoulder. Whispered, 'One more minute, it's all I need.'

The doc didn't say a word, just looked angry.

Walter glanced back at the girl.

She was writing again.

The doc came over to see.

T…H…A…N…X

'Thanks? Thank you?'

Faintest of nods.

'Thank you for what?'

F…O…R

'Yeah? What for?'

X

He glanced at the doc, then back at the girl. Her eyes were closed; the pen had fallen from her hand.

'That is enough, you must go now,' said the doctor, and the hand on Walter's shoulder, urging him to stand and turn and leave brooked no argument.

'But what is the X?'

'A kiss of course, it's not an X, it's a kiss.'

'Ah, that,' said Walter, 'I see,' he said, annoyed at his slowness, smiling to himself, as the doc waved him off down the corridor, as his medipager beeped.

Chapter Forty-One

Three years before.

Desiree's rapid progress was confirmed the day she received a letter from the Scientists' Society, advising her she was to be the year's recipient of the Sir Fred Berrington Memorial Trophy, a huge silver cup that most young scientists coveted. Everyone knew the Memorial Trophy was presented to the best young scientist of the year, though the Society was far too conservative to repeat that.

But, as with awards that came from the Palace, she was forbidden to tell anyone of her prize, not even her nearest and dearest. It had to remain a secret, a total surprise to everyone but the winner. Desi was desperate to broadcast her news, not least to Professor Mary Craigieson, who had in her day won the trophy twenty years before. Somehow Desi bit her tongue and kept the secret.

The award would take place at the Grosvenor House Hotel in Park Lane, London, before a thousand of her contemporaries. The Chancellor of the Exchequer would present it, amidst a blaze of smiles and flashlights.

Desi couldn't wait.

The clock seemed to slide backwards; days felt like years, as she counted down toward her big day.

Finally, it arrived, and Desi set off for London by train.

Chester to Stafford, change there, jump on the Glasgow to London Euston service.

It was a crushing bright morning as she stood on Stafford's Platform One, close to the rails, waiting for the connection. There were plenty of people about, and Desi knew the train would be full when it pulled in. She didn't want to be at the back; she didn't want to miss out on a seat; she didn't want to stand all the way to London.

Later that evening, she'd have to make a big thank you speech, and though she had rehearsed and refined it time and again, standing before her long hall mirror, rehearsing her gestures as much as the words, she still felt the need to go over it again, memorising things one last time, making slight alterations too, cutting out a phrase here, adding something there, trimming the silly jokes that had sounded fine and dandy when she was daydreaming in the Red Caves Social Club with Professor Jim McClaine. Some of his Antipodean cracks in the club were incredibly funny, but probably not suitable for the occasion. No, she would add something topical that was in the news, something in the papers that day, and she couldn't do all that standing up, she couldn't concentrate when standing on a train.

She wanted a seat.

She needed a seat.

She must have a seat.

Please stand clear!

The train now approaching Platform One will NOT be stopping at this station. Please stand clear.

She heard the tinny announcement and was pleased to see everyone taking a backward step. Desi did not. She stooped and grabbed her new maroon case and edged closer to the track.

She could hear the train approaching. She couldn't miss it. A Manchester London non-stop express, hurtling past the signal box at the end of the platform, entering the station, closing on the main buildings, closing on Desi, no hint of slowing down, thundering through.

The whole place shook.

The voice in her head returned.

Jump, bitch! Jump!

Go on!

Jump, bitch! Jump!

From nowhere she felt dizzy, unsteady on her feet.

Perhaps she had been working too hard.

She lifted her right foot to take a step… and stepped backward.

The train whistled through, less than two feet away, puzzled faces streaming by, as if Desi was flicking through a roll of film. Coloured, blurred faces, anxious faces, as if they weren't real people at all, fleeting spirits, as if in a movie, or a dream.

From behind, an elderly lady stepped forward and said, 'Are you all right, dear? You look awfully pale.'

241

Desi glanced down and focused on the lady's grey-haired face.

'I'm fine thanks, must have been something I ate.'

A mischievous glint formed on the lady's phizog.

'I've seen that body language before,' she said. 'In the way, are you?'

'In the way?' asked Desi.

'Yes, you know, expecting good news to come?' and she glanced at Desi's trim tummy.

'Oh God, no!' said Desi, her hand going to her mouth. 'God, I hope not. Impossible.'

The lady smiled and nodded at her knowingly and said, 'You wouldn't be the first girl to say that,' still believing that she was right.

The tinny announcer returned.

The next train arriving at Platform One is the eleven sixteen to London Euston, stopping at Nuneaton and London Euston.

'That's me,' said the lady.

'And me,' said Desi, and five minutes later they were sitting together, chatting, as they watched the gentle, green Staffordshire countryside rolling by.

The award ceremony went perfectly. The Sir Fred Berrington Memorial Trophy glistened in her arms. She'd collected it to thunderous applause, and embraced it as a long-lost lover. It was the second most prestigious prize of the night, only the all-embracing Golden Scientist of the Year Shield ranked above it in importance. Desi had already thought about that. She was determined to return next year and bag the Gold Shield. She possessed the ammunition to do that too, for she was on the verge of a mind-altering breakthrough.

Her speech went well; the audience laughed where they were meant to laugh, and more importantly, listened intently to the serious stuff. Desi had a talent for public speaking, she'd always known that, but that night it was reinforced.

Desi could hold an audience like an osprey gripping a slippery sea trout. She wasn't about to drop them, not until she was good and ready.

The following day she would return to her riverside maisonette, where she would set the glittering silver trophy down among her other spoils of war, like a proud magpie, in the spare bedroom, now crammed with the weird and wonderful flotsam and jetsam of her experiments. She would polish the cup every month, and when the day came to return it, it would be in better shape than ever.

In the meantime, she would occasionally glance at the prestigious names engraved there; going back fifty years, fifty eminent people, the best young scientists Britain had to offer, and there at the bottom, the very last name, freshly engraved, was Desiree Mitford Holloway, only the second woman to bag the prize, following in the pioneering footsteps of her tutor and mentor, Professor Mary Craigieson. How neat was that?

Desiree inwardly smiled. She was at peace with the world.

Chapter Forty-Two

The moment Walter left the hospital, he took out his phone and rang base. Jenny Thompson answered.

'Is Gibbons there?'

'Gone out, Guv. Had a bit of an alarm.'

'What kind of alarm?'

'A woman in a big house over at Curzon Park reported a maniac in the kitchen threatening her. We all thought it was another, you know, he-she thing attack. We've been trying to contact you.'

'Phone's off. I've been with Karen.'

'How is she?'

'Rough. What happened?'

'Nah, false alarm, it was that idiot Davey Seed.'

Jenny didn't need to say anymore. Davey Seed was a basket case who should never have been walking the streets. Made a habit of wandering into other people's houses, usually in the summer when side gates were unlocked and conservatory doors were thrown wide open. He'd stroll in and sit down and gurn at the householder and say, 'Tea? Tea? Any tea?'

'The lady's very shaken up,' said Jenny.

'I'll bet. The sight of Davey Seed would upset anyone who didn't know him. Forget about that. I want you to do something for me. Urgent.'

'Sure, Guv.'

'There was a case a couple of springs ago.'

'I wasn't here then.'

'I know that,' said Walter, keeping the irritation from his voice.

'Sorry, Guv.'

'Something about a death on a railway? Something to do with someone called Holloway. It must be on file somewhere. I want an address. Got that?'

'Sure, Guv. Holloway.'

'Find out all you can, oh, and can you drive?'

'Yes, sure, Guv.'

'Arrange an unmarked car, and change into civvies. You do have plainclothes?'

'Sure, Guv, in my locker.'

'OK, Jenny. Get on that, top priority. I'll be back as soon as I can grab a cab.'

Jenny was sitting at Karen's desk when Walter hurried in.

'Well?' he said, before he'd even sat down.

'Desiree Holloway met her end under a Glasgow-Euston express at Crewe Station. Several witnesses stated it was suicide, though there were allegations she had been pushed.'

'Allegations by whom?'

'Don't know, Guv. The records are not great. Think there was a big admin shake-up shortly afterwards.'

'Ah yes,' he mumbled, remembering the Mrs West big shake-up spring clean. Joan's shake and whack, the lads called it. He'd forgotten about that. It had to be done, but by God she milked the moment. 'Have you got an address?'

'Not Holloway's, that seems to be among the lost data, but I do have an address for the next of kin.'

'Where?'

'Iona House, Wrexham Road.'

'Good girl. We'll try there. Car organised?'

'Yep, though it's a bit crap.'

'Don't care, so long as it's in civvies and gets us there.'

'Shall I tell Mrs West where we are going?'

Walter gave her a look that said everything.

He unlocked his desk drawer and retrieved the Glock 22. Slipped it into his raincoat pocket. Jenny watched him do it and wondered what was going down, and what she had let herself in for.

'Come on,' he said, striding for the door, Jenny hurrying to keep up.

For a big man with a limp, he couldn't half shift when the feeling took him.

Walter was a decent driver, but he preferred being driven. It gave him thinking time when they were coming or going. Sometimes when he was driving he still thought about cases. Sometimes it had almost brought double trouble to his door. Hence Jenny was driving, and anyway he liked company, especially young company, especially on a case like this.

Jenny pointed the car south, past the Roodee, crossed the river, headed toward Wrexham.

'So what's this all about?' she asked.

'Not sure. Just an idea I had. It's not far now.'

He was right. The building was coming up, set on a brow on the right-hand side. You couldn't miss it, a late Victorian or early Edwardian detached house. As they drew closer, he stared up at the fascia. Built into the gable were the words Iona House, picked out in blue Mucklow bricks. It must have been a heck of a property in its day. It was divided into four spacious flats, as they discovered when they pulled into the driveway, set to the right side of the house.

There were two cars sleeping in the small rear car park, an old rusting Jaguar and a green Ford saloon that badly needed a wash. No smart Japanese hatchback. Disappointing. They went round to the front, their feet crunching on the gravel drive, and peered up at the four white bell pushes set beneath one another in a neat line. Before he could ring any of them, the front door opened and an elderly lady peered out.

'Can I help you?' she said. 'But I must warn you I never buy from cold callers, and I don't have any antiques I wish to sell.'

Walter smiled as gently as he could manage. Flashed his ID.

'Your name is?' he said.

'Mrs Hymas, Elizabeth Hymas, Betty to my friends, though there is no Mr Hymas,' she said, smiling at the pretty girl. 'You know how it is, went his own way, thank the Lord for that, liked the booze, you see,' and she pulled a crazy face. 'Got a bit handy with his fists too when he was worse for wear,' and she nodded slowly at the girl, as if it were a dire warning. 'Horrible man!'

'Which flat do you live in?' asked Jenny.

'Number one, though we prefer to call them apartments. I have the whole place to myself at the moment, everyone's out, so it's quite nice to see you. It gives me someone to talk to. Mr Kenson and Mr Watson, they have the top flats, they go away together every May, never miss. They rent a place in Spain for two weeks. But they are not homo-funnykins, and all that peculiar business, they don't sleep together, or anything like that, or at least I don't think they do,' and she grinned mischievously at Jenny, and added, 'But who knows?'

'And flat number two?' asked Walter.

'Nicest people you could wish to meet. Samuel and Samantha Holloway. They keep a lookout for me, run me on errands sometimes, bring me back heavy shopping, spuds and stuff, and the odd bottle of how's your father,' and she winked at the pair of them. 'Tell you the truth I don't know what I'd do without them.'

'They're husband and wife?' asked Jenny.

'No, silly... brother and sister.'

'And they are away at the moment?'

'Yes.'

'Do you know where?'

'No, but I do know something very important is about to happen.'

'Oh yes, like what?'

'He's a writer, you know. She does fashion, but it's him who's had the big success.'

'What's that, then?'

'His new book, of course. Been a huge hit in America, he was telling me the other day. He's going to the United States in a few days to collect his prize, a million dollars, can you imagine?'

'Is he tall?' asked Jenny.

'No, not really, not as tall as this big fellow.'

Walter and Jenny shared a look. Jenny wanted to giggle. Walter hid a scowl.

'And the sister; is she tall?' asked Walter.

'Pretty much. Not huge, but taller than her,' she said, glancing back at Jenny.

'Lovely slim figure, I'll bet,' said Walter.

'Oh yes, mine was like that one day, you know,' and suddenly she appeared guilty, as she ran her hands across her not overlarge stomach.

'When are they due back?' asked Jenny.

247

'Tomorrow evening, he was most specific about that, said they would be back tomorrow evening.'

'Tell me, Mrs Hymas,' said Walter, 'have you ever seen them together?'

'Pardon me?'

'Have you ever seen Sam and Samantha together?'

'Of course I have, well at least I think I have, I must have done, mustn't I? They have been in my flat many times.'

'And both at the same time?' asked Jenny. 'Say, had a meal together, you and the two of them round the table?'

'Well, no, we never eat together. We are not that close. But I get a separate card and present from them every Christmas. One from him, forward sloping writing in blue, and one from her, backward sloping writing, in black. Generous they are with their presents too, I'll say that. More so than misery guts Kenson and Watson, sounds like an estate agents, don't you think? Kenson and Watson. Yuck!'

Walter smiled.

Jenny did too.

'I want you to do us a big favour,' said Walter.

'Anything to help the police.'

'Don't tell Sam and Samantha we called. We want it to be a surprise. It's to do with the book, you see,' and he touched his nose and winked.

'Ooh, is it? How exciting. I won't say a word.'

'And one other thing.'

'Yes?'

'Would it be OK if we waited in your apartment tomorrow until they came home?'

'Sort of a nice surprise for them both?'

'That's correct,' said Jenny, 'a smashing surprise.'

'Of course you can. I'll tell you what I'll do; I'll bake some fairy cakes. My fairies have won prizes right across Chester.'

'Don't go to too much trouble,' said Walter.

'It's no trouble at all, tell you the truth, I'll enjoy the company, it'll make such a pleasant change.'

'We'll come just after lunch.'

'Come whenever you like. I won't be going anywhere. The kettle is always thinking of boiling.'

'That's the spirit,' said Walter. 'Thanks so much, Mrs Hymas, you've been most helpful.'

They smiled at her one last time and turned away and retreated to the car park.

She didn't go in until they were out of sight.

Round the back, Walter went to the window of flat 2, placed his hands on the glass to shade his eyes, and peered in.

'See anything?'

'Not really, these lace curtains don't help. Just a normal kitchen as far as I can see, maybe a stove.'

'You think it's him or her?'

'Not sure. As soon as we get back to the station, arrange a search warrant. If he doesn't show tomorrow, we'll turn the place over, see what's in there.'

'OK, Guv.'

'Yeah,' he said, thinking of something else, as he turned back the car.

'Guv?'

'What?'

'Would you ever think of kicking in the door, taking a sly look? You know, just in case.'

Walter turned back to her and peered at the door. Glanced at her again. Course he'd thought of it.

'That, WPC Thompson would be illegal, and in any case, if we did, and made a mess, and there was nothing of interest in there, it might warn the bastard off if he came home later when we weren't here. Understand?'

'Yes, Guv. I see.'

'Come on,' he said. 'There are things I want to research in the records.'

Jenny started the car and headed back toward the city.

Walter laughed inwardly.

He could hardly believe what he had just heard.

The young WPC advocating breaking and entering on the off chance they might stumble on information. What were they teaching them at Police College these days?

Showed initiative though, you had to grant her that.

Walter giggled.

Jenny glanced at him from the corner of her eye and wondered why he was tittering.

His mouth was dry. He needed a pint. He needed several pints.

Chapter Forty-Three

Karen was discharged the following day. She was young and fit and had rapidly recovered and they needed the bed. She wanted to go home but didn't want to be alone, so she rang Gibbons and asked him if he'd like to come over for a chat. He said he would, though his shift didn't finish until 8pm. He'd be round at ten after taking a shower and grabbing a bite to eat.

'Thomas Telford House,' she said. 'Number fifty, on the ring road, overlooking the locks.'

'I know it,' he said, 'I'll see you later.'

It was only a couple of hundred yards from his police digs; it wouldn't take two jiffies to get there.

Sam settled down in front of the television. Looking forward to seeing the news. See what spin they put on events at Chester racecourse. A tiny smile played across the lips.

Sam was in for a big surprise.

There was nothing on the national news.

That was weird. Why not? There should have been.

Wanted to see the fat black cop squirm; wanted to see him angry, to see him disconsolate, wanted to see him shaking with rage, wanted to see him feeling the loss.

The local news came on. A little common sense had returned. It was the lead story.

The sexy announcer carried that excited inflection in her voice only present when a major story broke.

They were showing library footage of the racecourse, hazy distant pictures of groundsmen preparing the track, mowing and clipping, and other guys with paint pots looking for something to paint white.

The breathy voice cut in.

A woman police officer was attacked in the toilets at Chester races on Ladies' Day. Thankfully, she is making a rapid recovery. Her injuries are not life threatening. The police are looking to interview a slim woman aged around thirty, black hair, wearing a navy blue suit and a member's badge.

How could the injuries not be serious?

Of course the injuries were serious!

They were lying. They were all lying.

In cahoots with the authorities. Liars!

Conspiracy, a pathetic attempt to trick Sam and the public into believing barefaced lies.

When someone is hung by the neck, when they blackout and are left for dead, the injuries are deadly serious. Get real. Be honest!

But what if she wasn't dead? What then?

Seven times over was seven times over.

Now they were saying it hadn't happened.

Six times wasn't enough.

Six times wasn't the deal.

Six times meant unfinished business.

10.30pm that night.

Still nothing on the national news. Nothing new on the local either. Same old cannon fodder. Something had to be done.

The man carefully dressed, all in black. Sweatshirt, jeans, socks, leather gloves, woolly hat, trainers, all black. Picked up the black sports bag and let himself out. Went downstairs to the underground car park. Opened the car, threw the bag on the back seat, jumped in the front, started the engine, cruised out into the black night. No moon, no stars, thick cloud, a cloaking mist creeping up the river on the late tide, a chilly night for May. The only light piercing the gloom, the cold orange sodium that was everywhere. He didn't have far to drive, three miles max, through the city centre and on to the northern suburbs.

In the city the early drinkers and diners were leaving town, the late night hard boozers and boppers and gamblers were going in. The centre was lit up like Christmas. All around young people filled the pavements, chattering like gulls, shrieking, laughing, pointing, threatening, punching, fighting, fainting, puking.

The man drove on, didn't see them at all, didn't see anything; just drove. The suburbs were quiet. He parked in a tree-lined boulevard, a hundred yards from the target. Slipped the car in amongst a dozen similar middle class vehicles.

Cut the engine. Turned round, grabbed the bag, stepped out, locked the car; walked away, not too quick; not too slow, heading down toward the house. Two sleepy squirrels in one of the trees above his head watched him go. He didn't see them. They cuddled up together and closed their eyes.

At the target property there was a dim light on in the front room. Nothing upstairs. All dark. He glanced around. No one about. Crept up the path. Opened the side gate, not too difficult, just the one bolt, no padlock, pushed open, not too noisy, slipped through, eased closed, stood still in the absolute blackness, eyes growing accustomed to the dark, tiptoed down the alleyway, hand out ahead; feeling for bins or bikes. All clear. Nothing there.

Somewhere nearby a dog barked, not next door, maybe three or four houses away. Not an alarmed bark, not a people come running bark, maybe a play bark, or an I'm hungry bark. At the back of the house, down the garden, beyond the hedge, he could see similar properties through the bushes and pruned trees. Some lights were on over there, all the curtains and blinds were closed; no one was looking out, no kid playing up at well gone bedtime. One house had security lighting illuminating a flat extension. Two cats were yowling and fighting there, the black and white one breaking off and dashing away. A fraction of light filtered over the hedge into the garden where he stood. The man shrugged and turned back to the house that interested him.

He stared up at the old home. Jammed on the rear of the building as an afterthought was a small single story extension, pebble-dash and brick, perhaps a kitchen. It boasted a wide window, three panes across, no curtains or blinds, nothing. There was no light on inside, just the hint of brightness filtering in from another room, or maybe from the hallway. The window frames were the original wooden structures. They had begun to perish. His gloved hand rubbed one corner. A little came away on his thumb. He set the bag on the floor,

253

stooped down, opened up, the metal zip sounding like gunfire, took out a small jemmy, stood up, inserted it in the vertical edge of the left window, and levered it back. Not too much force. Not too little. Gently does it.

The old window frame was no match for a modern tempered steel tool. The metal catch inside securing the window burst with a crack. The window came open in his hand. He stood quite still, half expecting someone to come running. No one did. The same dog barked again. No one paid attention. Somewhere over the back, a door opened, the metallic blurred sound of a TV or radio spilled out, drifting on the still night air, and someone yelled, 'Come in Felix!' and the door closed again.

Silence returned. The man bent down, returned the jemmy to the bag, picked it up, hooked it over his arm; pulled the window open. It came toward him like a small glass front door, four feet above the ground.

He stuck his head inside. It was a kitchen, dimly lit, but he could see what he needed. Someone had eaten a curry. The remnants were still there, a ready meal job, detritus scattered around the worktop, the coloured cardboard sleeve, the blackened, clear vinyl top, the plastic base, some rice still remaining, looking rejected, the smell, not korma, something stronger, tikka, Jalfrezi perhaps, he didn't care.

Put his hands on the sill, flexed his trainers and toes on the path outside, jumped and pulled himself up and through the window, landed inside on the vinyl floor. Stood perfectly still. Glanced around. Blue pilot light on the boiler. Green power light on the freezer. Red warning light on the burglar alarm sensor, not activated, couldn't have been. Thank God for that. No one came running. The freezer cut in with a loud hum, startled him for a second.

There was music in the air. Radio, television, maybe, coming from down the hall, maybe from the sitting room set off toward the left. He crept to the kitchen door; it wasn't closed, just pulled to, eased it open. A gloomy long narrow hallway much as he expected, coats hanging up on wall-mounted hooks, a small table, old-fashioned telephone on top, the room off to the left as he'd imagined, another door, another ajar, the music louder, but not too loud. Jazz of some kind, puke music, he would say, and slightly more light so he could see better. Total silence other than the music, no sound of anyone talking, no noise of anyone moving about, no newspaper being turned over, no gobbling irons scraping on china, nothing from upstairs, no bath or shower running, and yet as he eased inches forward there was another sound, heavy breathing, and more than that, snoring. The occupant was asleep.

How opportune was that?

Crept to the sitting-room door. Peered through the gap at the hinge's end between the door and the frame. Saw a coffee table covered in empty beer cans, three, no four of them; bent over in the middle as if someone had been flexing them in the hand, aids to relaxation, wreck the cans, while thinking of the day's events.

Irish stout. Fattening stuff. Sleepy stuff.

The snoring grew louder.

Eased the door open to a dimly lit sitting room. Stood in the doorway.

The weighty guy was sitting in a big old-fashioned armchair, wooden arms, his head back, eyes closed, sturdy furniture. The man in black glanced around the room. Flowery wallpaper, patterned carpet, needed a clean, old oak standard lamp trying hard to light the room, ridiculous flowery lampshade, writing desk, old books on the top, slab down, wide open, bills and cheques scattered about, matching armchair pushed into the far right corner, slight musty smell, and curry and beer and sweat. It all looked and smelt like something his great aunt might have had, or from a fifties Ealing comedy film. Same thing, really.

Old-fashioned brown telly, Grundig, sturdily made, last for years, never blew up, someone on the screen was blowing on a horn. At least it was in colour, a dusky woman was cooing along, sleepy music, and it was working well on the guy in the chair. Glanced back at him. Still fast asleep, completely out of it, as if he'd had a hard week, or maybe two. His frizzy grey hair standing on end as if he'd had an electric shock.

The man in black smiled and slipped four heavy-duty plastic cable ties from his bag. Set the bag carefully on the hall floor. Crept into the room.

The guy didn't stir.

Continued snoring.

The man in black slipped a tie through the wooden arm of the chair, around the black guy's right wrist, fastened it; eased it tight, but not too tight.

The guy didn't stir.

Moved around the back of the chair.

Same job, left wrist, same result.

The eyes remained shut.

Nothing would shift the tie, other than a sharp implement.

Crouched down. Slipped the third tie around the right ankle. It couldn't have been better positioned, next to the wooden foot. Eased it tight. Job done.

Back round the other side.

This one was tricky. The left foot was splayed away from the furniture, lazily resting on the heel, the aromatic worn carpet slipper half off. Fed the last tie around the wooden furniture leg, around the black guy's ankle, slipped one end through the loop, and yanked it tight, bringing the whole leg back with a jolt, securing it fast to the chair leg.

The black guy woke up.

'What the hell!'

Began shaking frantically, trying to free his limbs, realised he was stuck fast, stopped shaking, focused his tired eyes, stared at the man in black. He was busy revisiting each plastic tie, gently easing them tighter. The black guy thought of biting him, but by the time he'd thought of that, the man in black had finished and moved away. No one and nothing could break free from that chair.

The man in black stood in front of the TV, his back to the screen, bent down to the coffee table, grabbed the remote, fired it over his shoulder, and the music stopped.

The black guy stared up at the intruder.

Five feet six, slim build, small feet, nice lips, clear skin, pretty face, short neatly trimmed light brown hair, maybe a touch of blond, maybe a touch of highlighting, bright blue eyes, and a pert bum, a pretty boy, or a pretty girl?

Walter grinned.

The man in black grinned back.

'You recognise me?' he said.

'In a way.'

'Good, that's good, Walter. It shows if nothing else that you are not totally incompetent, pretty much, but not completely.'

The man retreated to the hallway, picked up the sports bag; came back inside; swept the empty cans from the coffee table with a metallic clang, set the bag in their place.

'You know why I am here?'

'I guess you have come to try to kill me.'

'Wrong! Incorrect! I haven't come to try to kill you. I have come to complete my task. I will kill you, in a few minutes from now. It's your own fault. You should have left the bitch to die. That was a big mistake. It's say your prayers time for you, Wally.'

Walter didn't answer. He didn't have anything to say. He was fighting his mind clear of alcohol. Thinking how he might get out of there. Glanced at his mobile phone on top of the TV. Couldn't remember if he'd charged it. Couldn't figure how to get hold of it. Couldn't think how he could use it. The landline in the hall might as well have been in Mongolia. The man in black began taking items from his bag, setting them down on the table before him.

Walter glanced at them.

He didn't like what he saw.

He didn't like what he saw at all.

Chapter Forty-Four

A year after Desiree won the Sir Fred Berrington Memorial Trophy, she was invited back to London, up for the big prize, the Golden Shield. The Shield was different because it was the top prize any British scientist could win, but it was different in another way too. The winner didn't know who had won it. There were five nominations, and the name of the lucky recipient was known only to the eight souls who sat on the Scientists' Society Committee.

Desiree was on the shortlist, nothing more, though secretly, she was confident of picking up the top prize, though she was far too modest to suggest such a thing, even to her mentor, Jill Craigieson. She had been poorly with a bout of serious back trouble. It happened often, and she was resting up at home. She rang Desiree the night before she set off for London and wished her well.

When she'd called, Desiree was in the process of giving the Berrington silver cup its final clean and polish. It was as she knew it would be, brighter, more gleaming, spotless; cleaner than when she'd picked it up and clasped it to her breast a year before. She imagined the sparkle would bring her luck, bring her the success her outstanding work deserved. She didn't want to hand it back, though she would happily exchange it for the Gold Shield.

This time the Chester to London train changed at Crewe.

When she arrived there, she found the station busy. The previous London train had been cancelled due to the wrong kind of leaves on the line, or the wrong kind of snow in the air, or the wrong kind of electricity in the wires, or the wrong kind of idiot in management, which was probably closer to the truth. Desiree wasn't alone in thinking that, as she checked her two bags were still at her side, the same smart maroon suitcase from the previous year, and the worn crinkly purpose built black case housing the Sir Fred Berrington Cup.

Whatever the reason for the non-arrival of the previous London service, passengers were backing up. The platform was crowded and becoming more so, standing room only, people nudging in from the rear, passengers flooding out of the waiting rooms, not wanting to be left behind, people dashing down the steps from the passenger bridge only to be confronted by thick crowds, travellers desperately trying to wheedle their way closer to finding a carriage door, when the train eventually arrived.

"Please stand clear! The next train arriving at Platform Three will NOT be stopping at this station. Please stand well clear!"

Desiree exchanged a nervous look with her neighbours and sniffed a rebuke. How could anyone stand clear when the pressure from behind was easing more people forward toward the track, toward the rails?

It was laughable.

A tall bespectacled man in a tweed suit standing at the front, three along from Desi, turned around and gawped across the packed heads, back toward the station buildings and shouted: 'Stop pushing at the back! We cannot move any further forward! Please stop pushing!'

The pressure eased for a matter of moments. Some people used the lull to edge into better positions, slip a tad forward, closer to the rails, reintroducing pressure, only more so than before.

Desi felt her feet being pushed forward and dug in her heels.

She glanced down at her bags. They were slightly behind her, as if some invisible tide was washing her out. She manoeuvred the maroon case forward with a touch of her toe, while picking up and cuddling the black one.

The non-stopping train was rumbling toward the station approach. Past the signal box, past the end of the platform, entering the main body of the station, a rhythmic, thundering beat as the heavily laden express began to whip through.

Out of nowhere, the voice returned.

She hadn't expected it.

She hadn't wanted it.

She shook her head and tried to obliterate it.

Jump, bitch! Jump!

Go on!

Jump, bitch! Jump!

259

The voice of destiny, and this time it was the unmistakable voice of the hateful Toby Malone.

No! I won't. Go away! Leave me alone!

Do as you're told!

Jump, bitch! Jump!

Let's face it darling… you know you want to!

Come and join me!

Jump! Do it! Do it now!

No! No! I don't! I won't!

Still more people had arrived at the rear, more pressure, more eagerness to get closer to the front, regardless of the massive weight of moving steel and wood and fabric and luggage and food and prams and bikes and humanity, all crammed together on the express train that was hurling itself through the station.

In the melee, Desi stumbled.

She grasped the Sir Fred Berrington closer to her heart as if it might protect her and fell.

The crowd gasped. The sound drowned out by the express.

Hands went to mouths. Eyes widened. Shocked mouths opened.

People looked away, not that there was much to see.

Desi was beneath the still moving last six carriages, as they hurtled over her remains. The crinkly black box had burst open on first impact, throwing the old and coveted trophy toward the centre of the track where it bounced once and stumbled under the far steel wheels, flattened beyond recognition, the passengers feeling the tiniest of jolts, not enough to be of concern. How were they to know that Sir Fred Berrington had been mutilated beyond use, beneath their restless feet?

Desiree Mitford Holloway hadn't fared any better.

Death was instantaneous.

Decapitation.

Mutilation.

An horrific death.

In five seconds flat Desiree Holloway ceased to exist.

'Oh my God!' shrieked a teenage girl, clutching her face. 'Did you see that?'

She glanced around at her shocked neighbours.

'I told you!' yelled the tall man, turning round and staring at the rear of the crowd as if they were personally responsible. 'I told you so! A poor lady's gone under the bloody train!'

Thankfully, no one had witnessed her final moment, not after Desiree had disappeared beneath the locomotive. It seemed an age before the long train cleared the station, cleared the view, and as the rear of the train dashed away, shaking people stared down at the bloody remains, strewn along the track toward London.

Unrecognisable.

Was that a head?

Is that really hair?

Isn't that her black jacket?

Poor woman!

Look, there! A hand, see, just beyond the brown sleeper. It's a hand, I tell you!

Everyone peered, but not everyone saw it.

'She jumped, you know!' someone said.

'She did not!'

'She bloody well did!'

'She stumbled under the weight of the crowd,' said a third.

'She jumped, I tell ya!'

"The train now approaching Platform Three is the eleven nineteen calling at London Euston only. Platform Three for the London Euston Train."

'Oh, my God; hasn't somebody sent for someone?' cried a woman.

The tall man turned round and yelled, 'Stop this! Fetch someone! Now! A woman has gone under the train!'

Still more people were funnelling down the steps, pushing onto the platform, urged on by the strident tannoy announcement. Latecomers and day-trippers and poor timekeepers and runners with pushchairs; and students with music in their ears, and coloured rucksacks slung over their shoulders; and a big man with a cello, and gaggles of confused foreigners, and school children on a day trip, and lots of them.

'What's all the fuss about?' asked one, jokily.

'Gawd, it's busy down here today,' said another suited man, as he pushed his wheeled bag before him, muttering, 'Make way, make way! I must get on this train. Matter of life and death.'

Several bystanders looked at him with disdain.

Eyewitnesses at the front, feeling more pressure from the rear, thought better of it, turned about and fought their way away from the trackside. They would go straight home, and not by train, leave it for another day when things were quieter, and safer, and they had re-gathered their nerve, and rediscovered some courage.

The London train was spluttering into the station as if it had a cold, unknowingly cloaking the horror, hiding the evidence. The passengers on the train thought the people on the platform looked a miserable bunch, even more so than usual.

A moment later, a hundred tried to get off. Had to push their way off and fight their way through the nervous throng. God, what was wrong with everyone today? The instant the doors pulled open, three hundred fought to get on, pushing and shoving and elbowing and cursing and grimacing.

Someone said, 'There's nothing we can do for her now, and I need to get to London.'

Another said, 'She jumped anyway, it was her own choice.'

'You cold bastards!' yelled the tall man, refusing to board the train, turning around, fighting his way back through more latecomers.

'Who's in charge here?' he demanded. 'Where's the station manager?'

People looked at him as if he were a troublemaker, a shilling short of a quid, there's always someone who wants to make a fuss.

'Bit of a loony,' someone suggested, as they hurried on by, and no one was going to argue. There were loads of loonies about these days.

'He looked a loony,' said someone else. 'Very tall people are often loonies!' and several people glanced around to see if they were standing next to anyone particularly tall.

Not everyone managed to board, though most of them did, crammed together like football crowds from years ago, trying to read their newspapers and magazines and devices over someone else's shoulder, trying to eat a cheese sandwich or a piece of spicy sausage out of a green packet, or a muesli bar without appearing to do so, trying to reach the packed lavatories, trying not to sniff someone else's armpit as they stretched, trying to read vital texts, trying to make or receive a phone call, trying to get online, trying to access their Bookface page to broadcast their vital news to the waiting and voyeuristic electronic world, of what they had seen and where they had been, and you should have seen it too, and how exciting it all was, and how incredibly bloody. My God! Better than the TV! Far better!

One standing passenger was heard to intone into his palm-pootler: 'I'm having a bad day, I'm on the train... but someone else has had a far worse one... they're beneath it!' Followed by a cold laugh, and hostile stares.

After the London train had slipped away, one or two remaining on the platform noted that the supposed severed hand had vanished. A few more were taking pictures with their mobile phones, hands in the air like weird worshippers to the modern God, Techno, to be sent on up ahead to wherever they were going, like a harbinger of doom.

Gross! Look at that. Yuck! I'll just take a few more, perhaps from over there, a better angle. You never know when you'll get another chance!

The sight of the remains of the person formerly known as Desiree Holloway would affect the minds of the unfortunate souls summoned to clear up the mess for years to come.

Didn't seem to affect the passengers much.

Belatedly, the station closed.

Services were suspended.

Police summoned, and cleaners too.

Passengers were still arriving.

It was nothing to do with them.

What the hell's going on?

Railways of today, eh? Waste of space! I remember when... blah blah blah.

Tempers flared.

They simply had to get where they were going. Had to!

But they wouldn't. And they couldn't. And they didn't.

Not for several hours afterwards.

263

It was an hour later before anyone noticed the fancy maroon suitcase, still sitting unattended on the platform, close to the edge where Desiree had placed it. Could it be a bomb, someone said. It contained her expensive dinner outfit, culled from the Manchester bazaars, never worn before, never worn again, not by Desiree Holloway, not by anyone.

The Scientists' Society Annual Dinner and Presentation went ahead as planned, oblivious to the bloody events up at Crewe. The committee were furious with the young woman for not turning up, but most particularly, for failing to return the much loved Sir Fred Berrington Memorial Trophy. No one had ever done that before. One crusty old sod said, 'That's what you get for giving it to a woman in the first place. We might have known!'

'Shut up, Lionel!'

The winner of the silver cup was a gawky tall girl wearing dreadful black specs. She was assured it would be hers, just as soon as it could be located. It had gone missing in transit. Nothing to worry about. Sorry about that. You'll have it in a few days. In the meantime, the committee went into emergency session.

Later, the Gold Shield was presented to the scientist of the year, Michael Fixington of Allied Chemical Industries, for his innovative work in non-drip paints. Michael was amazed, as was everyone else.

Three days later when the Society discovered the truth, the committee met in emergency session.

'I'd like to apologise,' muttered Lionel.

'I should think so,' sniffed three of the others.

'Well? What are we going to do about it?'

Many ideas were mooted.

A posthumous award. A special award. A citation. A press release. What exactly?

Then Lionel said, 'Maybe we shouldn't make such a big fuss about it. There is a rumour she committed suicide, after all.'

'Did she? I didn't know that.'

Doubts and rumours filled the room.

Much nodding and muttering.

The committee pondered for an hour and did nothing.

Desiree Mitford Holloway would soon be forgotten. There would always be a bigger, brighter star next year. There always was.

Nothing ever changed, not really.

There wouldn't be a Sir Fred Berrington Memorial Trophy though, leastways, not the original. They didn't even get back the few mutilated pieces of scrap metal that were found. A month later the gawky girl in the glasses was delighted to receive a gleaming replica.

It didn't bother her for a second. Why should it?

Chapter Forty-Five

Walter glanced back at the coffee table. At the bottles. Three full bottles, different coloured caps. They looked like spent indigestion relief bottles. They weren't spent any longer. They were full of scarlet liquid. Looked like blood to him, and he had seen plenty of that in the previous thirty years.

There was another smaller container too, a phial, he'd guess that's what you'd called it. Clear glass, clear liquid inside, tiny white label, tiny white print. He squinted, but couldn't read a thing.

He knew his best chance was to engage the man in black in conversation, to play for time. Walter's hostage dealing training kicked in. He'd been on a refresher course only six months before. Mrs West's idea, and for once she might have been right. Cresta Raddish would have loved it, been in her element, trying to read the mind of the hostage taker, concentrating on the central issue of having the hostage released in one piece. It was the only thing that mattered, except in this case, Walter was the hostage.

'So,' said Walter, 'how did you get into cross-dressing?'

The man was busy putting out another item on the table like a stallholder setting up at an antique fair.

Walter didn't like the look of that one either.

It was a large syringe.

The man in black let slip a sarcastic little laugh. A girlish laugh.

'Well?' persisted Walter. 'Did you get your rocks off on it? Was it Desiree Holloway? Was it her idea? Was she into all that kinky stuff?'

'You don't know anything!'

'You're right, I don't, but I'd like to. If you are going to kill me, what's the harm in telling me, you might as well, you're not ashamed of it, are you?'

'Course not!'

'So how did you get into it? And what do I call you, by the way? You must have a name.'

'Sam, you can call me Sam.'

266

'So, how did it happen, Sam, your idea or hers?'

'I know what you are after!'

'I'm not after anything. I'm hardly in a position to be after anything, am I?' said Walter, glancing down at the hand ties.

'Yes, well, just so long as you understand that. If I were in your position, I'd be saying a few prayers to your God, if I were you, if you believe in that kind of thing. You haven't much time left.'

'Do you believe in God, Sam?'

He thought about that for a second.

'Yes, maybe, sometimes.'

'And you're ready to meet him, knowing what you have done?'

'God will be merciful. And anyway, I have a sneaking suspicion that God is a woman.'

'That's a novel take.'

'Let's face it, Walter; none of us has any idea what God is like. God could be a gigantic chicken for all we know, and imagine how angry that great Cock in the sky will be when we meet it. Had chicken for dinner, did you? That's not going to go down well, is it? Sorry God, I've been eating your children for these past fifty years.'

That little laugh again. Some people might find that attractive. Predatory men, for example. This guy would be in big demand in a high security prison. How would he cope with that? Maybe he'd like it. Maybe it was time to change the subject.

'Tell me about Desiree?'

'Just you remember, Darriteau, this time tomorrow, you'll be long gone! Kaput!'

'There's not a lot I can do about that.'

'You are right there, pal!'

'Tell me about Desiree?'

'What do you want to know?'

'Everything. I've got time,' and forgetting his dire situation for a second, Walter couldn't keep a sly grin from spreading over his drooping chops.

'That's one thing you don't have!'

Walter glanced at the clock.

'It's only quarter past eleven. I'm not due on till eight. No one will miss me till nine. That's ten hours away. We've got plenty of time.

Tell me about Desiree? After all, it's what this thing's all about, isn't it?'

Sam backed away. Sat in the chair in the corner. Crossed his legs. Thought a moment.

'She was strikingly beautiful, not classically beautiful, but once you'd seen her, you'd never forget her.'

A moony look came over his fair face, the kind of look Jenny Thompson occasionally portrayed when she was reading those love novels in the lunch break.

'She meant a lot to you?'

'She was everything to me! She said we were soul mates. I was her other half, and she sure as hell was mine.'

'And you started wearing her clothes. Was that before she died, or afterwards?'

'Before, don't be ridiculous, long before!'

'Why did you do that?'

He closed his eyes, as if remembering, as if he were thinking things through, as if he didn't want to answer, as if maybe he was ashamed of the answer, thinking he might come across as some kind of weirdo.

'You can tell me, Sam, I'm going to meet my maker, remember. No one will ever know.'

'Just so long as you understand that! When we have finished talking, that stuff,' and he pointed to the bottles, 'is going into you!'

Walter glanced back at the table, and the bottles.

Didn't like what he saw.

'What's with the different coloured tops?'

Sam smiled. 'RGB, red, green, blue.'

'I can see that. What's the difference?'

Sam grinned again, not so pretty this time.

'Red… is rat. Green… is great ape; chimpanzee, to be exact. Blue is basset hound, pretty doggy to you and me. And the thing is, Walter, I am going to give you the choice of which you'd prefer. Interesting, eh?'

It was interesting all right, but not that interesting, and anyway Walter didn't appreciate the thread of conversation, preferred to talk about Desiree Holloway, didn't want to talk about the blood in the bottles at all. But before he could say anything, Sam was talking again.

'Come on, Wally; rat, doggy, or chimp?'

'I can't possibly decide that.'

'You don't make a decision, you get them all! And you get them now!'

It was a threat that Walter took seriously. Talking about it seemed to rile the guy, and that was always frowned on in hostage school. Rule number one: Never make the hostage taker mad, never antagonise them. Another rule broken. It wasn't the first; and sure as hell wouldn't be the last.

'What's in the glass phial?'

'Ah, now that's an interesting question. It's what we call witches' brew. Blow you away, it would, blow the whole street away, come to that, I haven't decided yet what I'm going to do with it. But take it from me, Wally baby, you don't want to get too close to it.'

'Suits me, Sam.'

'Red, green, or blue? Last chance!'

'Green.'

Sam relaxed in the chair.

'Great ape! Good choice. Any reason?'

'Our nearest living relative; seemed logical.'

Sam nodded and said, 'I'd have chosen green too, if I were in your shoes,' and he went into thinking mode again, and Walter didn't want that. You could never tell what the guy was thinking about, or what he would do next.

Walter said, 'Tell me more about Desiree?'

Sam smiled at her memory. He couldn't help himself.

'Tell me about how you got into cross-dressing.'

'Why should I?'

'I'm trying to paint in the background, to understand everything about the case, about you. It'll let me die happy, my last dying wish, if you like.'

'Desiree didn't die happy!'

'Why not? Tell me about it, Sam; it will do you good to get it off your chest. Why didn't Desiree die happy?'

'It's very complicated.'

'I am sure it is. We've got time, Sam. Tell me everything about Desiree. She sounds such a fascinating person. I'd really like to know.'

'She was a genius.'

'Really? A genius. Wow!'

Sam nodded.

'Far too good for this world.'

'Tell me all about Desiree, Sam, it's killing me not knowing.'

Pretty boy giggled.

'It's killing you knowing, that's your problem.'

'I can live with that.'

'You can die with it too.'

'We all have to die sometime.'

'Yeah, but not today, eh?'

He lifted his right hand and made a gun shape and pointed it at Walter's head and said, 'Bang, bang, you're toast.'

'Tell me about Desiree, Sam... please.'

It was the please that did it. Sam always knew he was a soft touch.

'You really want to know?'

'Yeah. Sure. Everything.'

'One condition.'

'Name it.'

'You don't tell anyone,' and he did that pretty boy laugh again.

'Agreed,' said Walter.

'All right, Walter, Wally, Inspector Darriteau. Why did you never make Superintendent, by the way? Don't answer that, I can guess, not clever enough, eh, sticks out a mile, now where were we?'

'You were going to tell me about Desiree.'

'Yeah, you got it, all right; just this once, and afterwards you get the green.'

'If that's what you want.'

'It is what I want.'

'You're the man.'

'Don't you forget it!'

Chapter Forty-Six

DC Gibbons arrived at Thomas Telford house at five past ten. Went to the door and pressed fifty. Karen's metallic voice appeared to one side of the door. 'Hello?' she croaked.

'Hi there.'

'Come on up,' and the door sprang open.

Up in the flat Karen whispered, 'Do you fancy a beer?' opening the fridge and demonstrating the well packed shiny green cans.

'Nah, rather have a coffee.'

She rather liked that. She'd always considered Gibbons to be some kind of boorish lager lout. She set the coffee machine burbling and told him to go through to the lounge area.

'How do you like it?' she said, straining what remained of her voice.

'Milk, dash of shug-shug.'

She brought the mug in and set it on the coffee table, and sat on the two-seater sofa. He was sitting in the chair by the window. The curtains or blinds or whatever she had, were still wide open, and he could see the headlights of cars dashing along the inner ring road, and occasionally heard the sound of a honking impatient driver or the beep-borp of an ambulance. The sodium light glistened on the damp road and bounced off the contrasting flat and still waters of the canal. It was a peaceful picture. It was a nice place to live. Gibbons couldn't wait to have a gaff like it.

'So,' she said, struggling to get out words. 'How goes it?'

'Yeah, good, Walter thinks we might make an arrest tomorrow.'

'Yeah? Really?'

'Yeah, that address you gave him, came up with a weird couple, Sam and Samantha Holloway. Walter thinks they are the same person, away today, back tomorrow, apparently. We're going in early doors to the flat next door. When they, or he or she, or it comes home, we'll be waiting.'

'God, I hope so. That's a relief, I can tell you. Have we been inside their place yet?'

'Nope, search warrant all ready, being turned over tomorrow.'

'It was Walter who put me on to it,' she said.

'Yeah, how?'

'He figured out it was someone with a major grudge. Holloway was the one that stuck out. Obvious really when you think about it.'

'It's always obvious afterwards.'

'Yeah, suppose so, I vaguely remember this guy, coming to the station three or four times, demanding that we investigate a suicide further, his girlfriend apparently. I never saw him myself, just remember the desk sergeant going on and on about this bloody nuisance who kept coming back. He was boring the life out of him.'

She coughed and tried to clear her throat. Perhaps she shouldn't be talking at all, thought Gibbons, and he said, 'So he thought, this guy, that the suicide was murder?'

'Must have done.'

'And could it have been?'

'Nah, several witnesses said she jumped in front of the train, middle of the morning. No doubt.'

'Bloody way to go.'

'Terrible way. The station was unusually crammed.'

'All pressed up against one another?'

'Yep, probably.'

'So someone behind could have given her the slightest of nudges, just enough to send her over the edge, and I suppose it was possible no one saw it.'

'Maybe. We'll never know now.'

'So his girlfriend is killed, accident, murder or suicide, we don't know which, and he broods about it for quite a while, and then goes on a murdering spree. Does that sound right to you?'

'Maybe, maybe not. Looks like something must have sent him or her over the edge. Maybe we'll find out tomorrow.'

'I bloody hope so; this case has gone on long enough.'

'You can say that again,' she said, reaching forward for her ice-cold cranberry juice she was sipping.

'What do we know about the dead girlfriend?' asked Gibbons.

'Not much. Bit of a high flyer. Worked in some chemical company down on the Cheshire-Shropshire border, from what I recall.'

'And what did the guy do?'

'Don't know, no idea, don't think we ever knew. Did you find out anything yesterday?'

'Jenny was telling me the old lady living next door said he was a writer; and a successful one, too. Apparently he'd won a million dollar contract in the States.'

'Do you believe that?'

Gibbons pulled a face. 'Seems far-fetched to me. Perhaps he's a Walter Mitty type guy.'

'Yeah, that rings true. Hopefully, we'll find out tomorrow.'

Gibbons sipped coffee.

'There's something that's worrying me,' she said. 'Something doesn't fit. It's why I asked you over.'

'Yeah, like what?'

'He tried to murder me, right?'

Gibbons drained his drink and said, 'Yep, he did.'

'Well, he now knows he didn't succeed, doesn't he?'

'He does if he watches telly.'

'Bound to, these people get off on publicity.'

'So what are you saying?'

'That he might come back, try again. Come here, maybe.'

'No, he can't. Does he know where you live?'

'Hope not, but we all know with the bloody Internet you can always find out where anyone lives if you try hard enough.'

'Don't worry about it. This time tomorrow he'll be behind bars.'

'Yeah, but he's not yet, is he? I don't want to be alone. Could you stay over tonight? Sleep in the spare room? I'd feel a lot safer.'

Gibbons pulled a happy face. 'Sure, if that's what you want.'

'It is; thanks. I appreciate it.'

Chapter Forty-Seven

Sam sat in the chair in the corner and closed his eyes tight. A picture of Desiree flooded into his head. It was so realistic, so colourful; so close, he could almost touch her, smell her; it was as if she was there with him. A contented expression spread over his cute face, and his eyes opened and he realised she wasn't there at all. His face turned sour. Not a good moment for Walter.

Then Sam said, as if remembering he'd told Walter he would tell him all about her before he put him out of his misery, put him out of this world for good like an old dog being put down.

'We were exactly the same size.'

'You and Desiree?'

Sam bobbed his head. 'Yep, identical, except for her narrower waist and boobies, of course. Same height, same weight, same shoe size. We seemed to fit together like two pieces of a jigsaw. I'd never experienced anything like it before, and she said exactly the same thing.'

'Go on.'

'We'd been out to dinner, some expensive place, she was doing so well in her work, didn't mind paying, can you imagine that, a wonderful, beautiful woman who couldn't get enough of me, and she paid as well!'

'For the meal?'

'Course for the meal. What do you think, sex? Geez, Desiree would never have to pay for sex; they were queuing round the block for her. She told me the other guys at work were always making passes at her, and back at uni too, almost every bloody day.'

'What happened next?'

'We had an extra bottle of wine; shouldn't have done, I suppose, but we did.'

'And all inhibitions flew out the window?'

Sam smiled at the memories.

'You could say that.'

274

'And?'

'Are you getting your rocks off on this, Walter? You dirty old bugger.'

'I am trying to understand.'

'Yeah, sure, I believe you, thousands wouldn't.'

'Well?'

'I took her dress off.'

'And?'

She said, 'Put it on.'

'I will if you will.'

'And you did?'

'Yeah, anything for a bit of fun. I mean not just the dress, every goddamned thing, knickers, suspenders, stockings, the whole shebang. She insisted on it. Her, standing there in my best suit and tie. She made me fix up the tie for her, she couldn't do it herself, me in her red shoes, her in my shiny black ones, oh man, it was a weird sight, and then she started on the makeup.'

'She made you up?'

'Yeah, made me up good and proper. Have you ever worn red lippy, Walter?'

Walter grinned at the thought. 'Don't think it would suit me.'

'No, you're probably right.'

'You enjoyed it?'

'I bloody did. That was the weird thing about it, never had any cross-dressing ideas before, but with her, it just seemed to be the most natural thing in the world.'

Natural behaviour wasn't how Walter would describe it.

Then she said: You need a wig... and tits.'

'There's nothing I can do about that.'

'No, she said, but leave it with me,' and we stood in front of the mirror, hand in hand, her in my grey suit, white shirt and tie, me in her red party frock, and lippy, drunkenly grinning at our images. 'You make a fabulous woman,' she said, and I have to admit, I did. I'd have fancied me if I'd seen that person in the mirror strolling through Tattersalls at the races on Ladies' Day. You would have too, Walter, I guarantee it.'

'Maybe I would.'

'She didn't make such a great guy, and I think she knew that. She didn't look like a guy, and secretly I think she was happy about that, and I sure as hell was, and then we slowly undressed each other, and you can guess the rest.'

'You made love?'

'You really want to know all the freaky little details, don't you, Walter? You naughty boy. Yes, we made love, but more than that, we made love like we had never done before, 'cept perhaps the first time, and afterwards Desi said exactly the same thing, and I believed her. She was freaky that way. Something had gone down at college. I think she had a wild time there. I never found out exactly what. But I'll tell you one thing, Walter, if your sex life is ever in a rut, put on a red frock and some lippy. You'll be amazed at the results, except, shame, it's too late for you now, Walter, isn't it? So don't go getting any crazy ideas. But at least you'll pass over with the benefit of my expertise.'

Walter's sex life was infrequent at best, but that was his business, and he had no intention of discussing it with the freak.

'I'll take your word for it.'

'Do you know what, Walter? I fancy a coffee. Have you got any coffee in? You don't mind if I help myself, do you? Course you don't,' he said, standing and giggling and patting him on the shoulder, and heading for the door, and then he said, 'You won't mind if I don't make you one, I'm not feeding you.'

'Help yourself. It's instant.'

'That'll do, and a pee while I'm at it,' and he went into the kitchen and put on the kettle, and ran up the stairs to the bathroom.

Walter bent down and tried to bite through one of the plastic ties. His teeth were not what they once were. He didn't make any progress, and visions of exploding teeth filtered into his head. Better to be alive with no teeth than dead with intact ones. Tried again, came off; looked at his handiwork, slight marks, nothing more. It wasn't going to work. Tried to stand up. Quite impossible. Tried to shake the chair toward the coffee table. Didn't go anywhere. Swung from side to side. Imagined he could turn the whole chair over, but with what intent? A picture came into his head of himself lying face down on the floor with the heavy chair on his back, like a bloated turtle, and Sam coming back and laughing and leaving him there,

276

undignified and uncomfortable, and vulnerable to injections from the rear. No, at least sitting there, up straight, he could see what the maniac was doing.

The cistern was running. He'd flushed the bog. Then he came down the stairs, singing or humming. The guy was a head case, no doubt about that, jauntily, making himself at home, went through to the kitchen, made a mug of black coffee, and came back and carefully set it on the table, next to the blood; rat, chimpanzee, and basset hound, and instant coffee, a strange mixture, the steam curling and rising away.

'I hope you don't mind me saying, Walter, but your kitchen and bathroom could both do with a bloody good clean.'

Walter rolled his eyebrows. He knew that to be true. He did once have a cleaner, but she was most unreliable, and often turned up smelling of gin. One morning she went up to clean the bathroom and Walter heard nothing more for the best part of an hour. Went upstairs and found her sleeping it off on his bed. He couldn't be doing with that, and Mrs Gretton received her notice, swore at him she did, called him a jumped up black fucking bastard! It was nothing he hadn't heard a million times before. Walter laughed it off, but had never got round to finding a replacement. If he got out of this jam, he would.

Sam picked up the coffee, cupped it in his hands, sat in the chair in the corner, and peered across at the dozy cop.

'Now where were we?' he said. 'Oh yes, I was about to tell you about the wig 'n' tits. Do you know something, Walter? You were right; I really am enjoying getting this off my chest. It's therapeutic. But don't go getting any ideas, remember, it's great ape for you, my man, just as soon as we have finished.'

'Wig 'n' tits?' said Walter, eager to keep the conversation flowing.

'Ah yes, they were amazing, those tits.'

'Yeah?'

'They were just like the real thing. Not like those ugly comedy jobs you see blokes strapping on the front of their shirts on rag days. No, these looked dead real, and felt real too. God knows where she got them, said they cost her sixty-five quid, came in the morning post, said cancer babes bought them, money well spent, I'd say. Stuck on my chest natural like, God knows how, no glue or nothing, just

277

natural adhesion. On they went, followed by Desi's red bra, and Bob's your uncle... or your aunty, to be more accurate. They were part of me, unmovable, except for the occasional flirtatious wobble. I've never been a hairy guy myself, never was, even now I only have to shave once a week, and it's more down than bristle, caused me all kind of angst during my teenage years, I can tell you, and I've always waxed my chest too, so they seemed like a natural extension. When I was younger, I always knew I wasn't gay, never fancied a bloke, ever, but I wasn't butch either, not like the other guys, different somehow, it was very confusing. Knocked my confidence, it did.'

'I can understand that.'

'Then she brought out the wig. Blonde bob thing it was, amazing, cost a packet, there was nothing cheap about Desi, and she did the makeup and painted my fingers and toes and dressed me, and when I looked in the wardrobe mirror afterwards, it was like there was a stranger in the room. I was looking round to see where I was because there were these two beautiful women, chatting and laughing as girls do, sipping a glass of white wine, and I was absent, missing, kind of vanished.'

Walter nodded as if he understood everything.

'Then Desi said, let's go out, and I was so unsure about the idea, but she insisted, called me a scared bitch, which kind of worked. So we rang for a cab, went to the station, and jumped a train to Manchester. Had lunch in the big hotel on the square, what's it called, The Albert, is that it? I can't remember, but as we were sitting in the lounge afterwards over coffee, these two ultra smart Dutch businessmen came in and sat close by, and starting hitting on us. Told us they were in electronics. Millionaires, they said, over here to buy some big company in Bolton. Thought it might impress us. Desi couldn't stop grinning at me, as these two handsome guys were pestering us for a dinner date that night.'

'They had no idea?' said Walter.

'Not an inkling! Man, it was weird, and then Desi suggested we went to the loo and that was weird too. The first time I had ever been inside a Ladies' lavatory. No one looked at me twice. Mind you, checking out some of the dogs in there, it wasn't surprising. These days I've become quite used to it. Occasionally, I make to go in there when I'm dressed as a man. Walter, you wouldn't believe

278

how confusing life can be. Then we went back to the coffees, and the guys, and gave our apologies and made to leave, and the tall guy stood up and grabbed my arm, and tugged me to one side and asked for my phone number. Just like that, practically begged me for it, said I was the most beautiful English woman he had ever seen, in that cute Dutch accent they have, and yes, I know he probably used that line on all the women, but hell, I didn't know what to do. Said the first thing that came into my head. Said I was engaged, and that Martin wouldn't approve, but by God, he was a persistent bugger. I didn't know men could be like that, refusing to take no for an answer.'

'How often did you go out with Desi dressed as a woman?'

'Couple of times a month, we'd make a big deal of it, get all dressed up, go somewhere really swanky, every time we went to Manchester for sure, hang around all the boutiques and department stores, sampling the perfumes, trying on ridiculous dresses, me sitting and waiting in the hairdressers while Desi had her black locks done, me reading Cosmo and giggling, as Desi had her nails done, and then she insisted I had my nails done too, fingers and toes. God, I thought the assistant must surely know, but she didn't, it was so exhilarating, and afterwards we'd scurry home to Chester and screw each other senseless. Geez, Walter, I can't find the words to describe it. Best days of my entire life. Best days.'

Walter allowed a decent pause. Sam had that far distant look back on his face. Then Walter said, 'You were in love with her?'

'Course I was! What do you think? Isn't it obvious? Head over heels, completely and utterly. I was mad for her. I'd never felt that way about anyone before. Never.'

'And she loved you?'

'Yeah, I think she did, though I know she found it hard to love anyone. That bastard at uni really hurt her. Messed with her mind. I have no idea what he did to her, and I don't want to know, and she never told me. But sometimes she'd wake up crying in a cold sweat, mumbling, Stop Toby, Stop! And I didn't think it was sex she was talking about.'

'What then?'

'Torture, my friend, that's how it came across to me. The bastard tortured her.'

Walter pulled a sympathetic face.

'That's when I asked her to marry me.'

'Marry you?'

'Yeah, right there at half-past three in the morning. The bed sheets soaked with her terrified sweat. I held her in my arms and asked her to marry me.'

'What did she say?'

'She said she couldn't possibly marry me; she couldn't marry any man because she never wanted to lose her name. She wanted to be famous, she was determined to be famous, and she wanted to be known as Desiree Mitford Holloway, and nothing else. I always knew she would achieve that too. She was so special in every way. Once she'd decided on something, hell itself wouldn't get in her way.'

'So what did you do?'

'I told her I wasn't an ordinary man. I think she knew that by then, and I told her we could still get married, and if need be, I would change my name to hers. I think that impressed her. I think it made a difference. You can do that, you know, if you really want to, if you go through the right legal procedures. It doesn't have to be the woman taking the man's surname, you can do it the other way round, so she agreed, and that's what we did. Got married in Chester Registry office as soon as we could, just a couple of friends there, and afterwards we flew to Barcelona for our honeymoon, and the moment we arrived we slipped on two identical little black dresses and hit the town. Wicked, it was, wicked. The club scene there is second to none. The best honeymoon ever, the best. It's all down in my diary. Did I tell you I keep a diary, Walter, have done for years, it's very therapeutic, Sammy Pepys had nothing on me. You should try it, but then again, it's too late for you, pal, isn't it?'

Walter ignored the question and said, 'So you were deliriously happy, and it stayed that way?'

'Damned right it did! We'd have our little quarrels like any couple, but when we made up, we really made up! I'd have spent my entire life with her. I never wanted to be with anyone else. I'd still be with her now... except you bastards murdered her.'

The spiteful look crashed back onto his face.

He stared across at Walter as if he were personally responsible.

'What do you mean?'

'You know damn well what I mean!'

'I don't, Sam, I don't, you tell me.'

Sam frowned. The black guy was playing for time. Sam knew that, and he was running out of patience. Stared at the blood. Stared at the syringe. Stared at the copper.

Walter saw him looking, pondering.

'Tell me about Desiree's death, Sam? Please.'

Chapter Forty-Eight

Karen glanced at the digital clock. It was ten to midnight. She'd enjoyed her chat with Gibbons, but she was tired and weak and began yawning. Gibbons yawned too. 'I'm going to have to go to bed,' she said, 'I'll show you the spare room.'

'Great,' he said, 'I'll just slip to the bathroom.'

Five minutes later he was in the spare room, in bed. He was knackered; it had been a long shift; it had been a long month.

In her room, Karen lay on her back staring out at the blackness, revisiting the horror of being yanked from the lavatory, being hung out to die. She knew she would never forget it. She wondered what kind of person could do that. To cold bloodedly attempt to murder someone they had never met, in a busy public place, without any fear of being discovered, and having no qualms about what they were doing. She wondered where he was now, the killer, and what he was doing, and who he was terrifying. Samuel Holloway, she contemptuously spoke his name, and she knew she wouldn't rest until he was stopped.

Walter peered across at the clock. Both the hands were super erect. Outside he could hear the old church bell announcing the new day, chiming across the city, somehow comforting, floating on the night air, and he wondered if the new day might be his last. Think positively! Always engage hostage takers in conversation.

'Tell me why you think we killed Desiree?'

'I don't think, I know!'

'But why?'

'You know why!'

'I don't, Sam, I don't. Please explain.'

Sam scowled and shifted in his chair. Thought the black guy was taking the piss, but he could wait a little while longer before he put him to sleep. Maybe he should recall and replay what happened to Desiree one last time, for her sake, to remind the copper of exactly

282

what they had done. Not that he didn't know already. Yeah, that's what he'd do. He'd go over it one final time for Desi's sake, and then he'd kill him. For certain. He'd murder him, sitting in that chair, in his own front room, and he was looking forward to it.

'Desi began bringing stuff home.'

'What kind of stuff?'

'Information, theories, samples, experimental stuff, top secret stuff, weird stuff, stuff most people wouldn't want in the house.'

Walter glanced at the table. Saw the bottles. Red, Green, Blue. Rat, great ape, basset hound. 'Like the stuff on the table?'

Sam nodded.

'Why did she do that?'

'She worried her work might be taken from her, appropriated by someone else. Eden Leys had a history of it. You know how it works, some brilliant scientist in her twenties or thirties makes a ground-breaking discovery, some supervising scientist in his sixties, looking for one last hurrah, jumps in and grabs the credit. She said it happened all the time, been going on for years. She said the senior ones said that was how things worked. They always looked after the older guys, the younger ones had plenty of time to break new ground, to make their name, and that they, when they were old, would be looked after by the younger ones in turn.'

'The world doesn't work like that,' said Walter.

'Damned right it doesn't!'

'So what happened?'

Sam pointed at the table.

'That blood came from animals she'd personally killed. She said she'd kept it for their memory. It kept her grounded. It kept her focused. Normally, it would be disposed of, thrown away, flushed down the drain. She said that wasn't right. Disrespectful, she said.'

Walter nodded, tried hard to imagine the fate of those unfortunate creatures, and especially the chimpanzees.

'So what happened then?'

'There was an Australian guy, I forget his name. He was always creeping round her when she was working; looking for hints of what she was up to, where she was going. He knew she was brilliant. She knew he would steal her stuff, given the chance. He was all smiles and charm, he'd take her down to the social club they had going on

283

the site, buy her a bottle of wine, and pump her for info. She grew wise to that; began feeding him duff stuff. The schmuck was so thick he took it all in and worked on it for weeks. It led nowhere, down a dead-end corridor, and you have to laugh at that. You had to admire her cunning. Not only was she pioneering her own work, she was staying up all night setting up faux avenues for pricks like him, theories that looked promising, and all the while they were nothing more than gigantic time-wasting exercises. Futile diversions. He was furious when he found out. Can you imagine? Wouldn't speak to her for weeks. Started spreading rumours about her, telling tales behind her back, said she was a lesbian, all sorts.'

'I can imagine.'

'Can you, Walter? Can you?'

'I think so. I'm on her side. What happened next?'

'She began bringing data home. Reams and reams of the stuff. Several years' work. I asked her if it would be missed. She said it was mainly copies she'd printed. She wanted it in case the originals ever went missing, or were stolen, or destroyed in a fire or accident of some kind Or in case she was relieved of her post.'

'She was worried about that?'

'Petrified. The place had a history of dumping high fliers who made life uncomfortable for the middle grounders who wielded the power. The brilliant ones put the dull ones firmly in the shade. There was an enormous amount of jealousy and backbiting. You wouldn't believe some of the stories she told me.'

'Did she have any trouble getting it out?'

'Not at the beginning. Security was a joke. She'd wear a long, heavy skirt with a big hem on the inside. I modelled it for her, as she did the alterations. There was a large false pocket inside. She showed me how she'd slip a file in there like a kangaroo's Joey and walk back to her car and drive away. If the guards stopped her, it was only to say hello, or maybe to wink at the striking dark girl, perhaps ask her for a date. At worst there was a casual glance in the boot of her car. They may have wondered what was beneath her neat skirt, but they would have been amazed to discover what was really there.'

Sam giggled in that pretty way of his.

'And then?'

'There was a big step up in security. They brought in new people. Everything changed. It was much harder to get anything out. That was about the time she started being followed.'

'People were following Desi?'

'Yes.'

'Who?'

'Your lot, of course.'

'What do you mean; my lot?'

'Government police, security police, how the hell do I know?'

Walter puffed out his cheeks, breathed out heavily.

'I can't see that,' he said, 'I certainly knew nothing about it.'

'Course you wouldn't. It was MI7.'

Walter zipped a sharp laugh through his nose.

'Now I know you're wrong, Sam. MI7 doesn't exist, except in the minds of spy writers, and in the movies.'

'No, no, no, you're wrong! MI7 exists. They followed and killed Desi. I know it may be unpalatable to you, Wally, but that's the truth. That's what happened!'

'MI7 existed during World War II,' said Walter. 'It dealt with propaganda and stuff like that, but it was disbanded, early sixties, I think it was. It doesn't exist anymore.'

Sam did the same sharp, dismissive laugh.

'Shows how much you know, Wally. Stop living up to your name, shows how out of touch you really are.'

Walter remained quiet for a moment, thinking things through, then said, 'Tell me everything you know about MI7?'

'Desiree told me it was reactivated soon after it was decommissioned. They had special responsibility for chemical warfare secrecy, weapons of mass destruction in the modern vernacular, hence their huge interest in Eden Leys. They were interested in everything that went down there. You must know that, and they weren't happy when the plant was semi-privatised, I can tell you that. For a short while they were replaced with contracted in security. That feeble lot couldn't detect an ant in an ant hill. Not surprisingly, they soon got pushed. Desi became tense. I couldn't get her to open up to me. I knew something was wrong. She said the whole place was subject to new American secrecy orders, she was bound to silence. It was too dangerous for me to know anything.

285

She had this spare bedroom full of stuff, data, samples; you name it, a huge amount of gear. She said we had to move it, and quick, so we switched it from her place by the river, down to mine at Iona House. We always kept on both properties and it was a good job we did. It took us three car rides to move everything, that'll give you some idea how much gear was involved. We did it on the Friday night. On the Saturday night we went out to celebrate, got dressed up, kissing cousins she called us, Desiree and Samantha, took a cab down to that fancy hotel in Cheshire where they do the ballooning, enjoyed a fab meal, danced for hours, curled up in bed together, made love, got up late on the Sunday morning, fab breakfast, cab back to Chester...'

'And?'

'Desi's place had been ransacked. Made a hell of a mess. We called the cops round. It wasn't you, was it? Don't answer that, I know it wasn't. They said there had been a spate of opportunistic burglaries in the area. Oh yeah, I'll bet, the ransackers, whoever they were, made it look realistic by breaking in and turning over the two neighbouring gaffs for good measure, but Desi knew was MI7. That's what she said as soon as the regular cops had gone, and I believed her. She also said the Aussie bastard had tipped them off.'

'Why did they do that? Break in and ransack the place.'

'Looking for evidence, of course!'

'Evidence of what?'

'Oh, come on, Walter, keep up, man! They were trying to find evidence that she was leaking stuff outside, taking stuff off prem. They thought she was feeding info to a third party, but the only third party was me. If we hadn't moved everything, Desi would have been arrested. They would have thrown the book at her; thrown the key away. God knows what she would have been charged with. That night she told me if she ever had an accident, ever disappeared without warning, leaving a letter behind saying that she'd gone away, or ever died suddenly, it would be the work of MI7.'

'Where's the stuff now?'

Sam thought about that for a moment.

'I still have it. There's no harm in you knowing. The knowledge you have will be extinguished when you go,' and he glanced at his petite, girlish wristwatch, and said, 'I'd say, Walter, you have just entered your last hour.'

Walter needed to pee, but didn't say. He wanted to keep talking. There were still things he didn't understand.

'What exactly goes on at Eden Leys?'

'Don't you know?'

'Course not. You tell me.'

'They are experimenting on live human beings.'

Walter laughed again.

'Don't laugh like that! They are! I've got the proof. Some of it is in my spare room, but most of it, the juicy bits, including photographs and IDs, are locked away in a solicitor's office miles from here.'

A picture of the offices of Lambourn, Harcourt and Snapes flooded into Sam's mind, and their luxurious suite on the sixth floor of the Royal Liver Building, Liverpool. Those fab rooms staring out across the wide and murky river, and the huge storeroom in the basement that housed the gigantic safe, a piece of kit that was too heavy to be set up anywhere but on the ground itself. In that vast safe lay the evidence, Desi's life's work, Desiree's masterpiece. Proof of what was going on. Proof of why she had been murdered. Sam paused, switched off.

Walter switched him on again.

'Tell me about the experiments on living human beings?'

'What do you want to know?'

'Everything you do.'

Sam pursed his lips, sorted his thoughts into some kind of order, and began again.

Chapter Forty-Nine

Karen tossed and turned. She couldn't sleep. She slipped from the bed and went through to the kitchen. Poured another glass of ice-cold cranberry juice. Sipped and swallowed. Sipped and swallowed. Her throat felt as if a piece of barbed wire was jammed down there. Her eyes hurt and her hands shook. She expected him to return, the killer, maybe that night. He had tried and failed to murder her, and he now knew it too. He'd tried to kill her for a reason, the seventh death in his reign of terror.

Maybe there was some significance to the number seven.

Seven was a strange number. She knew that well enough. When a group of people are asked to name a number between one and ten a huge majority choose seven. Why? Some people say it is a lucky number. Racing car drivers fight to have it on their cars. Others say it is dreadfully unlucky.

Seven days in the week, the seventh day is the Sabbath, the holy day, seven deadly sins, seven sisters, seven dwarfs, seventh son of a seventh son, perhaps Sam was a seventh son of a seventh son, seven wonders of the world, seven sacraments, seven heavenly virtues, seven stations of the cross, seven years bad luck if you break a mirror, seven-year itch, seven murders, or at least six killings plus one attempted, and an old rhyme came back to her from when she was a little girl:

One means anger
Two means mirth
Three, a wedding
Four, a birth
Five is heaven
Six is hell
But seven's the very devil himself.

A strange thing to teach a kid, she thought, and amongst it all were seven murders… but he'd only completed six. He was coming back; of course he was coming back. She went through to the spare bedroom. The door was ajar. Eased it open. Rays of light fed in from the hallway. Gibbons was asleep, lying on his back, snoring like a child. He'd said he was dog tired. He certainly looked it. The duvet cover had slipped down, revealing his chest. He was surprisingly muscular; she would never have guessed it from the grubby and worn flappy shirts he liked to wear to work. Perhaps they were a fashion statement, like ripped jeans, though she doubted it.

She wanted to wake him and talk some more, but he looked serene and peaceful. It would be wicked to wake him, a sin. Never wake a sleeping person, her mother always used to say, it's a sin, unless it's an emergency. Was this an emergency? Maybe, maybe not. He'd surely think her crazy, his neurotic female sergeant. She didn't want that. She pulled the door closed and went back to bed.

Sam took a deep breath, reflecting on his words, and began again.

'Desi said she was on the cusp of a breakthrough in the quest to find a cure for dementia and Alzheimer's, and yes, I know Alzheimer's is a type of dementia, but some people think of them as separate diseases. She was working on producing a pill that could reverse the aging process in the human brain. The idea was it would protect the brain. It had worked on rats and apes and she was sure, with more tests, it could work on humans too. The opportunity to experiment on live human beings was one she could not turn down. She said one final push, and she'd crack it. She had been experimenting on apes for at least a year before that. It's not such a big step from apes to humans. The people were handpicked. They had no known relatives. They were terminally ill and not expected to survive for long.'

'So what happened to these people?'

'They all died, according to Desi. Every one of them. Cremated on site. She always went to the funeral services. Most times she was the only one there.'

'And their deaths were covered up?'

'You tell me, Walter. You're the detective.'

'I don't know. I know nothing about it. Did she make any progress?'

'Progress, yes, a cure? I'm not sure.'

'How many people are we talking about?'

Sam pulled a face.

'Don't know for sure, twelve, maybe twenty.'

Walter's turn to pull a face. Between twelve and twenty deaths, if the guy was to be believed. Legal deaths? Or Illegal? Murders or mercy killings? He didn't know, but he wanted to find out.

Sam was talking again.

'It wasn't just experiments on live humans that Desi did. She was obsessed with all aspects of progress in the field. Her father had been struck down with it. That made it personal. She wasn't interested in much else. She'd developed a theory called Distant Consciousness. It's an idea that in severe cases memories can be stimulated by documents and items from long ago. Everyday items, but objects dear to the heart, things associated with beautiful memories, precious events, such as a programme from the 1951 Festival of Britain, an occasion attended with a loved one, a fiancé, a life partner. Or maybe an early Elvis Presley record, or tickets to an early Beatles concert when no one outside of Merseyside had ever heard of them. Even football programmes from big games like the 1966 World Cup Final, that kind of thing, memory jolters, she called them. People who'd not shown any sign of recognition of anything for years, recognised those items. She had genuine success with it. She was communicating with them.'

'Go on.'

'She'd visit country nursing homes, study the patients, and bring her research data and techniques back to Eden Leys. Adding that to the secret live experiments, she told me she was this close to cracking it,' and Sam held his forefinger and thumb half an inch apart, and jabbed them into the air. 'This close, Wally! And then you bastards murdered her.'

'I didn't murder anyone.'

'You know what I mean!'

'Why seven, Sam?'

'MI7 were responsible. It was just a number, it seemed fitting at the time, it stuck in my mind, seven times one is seven. You had to pay seven times over. They all had to pay.' Sam glanced at his watch. 'You've got fifteen minutes left, Wally, fifteen minutes. Said your prayers yet?'

'There are still things I don't understand.'

'Tough luck! Fifteen minutes.'

'Tell me about the day Desi died.'

The guy sighed hard, but started talking again.

'She was on the way to London to pick up some top scientific award. A train had been cancelled. The station was packed. She was desperate for a seat. She had work to do. Her speech to complete. She was standing at the front. The train came in. A little nudge from behind. It could even have been done with a muscular chest, thrust forward at an opportune moment; that would have been enough. Over she went, out of this world, out of my life forever, my darling Desiree, my other half, my soul mate, my reason for living... murdered in cold blood in broad daylight in a public place by some government assassin.'

Sam looked away and stared at the wall.

Walter gave him a moment, then asked, 'How do you know all this?'

'I studied all the police reports I could lay my hands on. I had to bribe one guy in your department, there you are, one juicy titbit of gossip you can take with you. You've got a mole who will sell their soul, cost me three hundred nicker, worth every penny. Plus the coroner's statement, everything I could find. It was obvious your mob was convinced it was suicide from day one. You never really looked at alternatives. You didn't give Desi a chance. You'd made up your minds.'

'I was on holiday.'

'Gee bloody whiz! Well, that's you off the hook, isn't it! I don't think so!'

For once Walter didn't have an answer.

Sam snarled and started again.

'Along with what Desi told me about unexpected accidents, and how scared she was, I knew she had been murdered. I just knew.'

'But didn't you say she was upset about something in her past; that she woke from nightmares. Couldn't that have had something to do with it? Couldn't that have been preying on her mind?'

Sam thought a beat and said, 'She didn't commit suicide, if that's what you think. But she did once tell me she was hearing voices.'

'Voices?'

'Yeah, you know, nasty voices in her head ordering her about. I think it went back to that Toby Malone character. I'd like to have met him. I'd like to have killed him, but thankfully someone else got there before me. Good and bad in everything. Good, that he's long dead, bad, that I didn't eradicate the bastard first.'

'Could Desi have murdered Toby?'

'Don't be ridiculous!'

'Really? Are you so sure? She was used to death after all, and if he hurt her so much…'

'She didn't! But even if she did, he deserved it, and even if she did, it had nothing to do with her demise.'

'You don't know that!'

'I visited the cop shop seven times. Seven times, Walter. Seven bleeding times! Pleading with your people to reopen their inquiry. Begging them to start an investigation into everything that was happening at Eden Leys. And what did they do? Damn all! That's what. Bugger all!'

'I guess your enquiries never made it past the station sergeant. I could have a word about that.'

'Too late now!'

'They are overworked and underpaid and are snowed under with crazy people coming in and demanding all sorts. It's not excusable, but it is understandable, that occasionally they may send the wrong people away.'

'Like me, you mean?'

'Yes. Maybe. Like you.'

'So you concede I might have a case?'

'I'd like to look into it further.'

'Too late, mate. Far too late!'

'Tell me something about the Chester Mollesters thing, and the bad spelling.'

'Not much to tell. A futile attempt to mislead, I regretted it afterwards.'

The landline telephone in the hall rang.

They both jumped.

A phone ringing in the small hours is far louder than during the day. Walter glanced at the clock. Sam at his wrist. Five to one.

'Who the hell's that?' said Sam. 'Who'd be ringing at this time of night?'

'No idea, probably a wrong number.'

The phone rang for ages, maybe thirty, forty, double rings.

Sam didn't answer, just cursed it. It still rang.

'Whoever it is, they're a persistent bastard!'

The ringing stopped.

Sam sighed. He looked nervous.

Walter did too. He wanted to ask another probing question, preferably one that might produce a thirty-minute answer. For a moment his mind went blank. He really needed a pee.

The mobile atop the television set began leaking sound. Karen had programmed it to chime that awful seven-note ringtone, the one that sounded like water splashing off the roof. God knows how she did it. He didn't care, didn't like it either. Each note lower than the last, splash, splash, splash, splash, splash, splash, splash, stop. Then the same seven splashes again and stop. Seven. And again. Seven and again.

Sam jumped from the chair. Went to the phone. Picked it up. Saw who was calling. Grinned.

'It's time, Walter, it's time.'

'Who is it?'

'Who do you think?'

'I have no idea.'

'The lucky bitch.'

'Karen?'

'Yeah! The very same. You're only in this position because of her; you know that, don't you? If you hadn't saved her, I'd have vanished. Mission accomplished. I'd have cleared off to Barcelona. Happy memories there, you understand. I would have enjoyed a second honeymoon, all alone, yet not alone at all. Sometimes dressed as a lonely lady, a striking woman in mourning, a woman with admirers. Wealthy old businessmen would have paid court to me, felt sorry for me, sent me flowers, dinner invitations. Who knows, I might even have let them buy me jewellery... I might even have let them live. You would never have seen or heard from me again, except you couldn't stop interfering, in your size ten clodhoppers. Big mistake, Walter. Fatal mistake.'

Walter fired off another question, 'Why did you leave it so long afterwards, before you began killing people?' He was desperate to keep Sam talking, encouraged in knowing that Karen was awake, and thinking.

'I'd been considering it for ages, planning it, wondering how I might go about it. I guess I hoped you might see sense and reopen your enquiries. But you didn't, and there was no sign you would. And then that guy came along on the highway. It was a spur-of-the-moment thing. There he was, nodding at me, and there was my foot hovering above the accelerator; and something in my head was shouting: Don't stop! Do it! Do it now! And I did, and I don't regret it, not for a moment.'

'He was an innocent family man.'

'Tough shit!'

'A decent person, don't you have any regrets?'

'Desi was a decent person! Devoted to searching for cures to save mankind, and look what happened to her!'

Sam stood up and went to the sports bag, took out a large pair of gleaming scissors, held them in the air, practiced a few snips. 'I still hoped you might reopen Desi's case, that justice would prevail, that you might see sense, get it right for once, but no...' and his voice trailed away.

He was suddenly busy, scissors in hand, cutting into Walter's right shirt cuff, clean through, up to the wrist, careful not to snip the plastic tie, and then all the way up to the shoulder, cutting off the raggy bits, exposing Walter's flabby arm, his wrist still firmly fixed to the arm of the chair.

'I'll reopen the case, you'll get your justice; we'll open the whole damned can of worms.'

'Too little, too late, Wally! Time's up. Here we go.'

294

'And the different coloured eyes?' he said, desperate to say anything to prolong the conversation.

'You know the answer to that. Contact lenses, of course, you can have any colour you like. There's a place in Manchester that sells nothing but weirdly coloured lenses, fab it is. We built up quite a collection, red, yellow, black, gold, purple, you can have any colour eyes you want.'

Walter sniffed and said, 'I know someone who'd adore purple eyes.'

'Do you? Who?'

'You don't know her.'

'Who, Walter? Who?'

'Cresta.'

'Who's Cresta?'

'The profiler on the case.'

'Ah yes, Cresta Parsnip, or whatever she's called, I read about her in the Sunday supplements. American, isn't she?'

'Raddish, her name's Raddish. She's not American, just studied there. Crazy about the colour purple.'

'Yeah, well, I considered doing her, taking her down. But your sweet chick was a more enticing target. Are you plugging that girl, Walter?'

'No, course not. I'm old enough to be her father.'

'Doesn't stop a lot of men, Walter, in case you hadn't noticed.'

Walter shook his head and said, 'Which killing gave you the most satisfaction?'

'Oh, that's easy.'

'Which one?'

'The Right Reverend, of course, the railway killing. That was so sweet, so poetic. I thought of Desi every second, as he was crunched under the wheels. It seemed somehow appropriate that there he was, a man of God, meeting his maker in an identical fashion. God could chew on that, part payment for my Desi's loss. Had to be that one, didn't it?'

'I still don't understand why Desiree was killed.'

'She was killed, Walter, because she was stealing information, you moron! That's how they saw it; they couldn't prove it; so they eradicated the problem. Simple as that. One day there's a big difficulty, the next day there isn't. You are beginning to annoy me! Great ape, you say?'

Walter glanced up at the guy. He was standing like a bartender waiting for the drinker to choose his poison.

'I said: Great ape did you say?'

His eyes were wilder this time, didn't look like he'd brook an argument.

Walter nodded.

'Good man,' and he carefully unscrewed the green cap. Fixed a large needle on the syringe. Slipped it into the bottle. Carefully drew it back, fully loaded, scarlet blood, foreign blood, killing blood.

'Byes-e-bye, Walter baby, it's been nice knowing you.'

In went the needle.

Walter grimaced. Said nothing.

Down went the plunger. In went the blood.

Walter cursed. Stared at the syringe.

Stared at the blood as it left the vehicle, entering his body.

Nothing happened.

He wondered how long it would take.

Sam grinned.

Mission accomplished, at long last.

Seven times over.

Seven times one is seven.

Seven deaths.

Desi avenged, at last.

The fat black cop on his way to hell.

Desiree could sleep easy in her grave.

100 Ways to Kill People.

Inject an Inspector with the blood of a great ape, this time a murdered chimpanzee.

Poetic. Truly poetic.

'Time to be going, methinks,' he said, 'I don't want to be here when the cavalry arrives, if indeed they ever do. Bye-bye, Walter, have a nice death.'

'You're sick in the head. You should see someone.'

'And you my friend; are dying. Make the most of the tiny time you have left, and just to be on the safe side, to make sure there is no mistake this time, I think a dash of rat is called for, don't you?'

The killer grinned and picked up the red-topped bottle.
Walter shook his head. He still needed a pee.

Chapter Fifty

Karen and Gibbons jumped from the car. Ran toward the house, Karen stumbling, still weak. Gibbons helped her up. 'Go on!' she said. There was a dim light in the front room. Someone was in. Perhaps the old fool had fallen asleep in the chair. She joined Gibbons at the open front gate. 'How do we get in?' he whispered.

'There's a key,' she said, 'under a big stone. We came back late one night for a chat, he'd left his keys in the office, and he said there was a key under the stone, but it had been snowing and we couldn't even find the bloody stone.'

'Whereabouts?'

'By the peony, Walter said.'

'What does a peony look like?'

'No idea, try that big stone there.'

Gibbons turned over the stone, nothing but wriggly worms and pregnant earwigs caught out in the streetlight. Turned over another. Same as before. Turned over another one. Faint light glinted from a rusty key, half buried in the mud. He grabbed it, wiped it on his sleeve, and raced to the front door. Slipped it in the lock. Gently turned. The door opened, with Karen at his shoulder.

Muffled voices came from the front room. They ran to the doorway, looked in.

Walter was tied to the chair.

There was a slight guy standing over him, dressed in black, stupid grin on his face, a huge syringe in his hand loaded with scarlet liquid. More bottles on the table, one empty, one full, one half empty, plus another smaller, clearer container.

'Are you all right, Walter?' screamed Karen.

'Oh no sister, he isn't,' said the man in black. 'He's on his way to meet his maker, a gigantic chicken, we believe. Have any thoughts on the subject?'

Gibbons ran at the guy.

Sam turned toward him, syringe first, jabbing it in the air between them, snarling, 'Come on hero boy, want some?'

Karen staggered to the hall, thinking about the Glock she'd left at work, went to the kitchen, rummaged in drawers, came back with two old carving knives, one sharp, one not, slipped one to Gibbons. Sam looked nervous. Karen moved around to the guy's left, Gibbons to his right.

'You're finished,' said Walter. 'Finished! Give yourself up before you get hurt.'

Walter didn't look well. He needed a pee.

'Shut up, old man! It's you who's finished.'

Gibbons thrust the knife forward, tried to knock the needle from the guy's hand. What was in that thing?

Karen lurched at the guy from the left, almost fell over. Sam had expected it. She was loyal to the end and seeking revenge. He jabbed the needle toward her face, aiming for the eye, Karen swayed left, missed by a whisker, but the needle grazed her right earlobe, not enough time for him to press the plunger. In the scramble he'd taken the knife from her, yanked it clear from her weak grasp. He was strong. Much stronger than he looked. Surprisingly strong, but she already knew that.

Sam hurled the syringe at Gibbons while jabbing the knife at Karen. The loaded needle turned over in flight and bounced harmlessly from Darren's shoulder. Sam turned on the balls of his feet and flashed the carving knife at Gibbons.

Gibbons slashed back. Both missed. Karen glanced at Walter.

His mouth was open, and he was breathing heavy. He didn't look well at all.

Sam and Gibbons were jabbing at one another like feuding pirates.

Karen saw her moment, rushed in from the side, used the last of her strength, issued a left-handed forearm smash, cack handed. Walter remembered she always took people by surprise, every time. It knocked Sam off balance. Gibbons waded in. He dropped the knife. He'd never liked knives, flexed his muscles and punched the guy in the chest, a thundering blow to the torso, a professional strike, honed in the gym he adored.

Walter managed a grin. Sam went down, falling backwards, over the coffee table, squealing and panicking and scattering the bottles of blood, and the scissors and the empty coffee mug, shattering the glass phial. Shards of razor sharp glass slipped into his body, injecting clear chemical into the small of his back.

They stared down at the immobile man in black.

At his startled and panicked eyes.

At his trembling and unmoving body.

At his quivering and silent lips.

At his final movements and moments.

At his death.

'Don't touch anything!' yelled Walter. 'It's some kind of chemical weapon; you'll need to ring HAZCHEM. And call an ambulance. Quick! He's injected me with foreign blood. And cut me loose! And get me a bucket! I need a pee!'

Chapter Fifty-One

The following morning the police arrived at Iona House, earlier than planned, Karen, Gibbons and Jenny Thompson, but no Walter. He was getting fixed in the Countess hospital, having his blood changed, tests run, a lucky escape, no rat, but the chimpanzee had been removed, just in time, along with all the rest, though it had been a close call. 'Where's the big black chap?' asked Mrs Hymas.

Gibbons and Karen shared a look.

'The big black chap is unavoidably detained. He sent his apologies,' said Karen.

'Oh, really? That's a shame. I've made him some fairies specially.'

'Perhaps we could take him some back.'

'Oh yes, would you?'

'Sure,' said Karen. 'You don't have a key, do you, for flat number two?'

'No. Why? What time will Sam and Samantha be back?'

'Sam and Samantha won't be coming back.'

'No! Why? They haven't had an accident, have they?'

'You could say that,' said Gibbons.

'How terrible.'

'We have a search warrant,' said Karen, flashing the document before Mrs Hymas's face.

There was a momentary pause, and something clicked in her old watery eyes.

'They have been naughty, haven't they?'

'What makes you say that?' asked Jenny.

'They used to spin me yarns. They used to think I was doodle alley, senile, and I am not.'

'Did they?' said Gibbons. 'Tut tut tut.'

'What kind of yarns?' asked Karen.

'Oh, crazy things. They said if I was ever naughty, they'd wrap me in Christmas paper and throw me in the river at midnight. Silly

301

things like that. Only a joke I know, but sometimes it kept me awake at night.'

'You don't need to worry about anything like that any more,' said Karen. 'We're going into the flat; we'll come back and see you later.'

'Do you want me to come with you?'

'No, you're all right. You stay here.'

'Shall I put the kettle on?'

'Great idea, you do that.'

The officers smiled and nodded and left Mrs Hymas to her fairies, crossed the hall and stared at the stripped timber door. Karen followed procedure and knocked. No sound, no reply, no surprise. Gibbons took out a small jemmy from his deep trouser pocket, placed it on the rim of the door, applied pressure, his biceps bulging beneath his shirt as he began levering; Karen and Jenny both noticed that. Three seconds and the timber split with a loud crack. One more jerk, and the door flew open, two chunky and rusty wood screws tumbling to the hall floor, as if in protest at being disturbed.

The officers slipped on latex gloves and went inside, with Walter's parting words ringing in Karen's ears.

'Find me that diary; and any details of any documents deposited with a solicitor.'

They'd entered a large sitting room with views out over the front lawn and the driveway. Karen wasn't alone in wondering what had gone on in that room. It was pretty ordinary. A little old-fashioned, too. A leather settee, modern TV, nothing of any great interest, clean and tidy, well cared for, but no obvious diary. They went through to the kitchen. A large solid fuel stove, long since gone out, ideal for disposing of bloody clothing, Karen imagined. No evidence of any kind in there, and no body parts. Who knows what had gone through that furnace?

Into the bedroom, nice double bed, everything clean and neat and tidy. Opened the floor to ceiling wardrobe, fine clothes, and lots of them, expensive too, men and women's, dozens of shoes on the floor, all neatly stored side by side, again, men and women's, similar sizes, very expensive, Karen noted that, top ticket designer gear, better than she could afford, and sitting on the shelving to the right-hand side, were four white heads, polystyrene models, topped with

302

trendy styled wigs, four different colours, black, blonde, red, brown, and very smart.

Gibbons thought he recognised the black one.

'Look at these,' said Jenny.

She'd opened a bedside table. Five contact lens containers, five different coloured lenses.

'Explains a lot,' said Karen.

'And these!' said Gibbons, brandishing a pair of touchy feely breasts in front of his chest. 'They're fab, just like the real thing!'

'Put them down!' said Karen, grinning.

'What's he like?' said Jenny.

But still no diary. Karen thought it might have been in the bedside table, last chore of the day, maybe, before a peaceful night's rest, update the terror records; update the murder diaries. She returned to the inner hallway, opened the door to the second bedroom.

'Oh…my…God!'

The other two hurried to join her, peering over her shoulder at the noticeboard she was gawping at. Seeing her picture staring back, a blown up black-and-white photo culled from one of the news conferences. Through the middle of her face in scrawled red ink was a splashed handwritten cross.

Next to her image was one of Walter, a large red question mark next to his likeness, and an unmarked one of Cresta Raddish.

'Proof if proof be needed,' said Gibbons.

'Look at this lot!' said Jenny.

Karen and Gibbons swivelled round and saw the bottles of what looked like blood, and specimens of what appeared to be living tissue stored in formaldehyde, animal or human, it was hard to tell. The blood and samples were sitting on a tall teak shelving unit that housed clear glass bottles, containing God knows what substances, some labelled, some not, and binders containing computer printouts, large red notebooks, smaller secretary sized notepads, all full of neat handwriting. No obvious diary, not that Karen could see.

'Look at that,' said Jenny, pointing to a steel craft knife. The blade was retracted, the tool partly hidden behind one of the larger glass jars.

'Potential murder weapon for killing number five, I'd say,' said Karen.

'Remind me which one that was,' said Gibbons.

'Cripps, Jago Cripps,' added Jenny, 'the one at the flat.'

'Ah yes, that's the fella,' said Gibbons.

'Give me a bag,' said Karen.

Gibbons pulled a plastic bag from his pocket and unfastened the top, held it open; Karen took the knife and slipped it inside, and wondered what they would find next.

Pushed against the far wall was a computer desk. On top, an ultra modern computer and printer with failed red printed notices discarded to one side. Gibbons recognised them from the Ladies' loo.

Toilets Closed For Cleaning.

He said nothing, didn't want to remind Karen of that dreadful day.

'Maybe the diary's on the computer,' suggested Jenny.

'Could be,' said Karen. 'Boot it up, Gibbo.'

Gibbons fired up the machine as Karen turned back to the info wall. Practically every newspaper article ever written on the case was up there, some with rude comments and threats scrawled over them, others blank. Gave her a weird feeling, staring at her own defaced face. She looked so worried up there, frightened even. Perhaps she was. Not an image any police officer would wish to portray. In future she'd address that. She shivered and turned back to the computer.

Jenny and Gibbons were standing over it.

'Need a password, sarge,' said Gibbons.

'Could be anything,' said Jenny.

'Try Samantha,' said Karen.

Didn't work.

'Let's try Desiree,' said Gibbons.

Didn't work.

'Try seven,' said Karen.

Didn't work.

'How about Sam the man or son of Sam?' said Jenny.

Neither worked.

'What about, murdering bastard?' said Gibbons.

'Don't be stupid,' said Karen.

Didn't work, anyway.

'Could be anything,' said Jenny again.

'Bag the lot up and take it back to the station,' said Karen. 'They have password detection programs there. Won't take them too long.'

Gibbons nodded and went outside to collect the police canvas bags from the boot of the car.

'What about these?' said Jenny, pointing at the samples and bottles.

'I don't think we should touch them,' said Karen. 'They could be hazardous. Think we need advice on that.'

Gibbons was back, overheard her, and said, 'I agree. You saw what it did to Sam the man.'

'Sam, the he-she thing,' corrected Jenny.

'Yeah, that to.'

Karen turned back to the shelves. Took out one of the red notebooks. Opened it for a better look, and noticed a date. It was a diary; they were all diaries, all seventeen of them, page a day diaries for the previous seventeen years.

Walter's gruff voice flashed into her head.

Bag it up and bring it home. Don't open it, don't read it, and don't give it to Mrs West or Cresta, not until I've seen it.

'Give me a bag, Gibbo.'

He passed her a canvas bag. She counted them in, seventeen in all. Seventeen years of what? Hatred, violence, murder, what? A step-by-step account of how to terrorise and murder people. And for what? The guy was sick in the head, but weren't they all? Bring back the rope, Karen thought, and yet, when it came to it, did she want that? To see and hear of criminals dangling to their deaths from the end of a rope?

She flexed her head and felt her neck beneath the dark polo necked jumper, still sore, still horribly marked. She remembered being hung, less than a week before. She recalled how it felt, the darkness of it, the panic, the final thoughts, the kicking of the feet, and all she could think about was the crazy image that when they found her, her knickers would be dangling around her ankles, and how crazy was that? She would never forget it. She could never forget it. Never, ever. She closed her eyes and shook her head. Bring back the rope.

Oh yes. Sooner the better!

Her mobile began bleating. She didn't recognise the number.

'Hello.'

'Have you found it yet?'

It was Walter, and he sounded even more impatient than usual.

'I haven't found it,' she said, but in the way she spoke, he guessed there was more to come.

'Well? What?'

'Seventeen.'

'Seventeen what? Diaries?'

'Yes, page a day, crammed full, some days with added extras.'

'You haven't read them?'

'Nope. Course not. When do I have the time to do that? How are you, anyway? Where are you?'

'I'm still in bed, still plugged up. The docs said if it had been a few minutes longer I'd have died. I had to play merry hell to get the phone wheeled down here. I hope to be back in the morning.'

'Is that wise?'

'That's rich coming from someone who's just suffered a hanging!'

'I was just thinking about that.'

'Well, don't.'

'I can handle it, I'm twenty-five.'

'Yeah, and I'm not, so what, big deal. I'll see you in the morning, and don't read them, and make sure fussy britches doesn't see them either, not before I do. Lock them in the cupboard in the spare room.'

'You're asking a lot.'

'I know. It's what I'm paid for; it's why you like me so much. Did you find any solicitor's stuff?'

'Not yet.'

'Keep looking. I'll have to go; the medical mafia are back, curtaining me off. God knows what torture they're planning for me now. I wish I was down there with you. Ta-ta… and well done.'

She'd wanted to ask him for advice on what to do with the bottles and jars. Never mind, Mrs West could rule on that. Another job for HAZCHEM, most likely, the hazardous chemicals division. They'd had a busy twenty-four hours, ended up with a couple of bemused boffins from Eden Leys perched on their shoulders. She took out a tin of throat lozenges and slipped one into her mouth. Offered them round. The pair of them shook their heads.

306

'The computer stuff's in the car, sarge,' said Gibbons.

'You'd better go and protect it because Guv would have our guts for garters if someone stole it now.'

Gibbons nodded, realising how right she was, waved at Mrs Hymas through the window on his way out. No tea and cakes for him.

'You'll have to stay here,' Karen said to Jenny. 'No one is to enter the flat under any circumstances. Understand?'

'Yes, sarge.'

'I may come back myself, depends on what ma'am says. They'll send some top brass down, but I won't forget you. See if you can find any details of papers lodged at a solicitor's. I'll get more people down here as soon as I can.'

'Thanks, sarge.'

'Talk to Mrs Hymas if you like, have some tea and cakes, perhaps collect some for Walter, but don't let her in here, and don't tell her anything. I don't need to remind you this is a major crime scene. Put some tape across the door. No one enters.'

'Got you, sarge.'

'We'll see if we can break into the computer.'

'Good luck with that. See you later.'

'Yeah, you will.'

Chapter Fifty-Two

Walter was a man of his word. He was back in the office first thing the next day. He looked dreadful, as if he'd had the lifeblood sucked from him, which was pretty close to what had happened. Karen was there too, and she looked little better. She slipped him the key to the metal cupboard, as Mrs West came in.

She barked a shrill Good Morning everybody, glanced at Walter, thought about saying: You look terrible, thought better of it, and mumbled: Good to see you back; and hurried toward her office, went inside, and closed the door. Walter and Karen shared a look.

'You're going to have to tell her,' Karen said.

'I know. I'll do it now, before she's wide awake.'

He stood up and limped toward her office door, knocked hard once so he wouldn't have to do it again.

'Come!' came the distant voice.

Walter went inside.

'Ah, Walter,' she said, 'sit down, I wanted a word with you. How are you anyway?'

He puffed out his cheeks. 'They tell me I'll live, which is good enough for me, and more than the unlucky six have to look forward to.'

'True, but at least, thanks to you and the team's fine efforts, there won't be a seventh.'

It seemed small compensation, though not much, and nothing for the relatives of the dead.

'So,' she said, 'you're wrapping everything up?'

'Busy on it now, ma'am.'

'And the general debriefing?'

'Arranged for this afternoon, half-past two.'

'Good. Is Cresta in?'

'Not yet, due in any minute.'

'So what can I do for you?'

Walter took a deep breath.

'The killer left a diary, ma'am.'

'A diary?'

'Yes, seventeen volumes.'

'And where are they?'

'Locked in the cupboard, ma'am.'

'And why wasn't I told?'

'With everything going on, I don't think they wanted to bother you with it.'

Mrs West sniffed. She didn't believe that. She grabbed her bag and took out an embroidered handkerchief and blew her pink nose. Walter glanced away. For some reason he found it funny and had to fight not to laugh.

Once done with the hankie, she said, 'Seventeen volumes, you say?'

'Yes, ma'am.'

'Well, I can't be spending all day reading that. I've staff assessments to complete, up to and including this case, on everyone, Walter, including yours, and God alone knows what else,' and she glanced at him over the top of her pink framed specs. 'They are probably full of childish ramblings. Could you read them ASAP and report back?'

'Of course, ma'am, if that's what you want.'

'Yes, Walter, it is, do that, and note anything important I need to know.'

'Fine, ma'am, I'll get on with it right now. When I have finished with them, is it all right if Cresta sees them?'

She thought about that for a second, pulled a face, and then said, 'Don't see why not.'

'Right-ho, ma'am.'

'And I don't think you should be here all day, you look bloody awful, go home and get some rest as soon as you can.'

'Yes, ma'am, thank you, I will,' though the thought of going home to a boarded up kitchen window, and an empty house full of all too recent memories of torture and near death, was not one to tempt him home early. He'd stay for as long as he could keep his eyes open. She nodded him away, and he was glad to be out of there.

'Well?' said Karen.

'I'm assigned to read them all, starting now.'

'Good. And am I in the clear?'

'Course,' he said, unable to keep a smile infiltrating over his drawn face. 'Would I dump you in it?'

'Don't answer that,' she grinned, as she watched him limping away toward the private office, key in hand.

They were maroon, all seventeen of them, made by the same manufacturer, and each one still had the price sticker affixed to the back cover. A seventeen-year record of inflation in the British stationery industry. He opened the earliest one, sat back and began reading, and was struck by the carefully constructed handwriting.

This wasn't a hurried record; this was a detailed account of the guy's life, a considered account, as if he had debated long into the night over every word. It soon became apparent the entries were not written on the day in question, but often some time afterwards, as if he'd left blank pages to be filled in later, as if he'd wanted to reflect on events before committing them to paper.

How many people could do that?

Keep a regular and detailed diary, but leave matters to mature before recording them. It was obvious he'd gone back, sometimes years later, to change and add material, perhaps recently recalled or discovered.

Walter had seen nothing like them before.

As in most diaries, Sam had recorded everyday events, met so and so in the pub, drank too much wine, Shirley was there and I fancied her. But also detailed personal items that many people wouldn't care to see written down. Intimate details of all the dirty little habits that everyone possesses, and everyone denies.

It didn't make for easy reading.

It was clear Sam hadn't enjoyed an easy life, but Walter had expected that. No one goes out and murders six people at random, and tries hard to complete the hand of seven, if they have enjoyed a comfortable and contented existence.

Or do they?

Walter pondered on the point.

Had there ever been a random serial killer who had enjoyed a trouble free, stress-free life, with nothing hidden in their background, to suggest at what was to come? He was struggling to name a case, and he had known more than enough.

The main point in studying the diaries, so far as Walter was concerned, was to see if there were any pointers or hints as to what he, Walter Darriteau, or his successors, could have done differently in the case. Or do differently next time. Any tiny thing that might have enabled them to apprehend the killer earlier; any missed fact that might have saved lives. That was the point of the exercise. Nothing more. No doubt Cresta would think and say different, and in due course, she would have her chance, after he had finished.

If he couldn't glean such intelligence, the time spent reading Sam's neat, but tiny handwriting, a style that enabled the guy to cram a maximum amount of information and trivia into those bound A4 pages, would be, in his eyes, wasted.

Cresta would end up writing some best-selling book based on the murder diaries, but Walter wasn't jealous about that. If she had the time and tenacity to produce such a work, good luck to her. He did not.

He ploughed on, pausing to scribble notes in not so neat handwriting on a foolscap pad. At eleven o'clock he needed a breather, went outside, and headed for the cloakroom.

Cresta glanced up from her desk. She was still writing her final report that she would portray as groundbreaking. Walter had returned and interrupted her train of thought with a comment of his own.

'Morning, Cresty, how are you?'

Cresta glanced up.

'Walter, there you are. It's Crest-A, Walter, as you well know, Crest-A, and you look somewhat pasty, if I may say, how are you feeling?'

Pasty, he thought, she'd look bloody pasty if she'd had the lifeblood sucked from her, but he resisted the temptation to make a joke, and came to the point.

'What would it be worth to the history of this case, and indeed to the whole subject of criminal profiling, if the killer had written a detailed account of his activities going back years?'

'A great deal, that goes without saying,' and then the penny dropped. 'He wrote a diary?' she asked, her eyes widening.

311

Walter grinned and nodded once.

'Where is it?'

'I'm reading it now.'

'Can I see it after you?'

'I might persuade ma'am to let me release it on one small condition.'

'What, Walter, what?'

'You buy me lunch at Pierre's. I'll be there at 12.30 if it's a deal.'

Cresta smiled in purple. What a devious man he was.

'I'll be there,' she said. 'I'll be there.'

'Good. They do a wonderful quiche, and I'll have chips with mine too, brilliant, it is, see you later.'

Chapter Fifty-Three

After an excellent lunch Walter retrieved the diaries from the locked cupboard, burped, and sat back in the chair. Pierre's quiche was the most expensive bacon and egg pie in the universe, but it was lovely, even if it encouraged indigestion. Blood making pie was how he described it to Cresta, and that brought a grimace to her purple decorated face. She'd chosen the cold smoked trout with a sprinkling of green leaves, which said everything.

'I need all the blood I can manufacture,' he continued, before she suggested they talk of something else, and most particularly of the murder diaries.

She wasn't bad company as it turned out, and hadn't Karen once intimated they would make a handsome couple? He wouldn't have gone that far, but away from the confines of the office and the competitiveness of that environment, she relaxed and was bearable. Perhaps she was being agreeable because she knew he had something she desperately wanted, and it wasn't his ravaged body. Walter sighed and shook those recent memories from his mind and began reading.

The first time I remember feeling uncomfortable about myself was the day I discovered I possessed initials that spelt a mildly rude word. It could have been worse, I suppose. I could have been christened Steven Harold Ian Truman, or Freddy Umberto Chapman King, or even, God forbid, Colin Uriah Norman Trethowan.

My name, by comparison to those horrors, and no doubt there are poor unfortunates padding around out there with initials such as those, could be considered comical, a joke. I didn't see it that way, it wasn't a joke to me, not back then, and I suspect most boys wouldn't have thought so either. It was strange I hadn't noticed it before Billy Freeman yelled at me in the playground: 'ASS by name, ASS by nature, you're a complete ASS!'

We were eight, and even then I had to ask him to explain what he meant. It was a small and silly incident that shouldn't have brought me discomfort, yet it did. Even now, looking back from years later, it makes me uncomfortable to think of it. You're an ASS! Maybe I am, who knows, who cares? I dumped the problem as soon as I could by ditching my first name. Who wouldn't have?

Walter flipped through the pages. It was an easy thing to do, to dip in and out, because though they were written on dated pages, oddly, they didn't come out in chronological order. It was all a little haphazard. The writer was either extremely gifted, or totally disorganised, and it was mighty difficult to decide which.

Karen knocked on the door and came in.

'I'm going to Iona to oversee the removal of the contents. Anything you want me to look out for?'

'Yes, the solicitor's name and address.'

'Besides that?'

'Nope, not that I can think of.'

'How's the reading going?'

'Confusing.'

'In what way?'

'Jumps about all over the place.'

'You've got Cresta jumping up and down.'

'Good. Well, she's going to have to wait, and for quite some time too.'

Karen grinned. He enjoyed winding Cresta up. Karen was surprised he'd told her about the diaries at all.

'OK, I'll see you later.'

'Yep, see you, oh; some more of those fairies would be nice.'

'I'll see what I can do.'

He turned over the page.

My life took a turn for the better the day I fell totally and utterly in love. It had been a slow burner. I'd known the girl for several years before I thought of her in any way other than as the quiet but cute vicar's daughter. Unlike my friend Dennis who the very first day I mentioned her, said 'Yeah, yeah. But would you fuck her?'

314

At the time that notion had not permeated my confused head, though a few years later that idea was fixed in my mind from first thought in the morning till the last at night. The second or third time I saw her I glimpsed her knickers, as she'd curled her legs beneath her at the vicarage tea party. I'd looked away and Dennis told me off about that too. It was an image framed in time that returned to me time and again. It still occasionally does. I know it shouldn't, but it does, locked in my head, as if to tease me, as if to remind me of something I never had, something I could never attain, as if to say: You've wasted an opportunity there! You ass! You're an ASS!

The ironic thing was that at one time she had a real crush on me. She bought me a rabbit's foot, especially for my big concert on the radio. I was too stupid or too embarrassed to notice her feelings, and it was a couple of years later, when she returned from college during the summer holidays, that I finally asked her to the pictures. It wasn't easy persuading her either. I had to ask her four times before she agreed. Later, I discovered she only consented because her father, the vicar, encouraged her to do so. Imagine how I felt. The girl at my side was there because her father asked her to be, not because she wanted to be.

That night I made a complete and utter fool of myself.

I wasn't the first young man to do so on their first meaningful date, and I won't be the last, but that doesn't erase the hurt one feels when looking back on it from some years later.

On the way home I pushed her against the back of the bus shelter and kissed her. She didn't resist; she didn't cry out; she didn't do a thing. Her response was spelt out through her icy lips. I imagine now that she must have grimaced through the whole experience, though I was far too smitten to realise that, and too innocent to understand that it was any different to how it should have been. Maybe I had an inkling. If I did, I buried it in the outer reaches of my expanding mind. I didn't want to know a thing, other than what I saw and felt and smelt in front of me.

Flushed with success, for I had dreamt of kissing those pink cherry lips for weeks, no months, nay years, I pressed onward, determined to achieve my goal, as any hot-blooded male might, strike while the iron is hot, show her you love her, as the agony aunt pages always say, tell her you love her, they always recommend. How is she ever to know how you feel if you don't tell her? So I did.

'I love you, Machara,' I said.

She didn't say a word. She was probably squirming with embarrassment.

315

I loved everything about her, even her name I found alluring. I had never met a Machara before, still haven't. I loved her to bits, and what does a passionate man do when he loves someone? Asks them to marry him, that's what, so I did.

'Will you marry me, Machara McGowan?'

She giggled derisorily.

I didn't look into her eyes; I couldn't, because my head was set to one side of hers. I was staring at her neat left ear that was poking through her bonnet of black hair, that ear, a white protuberance that resembled those ultra precious mushrooms one finds in the forest early on a Sunday morning, a variety you never see in the shops. That night in the bus shelter there was something particularly sensual about her ear, I still remember that, it's difficult to explain, I could have bitten it off, though I didn't understand it at the time.

When she spoke she said, 'I couldn't possibly marry you, you're no-ooo a Scot.'

She didn't reject me because I was too young, too inexperienced, too short, too nervous, too lacking in prospects, too ugly, too dull, too horrendous, she rejected me because I didn't belong to the Scottish race. Stupid girl! How peculiar was that? I suspect it was a condition that would one day come back to haunt her, and only two years after that she did indeed find her ideal man.

Robertson was six feet four inches tall, broadly built, sandy beard and hair, with a glint in his eye. His highland accent alone was enough to win Machara's heart, or so she imagined, and the fact that he wore a kilt, and his birth was registered in Fort William, would have clinched the deal.

When I heard the news, I was mortified.

I didn't understand how the love of my life could want to marry this huge ginger pig, this hairy legged oaf who delighted in prancing around in a green and yellow tartan skirt. But marry him she did, in her father's church, where I had once led the choir. I didn't attend, I couldn't bring myself to do so, for when the Reverend Blair McGowan stood up and uttered the immortal words: Is there any lawful impediment as to why these people should not be joined in holy matrimony, I knew I would have jumped to my feet and yelled: 'He's no-ooo a Scot!'

'Cept he was, and she did.

It didn't turn out well.

Robertson Brothy had a weakness.

Many men do.

316

His fatal weakness was not women, or girls, or even boys, or gambling, or money, or calories, or whisky, or drink, or lack of ambition, or laziness, or of being a bully, or of being violent, no, his weakness was one of egotism.

Robertson Brothy loved himself above all others.

He was used to getting his own way in all things. He possessed a booming voice and adored the sound of it. He would dominate conversations, he would talk others down, he would talk over people, and talk endlessly about himself and his life and his successes. He would cut others short, often in a rude manner, without ever seeming to notice, he would belittle people, especially anyone Machara liked, and he'd insist that people listened to him and his brilliant ideas, and especially his new wife, who at first tolerated it, but gradually retreated into her shell until she never spoke at all, unless he spoke first.

'I'd like some sirloin steak for dinner.'

'Yes, Robertson, I'll see what I can find.'

'And we'll go golfing again at the weekend. Carnoustie, I think.'

'Yes, Robbie, whatever you say.'

'And don't call me Robbie!'

Machara detested golf, but would never mention it, and would hack her way round Scotland's championship links, embarrassing her husband, infuriating committee members who would reluctantly ban her. Though it made little difference, for there are thousands of golf courses across Scotland, as they moved up the coast to the next untouched collection of fresh holes.

'You'll get the hang of it,' insisted Robertson.

'Yes, dear,' she would say, but she knew she wouldn't, and she never did. She didn't want to. She hated golf, and everything that went with it, and she grew to loathe Robertson Brothy.

Machara's father was against divorce.

Prior to the marriage he had taken his only daughter to one side and had lectured her on the sanctity of marriage, imploring his beautiful girl to be certain that Robertson was indeed the man for her, before she agreed to anything. Blair was not blind to Robertson's overbearing nature, (the Reverend liked Robertson to come calling at the vicarage for a day or so, but was mighty pleased to see him leave). But his daughter was blind to that. Sometimes love really is blind.

She had made her decision and would stick with it, whatever it took, for better or worse, however hard the rock strewn road became, however

317

unhappy it made her. She had chosen him freely and fairly, and anyway, she couldn't possibly divorce Robertson Brothy, because he was a Scot.

I confess I imagined the last part of the previous sentence, and I laughed at it too, maybe a little unkindly, when I did. I have made many dreadful decisions in my life and I take little comfort from knowing that I am not alone.

Would Machara do the same thing if she had her life over again?

Of course she would, because she was a passionate human being, and passionate human beings do not know their own minds. They make mistakes. They are guided by exterior forces, we all are. Our actions are often not what they should be, not truly our own. They are dictated by events and passion.

Walter set the diary down and paused for thought. Read that line again. *Our actions are often not what they should be, not truly our own. They are dictated by events and passion.*

Your actions, young man, were your own, and no one else's, and no amount of window dressing, or fiddling with history, could ever alter that.

I remember my eighteenth birthday well. Dennis's girlfriend, Jillian, had fixed me up with one weird girlfriend after another. I don't know why, but they all reminded me of animals, giraffes, meerkats, chickens, walruses; you name it, they were all there, as if they'd just vacated the ark. I wasn't a success with her zoo, and stopped taking the dates, or perhaps she stopped providing them. I can't remember which.

They left me that night to go to the cinema, and I picked up my brown paper parcel, and the present they had given me, a pack of string vests, the only gift I received that year, and later I walked around the city walls three times, alone with my thoughts, before I retreated to my flat where I opened my parcel, took out the first of my maroon diaries, and began making notes, recalling a haphazard history of my life. If you are reading this you will know what I mean.

Soon afterwards, I embarked on a series of brief affairs, more by luck than judgement, brought about through alcohol. Thinking back on it, I can't remember whether I was more or less drunk than the girls in question. Truth is, we were both stoned.

As you might gather from my coldness toward the business, they were not great successes. I'd discovered women, but I hadn't found my woman, and that wouldn't change for a good few years.

318

Chapter Fifty-Four

Walter was getting a headache. Sam's writing was tiny, and it took considerable concentration to get through it. Karen came knocking again and entered. Walter glanced up. 'How goes it?'

'OK, everything of interest is now out of Iona. No solicitor's details anywhere. Perhaps we should start ringing round the usual suspects and ask them.'

'It's a thought, but give it a little longer.'

'One bit of good news.'

'Oh yeah?'

'We've cracked the computer password.'

'And?'

'It was Ionahouse.'

'That was difficult. And?'

'Nothing much, love letters, the usual flattering stuff that men write.'

Walter wasn't sure what men wrote in love letters. He couldn't remember that far back. Come to think of it, he wondered if he had ever written a true love letter... or received one.

'Like what?' he said, striving to sound disinterested.

'You know, the usual cock and bull.'

'Like what?' he mumbled again, staring down at volume nine.

'You don't need me to tell you that; use your imagination. You can read them yourself if you like.'

'Mmm, maybe later.'

She glanced down at him. He seemed barely to notice she was there. She glanced at the diaries. She was becoming interested in those damned books. He seemed riveted, and she regretted not taking a quick peek when she had the chance. It was a pity they were going on the Cresta run next.

'See you later,' Karen said, and she let herself out.

'Mmm, yeah.'

My life changed the day I met the woman of my dreams.

As so often happens in matters of the heart, it was by accident. If I had been five minutes earlier, or she five minutes later, I would never have seen her, or met her. Our paths would never have crossed, and we would never have known of each other's whereabouts. The chances are, we would have gone through the rest of our days pining for the other half that we knew existed, but could never find.

It was a Saturday morning, and I was terrified.

Some idiot at the tax office where I worked at the time decided it would be a good idea to improve team bonding, and the best way to do that, they reasoned, was through skydiving. I confess I didn't want to participate, and would never go again, but the shame and embarrassment of being seen as a coward forced me from my bed that clear and dry Saturday morning.

A coach took us to the aero club where we'd gone through all the procedures and prelims. We were packed into our multi coloured gear and we headed outside. She was coming in. Some idiot at their place, Eden Leys, had had the same peculiar idea. Parachuting brought people together, they said, killed people too sometimes, I recalled, but there we are, and just this once, it did bring people together, though not as they imagined.

She was coming back, walking along the narrow tarmacked path. I was going out, same path, same place, same time.

We set eyes on one another at the same moment.

We were the same height and almost identical weight, and we even possessed the same sized feet. Eye contact was easy, straight ahead; there it was, eye to eye. Hello there!

I stared into her mesmerising dark eyes. She told me later my blue eyes were the first thing she saw, like lasers spearing into her soul. She said she couldn't look anywhere else. She felt as if she were being hypnotised. It was the same for me. I couldn't look anywhere else.

I paused on the path, maybe five paces away.

She paused too.

'Hi,' I said, ambling closer.

'Hi,' she said, her white teeth picked out against her rustic skin, as she smiled that special smile reserved for the one we love. I doubt if she smiled in precisely that way again in her entire life. I know for sure I didn't.

I was lost for words, said the first thing, nay the only thing; that came into my pounding brain.

'Just been up?'

She grinned and glanced down at her spent chute.

320

'Yep,' she said, still smiling beams as if from an ultra-violet lamp, pausing, waiting, hoping, for me to speak again.

I was struck dumb.

'Just going up?' she said.

'Yeah, looks like it. I'm so nervous.'

'Don't be, there's nothing to be nervous about, you'll be fine,' and she reached across and squeezed my wrist. Electricity charged into my arm, sweeping through my entire body. I swear to God I could hear it crackling, see it arcing.

Her friends had passed by and had moved on toward the buildings. One of them turned round and shouted back, 'Come on, Desi! It's your round!'

She glanced at them and shouted, 'Just a minute!' Glanced back at me and said the most warm and kind thing that anyone has ever said to me in my entire life.

'Would you like me to wait on for you?'

No one had ever said anything like that to me before. No one had ever wanted to wait for me for anything, not since I was a child. I could barely find the words to reply. Of course I would like her to wait.

I said, 'I'd love you to wait.'

She moved closer, smiled at me again, zipping sparks down my spine, as she said, 'I'll wait. For sure. What's your name?'

'Sam.'

'OK, Sam, mine's Desi.'

'I know.'

Alan Steadman, the office wet, turned round and saw me standing close to this dark and pretty girl, and shouted: 'Eh up, looks like yellow balls is ducking out. Come on, Sam, if you're coming,' and he started making chicken noises.

We glanced back at Steadman and scowled, and she said, 'You'd better go, Sam,' and she leant across and kissed me on the cheek. I couldn't believe it. I could feel the fire on my face. I cannot explain in writing how I felt back then. Certainly I had never experienced feelings the depths of which swept through my entire body at that moment, being kissed tenderly by a complete stranger, though of course we were not strangers, we never were. It was as if we had known each other since the womb, and I still cannot explain that, as I write this memoir of the earth shattering events of that late Saturday morning.

What kind of girl kisses a total stranger?

In broad daylight.

321

In front of other people.

How much courage did that take?

What kind of person could do that?

I know I couldn't.

Can you imagine how special I felt at that second?

I suspect there are no words in the English language to describe it.

Far better men than I have tried and failed. The closest I can get is to say that if the whole of a person's life could ever be compressed into a split second, then that second was that exact moment.

The Glendower Aero Club, I will love you forever!

'I'll wait for you,' she said again, 'Good luck, Sam, you'll enjoy it.'

I doubted that. But she smiled me away, and I ran after the others with springs on my feet, and bragged about pulling a new girlfriend. Me, the same guy who had pushed Machara up against the bus shelter and forced her to kiss me, the same boy who was rude to Jillian's friends, the same guy who had to be drunk to find a girl at all, and she drunker still.

They didn't believe me, of course, my friends from the tax office, that she said she'd wait for me, and I had my doubts about that too, and as I jumped from that plane, I volunteered to be the first to go. I was in a hell of a hurry to get back down to earth, and the moment before the chute opened, I thought that if ever God was going to be nasty, mean and wicked, now would be the moment to be so, minutes after I had found my life partner. He or she or it, or whatever God is or was, might have snatched that happiness away, by snagging my chute. I can't tell you how relieved I was when that multi coloured mushroom swirled open above me, and when it did, slowing the fall, I wished it had opened later, so that I could have been on earth sooner.

Desiree was a woman of her word.

She always was.

There she was, standing there, swaying back and forth, her hands clasped together behind her back like a little girl at her first school assembly, or a mother flushed with happiness when her first son learns how to ride a bicycle, beaming at me just as before, only more so.

She linked my arm, asked me how it had been, asked me to explain my emotions, and said she shared the same feelings, though neither of us wanted to talk about parachuting. There were so many more important things to relate, as we made our way back toward the buildings.

Her friends were still there, hanging about, becoming irritated.

'Come on, Desi,' one of them pleaded, 'We are going to the Snooty Fox!'

'Can't today, boys. I'm sorry, but I've met my old friend, Sam, and we have so much to catch up on. Don't we?' she said, pulling me closer and peering and smirking into my eyes.

I nodded and said, 'Yes, we do.'

And that is what we were. Old friends. Old friends who'd known each other minutes, yet we had known each other forever.

We had so much to say.

Everything that had gone before, we couldn't wait to share, and everything that was to come, we couldn't wait to see, and think about, and whatever the future held, we would share every moment, hand-in-hand. The good times and the bad, and there would be plenty of both. We didn't stop talking for hours. We didn't stop talking once, not until we were making love in her apartment that overlooked the River Dee, just above the ancient bridge.

She'd asked me if I'd like to accompany her back to Chester, and of course we both knew the answer to that. She'd led me back to her brand new Cayton Cerisa hatchback, while my friends and her friends gawped on in amazement, as if we were in a bubble, as if we couldn't see them, and they couldn't see us. And after that we'd driven to town, shared our first meal in some old pub in the main street, as we talked and talked, and begged each other to know where we had been all our lives, and why the hell we hadn't met sooner.

That night we made love on and off till the sun came up, and for longer still.

After that day, I never slept with anyone else.

I have never thought about sleeping with anyone else.

I have never desired anyone else, and she said the same thing, and I believed her.

I shall never lie with another woman.

Why should I?

Desiree Holloway was everything I desired.

Desiree Holloway was everything.

Desiree epitomised desire.

It was as plain and simple as that.

Desiree Holloway **was** desire.

When you have the best, nothing else will do.

Chapter Fifty-Five

Walter yawned and glanced at the clock. Twenty to six. He felt dog tired. Someone else's blood was gallivanting around his body, maybe donated by nine different people. Thank you, the nervous nine, I couldn't live without you. At least it was human blood. He set the diary down and ambled outside. Mrs West came out of her office wearing her going home face.

'You still here? Thought I told you to go home early.'

'Things to do.'

'Don't stay too late.'

'I won't, ma'am.'

She nodded and headed for the door, just as Karen was coming back in. She ambled over and said, 'How's it going?'

Walter pulled a face and nodded.

'Chapters and chapters of his love for Desiree Holloway. He was sure smitten.'

'Men get that way,' she grinned.

'Do they?'

'Have you never felt that way?'

He thought for a second, and said: 'No.'

She pitied him, but didn't say; then she wondered if he was being truthful. Men often aren't when it comes to such matters, women too, though men were far worse, in her eyes, they were. Much worse.

'Do you mind if I shoot off? I'm going to have an early night.'

'Nope, sure, fine, you get away, see you in the morning.'

He seemed distant.

'Are you all right?'

He focused his large dark eyes on her as if she'd just come in, and said, 'Yeah, sure, I'm fine, see you tomorrow.'

Karen collected her bag and smiled and bobbed her head and turned about and left.

Walter went to the cloakroom and pondered on what she had said.

Have you never felt that way?

Yes, once, maybe, but that was long ago, and there was little point in dragging up old sores. He washed his hands, blew them under the drier, and returned to the private office. And the diaries.

I have suffered many setbacks in my life; I am not alone in that, and I am not making excuses, and I don't want pity, but the knocks I took were bound to leave their mark.

My beloved mother died before I started school. My father took a mistress, the hateful and deceitful Donna Deary, who would slap me when my father's eyes were turned elsewhere. I suffered the loss of my beautiful house and garden where I played and learned of life. Then came the loss of my father in a violent and catastrophic accident, along with his new wife and my stepbrother, though I confess I did not shed a tear at their deaths. The loss of my inheritance, wasted in propping up a failing business, sucked dry by the scheming leech, Deary. The loss of my income and job at the flower shop I loved, the first true interest I ever developed, a love of flora that will remain with me always. Mrs Greenaway's surprising rejection, and the trauma of being taken into care.

The cancellation of my scholarship to King's, losing my dancing lessons I adored, the harassment and bullying at Saint Edmond's, the sickness to the pit of my stomach at being rejected by countless foster parents, who would stare down at me and force a closed mouthed smile, and shake their heads. He isn't quite right, they'd often say, or, he's not the one for us, just look at him! As they made little attempt to conceal their opinions or contempt or distaste, as if I were stone deaf to their spitefulness.

The shame and worry of being harassed, pressurised and touched by the vicar, Christian de Wyk, coming to terms with my weird adolescent appearance during those crucial formative years, and almost worst of all, the breaking and loss of my wonderful voice on the eve of my big broadcast concert, a festival that some forecast would change my life forever.

My silly falling in love and failed attempts at wooing Machara McGowan, and her trite and hurtful putdown, You're no-ooo a Scot! And my unsuccessful dates with Jillian's friends; and failed affairs with drunken women, old and young alike, some with teeth, some without.

Everyone suffers setbacks in their life. It is natural. That is what life is all about. Adversity, but few will have encountered as many as I.

And yet I would have traded all those losses in an instant to be rid of the one catastrophic blow that struck me down the day that Desiree was murdered. Something deep within me died that day. My love of life, perhaps, my love of people, my sanity. They all came under ferocious attack.

One month before she died, Desiree confessed her sins to me.

She had been keeping secrets from me, terrible things, appalling things, unbelievable things that at first I could not comprehend.

She was a killer.

I was living with a killer.

I was married to a killer.

She was killing innocent human beings.

The person I shared my life with, the person I shared my body with, the person I shared my mind and destiny with, my soul with, was killing other people.

Can you imagine how you would deal with that?

If the love of your life came home one day and spilled such wickedness, what would you do? What would you say? Would you want them to touch you again? Would you move out? Would you divorce them? Would you call the police?

If you loved someone as I loved Desiree, you would not do those things because you could not live without them. Yet you would never feel the same way again. It placed terrible strains on our marriage, and on our love.

Long after she was snatched from me, I saw the black policeman on the television. He was threatening me. Saying things like we would be meeting soon, he would catch me, and I would have to look into his eyes and deal with him. While he was talking he'd look at the blonde sergeant, and she would glance affectionately back, and I knew there was a close bond between them, and wanted to destroy that bond. I wanted to hurt them; I wanted to hurt them so bad. I wanted him and her to feel what it was like to lose someone that mattered, someone they deeply cared for. I wanted them to share my pain; I wanted to kill one of them, to see how they coped with that, and in time, I wanted to kill them both.

So, black policeman, if by some strange quirk of fate you should ever cast your bloated eyes over my diaries, as one day I know someone will, even if it is one of your successors, I want to recap the names of the dead, for they deserve to be remembered.

Pay attention.

Roll-call begins.

Harold James Craddock.

Hilda Mary Anderton.

George Bellway Milkins.

Ena Frances Marlow.
William Richard Amos Clarke.
Michael Patrick O'Leary.
Thora Joyce Beckett.
Not the names you expected, eh?
Seven names. Seven human beings. Seven deaths. Seven murders.
Seven criminal killings committed by my darling wife, Desiree Mitford Holloway, during her experimental work at Eden Leys. There were others too, but these were Desiree's personal work. Seven deaths that affected her profoundly. Seven deaths that cost her her life, seven deaths that provoked me to murder, seven times over.
Investigate that, why don't you!
If you dare.

Walter scribbled the names on his pad and set down his pen. Out of nowhere, he felt quite ill. He glanced at the clock. Ten minutes to eight. Stood up. His legs shook. Walking wasn't easy. He was hungry and wanted
to go home. He eased the diaries into the metal cupboard, locked the door, attached the key to his key ring, went outside, slipped on his raincoat, bade the skeleton night shift a curt goodnight, and limped away to find a cab.

Chapter Fifty-Six

Walter was back in the private office by 8am, wrote a note for Karen to come and see him as soon as she arrived, and returned to the quiet room, and the diaries.

You must think I am mad, and, as I have written before, I questioned my sanity. Perhaps that is why Desiree and I dovetailed so perfectly. She too questioned her sanity, and not without reason. But I am not mad when it comes to the information I have provided. Desiree killed those seven people. They lost their innocent lives in the headlong pursuit for a cure for Alzheimer's disease and dementia, and I can prove it. I possess all her case notes, all the gruesome and grizzly facts.

She showed them to me because she could see the doubt in my eyes. I did not believe her; I did not believe she was capable of such heinous acts. I sat on her balcony as the beautiful Dee gurgled by, and read in detail what she did, what drugs she introduced, what incisions she made to the bodies and brains, what tissue she removed, and what torture and torment she inflicted on the seven unfortunates.

I still find it difficult to comprehend, but I know it is the truth.

You will too when you read the evidence.

Desiree's file of terror is lodged at the offices of the Liverpool solicitor, Lambourn, Harcourt and Snapes, Sixth floor, Royal Liver Building, Liverpool.

The partner looking after the file is one Ms Bradbrook, though she likes to pronounce it Braybrook. For her to release the file, you will need to quote the password: Deliverance.

Walter set the diary down and picked up the phone and asked the operator to get the solicitor in Liverpool on the line.

The phone ran back a moment later, a sweet young girl boasting a slight Liverpool accent.

'Good mornin', Lambourn Harcourt and Snay-eeps.'

'Is Ms Bradbrook there?'

'Ms Braybrook, you mean?'

'That's the one.'

'Joost a mo, I'll put ya through.'

Karen knocked and came in. Walter beckoned her to sit. Musak played in his ear. He pulled the names off the pad, handed them to her, said, 'Suspicious deaths, all at Eden Leys, see what you can dig up.'

Karen glanced at the seven names and tried to whistle through her teeth.

'And organise a car.'

'Where are we going?'

'Liverpool.'

'Okey-doke.'

Elizabeth Bradbrook came on the line.

'Braybrook,' she said, as if she were busy and didn't care to be disturbed.

'Good morning, this is Inspector Darriteau, Chester Police.'

'I've been expecting you.'

'Really? You have something for me?'

'I'm not sure I'd describe it quite like that. I have paperwork here I can release… on certain conditions.'

'You have a file for me and I want it and I shall have it.'

'We both know you would need a court order to do that, unless…'

'I have the client's password?'

'Correct. And do you?'

'Your late client was a mass murderer.'

'Yet to be proven, I'd say.'

'He tried to murder me!'

'Oh dear. That was unfortunate. Do you have the password, Inspector?'

'I do.'

'Why didn't you say?'

'I'm trying to.'

'What time do you want to come?'

'Eleven.'

'I can do that.'

'I'll see you later.'

Karen drove as she always did, too fast, zipping up the M53 in the unmarked jag, and on through the new Mersey tunnel that was no longer so new, before turning back toward the river and the Liver Building, the largest of the impressive structures known as The Three Graces, set facing the Pierhead overlooking the river. Karen found a metered parking space as Walter took a police badge from the glove compartment and set it in view. They stepped out into the windy sunshine, glanced at the grey river, back at the grey building, and the big clock at the top that said five to eleven.

Ms Braybrook didn't keep them waiting. She was older than she sounded on the phone and came straight to the point.

'The password is?'

Walter glanced at Karen.

'Deliverance,' she said.

'Good. A little dramatic maybe, but there we are. Sam was always that way inclined.'

'You can say that again,' said Karen under her breath.

'Sign here, please.'

Ms Braybrook pushed a document across the table with a pen. Walter picked it up, scanned the paper and signed it.

'Good,' she said, retrieving the authorisation docket. She opened her desk drawer, pulled out an orange card file, perhaps two inches thick, and slid it across the table. 'I'm sure you'll find it interesting reading.'

'I am sure we shall,' said Walter, as Karen stood and scooped up the file.

'Have you made copies of the contents?'

'Of course not! I am a solicitor.'

Walter sniffed and nodded and stood up.

Ms Braybrook frowned and stood and nodded too.

Three minutes later, and they were back in the car.

'Look at that!' he said, pointing at the window.

A green parking ticket in a plastic raincoat jammed under the wiper. Karen laughed and jumped out and retrieved it.

'So what's in the file?'

'Proof of deaths at Eden Leys, if Sam's diary is to be believed.'

'Criminal deaths?'

'Are there any other kind?'

330

'Course there is; natural causes, accidents, deaths in war, for example.'

'Those Alzheimers' patients were not at war.'

'Only with their own minds.'

'Precisely.'

'You're determined to follow this up, aren't you?'

'As far as I can.'

'Could be tricky.'

'Life can be tricky, Karen, as we both discovered this past week.'

'You can say that again,' she said, and her hand returned to massaging her still sore neck.

'Start the car, let's get home.'

As she drove he said, 'That night when Sam was at my place; what made you think I was in trouble?'

'I figured he was determined to do seven. He thought I was the seventh, but when he discovered he hadn't finished me off, that he hadn't completed what he'd set out to do, I was convinced he was coming back, to try again. That's why I asked Gibbons to come over to keep me company. But when the killer didn't come, something told me he'd switched his attention to you, and when you didn't answer either of your phones, alarm bells went off. I had to come and see for myself. I had to check.'

'Good job you did.'

'Yeah,' she said, 'though if I hadn't bothered I might have been promoted by now.'

He glanced at her grinning face.

'Do you want my job that bad?'

'Course I do.'

'Do you think you're ready for it?'

'Yes, I do. Don't you think so?'

Walter thought about that for a second. If he'd been asked the same question a week before he would have said a resounding no. But now he owed his very existence to her detection and reasoning skills, he knew she was ready. He just wasn't sure he wanted to tell her.

'Maybe,' he said.

'That's a huge improvement,' she grinned. 'Last time we discussed this you said I was nowhere near ready.'

Walter turned to his left and smiled at the green fields of the Wirral hurtling by. Glanced at the dash. 95mph. Geez!

'Not so quick!'

'Sorry, Guv.'

He didn't say anything else for a while until she said, 'So is that it then? The Sam serial murder case is over?'

Walter sniffed.

'Pretty much, it's now down to the coroner, though I should think it's fairly straightforward. Six cold-blooded murders, he confessed them all to me, and the murderer dead too, attempting to escape the full force of the law.'

She giggled at that. The full force of the law. Her, as weak as a kitten who could barely speak, drink or breathe, and him lashed to the chair, looking helpless. An image of Walter strapped to his seat swept back into Karen's mind. God, how ill he looked, and then on to the last moment when the man in black fell on the phial. She never discovered what was in that damned thing. She didn't want to know either. She wanted nothing more to do with it.

Then she added, 'And two attempteds, don't forget that.'

'Ah yes, that too, two attempteds. No one will be charged with those.'

'No one will be charged with any of them.'

'True.'

'Saves us the hassle of going to court, giving evidence.'

'That's true too, though I quite like that part, of seeing them in the dock before their peers, of witnessing justice being meted out.'

Karen could take or leave that experience; so long as they weren't free to re-offend, that was the only thing that interested her.

Walter yawned and said, 'I'd liked to have seen Sam in the dock much earlier.'

'Goes without saying.'

'No, the real question is, how much did the knowledge that Desiree was involved in the deaths of innocent civilians, assuming that to be true, after her confession to Sam, how much did that tip him over the edge?'

'I think there was murder in him, it just needed a catalyst.'

332

'You could be right, we'll never know.'

'There is one other outstanding question,' said Karen.

'And that is?'

'How did Desiree die? Accident, suicide, or murder?'

'The coroner said suicide.'

'Coroners can be wrong.'

'We can all be wrong, Karen.'

'You're right there, Guv.'

Chapter Fifty-Seven

When they arrived back at the station, Walter went straight to see Mrs West. He told her of the file. She kept it, told him there were things she needed to bone up on. Walter was disappointed but returned to reading the diaries. He had almost finished.

When I was younger, I toyed with the idea of becoming a minister. To tell the truth, it was not my idea, but that of the vicar, Blair McGowan. I would never have considered such a thing without his input. I studied hard and took the first informal examinations that I passed. The Rev was mighty happy at that, and I guess at the time I thought it might have impressed Machara.

All the while there was something bugging me. I found it hard to convince myself there was a Christian God. I mean, if there were, would there be so much suffering and evil in the world?

Or was the doubt in my mind the devil's work?

Perhaps it was. But the thing that made me bin the whole preaching ethos, was the overwhelming feeling that the devil's work was a damned sight more exciting, more alluring, more tempting, than anything our so called God had to offer. The big D puts temptation in all our ways, if you believe the Christian doctrine, and that much is easy to accept. My problem is I was always more inclined to bite the apple than walk away. I figured out pretty early that a potential vicar shouldn't think that way.

Now, as I am coming toward the end of these diaries, you might think I should say sorry for what I have done. I can't do that. I'm not sorry. I enjoyed my work. Desiree's murder was worth at least what I accomplished in revenge. Maybe more so, despite the terrible things she did. To my mind, it was repayment to the world for her loss, and for my loss too.

If I had my time over again, I would do the same thing. Looking back on it now, as I write these words, the only surprise is that it took me so long to begin. If there is something eating you, whoever you are, wherever you are, something you need to accomplish, then do it now before it is too late.

I doubt I shall write much more. Things are coming to a head. Whosoever readeth these words, you may be assured they are the truth as I see it, and nothing but the truth.

I am not sad; I am not even disappointed; I am satisfied.

I can't wish you well. I don't wish any of you well. Just the opposite. I wish you all great unhappiness, and especially that black copper. I hope he rots in hell, and sooner rather than later. I hold him responsible. And remember this, Walter Darriteau, you and I will meet soon, nothing is more certain, so think about that!

Recognise those words?

They were among the first words you spoke to me - you pompous bastard!

The difference is, beyond the curtain, I shall be waiting for you, with a grin on my face, and a sharpened knife in my hand.

Armitage Samuel Holloway, nee Shelbourne, Iona House, Chester.

Walter sighed and closed his eyes. He set the book down and stretched his arms and legs. He still didn't feel quite himself. Perhaps it was to be expected; perhaps he was getting old. Though he would never admit that, not even to himself. Threats from beyond the grave, from a psychopath. Was that a first?

He strolled outside and sat opposite Karen.

Cresta glanced across the desks.

'Well?' she said. 'How are you doing?'

'Finished. You can have them.'

'Great!' she said. 'Not before time,' and she bolted to the private office before he changed his mind.

'Well?' said Karen. 'What's on your mind?'

'He threatened me with hell from beyond the grave. Said he'd be waiting for me.'

'Does that bother you?'

'Course not! I'm not going to hell.'

Karen grinned her cheeky grin and said, 'I wouldn't be so sure.'

Walter sniffed a laugh. He thought she was looking better, and as he was thinking of that, two strangers entered the office and strolled across the room as if they owned the place, as if they knew their way round blindfolded.

They were both just north of thirty and north of six feet, fit looking blokes, like rowers. The leading one, a grammar school boy judging by his accent, white skin, short mousy hair, tiny nose that looked as if it belonged on a rabbit. The other was fractionally taller, tanned, overlong straight and floppy blond hair that he adjusted with his palm, loud voice speaking poncy English, as if he couldn't care less who heard what he had to say. Dai Williams over at Prestatyn had a name for men like him, Rodneys, he called them, and Walter could empathise with that.

They hustled through and disappeared into Mrs West's room without knocking.

'Who are they?' asked Karen.

'Dunno,' said Walter, though he had a good idea. 'Anything else happening?'

'A newsagent in Boughton got attacked, some dispute over a lottery ticket.'

'Serious?'

'He'll live.'

'Anything else?'

'A bloke at Blacon was attacked by his wife.'

'Oh, aye?'

'She hit him over the head with his computer gaming machine; he had to go to hospital.'

'Poor love.'

'You're not really interested are you?'

'Nope, I'm not, but I'll tell you what does interest me.'

'Go on.'

'I want you to look into the deaths at Eden Leys. They're bugging me, I can't think of anything else. If any laws have been broken in that hellhole of a place, I want to be the man at the front of the queue asking the questions.'

'OK, if that's what you want.'

'It is what I want.'

'Where do we start?'

'Coroner's reports would be a good place.'

'I'll look at it now.'

Walter bobbed his head and tried to imagine what had gone on in Eden Leys. He'd checked their bland website, edenleys.com. Didn't

336

tell him much. No surprise, there. Bland exterior, bland content, bland words, but inside? Who knows what?

Mrs West's office door opened. The two guys came out looking pleased with themselves, closed the door behind them, and marched across the room without looking round. Headed straight for the exit, and within seconds they were through and away and out of the building.

'Correct me if I'm wrong,' said Karen, 'but didn't the blond twerp have our file under his arm.'

'Looked that way.'

'And you're not going to do anything about it?'

'What do you suggest I do? Limp after him and snatch?'

Karen pursed her lips and sighed.

The phone before them burbled.

She snatched it up, said 'Sure,' and handed it to Walter.

'Step inside, Walter, please,' the voice commanded.

He didn't answer, just set the phone down; shared a look with Karen and limped away toward the door. Once inside, she pointed to a chair and began speaking before he'd settled.

'The Desiree Holloway case is closed.'

'Just like that.'

'Just like that, Walter.'

'Who were those guys?'

'Don't be dim, Walter. You know the answer to that as well as I do.'

He exhaled a huge breath as if he had been holding it in all week.

'People down there,' and he pointed south, adjusting his arm toward Eden Leys twenty-five miles away. 'People down there are killing innocent people, and they are getting away with it, and we don't seem to give a toss.'

'You can't prove that.'

'I could have proved it!'

'You can't prove it now, and that is all that matters. They have assured me nothing like that is happening today.'

'Oh, bully beef!'

'Don't be rude, Walter.'

'I am not happy about it, ma'am.'

'There are lots of things I am not happy about, but we have to get on with it. We are a small cog in a big machine. It's best to keep on turning as if we are well oiled. Best not to jam and screech and bugger up the works,' and she glanced at his lips-pursed face. 'Don't look so offended, Walter, it's nothing personal. We've put a stop to our killer. That's the important thing, that's what will be remembered. Let's be thankful for that.'

She paused a moment and forced a smile and said, 'Now, what's next? I believe there is a problem over at a Boughton newsagent. I think you should pay them a visit and show the flag.'

Walter's mind was still elsewhere.

'That is all, Walter. Good morning.'

He heaved himself from the chair and muttered something she didn't hear, and went outside.

'Well?' said Karen.

'The Desiree Holloway case is closed.'

'Can't say as I am surprised.'

Walter sat heavy in his chair.

'Closed but not forgotten, Greenwood. So long as I live I will monitor that place. Somewhere down the track an opportunity will arise to reopen it, and when it does, I shall be there, grinning at those responsible like the grim reaper, waggling a big stick.'

Karen smiled. She could imagine that. He was like a huge Scotty dog, and a hungry one at that.

'Do you still want me to dig out the coroner's reports?'

'Not officially,' and he winked at her.

'Got you, Guv, leastways I think I do.'

There was a pause for thought, and then he said, 'What are you doing later?'

'Why do you ask?'

'Thought we could have a few jars, celebrate the closure if you like, maybe a nice meal afterwards, my treat, on me, say Pierre's, I love it there.'

'Oh sorry, Guv, I can't, not tonight, I've promised to cook a meal for Darren.'

'Who's Darren?'

'Gibbo, Guv, Darren Gibbons, you know, our colleague.'

'Oh, yeah, DC Darren Gibbons, he of the youth and body building muscles and a solid punch.'

'It's a little treat for him for coming over to my place the other night.'

Lucky Gibbo, Walter thought, but didn't say.

'I see. Ah well, never mind, another time, maybe.'

'Yeah, sure, anytime, just say.'

Walter left the office at just on seven. He ambled away and limped up the high street, bought an evening newspaper from Reg the Rag, and went into his favourite watering hole. It was a popular place and already half full. He knew people there, enough to exchange nods, and many of the drinkers recognised him from his recent TV appearances. But he was in no mood to chat. He took up his usual station at the end of the bar and ordered a pint of stout.

There was something bugging him. Sam told him he'd bribed one of his officers to release secret files. Who'd do that? Gibbons? He thought of him enjoying a meal over at Karen's place. No, he didn't think it was him. And someone had tipped off the press as well. Who'd do that? Jenny? Surely not. Gibbons maybe, and he thought of him again, enjoying a lovely meal over at Karen's place. Bugger it! Forget about it.

There was a stinking mole in the team somewhere, and he would make it his business to snag him, or her, and something else that Sam had said came back to him. Walter's bathroom and kitchen were dirty. Maybe they were. Most men didn't notice such things, leastways not normal men. He'd stick a card in the post office window the next day for a cleaner. No visitor would enjoy a dirty bathroom and kitchen. No female visitor.

He sank half the pint in one swoop and began thinking of the dead.

Colin Rivers, the Lay Preacher with a penchant for going out late, planning church events, run down and smashed on the ring road. The Right Reverend James Kingston, upwardly mobile through the cathedral ranks, talked of as a future bishop, pushed under a train in an almost replica death to Desiree's. William Camber, the lonely old fisherman, drowned in the New Cut. Maggie O'Brien, a gentle old lady who never hurt a fly, drugged and gassed to death in Delamere

Forest. Jago Cripps, the confused young guy, dabbling in drugs, trying to make sense of life, had his wrists sliced open with a craft knife. Sally Beauchamp, another young kid, caught up in high-class prostitution, drugged and suffocated with brown parcel tape, wound repeatedly around her head and neck until she looked like a brown mummy, her body dumped in a North Wales' quarry.

And what about the seven deaths at Eden Leys?

Walter was ashamed to think he could not recall their names, plus the two attempteds, as Karen called them, one on her at the racetrack, his sergeant, his oppo, hung out to die, and one on him, in his own house, for God's sake, the bloody cheek of it, in his front room, in his favourite chair, injected with foreign blood. He shivered at the memory of the syringe emptying its poisonous cargo into his body.

What had it all been for?

There was still something bugging him.

How many of those deaths could have been avoided if he'd been on top of his game? How many lives could have been saved? How many of those people would still be walking round the city, perhaps in this pub, enjoying a quiet pint, if only he had apprehended Armitage Samuel Holloway, nee Shelbourne, sooner?

One, two, three, four, five, six, how many?'

Had he failed them?

He hated to think of it that way. Maybe he had.

It wouldn't be the first time.

He had attended all the funerals, looking the relatives in the eye, seeing the confused mixture of respect and doubt that lingered there, and all the while he knew what they were thinking. Why my son, my daughter, my husband, my aunt, my father? Why oh why oh why?

It was a question he couldn't answer.

It always was.

His glass was empty.

He nodded the barman over and bought another pint, extra cold.

Forced a smile and paid the guy.

Drank a silent toast to all the dead.

Seven times over.

Author's Notes

This is a work of fiction. Any resemblance to real characters, living or dead, is coincidental. Many of the places mentioned in the book are real. The Shroppie Fly at Audlem, for example, is an excellent place to spend a sunny afternoon. But many places are fictional, such as the Eden Leys complex, which has never, and will never be built. Rumours persist operations were carried out on live Alzheimer's and dementia patients at the Porton Down site in Wiltshire. Do they still? Let us hope not.

Please don't write and tell me that Mostyn Station doesn't exist. I know that, but for the purpose of this book it does. Artistic licence, if you will. The station was closed in 1948, though some buildings remain, and trains still rumble through there. Perhaps one day, with a more user-friendly attitude to rail, the station might re-open, and if it does, let us hope it avoids any fatal accidents. And I know the Chester Police HQ is no longer in the city centre, but for this series of books, it is!

MI7 existed, though it was reported to have been closed after World War II. Could it still exist today? Of course it could. Whether or not it does, I shall leave you to speculate. Special thanks to Anne Sellars, RMN, who knows more about people with dementia type illnesses than most, having nursed such patients for more than thirty years. She put me right on technical matters and also thanks are due for her proofreading skills, advice, and encouragement.

I hope you enjoyed the book. If you did, you might like to know there will be another Inspector Walter Darriteau story released next year. I am very excited about that and so is he! Please look out for it. There are three other Walter Darriteau cases I'd like to mention. "The Sound of Sirens", "The Twelfth Apostle" and "Kissing a

341

Killer", all available in paperback and as ebooks. You might like to check them out. There's a full list of the books at the front of this one.

When you have a few spare minutes I would love it if you could place a brief review on any of the main bookselling sites. It doesn't have to be long, a single paragraph would suffice. It does help me, and that would be very kind of you.

Thank you for reading, I appreciate it,
Have a great day,

David.

Printed in Great Britain
by Amazon

83768775R00200